FRINGE PATRIOTS

By

Carl R. Smith

To: Joe

Carl R Smith

ISBN: 1-4107-0088-7 (e-book)
ISBN: 1-4107-0089-5 (Paperback)
ISBN: 1-4107-0090-9 (Dustjacket)

Library of Congress Control Number: 2002096366

This book is printed on acid free paper.

Printed in the United States of America
Bloomington, IN

1stBooks - rev. 01/28/03

Foreword

"The spirit of our nation dates before the first battle was fought and before the first word of our Constitution was scribed. Before governments and armies, before war and hate, the self-evident truths of man's freedom and rights existed in our Creator and were given to us. The spirit of our nation is not found just within the borders of a map but within the hearts of people from all over the world and from all points in history. Therefore, even if a man may prevail against a nation, he cannot prevail against the spirit. The United States of America holds to that spirit and those truths better than any nation ever has. Our Constitution reflects this eternal spirit in such a strong and clear way that this invincible spirit of freedom may now b e given a name: The American Spirit."

—Kevin Alexander Smith, 1st Lieutenant Tennessee National Guard

Penned by my youngest son shortly after 9-11.

Introduction

I was flattered when Carl asked me to review this incredible book. Then I was amazed, and had to ask, "Will the real Carl Smith please stand up! This amazing first book, a chronicle of the past, has produced a sound rendering of reality mixed with fiction in an arena of war that often deprives youth of innocence, it tells who, what, when, where, how, and why.

It is all the more frightening because Carl has carefully separated myth from reality while demonstrating that the past often reflects the present, and the future, with its understandable possibilities and risks. Writers and soldiers have traveled a familiar path throughout time. History is all around us, and of course we use it every day with barely a moment's thought.

There are "fringe" patriots and real patriots and they are both here. Don't stop now, Carl! It can be comforting to know that others faced great difficulties and survived. From the readers' perspective, waiting for more of this incredible energy and inventive zeal will not be easy!

David G. Gerkin, MD
Brigadier General
TNSG

Prologue

This book was written to encourage other young men like myself, whose upbringing would not be cast in a Norman Rockwell painting. I was what many would call a throw-away. A young lad discarded by those in his life whom God had put there to offer love, security, and understanding. When my mother left me by the side of the road with all my worldly goods in a cardboard box at the tender age of twelve I couldn't understand. In some convoluted way, that day undoubtedly served to make me a stronger individual. I can't at this moment remember the day or the time but I assure each and every reader that I became resolved to prove my worth to the world.

In high school I had very little; therefore, in order to be accepted I became the toughest boy in my class. I never picked on anyone, but when someone else was picked on I took his or her part. Consequently, I became very close to my assistant principal. I was a very good student and studies came easy for me.

I joined the military to find a home, and to further my education. What I subsequently found was many great men, and a few who would use others for their own self-aggrandizement. I paid close attention to those around me, especially those in authority, but I said very little. I was there during the raising of the Berlin Wall, during the Cuban Missile Crisis, and I was there during the height of the Viet Nam conflict.

After finding the perfect wife, we had three incredible children, and a family life to be envied by most anyone. In my thirties people would tell me I was the luckiest man they had ever met. I would simply smile and say, thank you. For years I thought God was trying to make up for my abject childhood.

This is a story I had to write, and there are four more books on the way. Many of the same characters, like me, are part of this amazing chronicle. These people made me what I am today, a man of honor, integrity, and determination. I guess when it's all said and done, one could ask for nothing more.

My greatest desire in penning this work is to encourage others. Whatever the beginning, the ending is up to you and you alone. Be an individual who walks in when everyone else walks out.

Chapter 1

Clay sat quietly in the old Citron that Johnny had acquired for him to use. It was a beautiful, star-studded night on the coast of France. The rain had subsided about dusk as a brisk breeze hurried the clouds away, leaving in their wake air so crisp it could be tasted. The moon and stars were as brilliant as he had ever seen. *What a night to end a man's life,* he thought. However, he continued to watch the small bungalow some two hundred yards away.

Clay waited for more than an hour after the lights were extinguished before making his move, knowing exactly where to enter the house and what he had been commissioned to do. He went to the side door just off the man's bedroom, and prepared to pick the lock, but there was no need. *How can this man, a widowed science teacher, be so dangerous?* Clay wondered. *He doesn't even bother to lock his doors at night.* But, like a good soldier, Clay dismissed the thought. Orders were orders. He cautiously opened the door and walked into the man's bedroom. Putting the gun to the man's head, he pulled the trigger. The man's body made a small jerking motion, and then he was still.

Quickly, he retraced his steps, departing the way he had entered; but the one-hour drive from La Rochelle to St. Nazaire took more than two hours this time. While his driving was mechanical, his thoughts bounced around his brain like jumping beans. Struggling to concentrate, he found a parking place on the Rue De'laine, barely able to read the sign in front of the Canary Bar. Dr. John Murphy was waiting patiently at a booth in the far corner of the dimly lit establishment. Even the bad lighting couldn't hide the anguished look on Clay's young face.

As he slumped into the empty seat, Johnny spoke quietly. "You look like shit, Old Buddy. Was there a problem? Did something go wrong?"

"No, nothing went wrong. The man's dead."

"Well," Johnny replied. "I guess you don't feel much like celebrating. Tell me what happened."

Clay stared at him. "Just shut up. I did the job, okay? I don't wanna talk about it anymore. Get us a drink; in fact, I'll take a double."

They sat in silence for a long time, speaking only to order more booze.

After several drinks, Clay leaned forward trying, without success, to remain in control. "Johnny, I can't do this anymore."

Johnny simply nodded.

They both drank too much, and the next morning, Clay's throbbing head was a glaring reminder. He took more time than usual to shower, shave, and get dressed. When he came out of the

2

bathroom, he found a note from Johnny telling him where and when they would meet for lunch. He was on time and Johnny was already waiting for him.

Johnny folded his newspaper. "How you feeling, Old Buddy?"

"I haven't changed my mind, if that's what you mean," Clay snapped.

Moving uncomfortably in his seat, Johnny smiled. "Okay, but tell me what happened to the car? It smells putrid."

Clay paled. "I got sick and threw up. The first time I couldn't get out of the car quick enough, I'm sorry, Partner, I tried to clean it up."

Johnny leaned to his right, putting his arm around Clay's neck. "Don't worry. I took care of it."

They ate their lunch in relative silence. Clay's thoughts of what he had done were beginning to haunt his very existence. He wanted out. *But how?* He knew Johnny was a little apprehensive; but Johnny hadn't been the one to blow a man's brains all over his pillow. Some hard decisions had to be made, and soon. Clay was supposed to be in Salem, Oregon in three days to kill once again, in the name of patriotism.

"Let's find some women and get laid," Johnny said, excitedly. "I bet that'll make us feel better."

"Are you crazy, Johnny? I haven't touched a woman in so long I wouldn't even know how."

Johnny reached for Clay's arm, stroking it as though he were a father attempting to comfort his child. "Clay, are you *really* finished?"

3

"I can't help it, Johnny. I can't kill someone without knowing the why's and the what-for's. I'm going back to Germany to explain things to the colonel, and I hope he doesn't have me shot as a deserter. Johnny, we've been friends forever, and I love you more than a brother. I'd kill someone to save your life, but not like this; never again like this."

Clay came unsteadily to his feet, fighting with his emotions. Johnny stood and they embraced. "I love you too," Johnny whispered.

As Clay withdrew he could see the tears welling in Johnny's eyes. "Take care of yourself, Johnny, and keep in touch, my friend." Clay walked away without looking back. Somehow, he knew that Johnny could handle this and he didn't feel badly toward him. He just knew they were different.

When Clay returned to Germany, the MP's arrested him before he could get to the colonel. The next day the colonel walked into his cell, irritation deepening the lines already weathered on his face, "Clay, my boy, I think you're making a huge mistake. You only leave yourself one option; however, if your mind is made up, tell the Court Martial Board you've been on a drinking binge and lost track of time. They'll take your stripes and ship you to Vietnam. What has taken place must never be discussed, but I'm sure you understand, don't you?"

"Yes, Colonel, you know I can be trusted."

"Good luck, Clay. Try not to get yourself killed." The colonel paused, and then continued. "Clay, if you have a change of heart, let me know. I'll get you out of that awful place." He smiled, but his deep set eyes told an entirely different story. Clay had not seen this expression before, and it gave him cause for grievous concern.

The war in Vietnam was just getting hot and heavy. Once again, Clay did as he was instructed. He stood alone before the military court and pled guilty to being AWOL (Absent Without Leave). He was demoted to private and lost a month's pay. Within ten days, he was, quite literally, on a slow boat to China. This time, there was no special treatment. He was on KP (Kitchen Police) for the entire twenty-three days.

Chapter 2

The story began on the first day of June nineteen hundred and sixty-one. It was unusually cold and the rain was surging from the heavens in great waves. Clay and Robert waited patiently with sixteen other young men to board the short flight that would take them to Fort Knox, Kentucky. The United States Army had claimed these men to serve their country. It was uncommonly quiet, each man deep in his own world of thought.

Henry Clay Smith was two days shy of his eighteenth birthday. Robert Lee Hurst, Clay's brother-in-law, was nearly twenty-two. He and Clay had made the decision to join under a new enlistment program called the "buddy system," which guaranteed they would be together during basic training. For Clay, it made the process less frightening and a great deal more appealing.

While waiting, Clay began to relive, in his mind, his reasons for choosing this path. His five living siblings, four sisters and one brother, were married, some with children of their own. One brother, Lynn, had died from spinal meningitis as a baby many years before Clay was born; and yet, this brother's life and subsequent death had greatly impacted Clay's own life. According to the older children, it had been this tragedy that had changed Clay's father, Alex, from a loving, caring father to one who dispensed abuse, mentally and physically, to his family. Clay, the youngest, and the only other male child to be born after Lynn's death, received most of the physical mistreatment. Alex would fondle the girls and beat Clay.

Before Clay's twelfth birthday, Alex had abandoned the family for the third and last time. Clay no longer had to endure abuse from his father, but his suffering had not ended. Two years later, Molly, Clay's mother, met a large man named Bill who had short gray hair and wild blue eyes. After knowing him for only three days, Molly had introduced Bill to Clay with words that caused Clay to shudder every time he remembered them. He could still feel the cold chills that ran through him as she had announced, "I want you to meet your new stepfather. We were married this afternoon at the courthouse."

The next day, Molly, Bill, and Clay had moved from Knoxville, Tennessee to Dayton, Ohio where Bill worked as a cook. By the end of their first week in Dayton, Bill informed Clay that he was no longer welcome to stay and would have to leave. No reason was given. As Clay packed his few belongings in a cardboard box, Molly stood in silence, never offering a comforting word as Clay disappeared into the night; acutely aware that his mother had traded her youngest child for a large, ugly, old man who had a huge potbelly and stank of grease.

Clay made it back to Knoxville, but had not found any loving, or even sympathetic, arms to welcome him. His older brother and sisters had no place for him in their lives or among their own families. Clay, being only fourteen at the time, was placed in the John Tarleton Institute for Orphans.

Robert interrupted his thoughts. "Clay, they're calling our flight."

"I'm sorry, Robert. I guess I was daydreaming."

He and Robert grabbed their bags and got in line along with the other young men. When they were seated on the plane, Clay again retreated to his thoughts of times past. The pain of his family's rejection often grabbed him unexpectedly.

Alex had abandoned the family three times and each time in the arms of a different woman; but when he had become tired of each new companion or simply had run out of money, Alex would come crawling to Molly, begging for forgiveness. She had always taken him back. When Clay was eight, Alex had returned home after several months of being gone, but this time Jo and Lucy, the only two girls still at home, had pleaded with their mother not to take him in. Subsequently, Molly had told him to leave, but afterwards, she had become hysterical.

"Kids, run, go bring him back," she cried.

Clay had run as fast as his little feet would carry him, giving no thought to the consequences. However, Jo and Lucy had hated him for bringing back their tormentor, and they had set about to make him pay. Even the brother and sisters not living at home had expressed their displeasure. At times, Clay believed he deserved their rejection, but the actions of a frightened eight-year-old boy were, surely, not so terrible that he should be abandoned, left alone.

Through all of this, Clay had had only two allies, his Aunt Ella and his friend, John Wayne Murphy. Of all the neighborhood children, only Johnny had continued to be his friend. Instinctively, he had understood and had stuck by him. When Johnny's father was transferred and they moved away, even Clay's Aunt Ella had been unable to console him.

Ella had lived with the Smith family for as long as Clay could remember. She was devoted to him and was, in fact, the mother that Molly never was. It was Ella who had stood between Clay and Alex to protect the child from this monster, taking as much of the suffering and abuse upon herself as possible. Then, several months after Johnny's move, Ella met a man named Noah. They were married three months later. Clay had wanted to go with her, but Noah's meager income made that impossible. Besides, Alex would never have allowed that to take place.

"Clay, wake up! The plane is landing." Robert said, shaking him repeatedly.

"Okay, okay, I'm awake. Stop poking me."

Chapter 3

Clay stood quietly with the others on the tar-mac as the army green bus pulled along side the plane, offering transportation for the final leg of their journey to Fort Knox, some thirty minutes away. He was looking forward to seeing his new home for the next eight weeks.

When they arrived, they were greeted by a cacophony of shouting and cursing.

"What's the matter *girls*?" the Drill Sergeant screamed. "We're not afraid of a little rain, are we?"

Robert was shaking, "This guy's crazy. I think we've screwed up. This may have been a big mistake."

"Shut up!" Clay said, through clinched teeth, trying not to move his mouth. "You're gonna get us in trouble, just listen."

"My name is Sergeant Scribner, and I'll be your mommy for the next eight weeks. I'll change your diapers and see to your every need. You may call me Sergeant Scribner, you may call me Sergeant, but do not call me Sir."

After an hour of standing in the pouring rain and enduring Sergeant Scribner's screaming, barracks assignments were made.

The first two weeks of Basic Training were used for testing. It gave the sergeants the ability to categorize each individual. In every test, whether mental or physical, Clay was at the top of the class. Robert didn't do badly either. By the end of the second week, Clay became a platoon leader as did Robert. There were four platoons in each barracks. Clay was platoon leader for the first platoon, and the third platoon belonged to Robert. Throughout the next six weeks, they were in constant competition with each other.

Knestric, one of Clay's charges, came to his bunk late one evening. "The second platoon is going to throw you a blanket party. I thought you'd want to know."

Clay rose to his elbows. "When's this gonna happen?"

"Tonight."

"Is the 'Turk' still in the latrine?" Clay asked.

"Yes, and he's alone."

"Get some of the guys and watch the door. Don't let anybody else go in until I have a talk with Mr. Turkey Rollins. Do you understand?"

"Yes, Clay. I'll get Mitchell. Nobody messes with him."

Knestric moved away, and Clay headed for the latrine. Turk, the leader of the second platoon, was still in the shower. The stalls were huge and able to accommodate ten or twelve men at a time.

Turk glared at him. "What the hell do you want? I assume you're not taking a shower since you have your clothes on."

"We need to talk," Clay said calmly. "If you have a problem with me or my men, let's settle it here and now."

Turk turned off the water and walked toward him. "I'm gonna kick your ass and knock that smile off your stupid face."

"Don't do something we'll both regret," Clay said. "I'm not gonna let you hurt me or any of my men."

Clay was acutely aware that his calm approach was driving the Turk over the edge and, consequently, working to his advantage.

"You smart aleck son of a bitch." Turk swung at him with his right fist. "I'm gonna —"

It was over. As Turk swung, Clay stepped to his left. With his right foot, he kicked the Turk on the side of the right knee, and the leg snapped like a twig. Turk lay on the floor, his mangled limb resembling a pretzel, a pool of blood forming under his right knee.

"Damn it, Turk, you brought this on yourself. I wanted to settle this like two adults." Clay reached for a towel. "Here, wrap this around your leg until I can get you some help."

"You go to hell," Turk yelled.

"Turk, you're a real piece of shit, you know that? You better listen real close. If you even think about messing with me or any of my men ever again, I'll send you home in a bag. This conversation is over." Clay turned and walked out.

When Clay exited the latrine, he looked at Mitchell. "Get the Medic. Turk's had an accident."

The next day there was a new platoon leader for the second platoon.

Sometime later, Robert asked Clay what had taken place in the latrine.

12

"Look, Robert, I decided some years ago that no one would physically hurt me ever again. I did what I had to do. The guys will learn from this, and maybe the others can share in a lesson learned by one."

"Hey," Robert grinned. "I'm on your side, remember?"

"I know. I didn't mean to snap your head off."

Clay couldn't help thinking about all the times his dad had beaten him. He remembered being tied to a giant oak tree in the yard, being beaten so severely he had lost consciousness. When he had come to, he realized that the neighbors had called the police. After that, his father simply locked him in the storm cellar after a particularly severe beating. At six, Clay had received a badly broken nose. Ella had treated him the best she could; there had been no money for doctors.

For years, the scars and the misshapen nose had made him look much tougher than he really was. However, while living at the orphan's home, he learned to box and became coached in the martial arts. His instructor had called him a natural because he was fearless and exceptionally strong. The instructor spent countless hours teaching him how to harness his fear and anger and how to win by taking advantage of his opponent's actions and reactions. Coach would say, "Never get angry. Be calm, and you will usually defeat your enemies." Coach had had many such sayings, which he repeated almost daily. Coach was one of Clay's fonder memories.

After the incident in the latrine, the entire company gave him more respect. However, he was sorry it ever happened. He took no pride or pleasure in having to hurt someone.

At the end of the sixth week of training, Clay learned that weekend passes would be given to every member of the number one rated platoon. Determined to win, even if he had to work his guys to death; he taught his men quicker ways to do almost everything. In fact, Clay's platoon was the one made up of guys with the higher IQ's. There was only one problem. The men with above average intelligence were not in very good physical condition; consequently, this was the area where he spent most of his training time.

Clay made sure everyone else knew how hard he was pushing his men. Then, two days before the most physical event, the obstacle course, he rested his platoon. They did nothing but stretching exercises while everyone else was worked to the point of total exhaustion. His strategy worked. On the day of the event, his platoon walked all over the other three.

As a way of saying thanks, the entire platoon chipped in and decided to get Clay his first woman. The big event took place at the Henry Clay Hotel, in downtown Louisville.

Afterwards, as Clay came strolling out of the hotel, Mitchell, along with a bunch of the other guys, came rushing toward him. "Well, how was it? Give us the lowdown."

"Ya know, when you pay money, you'd think the woman would at least take off her clothes," Clay grinned. "Although, having the hotel named for me; now, *that was awesome.*"

It was August, and graduation day was imminent. Everyone was anxiously awaiting new orders, orders directing each man to his next duty station. On Wednesday, before Friday's graduation, the orders were posted on the bulletin board. Clay and Robert would both be returning to Fort Knox, Clay to Clerical School and Robert to Engineering School.

All recruits were granted two weeks leave time between basic training and their new assignment. Robert went home to Lucy. Clay returned to John Tarleton to visit the kids. There was a special little boy named Kenny whom he was anxious to see. For months he had taken Kenny under his wing and protected him from all the bigger boys. Some of the children had living parents but were unable to reside with them for reasons too numerous to mention. They were, however, allowed to visit. Every Sunday, Kenny sat on the front steps, waiting for his mother. In almost three years, she never came. But, Kenny sat there every Sunday, without fail.

Clay knew only too well how cruel children could be to each other. The other children had made fun of Kenny for his devotion. Most of the children had given up hope a long time before. Actually, Kenny had made them feel bad about themselves because he had refused to give up. So the other children had picked on him as a defense mechanism in order for their own feelings to remain below the surface. Most of these young people had been lied to and taken advantage of all their lives. So, they had built walls of protection around themselves to minimize further damage to their bodies, minds, and, most especially, their hearts. Clay had experienced those very same feelings, and his insight came from first-hand knowledge.

Clay also learned, through this trip to Knoxville, that the majority of his sisters and his brother considered him more of a bother than anything else. As painful as that was, he accepted it. He hoped to correct the problem someday, but doubted it would ever happen.

Clay returned to Fort Knox and reported to his new duty station. He was immediately put in charge of his barracks, mainly because he had been a platoon leader in Basic. His good record had preceded him.

Clerical school was a breeze. It was nothing like basic training. There were passes almost every weekend. The nights, after 1700 hrs, were also free. Clay spent most of his time at the education center studying for his G.E.D, knowing that, if he could pass the test and get his diploma, he could start taking courses from the University of Maryland through the education center on base. Before finishing his second eight weeks of training, he had done so. Clay was well on his way to completing his first semester at the University.

As the second eight weeks of training was about to come to an end, once again, everyone was awaiting orders for their next assignment. Clay's next assignment was Transportation School at Fort Eustis, Virginia. Robert was reassigned to Headquarters Company at Fort Knox because he was being mustered out of the army on a hardship discharge. Lucy was pregnant and having some medical problems. Clay didn't know the particulars and he decided not to ask. A well-composed letter the following week was his way of showing concern, offering any help he might be able to render. They never wrote back.

Chapter 4

Fort Eustis, Virginia, the home of the Wheels was Clay's next address. When he arrived, he received another set of orders promoting him to E-3, Private First Class. That promotion was at least two steps above where he started some six months earlier. As a transportation specialist, he learned how to move troops from one spot to another. He was taught how to load and unload ships, trains, and airplanes, and was trained to be a manifest technologist. Ocean manifests were the documents used to load ships. It was like a blueprint, instructing the loaders where to place each piece of cargo. If the manifest wasn't followed and a ship got into some bad weather, it could be disastrous. Clay was good at his assignment; so good in fact, that he received a commendation from the Battalion Commander.

One of the instructors was a lady captain named Sarah Wyne. Sarah was about thirty and a good ten years older than Clay. Because Captain Wyne was one of the better instructors, she was at liberty to choose certain students to assist her on special projects. One evening, as she and Clay were working late on just such a project, she seemed a little overly friendly.

"Clay, would you like to take a short break?" Sarah asked. "My feet are killing me."

"Yes, Captain, anything you say."

Sarah walked from the classroom into the adjoining office, motioning for him to follow. She sat on the sofa and removed her shoes.

"Is there something I can do, Captain?" Clay asked, his voice breaking like that of a thirteen year old in the church choir.

"You could massage my feet," she replied. "Also, when no one else is around, you can call me Sarah."

"Okay, Sarah. I'll try, but don't get angry if I'm not very good. I've never massaged anyone's feet." Clay made every attempt to remain cool, taking a seat on the other end of the sofa.

Sarah smiled widely. "Clay, you have great hands. I'm feeling better already."

For the first time, he realized how really attractive Sarah was. She had short blond hair and green eyes. She was small in stature, but put together extremely well. Clay was trying hard not to act like a child opening a new toy, for, in reality, he could barely breathe. The only thing keeping his hands from shaking was the exercise of gripping and massaging. Knowing full well, if he was misreading her signals, he might get into a lot of trouble. Sarah lay back against the arm of the sofa where they were sitting and began to move ever so slightly. Clay squirmed, trying to readjust himself without doing any permanent damage.

Sarah pulled her legs back and sat straight up facing him, her eyes dancing mischievously. "Have you been with many girls?"

Clay's cheeks flushed, his gaze dropping to the floor.

Inclining her head Sarah ran her fingers across his lips. "Kiss me, Clay."

As if in a dream, he was going with the flow. Gently, Sarah's tongue began to explore. With passions rising and their bodies pressed firmly together she could feel his excitement. "Oh my, Clay," she said huskily, and, without the need for more words, she led him into the adjoining bedroom.

Over the next few weeks, Sarah taught him many ways to please a woman, things he'd remember forever. Clay considered it a time when boyhood gave way to manhood. Erudition from the book of Sarah was like encyclopedic mastering, the art of physical and sexual fulfillment 101.

Clay was now in his second semester at the University of Maryland and doing well. He intended to finish at least the first two years through the education center at Fort Eustis. With any luck, he would actually go there and finish the last two years on campus. However, the army had other ideas concerning his future. As Transportation School was drawing to a close and graduation time drew near, new orders came. Clay was ordered to report to the 105th Transportation Company right there at Fort Eustis, Virginia. The greatest part was no Viet-Nam. There were other perks as well, and not having to leave Sarah topped the list.

Clay had four days before he was to report to his new duty station so he decided to spend some time in Richmond, Virginia, about sixty miles to the northwest. Sarah was away on temporary duty until Sunday evening and there was little else to do. The Greyhound Bus took less than an hour and a half to make the trip. When he checked into the John Marshall Hotel in the downtown area, he was extremely tired for he and Sarah had been up most of the previous evening celebrating. After taking a quick shower, he lay across the bed. It was early Thursday evening and beginning to get dark outside as sleep overtook him.

Clay was awakened by a knock on the door. When he looked at the clock he was astonished to learn it was Friday morning. The knock was repeated.

"Who is it?" He asked rather loudly.

"Housekeeping. Would you like your room cleaned, Mr. Smith?"

"Could you come back in an hour? I'll be out of here by then."

"Yes, Sir, I'll be back later."

Clay quickly shaved, showered, got dressed, and headed for the elevator. He decided he would spend some time walking around town. The hotel where he was staying was on Main Street, two blocks south of Broad Street, which was really the main street in downtown Richmond. As he turned west on Broad, he suddenly realized he was hungry and made an about-face. According to information from some of his buddies at the base, about two blocks in that direction was the U.S.O. They said it was a nice place, and the food was good. When he arrived, there were only a couple of other guys in the place and they

20

were playing pool. The lady behind the counter was the motherly type. She kept patting Clay on the hand.

"Young man," she said. "We have a big dance here tonight. There'll be a lot of nice girls to dance with. It starts at eight o'clock. There'll also be lots of food and plenty to drink."

Clay looked at her. "I don't know much about dancing."

"That doesn't matter. I promise, you'll have a good time." She was very insistent, and, again, she patted him on the hand.

Clay played pool with the other guys and then finished his walk around town. He couldn't seem to get the idea of the dance out of his head.

Oh, what the hell, Clay thought. *I'll go back to the hotel, shave, shower, and go to the dance. It might be fun, at least I can watch.*

It was almost nine before he got back to the U.S.O. The place was really jumping. Clay ate a little of everything, and drank enough coke to sink a battleship. Feeling a little out of place, he decided to have one more bite then take in a movie. As he was filling his plate, they called for a ladies choice. When he turned around, a cute little girl with black hair and the sweetest smile took his arm.

"Would you like to dance?"

"I'm not a very good dancer," Clay said nervously.

She surveyed every aspect of his face, with a warmth in her gaze that would melt the heart of a child. "Heck, it doesn't matter. Margaret, the woman you were talking to, told me you were a little shy. She also told me your name is Clay; well, my name is Taylor, c'mon lets dance."

Dancing partners rarely seem to fit; but he and Taylor were a perfect match.

"Thank you for asking me to dance," Clay said, feeling much more at ease. "I'm glad I didn't embarrass you. I didn't, did I?"

Taylor smiled. "No, you didn't embarrass me. Clay, would you like to come and sit with me and my friends? We'd love to have you join us," Taylor spun around. "Wait a minute. 'It's all in the Game', by Tommy Edwards. I love this song. Let's dance."

They hit the dance floor once again.

"What kind of music do you like?" Clay asked.

"Gosh, I like a lot of different kinds. Although, I guess my favorites would have to be soul and beach music," she replied. "What about you? What do you like?"

"You probably won't believe me, but soul and reggae are my favorites, too."

When the song was over, she took him by the hand and led him to the table where her friends were sitting.

"Clay, this is my friend, Lillie, and the big lug is George. He's in the navy, stationed in Norfolk."

"It's nice to meet you guys," Clay said, holding Taylor's chair, "Say, George, are you in just for the weekend?"

"Yeah, I'll go back Sunday night."

The DJ had been gabbing for a while between songs. When the music started once again, Clay interrupted. "'Ain't too Proud to Beg', now, that's one of my favorites."

"Well, get up," Taylor said, grabbing him by the arm. "Let's boogie."

"No way! I don't know how to fast dance," Clay said, pulling away.

"Ah, c'mon," she urged. "Look, boy, you do have rhythm, don't ya? Just keep time with the music. Look around and do what the other people are doing. Just move with the music."

"Okay." Clay replied, "But you'll be sorry."

Taylor grabbed his hand and literally pulled him onto the floor. "Look, just snap your fingers and keep time with the music. That's all I do. There are so many people out here; we won't even be noticed anyway." When the song was over they collapsed in the chairs at their table.

"Can we do that again?" Clay asked, perspiration becoming evident. "How was I? Did I look as funny as I felt?"

"You did great, and you do have rhythm," she teased.

They were once more on the dance floor.

"Thanks for encouraging me, Taylor. I never would've done this on my own. Dancing is a lot more fun than I thought."

"That's what I'm here for," Taylor replied. "To dance with the servicemen."

Clay looked at her, the smile, now absent from his face.

When the dance was over, they returned to the table. Clay continued standing. "It was nice meeting you, George, and you too, Lillie. Thanks for the dance, Taylor. I've got to be going."

Clay turned abruptly and headed for the door. Outside the cool breeze felt good on his face.

"Clay, stop," Taylor yelled. "Where are you going?"

"What do you care?" Clay replied angrily. "I'm just another serviceman to you. Hell, there are a hundred more inside. You better hurry back; you might miss dancing with one. As you said, you're just here to dance with the servicemen, right?"

"Clay, please don't leave. I'm sorry. I didn't mean to hurt your feelings. We can just sit and talk if you want too. We don't have to dance anymore."

"I don't think so," he replied. "The people inside may get upset if you're not dancing with the other guys."

"Then take me with you. I'll go wherever you're going," she said, reaching for his hand. "I'm afraid if you leave, I may never see you again, and, for your information, I have never danced four times with the same guy, ever. I don't know why, but I just can't let you go. Don't make me beg?"

He looked at her, "That's the way I felt from the first time you touched my hand."

"Then please don't do this. Come back inside with me. I promise I won't dance with anyone but you. Please!"

"Are you sure that's what you want? Taylor, you don't really know anything about me."

"But I want to know about you. Don't you want to know about me?"

"Yes, Taylor, of course I do."

"Then stop being so stubborn." She took his hand and they walked back inside.

George and Lillie had decided to leave so he and Taylor had the table all to themselves. They danced a few more times, and, between dances, they talked and talked, until there were only a handful of people left in the place.

Taylor looked at her watch. "Clay, it's getting really late. Would you walk me to my car? I need to get home. I don't want to worry my mom and dad."

They left together. When they got to Taylor's car and were just about to say good night, Margaret came walking toward them. "Did you two have a good night?" she asked.

"I most certainly did," Clay replied.

Margaret smiled, "It's getting awfully late, Taylor, don't you think you better be getting home?"

"Yes, Ma'am, I was just leaving. Clay, I have to go. She's watching us," Taylor whispered. "I'd drive you back to the hotel, but that's not allowed." She gave him a hug and a little peck on the lips and away she went.

Some twenty minutes later, as Clay returned to his hotel, he suddenly realized that he not only forgot to get her telephone number, but he didn't even know her last name. *Damn, I hope she's there again tomorrow night. How could I have been so stupid?* As he opened the door to his room, the telephone was ringing.

"Hello, Clay, it's Taylor. You told me where you were staying, remember? I'm sorry I couldn't take you back to your hotel, but we're

25

not supposed to leave with any of the guys. That's one of the rules we promise to follow."

Clay couldn't stop grinning. "Boy I'm glad you called. I was scared to death I might never see you again. I didn't know your last name or your telephone number."

"Do you want to see me again?"

"What a silly question! You know I do. I've never had a better time. I guess that sounds pretty square, doesn't it?"

"It makes me feel pretty important," Taylor replied.

"You should feel important. You have all of a sudden become very important to me," Clay said, trying hard not to sound too stupid.

"Clay, I thought about you all the way home, and I couldn't wait to hear your voice again."

"Thanks. Is there any chance I could see you tomorrow night?"

"Absolutely, I'll meet you at seven-thirty. There's a restaurant on Broad, not far from your hotel. I'll meet you there, okay?"

"I'll be there, but it might help if you'd give me the name of the place. I think I could find it faster that way," he started laughing.

"Cut it out, Clay. The place is called Joy Gardens. It's the best Chinese restaurant in town. Did you get all that?"

"Yes, cutie. I heard every word, loud and clear."

They talked, and talked, and talked.

It was wonderful, and, this time, he not only got her last name but her telephone number as well.

Clay put the "Do Not Disturb" sign on the door and slept like a baby until late that afternoon. He shaved and hit the shower. Clay was twenty minutes early, Taylor was ten. She looked beautiful, and he promptly told her so. Taylor had dark brown eyes, almost black, and, when she looked right at him, it made him feel warm all over.

"I hope you like Chinese food, Clay."

"I just wanted to be with you. To tell the truth, I've never eaten much Chinese food, so I'm not really sure."

"That's okay. You might want to order the sampler platter. That way you can try all kinds of stuff."

"That's okay with me."

She reached across the table and touched his hand. "Well, we have to start out with hot tea. You have had hot tea, haven't you?"

"I've had iced tea. Does that count?"

She ordered for the two of them.

"Taylor, what kind of work does your father do?"

"He's an engineer for the telephone company, and my mother's a school teacher."

"What does she teach?"

"English."

"Look, Taylor, I'm just a country boy. I just finished my first semester at the University of Maryland, and I did that through the education center on base."

"That's really nice. What are you studying?"

"I'm going to major in math, but that's not important," Clay said nervously. "I love talking to you and being with you, but, let's face it, Taylor; you're way out of my league. Hell, I was raised in an orphan's home, and what family I do have wants nothing to do with me, and I—"

She reached across the table once again and took his hand. "Hush, don't talk like that anymore. I don't give a damn what your family thinks. Clay, you're going to be very successful someday. I'm betting on you. Now, let's talk about something else."

Taylor was extremely anxious for Clay to meet her parents. She wanted him to come to her house the following afternoon. He was scared to death but he agreed to come. She took him back to his hotel and they kissed goodnight. The kiss was so natural they both laughed. When Clay returned to his room, he turned on the TV hoping it would take his mind off Taylor. He was startled, suddenly, by the ringing of the telephone.

"Clay, I can't seem to think about anything but you. I guess telling you that is pretty stupid, huh?"

"Taylor, I feel the same way. I've never felt like this before, about anybody. I've talked to you more in the last two nights than I've talked to my sisters or my brother in my entire lifetime."

She started laughing. "My brother, Sydney, says we're in *love.* Sleep well, Clay. I'm looking forward to tomorrow and so is my family."

"Goodnight, Taylor."

Sunday afternoon came quickly, and Taylor arrived right on time. "Clay, don't be scared. My mom and dad are very nice and you are the first serviceman I've ever brought home. They're gonna love you."

As they drove into the big circle driveway in front of Taylor's home, Clay saw how huge and beautiful it was, even from the outside. His mouth was so dry he could hardly swallow. When they walked into the front room, her brother greeted them.

"Hello, Clay. I'm Sydney. Don't be nervous. We're just regular folks." He flashed a warm and infectious smile. "Taylor has told me all about you, but I wanted to meet you anyway."

Clay laughed "Well, I appreciate that."

They both smiled as Taylor punched Sydney in the stomach. "Sydney, I told you not to be a jerk."

Sydney grunted, grabbing her and kissing her on the forehead. "Just trying to help the boy relax."

Mom came next. She was a tiny woman, about five foot nothing and probably weighed less than a hundred pounds. Taylor's father was another story altogether. He was about six foot four and could have weighed as much as three hundred pounds, a very formidable man. Clay was amazed at the size of his hands and the strength of his grip. They all sat in the library where the questions began. It was obvious that Taylor had told them quite a lot; and, for that, Clay was grateful.

Fortunately, before her parents could probe too deeply, Taylor intervened. "Mom, Dad, I'm sorry but we have to leave. We're meeting with Lillie and George in a few minutes. There'll be plenty of time to talk later."

Clay stood. "It's been a real pleasure, but I also have to be heading back to the base pretty soon. Sydney, it was nice meeting you also, and you're a lot nicer than Taylor led me to believe."

"Touché, Clay," Sydney saluted. "I'm gonna enjoy having you around. You guys be careful."

Taylor drove Clay to the hotel. She waited in the lobby while he gathered his belongings. They drove to the Greyhound Bus Station where Clay could catch the bus to Fort Eustis. They sat together in the car for as long as time would allow, each promising to write. On the sixty-mile ride to the base, Clay slept, not wanting to think about anything. But, Taylor was there, in his dreams, tugging at his heartstrings.

The next morning, he reported to his new Commander, and was promptly given the rest of the day off to organize his gear. He was to report the following morning to the Battalion Commander's Office for his new duty assignment. When he finished putting his things away, there was a call he had to make. His hands were shaking as he dialed the number.

"This is Captain Wyne, how may I help you?"

"Hi, Sarah, may I see you tonight?"

"Absolutely, handsome, I'll meet you at the B. O. Q., (Bachelor Officer's Quarters) how about seven-thirty?"

"That's great, I'll see you then."

When Clay arrived at the B.O.Q., Sarah was waiting at the bar. As Clay explained what had taken place over the past three days, Sarah's expression never changed.

"I understand," she replied, her eyes beginning to moisten. "I knew this couldn't last forever. Clay, could we have one last night together? I'd love to feel you next to me once more."

"God, I'm sorry, I can't." Clay replied, avoiding the pleading look in her eyes.

He kissed her good-bye carefully, so as not to draw any attention to them; after all, they were soldiers, and she was an officer. As he walked out, he could feel a huge lump in his throat.

It was time to place a second call. Now, he was feeling better. The blues seemed to melt away with the very thought of talking to Taylor. Clay told her about his day, never once mentioning Sarah.

"I have to report to the Battalion Commander's office at 0800 hours tomorrow morning. I don't know why, however, when I do know, you'll know. Taylor, I miss you terribly. I can't wait until Friday when we can be together again. I'll call you Wednesday. Is nine o'clock alright?"

"That'll be fine, Clay. I think about you constantly, and, if I close my eyes and concentrate real hard, I can feel your touch. Please be careful and good luck tomorrow with your meeting. I'll be praying for you."

"Thanks, Babe. Tell Sydney and the rest of the family I said hello. I'll talk to you Wednesday night. Good-bye, Love."

As Clay began walking back to his barracks, he was in a world of his own, a world filled with thoughts of Taylor, Taylor, and, ah yes … As Clay turned the corner by the bowling alley, he heard someone scream.

31

What the hell was that? Clay said aloud. Stopping, he looked in all directions, but remained still. As he began to walk on, it happened a second time. This time he saw a man and woman struggling in a car on the other side of the parking lot. Clay sprinted toward the car. Reaching through the window, he grabbed the man forcing him to release the woman. Cursing and screaming the assailant pulled a gun. As he brought it through the window, Clay spun around knocking the gun from the man's hand. As the car door began to open, Clay jumped straight up kicking the door with both feet. The sound of tearing flesh and breaking bones filled the night air. It was about this time when the MP's arrived, late as usual.

Clay stepped back. "He's all yours, Sergeant."

The Military Police sergeant pushed Clay even further back. "What's going on here? Ladies first. What happened, Ma'am?"

"I've only been out with this idiot one time. I pulled into the parking lot and he jumps in the car and starts cursing me and hitting me. He said he was gonna kill me, and he might've had it not been for that young man. Thank you, Son."

After getting the whole story, the MP's transported the man to the hospital "under arrest".

All Clay wanted was to return to his barracks and get some sleep. After giving the second group of MP's his name, rank, and service number, he was allowed to do just that.

His sleep was fitful. The anxiety concerning his appearance before the Battalion Commander the next morning had him spooked. He had, however, done his homework, and he knew as much about the colonel as one possibly could in such a short period of time. Colonel Essex was six feet four inches tall with brown hair and brown eyes. As a Princeton graduate and a Rhodes scholar, he had moved up the ranks quickly. Scuttlebutt was, he would be a general before he was forty. The colonel was married to the daughter of a senator from Georgia, and they had two children. As an Airborne Ranger, he had been highly decorated during the Korean conflict. He was said to be hard-nosed, extremely thorough, but fair.

At 0800 hours the next morning, Clay was sitting outside the Battalion Commander's office. The sergeant major came out to greet him and to escort him into the colonel's presence. Clay saluted and Colonel Essex stuck out his hand. They shook hands, a rather uncommon occurrence for officers and enlisted men. The colonel had already been informed about the events of the previous evening and he was very impressed.

Colonel Essex began, "Son, how'd you like to be my Aide de Camp, as well as my driver?"

Clay was shocked, but he could still give an affirmative reply.

"You'll be promoted to E-4, Specialist Fourth Class," the colonel explained.

"I wasn't aware of that, but I'll take it," Clay replied.

They both laughed.

The colonel continued, "You'll also be required to go through some extensive martial arts training. I hope that meets with your approval as well."

"Yes, Sir. I'd enjoy the opportunity to learn. I've had some training over the last several years."

"I'm aware of that," the colonel replied. "It's part of your personal history."

"Of course it is, Sir. My apologies, Colonel."

"That's okay, My Boy. I like a young man with grit, and you most certainly have that. Clay, I'm looking forward to having you on my team."

Clay was told to report back to the sergeant major's office for further instruction. His mind was racing. *Maybe I'll bring myself up to Taylor's level after all. What a wonderful thought.*

Upon returning to the sergeant major's office, Clay was given explicit instructions, telling him where to go and what to do. First, he was to report to the Quartermaster for a new clothing issue along with the proper gear. He was issued a side-arm, a 45-caliber automatic with holster, to be worn at all times while on duty. Next, he went to the Special Forces training area where he met Sergeant Glenn Shackelford who was to be his personal trainer. The sergeant stood about five foot nine and weighed one hundred sixty pounds. Clay thought his short, brown hair, cut in a flattop, green eyes, and chiseled features made him look like the model for G.I. Joe. The sergeant was a fifth degree black belt and an army Green Beret.

Clay returned to the sergeant major's office after having lunch in the mess hall. Immediately, the sergeant major informed him that the entire battalion was on a Round-Out Alert. The alert was in response to the announcement of trouble in West Germany concerning the construction of the Berlin Wall. The entire Eleventh Battalion, which included the 105th Transportation Company of which Clay was now a member, would be headed overseas within two weeks. Colonel Essex wanted to see Clay in his office at 0730 hours the next morning.

Clay spent the rest of the afternoon and most of the evening with Sergeant Shackelford. They worked on a few things at the gym. After being knocked on his ass more than a dozen times, Clay mused, *this isn't going to be as easy as I thought it would be.*

"Hey, Sergeant, don't you think I've been abused long enough?" Clay said, about half way serious.

"Yeah, I guess so," Shack replied. "Let's go get a beer."

Clay found out in a hurry that Sergeant Shackelford could really drink beer. Fortunately, Clay made no attempt to keep up, but he still drank too much.

The next morning, Clay, headache and all, stood waiting at the colonel's office when the sergeant major arrived. The colonel pulled in a moment later.

"Smith," the Sergeant major said. "Wait in my office. I'll let you know when the colonel can see you."

"Yes, Sergeant Major."

Clay waited less than five minutes.

"You can go in now," the sergeant major informed him.

The colonel was standing in front of his desk. "Clay, it looks like we're in this thing together. I'm going to take a few days leave and you should do the same. I'll see you back here on the twenty-first. Keep your nose clean, My Boy. I have great plans for your future."

35

"Thank you, Sir."

"You're welcome. Now, go see that girl in Richmond. What's her name? Taylor, that's it." The colonel started laughing. "You see, Son, I do know everything. Wish her a Merry Christmas for me."

Clay stood for a moment with his mouth wide open. "I'll do that, Sir. Thank you again, Colonel."

Clay was given ten days leave, starting immediately. He was to be ready to move out as soon as he returned, which would be just before Christmas. The last few days had been too much. Clay was traveling on an emotional roller coaster. He was pleased to be able to return to Richmond for a few days; however, he had no idea how he was going to break the news to Taylor. Clay thought, *it's a hell of a lot better going overseas on a round-out alert with a state-side battalion. That way I'll be gone less than a year*. Being sent to an existing overseas battalion would have meant two years minimum. *That has to be worth something,* he thought, packing his gear once again.

The news was going to be one heck of a Christmas present for Taylor. Clay was sick inside, but he knew that spending the next few days with her would be wonderful.

Maybe I shouldn't tell her right away, he thought. But, he decided, the best way to handle this was to be up front with her and hope for the best. He knew it was going to be hard for the both of them. *Perhaps, if I explain the one-year, two-year deal, she might accept it more readily. Surely, she'd rather I be gone for only a year.* Clay slung his bag over his shoulder. It was a long walk to the bus station, and he was in a world all his own. *How in the hell did the colonel find out about Taylor, that makes no sense.*

"Hey, Soldier, want a ride?"

Clay turned to see Sarah's smiling face. "Absolutely," he replied.

Sarah delivered him to the bus station in a matter of minutes. They embraced in private, and, for Clay, it wasn't the least bit uncomfortable.

Clay saluted, and the captain returned his salute. "Good luck. I'll never forget you, Sarah," he whispered as he turned and walked away.

Chapter 5

When Clay arrived in Richmond, he decided to stay at the same hotel because of the familiar surroundings. After checking in, he called Taylor at work. She seemed puzzled, but happy to hear from him and immediately agreed to meet him for lunch. It was only about five blocks from the hotel to the place where she worked. He was there in less than twenty minutes. Taylor took ten minutes to show him off to her co-workers and then they were off, hand in hand, down the street.

The two of them talked and giggled and ate very little lunch, but they had a wonderful time together. Taylor agreed to pick him up at seven that evening, in front of the hotel. It was Wednesday afternoon and Clay had almost six hours to kill before he would see her again.

He walked around town until he found himself outside a jewelry store. The salesperson was very patient, showing him almost everything in the store. Suddenly, there it was the one he knew would be perfect. When she showed him the price, his disappointment became evident.

The salesperson never batted an eye. "You're a serviceman, aren't you?"

"Yes, Ma'am."

She smiled, "If you'll put a little money down, you can charge the rest and pay a little each month."

Clay had never before charged anything, but this was so important that he quickly accepted.

The remainder of the afternoon dragged by like a minister's sermon on a warm Sunday, when the thoughts of fishing or playing stickball were foremost in a young boy's mind. Clay was pacing, tediously, counting every crack in the hotel sidewalk when Taylor's car pulled to the curb.

He slid into the seat beside her. "Where're we going?"

"I'm taking you to Grove Park," she replied. "You'll love it! It's the most beautiful place."

He had to agree it was a magnificent place. Even though it was December and there was a certain chill in the air, they walked and talked for hours.

"Clay, the company I work for is having a Christmas party a week from Friday. Will you go with me?" Taylor pleaded. "It would make me very happy."

He nudged her playfully. "Of course I'll go, silly. Now, can we go back to the car? I'm freezing."

She put her arm around his waist. "Sure, Babe. It's getting colder by the minute."

The next evening they took in a movie, and, afterwards, Taylor had a major announcement.

"Clay, I promised my parents that we'd have dinner with them tomorrow night. I hope that's okay. Mom and Dad are really looking forward to it."

"Sure, that'll be great. I don't think I'll be as nervous this time. Is Sydney gonna be there?"

"I'm afraid not. He'd already made other plans, but you'll be glad to know he tried to change them."

Clay knew he wanted to pop the question at dinner the next evening. But, he didn't know exactly how he was going to pull it off; nonetheless, he felt the timing was right.

When they arrived at Taylor's home the next evening, he was amazed. Since he had been there five days earlier, the entire place had been transformed into a winter wonderland. The sheer beauty of the Christmas decorations resembled a department store window.

Finding the right opportunity, Clay nudged her father. "Sir, may I speak to you alone for a moment?"

They went into the next room. Clay was nervous, but he tried to speak calmly. "Sir, I want to ask your daughter to marry me, and I'd like to have your blessing."

Her father never changed his expression, and the silence lasted much too long.

"Sir, I know I'm not good enough for your daughter. Our backgrounds are totally different, but I'm a hard worker, and, when I finish college, things will be great. I swear. I love her very much."

Then he spoke, "This has happened awfully fast, but I think my daughter honestly loves you, and I do appreciate your coming to me first." He looked Clay right in the eye. "Love her as I have loved her for all these years."

Clay asked him to speak to Taylor's mother before dinner in order to let her know what was about to happen. Her father put his huge arm around Clay's shoulder. "Welcome to the family, My Boy."

The dinner table was exquisite. The meal was fit for a king. The entire setting was beyond perfection. "I must tell you ladies," Clay quipped, "this may have been the finest meal I've ever eaten."

Dinner was over and the ladies were about to serve dessert. Clay excused himself and went to the bathroom. He had to summon his courage for what was about to take place. As he returned to the table, he noticed Taylor's mother struggling to keep her composure, as the old man gave him an approving nod. Everything was ready. Clay stood beside Taylor with his hand on her shoulder. She turned to look as he bowed on one knee.

"Taylor, I can't imagine spending the rest of my life with anyone else. Will you marry me?" Clay asked, nervously holding the ring in front of her.

Taylor was shaking as she reached for him, eyes moist. "Henry Clay Smith, I love you more than anything else on the face of this earth. Yes, I'll marry you."

He placed the ring on her finger, and all was right with the world.

The next few days were incredible as they talked about and planned their future together. Clay spent the times when they were apart reading or working out. He would do anything to pass the time until they were together again.

The night of the big Christmas Party was almost upon them. Clay could hardly wait, except that every day they spent together was one day closer to the time when he would have to leave. Clay knew he had to get Taylor a Christmas present, but he didn't have a clue what it should be. He shopped almost every day while she was working. One day, he happened upon a little portrait shop, and the light went on in his brain. A calendar and twelve pictures, with a poem from his heart under each picture; Clay felt sure that would be perfect.

Friday came and Taylor was to pick him up in front of the hotel. Clay had bought a new black suit with little pin stripes. It had a vest and two pairs of trousers. The red and black tie he wore made him look like he had just stepped out of "Gentlemen's Quarterly". When Taylor arrived, she pulled next to the curb and he got in on the passengers side.

She was beaming. "Wow, you look great!"

"I feel great," Clay replied, moving closer.

"Woe, Big Boy! Don't disturb my make-up. Mom made me promise that we'd come back by the house so she could take our picture. It's really not much out of the way."

When they got to the house and Taylor stepped out of the car, Clay gasped, what a vision of loveliness, so pristine. She was wearing a straight black dress with little spaghetti straps over the shoulders. Her dark hose and black spiked heels accentuated her beautiful legs. She was wearing her mother's pearls and little pearl drop earrings. The two of them made a handsome couple. Taylor's mother had them posing all over the place. Wanting one more pose, her mother asked

Clay to take off his coat and very casually sling it over his right shoulder. He was to place his left arm around Taylor and lean against the car.

Taylor threw up her hands. "Don't anybody move. Stay right there. I'll be right back."

She ran into the house and returned in the blink of an eye, carrying a beautifully gift-wrapped box, which she promptly handed to Clay.

"Merry Christmas, Darling. I was gonna give this to you later, but now's the most appropriate time. It'll look really great in the picture."

He opened it as Taylor was fidgeting. It was the most beautiful watch Clay had ever seen. It was a Bulova; yellow gold, and self-winding. He was uncharacteristically speechless. It was, by far, the finest thing Clay had ever received.

"Thank you, Darling. I love it. Your present is back at the hotel —"

She put her fingers to his lips and whispered, "Later, Babe. It's all right."

Finally, they were on their way to the party.

"Clay, stop biting your nails," Taylor said, putting her hand on his knee. "And you're gonna wear a hole in those new trousers if you don't stop bouncing your leg up and down."

"Sorry, Love," he replied, pulling into a parking space.

Taylor took his hand as they walked from the parking lot to the front door. "Relax, Clay. It'll be all right. Most of these people have been drinking for over an hour and they wouldn't care anyway. Hell, we'll be the best looking couple in the place. Let them eat their hearts out."

An older distinguished looking gentleman greeted them at the door.

"Hello, Taylor. Is this the famous Clay we've all been hearing so much about?"

"Yes, this is Clay Smith. Clay, this is Mr. Swimmer, one of the big bosses."

"Hello, Mr. Swimmer, it's nice to meet you. I love your tie."

"Thank you, Clay. Brenda will show you to your table. You two have a great time."

They were directed to their table and were seated next to Janet and her husband, Jim. Clay had met Janet at Taylor's office. The familiar face made him feel a little more comfortable. Jim and Janet were already eating their salads, and, before he and Taylor could catch up, the entree was in front of them.

When dinner was over, a number of company executives spoke, wishing everyone a Merry Christmas and Happy Holidays. Thankfully, in less than twenty minutes the band was playing, and everybody was having a good time. When Clay began to realize how much they were drinking, he consciously started slowing down. *Someone has to drive home and I'm not going to ruin Taylor's night,* he thought.

On the way home, Taylor laid her head in his lap and fell asleep. When they arrived at her house, Sydney was the only one still awake and moving about. He helped Clay get Taylor into the house. She

44

kissed Clay goodnight, and Sydney helped her to her bedroom. When Sydney returned, Clay was sitting on the front porch.

"Clay, would you like some coffee?" Sydney offered. "I'll bet I'm the only person who can drink a pot of coffee at night, then go to bed, and sleep like a baby."

"That is a little odd," Clay admitted. "Actually, I'm so wired a cup of coffee would taste good about now."

Sydney retreated back into the house. He returned with a large tray containing a pot of coffee. "There's cream and sugar on the tray. Help yourself, Clay."

"Are you very religious?" Sydney asked.

"Not really."

"Taylor told me that your father was a minister and that he ran out on the family when you were small. What religion was he?"

"Baptist," Clay replied reluctantly.

"Clay, do you have a problem with ministers?"

"I think there are some who are called of God, but mostly I think they are men who can't do anything else or are simply too lazy to hold a real job."

"Hell, Clay, I'm sorry. I can see this is making you uncomfortable. Let's talk about something else."

They continued to talk until the coffee was gone. Sydney suggested that Clay take Taylor's car back to the hotel, but not before writing her a note.

Clay finally got to bed at dawn and fell asleep straight away. He heard the telephone ringing, but it took him a moment to find the receiver.

"Hello, Clay. Are you there?"

"Yes, Ma'am, I'm here. How can I help you?"

"I simply wished to thank you for taking such good care of my daughter. Sydney told me what you did, and I appreciate that. I'll have Taylor call you as soon as she is up and around. I'm sorry if I woke you. But, what you did means so much."

"It's okay, I'm glad you called."

Clay fell back to sleep and then awoke some twenty minutes later with a start, not knowing what time it was. He got up and headed for the shower, standing for a long time under the spray, trying to come alive. When he finished shaving, he brushed his teeth twice. Then, he lay back across the bed waiting for Taylor to call. He didn't have to wait long. Taylor was wide-awake and anxious to see him.

Clay got dressed and headed that way. When he arrived, there were people everywhere. Taylor's parents were giving him a surprise going away party, and he was surprised indeed. He was introduced to many of the other members of the family, and they all wanted to shake his hand. The local newspaper had picked up the story about his saving the lady at the bowling alley. The article made him look like a hero. He hadn't mentioned anything about the incident to anyone, not even Taylor. Now everyone knew and they were all very proud to have a hero joining the family.

The whole thing embarrassed Clay; however, it was nice to see the pride on Taylor's face. The party went on until almost eleven. At that point, a hush came over the room; the big man had something to say. "It has been a great evening, but I think it's about time we let the two love birds have a little privacy."

Clay turned to face the crowd. "As most of you know, I'm leaving tomorrow. But, I'd like to thank each and every one of you for making me feel so welcome." He flushed. "No offense folks, but I would like to spend my last few hours with the girl I'm going to marry."

Sydney raised his glass. "A toast to the ideal couple. God be with you, Clay."

The cheers could be heard throughout the neighborhood.

He and Taylor said their good-byes to the family and headed for the car.

Taylor squeezed his arm, "Honey, would you mind driving?"

"Not at all, where do you wanna go?"

"Let's go back to the hotel. I want you all to myself."

Clay swung the car onto the main road and headed downtown. Taylor snuggled close to him. Traffic was light, and in less than fifteen minutes they were parked and walking arm in arm into the hotel.

When they approached the door to his room, she tugged at his arm. "Would you carry me over the threshold?"

He picked her up, and whisked her inside, moving quickly across the room he sat down in a big overstuffed chair Taylor landing softly on his lap. They sat there holding each other, her head on his left shoulder.

"Clay, I think I must be the happiest woman in the world and maybe the luckiest."

"Hold that thought," he said. "I have something for you."

Clay stood, turned, and dropped her gently in the chair. Crossing the room, he retrieved a brightly wrapped package from the bedside table and returned to where she was sitting. He knelt in front of her. "Here, I hope you like it."

"What is it?"

"Open it and you'll see. It didn't cost as much as the gift you gave me, but it came from my heart."

Taylor removed the paper. She looked at every picture and read every poem, crying all the while. "You know that I love you more than the air I breathe. I can't imagine how wonderful our life together is going to be. Clay, I want to stay with you tonight."

"Sure you can, and ditto."

They both laughed. Ditto was their special code. When Clay would call her at work and tell her he loved her, she would just say ditto. That let him know there were lots of people around and she wasn't free to talk, but that she loved him too.

She stood before him and began to unbutton her blouse. That's when he understood. He reached for her, putting his arms around her waist.

Taylor began, "I've never been with a man."

Clay nodded.

"I know you've been with other women, and that's okay. I want you to remember this night in the days to come. All I ask is that you have patience with me."

He picked her up for the second time; however, this time he carried her to the bed and laid her there; stepping back, to once more drink in her beauty.

"Lay beside me," she pleaded.

He complied, instantly.

As Taylor's blouse fell open, he brushed her soft skin with his lips. She began to tremble.

"I have dreamed about this night since we first met. Am I pretty enough for you, Clay?"

"Yes, Love. You're the most beautiful woman I've ever seen."

Sliding his left arm under her neck he brought her mouth up to meet his. His right hand moved down to her flat stomach and under the waistband of her skirt. She forced his hand even lower. Clay began to massage her just as Sarah had taught him. Taylor's body suddenly stiffened and she screamed. "Oh, my God, I love you, Clay."

"I want to make you feel that great. Show me how," she urged.

"You have always made me feel great," he responded. "I love you, Babe."

Taylor excused herself and went to the bathroom. When she returned, she was totally naked. She stood in the doorway and let him look at her. She was magnificent.

"Teach me how to make love to you," she said. "Show me what you like."

Clay knew that he could very easily hurt this beautiful young girl, but he had no intention of doing so. Soon, and quite suddenly, they came together as one.

Afterwards, they lay together, holding each other. Clay knew he would never again love anyone as he loved Taylor. He felt this would be the last woman he would ever make love to, and that pleased him.

Clay picked her up and carried her into the shower. While bathing, they found new ways to show their love for each other. She was like a kid with a new toy, and determined not to let him rest. It was morning when they fell asleep in each other's arms.

When Clay awoke, it was almost noon. He could hear Taylor in the bathroom. He went to the bathroom door and knocked gently. "May I come in and brush my teeth? I promise not to attack you."

When he opened the door, there she stood in all her resplendent glory. She was even more beautiful than the night before.

She nudged him as he reached for the toothpaste. "Clay, the past twelve hours were absolutely the most wonderful time I've ever spent. I love you very much."

He loved the way she kissed, so soft, sometimes, or maybe most times, and then like a savage when the time was right.

Taylor looked him straight in the eye. "Darling, I want you one more time before we have to leave."

He looked at her with a smile in his eyes. "You got it, babe."

They were made for each other and they knew. They lay together, vowing their undying love until it was time to go.

"I don't know what to say," Taylor admitted. "I want to say something very profound, but I can't find the right words. Clay, I'm so afraid of losing you. I'll write you every day, I promise." Her body began to shake uncontrollably. She was crying now and unable to stop.

Clay just held her and let her cry. "Taylor, I'll call you tomorrow morning before we shove off. That is, if you don't mind getting up at five o'clock. We are leaving at six, and I sure would like to hear your voice one more time before we leave."

"I'll be waiting for your call, Clay, I ... "

"It's all right. The time will pass quickly," he said, desperately trying to keep his own composure.

Clay was certain that God had brought them together. He felt that it was some kind of payback for all the love he'd been missing for most of his life. Also, for the first time, life was worth living.

When he called her the next morning, it became evident; Taylor had been waiting by the telephone for his call.

"Good morning, Darling. There's someone here who'd like to speak to you."

"Clay, old boy. I fully expect to be the best man at your wedding," Sydney said. "So don't go doing anything stupid, you hear? We'll all be praying for you."

"Thanks a lot, Sydney. Don't worry I'll be fine. Take care of my girl."

"I'll do that. Here she is."

"Sydney and I, we've been talking all night. Clay, can you tell me where you're going and what's gonna happen next?"

"I'll try. We're taking a train to the Brooklyn Army Terminal. From there we'll be boarding the U.S.N.S. Gordon, a Navy transport vessel. It will take us to the Port of Embarkation at Bremerhaven, Germany. I don't know where we'll be going from there, but we're to arrive there on December thirtieth. Merry Christmas, Love, I'll call you at nine AM sharp, your time, on New Years Eve."

"Clay, I'm going to my aunt's the day after Christmas, and I won't be coming back home until January second. She lives in Ohio. You'll have to call me there, okay?"

"That's fine. Give me her number."

Taylor gave him the telephone number where she could be reached. "I love you Clay, with all my heart. Please take care of yourself. If anything were to happen to you, I wouldn't want to live. I'll pray for you every night."

"Taylor, I love you more than anything. Don't worry about me. I'll be lonely, and I'll be sad, but I'll take special care just because you're in my heart. I've been thanking God everyday for bringing you into my life. You have a peaceful and glorious Christmas."

It was so very hard to hang up the phone, but when duty calls, a soldier must respond, and Clay had to go.

Chapter 6

Clay picked up Colonel Essex at 0600 hours sharp at his quarters and they were off to the train station. When they arrived, the sergeant major was already there. He had everything under control. Clay was directed, along with the colonel, to a Pullman car. Their gear had already been put in place. The colonel's quarters were two single cabins with the partition removed in order to give him additional space. Clay's was only a single; however, it was a great deal nicer than that of the regular troops. So far, being the colonel's aide really had its perks. Clay was told he would not be needed again until they arrived in New York the next morning. Therefore, he retired to write his first letter to Taylor.

That evening, at about 1700 hours, there was a knock on Clay's door.

"Clay, how about having dinner with me in my car. It's got to be better than eating with the regular troops."

"Yes, Sir, Colonel, I'd love to."

"Good man. Wash up and come on over."

"I'll be there in ten minutes, Colonel."

They ate at 1730 hours and discussed the colonel's strategy concerning troop deployment until almost 2200 hours. The colonel was a brilliant tactician. Clay knew he could learn a lot from him if he would only listen and ask the proper questions.

The following morning was pure madness. Trying to relocate everything to the colonel's quarters on the U.S.N.S. Gordon was a major undertaking. When everything was ship shape so to speak, Colonel Essex, the sergeant major, and Clay were invited for drinks in the captain's cabin. Actually, Clay knew he was just allowed to come along.

While having drinks, the captain inquired if anyone could play Bridge. It seems they had three players, the captain, the colonel, and the sergeant major. They needed a fourth.

"Clay, my boy," the colonel said. "It looks like you get to be the dummy."

Everybody started to laugh. Fortunately, Clay didn't understand, but he knew he felt uncomfortable.

"Its okay, Clay," the colonel continued. "Men, give me a few minutes to teach my partner the game." Then, he gave Clay about five-minutes of instruction and introduction on how the game was played. When they had played the first rubber, everyone was amazed at how quickly Clay caught on. In no time, he and the colonel had made their first of many grand slams.

"Damn, Sergeant Major, I think we've been had," the captain said, about half serious.

"I think you're right, Captain."

"I swear, Gentlemen, I've never even heard of this game before tonight," Clay said, trying his best to look serious.

"Honest, Fellows, I assure you he's telling the truth," the colonel said. "Some people just catch on quicker than others, and Clay is a very bright young man."

"That's right," Clay reaffirmed. "Well, not about the bright young man part. But, I've played a lot of Poker, and other card games, but never Bridge."

They were playing for only a penny a point; however, by the end of the evening, he and the colonel had won about fifteen dollars each. As they were leaving, the colonel nudged him. "Meet me in my cabin and we'll have a nightcap. You did real well, My Boy. We make a helleva team."

Clay was waiting outside the colonel's cabin when the colonel showed up.

"C'mon in. Scotch and soda, right?"

"Yes, Sir."

The colonel handed him a drink. "Here, Son, you take the money, you earned it. You played brilliantly, Clay, you always knew what cards had been played, and which ones were still out."

"Please, Colonel, we're partners. Don't make me take the money."

"Very well, My Boy, but how did you do that?"

"I don't honestly know. Some years ago, I was told that I have a photographic memory. I can remember numbers and a great many other things. I just see them in my head. Plus, Colonel, I don't like to lose at anything. I guess I'm just a little too competitive."

55

Colonel Essex put his arm around Clay's shoulder. "I don't ever like to lose either. Hell, the money means nothing, but losing makes me ill."

The colonel poured them each another drink. "I'm going to take very good care of you, my boy. Let's just let this photographic memory be our little secret. It might come in very handy someday."

"Anything you say, Colonel."

"Clay, I know about most of your background. You've been treated badly most of your life. Well, your future looks bright. As I've said before, we make one helleva team. You get some rest, and we'll talk some more tomorrow." The colonel patted him on the back.

"Yes, Sir, and thanks, I'll see you tomorrow, Colonel."

"Goodnight, Clay."

After the nightcap with the colonel, he went up to the main deck. He wanted to watch and listened to the ocean. Taylor was swimming around in his head and it was wonderful thinking of her. He had already postmarked his second letter. Tomorrow was Christmas Eve. *I wander what she and the family are doing about now*. He could picture them sitting in the den around the fireplace, drinking hot cocoa and having pleasant conversation, Taylor's radiant smile glowing in the backdrop of the flames from the fireplace. Clay decided he would retire for the evening. Maybe, if he were lucky, he would dream of her, as had been the case since first they met.

Christmas Eve came and went with little or no fanfare. The colonel was in meetings most of the day. Clay had very little to do but think, and that made him miss Taylor all the more. On Christmas Day, there was a grand meal prepared for everyone on board. After dinner, the captain wanted his revenge at the bridge table, and the four of them sat down to play. Once more Clay's ability to remember numbers gave he and the colonel a decided edge. This time, they walked away with over twenty-five dollars each.

It was amazing to Clay that the colonel was so open with him. The colonel seemed totally unafraid when it came to sharing his thoughts.

Clay spent the remainder of the evening, once again, on deck. He had not heard a word from his family and he wondered how they were getting along during the holidays. *They don't even know about Taylor*, Clay thought. *But, hell, they probably don't care anyway*. What a sad state of affairs.

He and the colonel were becoming very close. The card games were really just a diversion, something to occupy the mind. However, winning money was a great way to pass the time as far as he was concerned. By the time they were ready to dock in Germany, he and the colonel were ahead approximately two hundred dollars each. To Clay, that was a pretty good chunk of change.

The day of arrival was at hand. Again, it was sheer bedlam trying to get everything organized. When the colonel was finally settled in his new surroundings, Clay was housed nearby. It was close to midnight when he finally got into the shower, knowing that before long he would hear Taylor's beautiful voice. Waiting was the most difficult part. He wanted to tell her again how much he loved and missed her. Clay wanted to fall asleep fast and then it would be time to make the call to the states. The colonel had worked it out with the base operator, and Clay was very grateful.

Clay awoke suddenly with someone pounding on his door. He hollered to let them know he was coming but it didn't help. Finally, he got to the door and opened it, there stood the sergeant major.

"Clay, something has happened. Meet me in the colonel's quarters in fifteen minutes. I can't tell you anymore than that."

"Yes, Sergeant Major. I'll be there in ten," he replied.

Knowing this had to be something really big; he was simply resigned to waiting for a few more minutes. He looked at his watch Taylor had given him. There was still more than two hours before he could make his call. *God, I hope we're not going to war over the Berlin Wall*, Clay said, aloud, but to an empty room.

When he arrived at the colonel's quarters, his imagination was running wild. He could feel the hair standing up on the back of his neck. Colonel Essex was visibly upset, and having a drink.

The sergeant major handed Clay a drink. "Drink this son, you're gonna need it."

Clay looked at him quizzically, saying nothing.

The colonel was pacing the floor and avoiding eye contact. Finally, the colonel looked straight at him.

"Son, I think you should sit down. This ain't gonna be easy. Clay, there's been an accident. While visiting her aunt in Ohio, Taylor has been killed. It seems she was sleeping in an attic room when the house caught fire and she was unable to get out. She was buried yesterday. They would've notified us sooner; but having been on the ship, there was nothing anyone could have done. Clay, I have her family on the telephone in the other room. They want to talk to you."

The tears were flowing down Clay's cheeks and he didn't even realize he was crying. He tried to stand and walk but he couldn't seem to move. Even the colonel had tears in his eyes. With the colonel's help, he finally moved to the bedroom to take the call. When he said hello, he heard Sydney's voice.

"Clay, I'm sorry. It must have been the will of God. There was no warning. They told us she probably died from the smoke, and that would have been relatively painless. Taylor loved you very much and you'll always be a part of this family. Please, let us hear from you," Sydney pleaded, his voice breaking up so badly Clay could barely understand. "If you need anything, call me. I hope we'll always be close."

"Thanks, Sydney. I hope she didn't suffer. I'll call you as soon as I'm able to put more than two words together. Give my love to the family, and, God bless you too."

They said their good-byes. Clay didn't know what to do. He just sat there on the side of the bed, motionless. After awhile, he lay across the bed and fell asleep.

When he awoke, the room was dark, and someone had covered him with a blanket. He knew it was real but he still didn't know what to do or where to go. When he emerged from the bedroom a PFC Hensley sat waiting.

"Specialist Smith, the colonel has given me orders to see to your every need. Your emergency leave papers are waiting for you at headquarters. I'll help you pack and you can be on the next plane back to the states."

"Who covered me with the blanket, and turned off the light?" Clay asked, almost in a whisper.

"The colonel, I suppose," Hensley replied. "He said you were shivering. And, I was told to let you sleep as long as possible. Instructions were given to the sergeant major to prepare your leave papers for his signature."

Clay straightened his uniform, "I wanna speak to the colonel."

To headquarters they went. "Sergeant Major, may I please see the colonel?" Clay asked.

"I think that can be arranged," he replied. "Wait here for a moment."

"Yes, Sergeant Major."

The sergeant major came out of the colonel's office and motioned for Clay to enter.

"Clay, are you all right?" the colonel asked.

"No, Sir. And, Colonel, I don't wanna go back to the states. Taylor has already been buried, and there's nothing for me to do. Colonel, with your permission, I'm gonna get drunk for the first time in my life, and it would be wise if no one got in my way."

"You go ahead, Son, get drunk, but I'm sending Hensley with you to keep you out of trouble." The colonel rose, "Hensley, stay with him and call me personally every couple of hours. If he needs anything, I want to be the first to know. Do you understand?"

"Yes, Sir," Hensley answered. "You can count on me, Colonel."

As they left the colonel's office Clay didn't know how he was supposed to feel, but it felt like something was tying knots inside his stomach, and when he tried to take a breath his lungs would no longer expand. He wasn't much of a drinker; but, on this night he tried real hard to remedy that. He overheard Hensley informing the colonel, by phone, telling him that Clay was too drunk to walk.

The colonel showed up personally, at the bar, and helped Hensley get Clay back to the base and into bed. The colonel mumbled something about talking to him later.

Clay didn't know how long he had slept, but it was late the next afternoon when he crawled into the shower, sick as a dog. It was New Years Day.

Beginning on the second day of the New Year, Sergeant Shackelford showed up.

"You have one more day to feel sorry for yourself, Soldier," Shack said, almost glaring at him. "Starting tomorrow, I'm going to kick your young ass all over West Germany. I'll pick you up at 0400 hours, be prepared. Do you hear me, Soldier?"

"Yes, Sergeant, I'll be ready," Clay replied. This time there was no buddy/buddy bullshit. The sergeant was all business.

Again, the sergeant's job was to train Clay in the martial arts, sometimes as much as twenty hours a day. Sergeant Shackelford almost broke him. But every time Clay was ready to quit, Shack would make him so mad he wouldn't give up. During this time PFC Hensley was doing Clay's normal job. Clay felt that the colonel had put him out of sight and out of mind. He felt as though the colonel no longer wanted him around.

By the end of the toughest eight weeks of Clay's young life, he was finally putting it all together. At the end of this period, and when he was at his peak and beginning to mellow out, the sergeant major called for him.

"Specialist Smith," the sergeant major began. "Life has been very unkind to you at times, but you have also been given a great gift. Your photographic mind and memory can be of great service to you and your country. The colonel and I, think it's about time you were allowed to use it. Using your gift properly can help your country and millions of people around the world. Look, Soldier, you really have no one. Taylor is gone and you never seem to communicate with your family. According to you, the only person left on this earth you really love is your Aunt Ella. I'm told that she's the one you're sending part of you're pay to. Do I have the facts correct?"

With a bewildered look, Clay admitted that he was right. "What're you trying to tell me, Sergeant Major?"

The sergeant major looked extremely uncomfortable. "Clay, it seems, we're always sharing bad news."

"What bad news? Have I done something wrong Sergeant Major?"

"No, you've done nothing wrong. The chaplain was just here. It has to do with your Aunt Ella, she is very sick. She's in the hospital in Jefferson City, Tennessee. The colonel and I think you should go there."

"Is she dying?"

"I don't know the answer to that. She's asking for you and I think you should go. When you return, we have a very important job for you. We hope that you'll be as anxious to accept as we are to make the offer. If Colonel Essex, in all his wisdom, had not put you through these last few weeks of intensive training, you might very well have taken your own life. The colonel really cares for you, Young Man."

That was the most emotion Clay had ever witnessed from the sergeant major. Unfortunately, it didn't last very long. In only minutes, he was back to being the tough leader everyone admired.

"Specialist Smith, you be back here at 1400 hours tomorrow. In the meantime, I'll make arrangements for your journey. Clay, you need to be home with your aunt. Now, get out of here. I'll see you tomorrow."

The sergeant major offered his hand in friendship. "It'll be all right, Clay. We may not understand, but God's in charge and he knows exactly what he's doing."

Clay was still somewhat confused. He thought the colonel had forsaken him when all along he was really trying to help. When Shack admitted to him that the colonel had personally followed his progress on a daily basis, he felt much better. A great sorrow was lifted from his shoulders. He liked the colonel a great deal, and had enormous respect for him.

The next day, when 1400 hours came, Clay was sitting in the sergeant majors office.

"I'm ready to go, Sergeant Major. I'll be back in about two weeks. Will that be all right, Sergeant Major?"

He nodded his consent and motioned for, Clay, to wait. When he finished, he looked up from his desk. "Clay, the colonel wishes to see you before you go."

Clay flashed a wide smile. "Thank you, Sergeant Major, I was hoping to speak to him before I had to leave."

He walked into the colonel's office, came to attention and saluted. The colonel returned his salute, then walked around the desk and gave him a big hug.

"I'm very proud of you, Clay. When you return, we'll have a lot to talk about. God bless you, Son, and be careful. I have a lot riding on you."

Clay didn't understand but he knew that now was not the time to ask. There were so many questions running around in his head. But answers would have to come at another time.

"Colonel, may I say something?"

"Certainly, what do you wish to say?"

"I want to thank you, Sir, for your kindness."

"We're all on the same team, My Boy. I hope things go well for you back home."

It was almost noon on Thursday when he arrived in Jefferson City. Clay decided to find himself a motel room and freshen up before heading to the hospital. He found a room at the Cherokee Motel. It was a small place locally owned. Most importantly, it seemed very clean and that was important to him.

Upon his arrival at the hospital, Clay was told that his Aunt Ella had lung cancer and wasn't expected to make it through the next seventy-two hours. The nurses told him that she had been asking for Noah, her husband. She had been there for six days and Noah hadn't been there for the last three or four days. When Clay came into the room, she was so glad to see him she wouldn't stop hugging him. She began to cough so hard she spit blood.

"Ella, please calm down. I'll be here for as long as you need me."

"Clay, I'm so glad you're here. Will you find Noah for me, please?"

He wiped her mouth and washed her face. "Ella, hold on," Clay said, kissing her on the cheek. "I'll be back as soon as possible."

"Where are you going, Clay, you just got here?"

"I'm going to find Noah."

He kissed her once more and held her close to him. She tried to kiss him back but she was too weak.

"Clay, tell Noah I'm not angry with him for not coming to see me. I know its harvest time and he's working very hard. Tell him if he could come for only a minute or two, it would be all right. Clay, tell him I love him very much."

As he left the room, he ran into his Uncle Bassell.

"Clay, I'm glad you're here. How's she doing today?"

"Not very well, I'm going to get Noah."

"I'm afraid you can't do that."

"The hell, I can't. I'll bring him if I have to drag him here."

"Clay, Noah's dead. He had a massive heart attack and died while hanging tobacco in the barn. I didn't wish to tell Ella because I knew how upset she would become."

"Hell, Uncle, she's already as upset as she can be. I cannot go back in there and lie to her."

"Look, Clay, she could go any minute, let's not make it any harder for her. She knows its harvest time. I told her he'd be here in a couple of days."

He didn't like the idea, but he said he would honor his uncle's wishes; after all, Bassell was her brother.

Clay finally got to talk to most of his sisters and his brother John. It seemed to him that everyone was just sitting around waiting for her to die. This went on for several days. Clay stayed with her at the hospital almost day and night. The doctors were giving her so much medication she barely knew the world she was in. When she had a lucid moment, all she asked for was Noah. The doctors didn't know what was keeping her alive but she kept hanging on.

Clay informed the rest of the family, including his Uncle Bassell, that if she made it through one more night, he was going to tell her about Noah. He had been up with her all night, continually wiping the spittle from her mouth and rubbing her back to help her breathe. He went back to the motel about daybreak to get some sleep. When he returned in the afternoon, he decided to tell her. Clay sat for more than an hour holding her hand.

"Ella, I need to tell you where Noah is. Can you understand what I'm saying?"

Her eyes opened and all of a sudden she was alert. Clay thought, *it's truly remarkable what can trigger the mind.*

"Ella, you know how much I love you. I want you to know that the rest of the family has your best interest at heart. They didn't tell you the truth, because, for some strange reason, they thought they were protecting you. They didn't mean to be cruel."

"Where is he Clay?"

"Uncle Noah died the other day while hanging tobacco in the barn," he said, tears streaming from his eyes.

Ella patted his hand and closed her eyes. When they opened again, she looked at him and a great smile came to her face.

"Thank you for telling me. I've been waiting for him all this time. Clay, I love you. You know that you're the child I was never able to have. Son, I will always be with you."

Ella squeezed his hand and closed her eyes one last time. She emitted a huge sigh; then, she went to be with her beloved Noah.

The subject of Noah was never mentioned again. Clay knew many of the family blamed him, thinking, Ella would still be alive if he had not told her the truth. They were sure that the sudden shock of hearing about Noah was the final blow that killed her. After the funeral, he packed his bags and left. No one came to the airport to see him off. It was a hurt he chose to ignore. Clay was glad to be going back to the Army. At least there he felt wanted and of some use. He was anxious to be with Colonel Essex, and even Sergeant Shackelford. *I wonder what important job they have for me. It must be something with substance, if the colonels involved. Whatever it is, I'll make them proud of me.*

67

Chapter 7

He arrived back in Bremerhaven, Germany, on Sunday afternoon. The sergeant major told him that a briefing would take place on Monday morning at 0800 hrs. Clay's sleep was disturbed by all kinds of crazy dreams. When he awoke, it was barely 0500 hours but he got up anyway. It seemed like 0800 hours would never come. But, it did; and in the conference room that morning was Colonel Essex, Sergeant Major Russ, and a general with four stars on his uniform.

Colonel Essex began, "Clay, in order for the United States to remain dominant in the world, a few select people must die. It is impractical for hired agents to be used and using any sort of military force is out of the question. Clay, we're recruiting you to work as an operative for a group of patriots that even the CIA doesn't know about. In order for this to work, it has to be completely undercover."

"Colonel, I trust you with my life. I'll do anything you ask of me. You've been good to me, like the father I always wanted."

"Thank you, Clay," the colonel replied.

Sergeant Major Russ began speaking. "Clay, you would have to go AWOL and simply disappear, at least as far as the Army is concerned. It will be assumed that, due to all that has happened in the past couple of months, you simply went off the deep end. All the Army will know is that you are AWOL and they would be actively looking for you.

"But where would I go?" Clay asked.

"Clay, in order to throw everyone off your trail, you'll be given a new identity and the proper papers to enable you to travel. All the instructions will be written down. You must read them and then destroy the information," the sergeant major explained.

"Clay, my boy, I knew from the very beginning that you were the man for this assignment. Sergeant Shackelford was your last test and you passed with flying colors," the colonel said, proudly. "Will you do this, for your country, and for me?"

"Yes, Sir. Thank you for putting so much faith in me, I won't let you or my country down."

"Clay, the General and I have other matters to discuss, please go with Sergeant Major Russ, and he'll take care of all your needs." The colonel walked around the table and shook Clay's hand and patted him on the shoulder.

Clay followed the sergeant major to the outer office. The sergeant major handed him a large manila envelope.

"Follow these directions to the letter, and if you need anything further, Sergeant Shackelford will handle it for you. Go with God," the sergeant major continued. "You are a good man; let your heart be your guide. Clay, be very careful, and don't be taken in by the way people treat you. Trust in God, and you will not go wrong."

The sergeant major had more to say, but Colonel Essex and the general walked out of the conference room, and he said no more. However, the look on the sergeant major's face was very puzzling, but Clay knew to keep silent. *What did it all mean?* He wondered.

Clay was instructed to pack his bags once again, leave as he came and return to the states. Upon arriving in the states, he would take a bus from New York City to Richmond, Virginia; however, he would get off the bus in Washington D.C. where the bus would make one of its normal stops on route to Richmond. When safely in D.C., he would go to Alexandria, Virginia and meet with Sergeant Shackelford in a small bar just outside Fort Belvoir, Virginia.

Shack would take care of getting him back across the ocean to a place in France called St. Nazaire. He was to check into the Hotel Royalle where someone would contact him. According to the sergeant major, he was in for a very pleasant surprise. But all he really knew was that the person who would meet him there was a doctor from the U.S. Navy.

Clay did exactly as he was instructed.

After checking into the Hotel Royalle and putting his things in his room, he went out for a bite of dinner. After a big meal of something he hoped was steak, he headed back to the hotel. On almost every corner, he noticed at least one lady selling herself for whatever the market would give.

When he returned to the hotel and was just about to put the key in the lock, the blood rushing through his veins seemed to chill, and the hairs on his arms were standing straight up. *What the hell. The colonel wouldn't have turned me in yet, but something's screwy.* He decided to stand back and give this some thought; knowing, to this point he had done nothing. *It must be the food,* he thought. *Maybe I'm just nervous; no one could be after me.*

When he opened the door, the only light was coming from the windows across the room. As he walked in that direction, searching for the lamp switch, something moved. The movement was coming from the vicinity of the chair in the corner of the room. Clay was foolishly unarmed. He thought of throwing the lamp and trying to make a run for it. Before he could do either one, a voice clearly said, "God, it's been a long time. Hey, Dummy, will you turn on the light if I promise not to hurt you? It sure is a small world, isn't it, Old Buddy?"

It was Captain John Wayne Murphy, his dearest childhood friend. When they parted as children, Clay thought they would never see each other again; although, Clay had thought of him many times over the years. They hugged and damn near cried.

"I'm sorry for the cloak and dagger bullshit, but I couldn't just hang around the lobby. When they told me yesterday who you were, well, I haven't slept since then."

"Damn, Johnny, they didn't tell me the name of the person I was meeting. They did tell me, however, that I'd be pleasantly surprised. I've thought about you a million times. How's the family?"

"I lost my dad a couple of years ago. He had brown lung disease from working in the coalmines all those years. Mom and Robert are doing quite well. Are your dad and mom still together, or did he finally leave and never return?"

"That's exactly what he did. If we get drunk enough sometime, I'll tell you all the gory details."

"How's your Aunt Ella?"

"I was at her funeral a few days ago," Clay said, choking back the tears.

"Sorry, Clay. I didn't know. I would love to have been there." Johnny put his arms around him. "Life really sucks sometimes."

Johnny filled him in on the major events of his life since his family left Knoxville, Tennessee. He graduated high school at fourteen, college at seventeen, and medical school at twenty-one, while in the Navy. Doing government service was the only way Johnny could, financially, make it all happen. That's how he got involved with the colonel.

"Johnny, your family must be very proud of you." Clay said, punching him on the arm. "I know I am."

When they were children, they were inseparable. Now, they were together again. Clay didn't know what lay ahead; but with Johnny by his side, it probably didn't matter.

"Listen, Clay. I'll supply you with everything you need for each assignment."

"That's great, Partner. Do you get your information from the colonel?"

"I don't know who it comes from, but it comes in big brown envelopes by courier, from Washington D. C.," Johnny replied.

"Some of the targets will be well guarded, and some will be totally unguarded and unsuspecting."

"Who are these people, Johnny? Have you ever heard of this guy in La Rochelle?"

"I only have details on three of them at this time, and I've never heard of anyone of the three."

They decided to make the first hit the very next day. It was a high school science teacher who resided about sixty kilometers from St. Nazaire, south, outside La Rochelle. He was a widower who lived alone.

"Have you done this before?" Johnny asked.

"Are you kidding? This will be the first time I've ever knowingly taken another person's life," Clay replied.

"Well, I sure am glad we're together again," Johnny said, smiling from ear to ear. "Just like The Lone Ranger and Tonto, huh, Old Buddy?"

"Yeah, I reckon so. But, if memory serves me well, you always got to be The Lone Ranger, and I had to be Tonto," Clay replied, laughing all the while.

"But I was older and smarter," Johnny declared.

Clay was still laughing. "Well, I'll go along with the older part. However, truth be known, you were probably the only black Lone Ranger in the south."

"Yeah, I'd have to agree with that statement. God, I'm glad you're here, Clay."

"Me too," Clay replied, unable to wipe the smile from his face.

Johnny's demeanor changed. "Clay lets get something to drink. I'll brief you on the first assignment tomorrow after lunch. We have plenty of time; it'll only take about an hour to get to La Rochelle, and anyway, the information needs to be fresh in your mind. I know just the place; it's called the Canary Bar. Clay, tomorrow night, when you've finished job number one, we'll meet there for a celebratory drink, okay?"

"Sure, Johnny. I'll meet you there when it's over."

Chapter 8

Clay still cringed every time he remembered La Rochelle. He had killed a man in the name of Patriotism, and with the thought of killing a man in his sleep still fresh in his mind, heading straight into the Vietnam War didn't seem so frightening. He was also sorry that Colonel Essex, who had been like a father to him, was disappointed in the choice he had made. However, he felt as though he'd been given his life back, what there was of it. After arriving in Vietnam, he was assigned to another transportation company. This company was responsible for aiding the Quartermaster Corp. Their primary function was to get supplies to the troops. Clay was great at his job and before long he got his stripes back.

Clay had not seen any real combat, except for the times when their convoys would get ambushed. He had been in Vietnam almost eleven months and hadn't fired more than a hundred rounds of ammunition. Many of his friends were not so lucky. As luck would have it, about a month before he was to go home, or at least back to the states, a sniper got him. On guard duty that faithful evening, he had been assigned to a nearby water tower. He climbed the ladder up to a landing and from this landing he could see for a great distance. The landing was more than a hundred feet off the ground. As he was walking his area, the sniper found his mark. The bullet hit him behind the left knee. It was a superficial wound; however, the landing was only about a foot wide. The impact from the bullet was of such force that it knocked him off the tower. His body dropped more than one hundred feet into a rice paddy.

Remembering very little, he awoke in a field hospital, with two broken vertebrae in his lower back and a separated pelvis, and there was a considerable amount of nerve damage in his lower back and down his left leg. It was a miracle he was alive. If he had not fallen into about a foot of water and the soft ground of the rice paddies, he would have surely died. But Clay was alive and his prognosis was good. The Army sent him to Lettermen Hospital in the western part of the United States. Then, in order to be closer to his home, he was moved to Walter Reed Army Hospital close to Washington D.C.

Even after many months of physical therapy, Clay was still walking with the aid of short arm crutches. The doctor in charge of his case was Dr. Robert Delong. There were many other doctors in the orthopedic clinic that treated him, but Dr. Delong was his primary physician. Clay and Dr. Delong became very good friends. As he began to improve physically, Dr. Delong would allow him to come down from the hospital ward and work in the orthopedic clinic during the day. It gave him a since of worth and made the boredom more bearable.

Clay made a lot of friends while he was in the hospital. Many of the officers' wives served as volunteers at the hospital. He became very close to one of the volunteers named Leila. She was tall, thin, and very attractive. Leila was in her mid to upper thirties. Her husband was a high-ranking officer who was away on temporary duty. Leila worked on Tuesday and Thursday afternoons as a receptionist in the orthopedic clinic. The two of them enjoyed spending time together. She would tell him about all the young girls working there who had an eye for him. Leila was quite the little matchmaker. Clay showed no interest, and he believed that's why she kept trying. To Leila, it became a personal challenge.

One day in early November, Leila posed a question. "Clay, do you know anything about putting together a children's swing set?"

"Do you have the directions?" he asked.

"Sure," she answered. "Do you think you could come this weekend and help me put it together?"

"If it's okay with the doctors, I'd be happy to help. I'd do almost anything to get away from this hospital for a while."

Clay found Dr. Delong at a time when he wasn't too busy to talk. "Hey, Doc, do you think I might be able to get a two day pass? I need to leave the hospital this weekend, if that's a possibility? I want to help a friend erect a swing set for her kids."

"I think it'd be a great idea for you to get out of this place for a couple of days. You must promise, however, that you'll take it slow, no heavy lifting. Can you promise me that?"

"I promise."

"Well, okay then. Go to the administration office and have them type up the pass. Then bring it to me for my signature."

"I'm on my way. Thanks, Doc."

The following Saturday, Leila picked Clay up in front of the hospital about eight o'clock. It was a cold morning, and by the time they'd driven the fifteen miles to Leila's house, it had gotten even colder. They began working right away. With a little luck and help from the children, the job was complete by early afternoon.

"Clay, you did a marvelous job. My children are going to enjoy your hard work for years to come. Let me show you to the bathroom where you can take a shower. When you're finished, you may take a short nap, doctors' orders. I'll call you when dinner is ready."

"Thanks, Leila. I'll do that, unless you need help with dinner?"

"Absolutely not, you've done your part. Take a shower and get some rest," she insisted.

Leila came in later and told him that dinner was almost ready. He went to the bathroom and then downstairs to the dining room. The children talked nonstop throughout the entire meal. As they were about to finish, someone rang the doorbell. Everyone went rushing to the door and left Clay sitting alone at the table. There was a lot of commotion and then it was quiet.

When Leila returned to the table, she was smiling. "The kids are spending the night with friends. They just left. Would you believe it's snowing really hard?"

"Snowing? Oh, Mommy, can I go see?" Clay said, in an attempt to be silly. He loved to watch it snow. *Wow*, Clay thought. *It's really coming down*. They stood on the back porch and watched for a long time. It was so quiet one could almost hear one flake land upon another.

"Clay, would you mind staying overnight? I really don't want to drive all the way to the base and back in the snow. Especially after dark."

"That's okay with me. Do you think it'll be all right?"

"I'm sure it'll be fine," Leila replied.

"You wouldn't happen to have an extra toothbrush lying around, would you? I sure would like to brush my teeth."

"Would you like to watch a movie with me?" she asked, looking through a kitchen drawer until she found a new toothbrush still in the wrapper. "Here, Clay, this ought to do."

"What kind of movie?" He asked, secretly praying that it wasn't some sappy love story.

"It's a double feature. 'The Wolfman, and the Bride of Dracula.' I love to watch horror movies, but I won't watch them when I'm alone. If I do, I get really scared, and then, I'll have nightmares."

"Don't worry your pretty little head, I'll protect you from the monsters," Clay said, trying hard to keep a straight face.

Leila shoved him towards the bathroom. "Smart aleck."

They had popcorn and some kind of warm rum punch. Leila turned on the gas logs in the fireplace. Clay thought this must be what it's like to have a real home and family. They sat on the couch together, laughing and talking. By the time the Bride of Dracula came on, they were not drunk, just all warm inside.

Clay hadn't been with another woman since his last night with Taylor. That had been well over two years. He and Leila had talked a lot about Taylor and Leila knew how long it had been. By the time they were well into the second movie, Leila had her head in his lap. All of a sudden, she turned and looked up at him.

"Clay, you know I planned this, don't you? Well, I didn't plan the snow, but I'm sure glad it showed up."

"I'm not sure I understand," he replied.

"Clay, you're bright, sensitive and, next to my husband, the sweetest man I've ever known."

His face became bright red. "What a nice thing to say, thanks."

Leila rose to a sitting position, legs tucked under her. "Clay, I'm probably fifteen years older than you. But, regardless of the years, I really care for you. I may even love you just a little."

Clay adjusted his body in order to face her. "What are you trying to tell me?"

Leila reached for his hand. "Clay, I can do almost nothing for you medically; however, I can help you mentally and spiritually. I'm sure I can give you back at least a part of your life, and I hope you'll thank me someday."

Clay was taken by surprise but he never moved. "Leila, you're a very beautiful woman and I'm flattered; however, I really don't think I'd be worth the effort."

Leila's hand moved to his leg and began drawing circles with her fingers. "Don't be silly. Of course you're worth the effort."

Clay continued, "Leila, you're class and I'm trash. At least, that's the way I'd compare the two of us."

With that, Leila came straight up off the couch with fire in her eyes. "Don't you ever say that again, to me or to any other woman? If it's me, and you don't want me, I understand. I already acknowledged our age difference. If that's the problem, maybe I'm not good enough for you."

Now, Clay was angry. "Leila, you know perfectly well there's no other woman in my life. If I wanted sex with anyone, you'd be my absolute first choice."

Leila reached again for his hand, bringing it up to her breast, drawing them close to each other. "I'm sorry, Clay. I didn't mean to upset you. Don't let me spoil a beautiful evening."

"May I have another drink?" Clay asked, trying to lighten the mood. "Maybe if I get smashed, you can just have your way with me."

Leila threw his hands away. "That's not funny."

She did, however, fix him another drink, and they sat together throughout the rest of the movie and didn't say much. Finally, Clay reached over and pulled her close. Her body just melted against his, like a hand in a glove. He could feel her rhythmic breathing. They held each other close until the movie was over and it was time to go to bed.

Clay turned to face her, their faces only inches apart. "Leila, you are a dear friend and your husband is a very lucky man. I'm just not ready."

Leila showed him where he could sleep and they said good night to each other. After lying in the bed for the longest time, wide-awake, he finally got up and went into the bathroom. Another shower was in order. *Where is that toothbrush, I laid it here someplace.* Teeth clean, he walked down the hall to Leila's room.

When he spoke her name, she was awake and pleased that he'd come. He lay down on the bed next to her.

"Leila," Clay whispered. "I think, I want you, but —"

Leila put her fingers to his lips.

She began to kiss every part of his body, sliding her mouth down his chest. Leila was certainly no novice. When she found what she was looking for, she paused.

"Oh my word, how can you do that?" He asked, not really wanting or expecting an answer.

"I've always wanted to find a man that could fully satisfy me. Clay, you might very well be that man."

They came together with great precision.

"Clay, that was incredible."

This time, when he and Leila reached their peak together, she went crazy. Leila was fortunate, Sarah, had taught him so many things he seemed like a pro. When it was over, they lay quietly.

"Clay, I never thought I'd ever let another man touch me. You're the only one I've slept with since I got married, and you've given me a night I'll remember for the rest of my days. You should feel good about that."

"I'm glad I didn't disappoint you. You mean a lot to me, and I wouldn't want to mess that up," He said, as he pulled her close.

Leila turned to kiss him. "You know, if we were smokers, this would be worth the whole damn pack."

When Clay woke up, he could hear Leila cooking in the kitchen. The snow over night measured about seventeen inches. They had breakfast, and then, spent the next few hours playing in the snow. They made a huge snowman; it must have been eight feet tall. The children were supposed to come back home that afternoon; however, they decided to stay another night. As a result of the snow, there would be no school the next day. Clay called the hospital to inform them that he was snowed in. Clay was back on track, and he had another twenty-four hours to spend with this beautiful and vivacious seductress who could pretty much handle all he had to give.

The sex was great, but he knew that Leila's original intention was to help him get back into the world, as a player, and a sexual human being. He believed she was a sweet and caring person, and he wanted to believe that she loved her husband. Clay, being a little old fashion, had some pangs of guilt.

Clay was able to get back to the hospital the following evening. When he walked in, there was a young Wac standing in the middle of the lobby. She was a mess, with mud from the top of her short-cropped hair to the bottom of her rather large feet, and she didn't look particularly happy.

"What the hell are you laughing at?" She yelled. "Haven't you ever seen someone who's fallen in the snow?"

"I'm sorry, Kiddo, but you're a mess," he replied, still laughing.

"Well, I'm supposed to be reporting for duty here at the hospital. However, I think I've injured my pride." And with that, she broke up.

He walked over and offered his hand. "My name is Clay Smith. C'mon, I'll show you where you can clean up a bit before reporting in."

"Thanks, I'm PFC Susan Weidenberg, and you have a great laugh. I'm a physical therapist, and I've just been transferred to this hospital. Now, stop laughing, and show me where I can wash up."

Susan was close to six feet tall with short blond hair and green eyes. She was very beautiful once the mud was removed. She was something of a Marilyn Monroe, in an extra tall. She had beautiful skin, and great legs.

Over the next couple of months, they became very close. There was nothing physical between them, partly due to the fact that Susan was gay. Clay, being from Tennessee, had never known a gay person, at least not to his knowledge. He didn't know what a lesbian was supposed to look like, but he was certain, Susan, didn't fit the mold.

As a physical therapist, Susan worked with Clay's back almost everyday on her own time.

She said, "Clay, you're doing remarkable well, with the exercises I gave you, but don't let up."

"Thanks, Susan. I'm trying real hard to help my flexibility. It seems to help with the pain, at least for the moment."

Clay was about to be retired from the Army, for medical reasons. Soon he would have to go before the Medical Boards for his evaluation. This would decide the percentage of his disability. That percentage determined the amount of money he would receive each month as payment for sustaining his injury while serving on active duty. He wasn't very concerned about it; although, he knew that Dr. Delong, Leila, and Susan were. The three of them encouraged him constantly to get the best deal.

Dr. Delong's advice made good sense. "Clay, you might look fine now; but in the years to come, your quality of life will most certainly be affected by your injury. The army always tries to get injured young men to make a settlement rather than take a monthly retirement check for the determined percentage of disability. The settlement amount could be as much as twenty-five thousand dollars. That's a lot of money for a young man to turn down when the alternative might be only a couple of hundred dollars a month. On the other hand, agreeing to a settlement would absolve the Army of any further responsibility. Any medical cost in the future would be your responsibility. Over the years, that could amount to a great deal of money."

Clay was convinced; there would be no settlement. His decision to take the monthly retirement checks was solidified even more when he came to realize how much money he had in his Soldier's Deposit Account. He had been in the hospital for a very long time. In all that time, most of his pay was going into the bank, (Soldier's Deposit). He had saved over ten thousand dollars and now he could take it out and spend it anyway he wanted. A new car and college were his top priorities.

He knew the car he wanted cost about three thousand dollars. By the time he had to pay for his car insurance and bought some new clothes, he would only have spent about thirty five hundred. Also, he had inquired about the cost to finish his last two years at the University of Maryland. After doing so, he found he still had plenty of money left.

Susan was about to be discharged from the service. So, the two of them, decided to spend a little time traveling across country in Clay's new car. One evening, while he and Susan were sitting in the hospital cafeteria finalizing their plans, Susan was particularly preoccupied.

"What's wrong, Susan? Are you worried about something?"

"Clay, There's something I need to talk to you about. There's this girl, her name's Gidget. Her father is some kind of general in the air force, and he's stationed in California. She'd really like to make the trip with us, at least as far as California."

He looked at her pensively. "Are you having sex with her?"

"Hell no! She's just a friend, and anyway she likes men."

"When can I meet her? She's not some kind of weirdo, is she?"

Susan pushed away from the table. "Well, she should be here any minute. I didn't tell her she could go. I simply told her she could talk to you. She can, can't she?"

He looked up again from the map he was working on. "You dirty rat! Yeah, I'll talk to her, but you owe me one."

When Clay looked up again, there she was.

"Hey, Guys, I'm here. Did you talk him into it yet, Susan?"

"No, Gidget. I didn't, that's your job, dummy."

Clay stood, making an attempt at being polite. "Why do you want to go home?"

"I really don't want to go home, but my mom's health is not too good, so I think I should go. Please, I won't be any trouble; and as you can see, I don't take up much room."

This was a most unlikely trio. Susan was gay and not embarrassed by it. Gidget was an absolute nymph and she was also pretty proud of that little fact. Susan and Gidget were both in their early twenties. Gidget was just as short as Susan was tall, one being about five feet and the other about six.

Clay said, "Look, Girls. There will be no screwing around between the three of us. Is that understood?"

"That's not a problem," Susan replied.

Gidget said, "Me either, but can we have sex with other people?"

Clay tried not to smile. "That's all right, as long as it's consensual, and doesn't interfere with what we are doing at the time."

"No problem," the girls' agreed.

He looked at Susan and then at Gidget. "One last thing, no matter what, I'll be back in time to start classes at the university in September."

Clay knew that saying good-bye to Leila was going to be difficult. He was also going to miss Dr. Delong. He wanted them to always remember him and the time they had spent together. Being a poet of sorts he wrote a poem for each of them. Because the three of them had talked so much about friendship, he titled the poem "Friends", and signed them, "With love, to a dear friend."

Chapter 9

The three unlikely amigos hit the highway. The first night was spent in Charlotte, North Carolina. They arrived there without incident. They were so excited they hardly slept that first night. The following day it was on to Nashville, Tennessee, "Music City." They wanted to take in the local culture. On the first night, they went to the Grand Ole Opry. Afterwards, they went to a bar that Clay found quite amusing. All the guys kept hitting on Gidget because she was very pretty. The taller men also hit on Susan. She was tall but even prettier. They were, of course, unaware of her sexual preference and she never let on.

On Monday they headed for Memphis, about three and a half hours due west from Nashville. By early afternoon they were on Beale Street listening to some great Jazz.

Susan said, "Hey, Guys, can we go to the Music Box? It's a gay bar, and I really want to see what it's like. You'll have a good time, I promise."

Neither Clay nor Gidget had ever been to a gay bar. However, after much begging from Susan they decided to give it a try. Clay was certain they were the only two straight people in the place. Nobody seemed to mind, especially when Gidget seemed to enjoy the attention she was getting. Gidget even danced with a couple of the ladies. It was during the last dance that things got out of hand.

"What the hell do you think you're doing?" Gidget screamed. "That was a bad move."

Clay jumped from the table, but Susan got to her first.

"What's the problem?" Susan asked, calmly.

Gidget was foaming at the mouth. "She tried to stick her tongue down my throat, and I slapped her."

Susan said, "I'm sure she didn't mean any harm."

"Harm, my ass." Gidget was still steaming.

"I'm sorry," the lady said. "You're just so damned beautiful."

That helped, Clay thought.

Susan gently pushed Gidget toward the door. "Get our things, Clay."

By the time Clay was able to retrieve the girl's purses from the table, Susan and Gidget were already out the door.

"Sorry everybody," Clay said, as he exited the place.

Gidget was still ready to fight. "I'm sorry guys, but she really pissed me off. The worst part was her stupid tongue was like gritty cornbread, and her breath was bad."

"Otherwise, it was pretty good, huh?" Susan said, ducking behind Clay.

Clay couldn't help snickering. "Come on, cut it out you two."

"Clay," Susan said. "I found someone I want to be with for the next couple hours. I'll meet you two back at the motel, alright?"

"Sure, Susan. You have a nice time."

Clay and Gidget left together. The next bar they went to was straight. This time, Clay looked on as Gidget found her a playmate.

"Look, Gidget. Here's the key to the motel room; however, you have him out of the room by three, do you understand? And, don't mess up both beds."

"I understand. Thanks, Clay. What are you gonna do?"

"I'll just go on down the strip until I find something I like," he replied. "Don't worry about me, and be careful."

Clay listened to a lot of different kinds of music, and even had some breakfast at the Huddle House. It wasn't fancy, but he was impressed at how clean it was. He returned to the motel at ten minutes past three and went by the desk to get another key in case the girls were already asleep.

He took his time getting to the room. When he arrived outside his door, he could here a lot of noise. Gidget was pleading with her guy to leave. Clay opened the door. It didn't take him long to realize that the guy had been using Gidget for a punching bag. He had no way of knowing how long this had been going on, but he knew Gidget was ready for it to stop.

Grabbing the guy by his hair he threw him across the room. The man came flying back at him. Clay simply stepped aside, letting the man's own momentum carry him head first into the wall.

"Ouch, that must've hurt," Clay smirked.

Clay quickly came to a conclusion. If he allowed this to continue, someone in the motel might call the police. He didn't want to be up all night explaining what had taken place, not to mention how embarrassing it would've been for Gidget. So this time, when the man came at him, he turned sideways and put his foot into the middle of the man's chest. The man stopped, grabbed his chest and went to his knees. Clay, with all his force, slammed both opened hands on either side of the guy's head. The impact was so hard blood spurted from the man's ears. The man just sat in the floor, whimpering and bleeding. Clay turned his attention toward Gidget as she lay crying on the bed.

"Gidget, are you okay?"

Gidget looked at him and tried to smile, "I'm okay. Would you please make him leave?"

Clay turned back to the guy. "Okay, move it, Asshole."

He took most of the man's clothes; all but what the man was wearing, and threw them into the hallway. "Get the hell out."

"Screw you," the man said. "I'll cut your damned head off."

"Man, you're really stupid," Clay said, angrily. "I was going to let you leave but you really need to learn not to hit on little girls."

With that, Clay raised his right foot and with great force stomped the guy across the top of his bare foot. He could feel the man's arch give way. Even Gidget could hear the bones break. Clay proceeded to again grab him by the hair and threw him into the hallway.

"I'm gonna shut this door," Clay said. "I'll open it again in exactly one minute. If you're still here, I'm gonna break the other foot. Do you understand?"

The man nodded his understanding and Clay shut the door.

He began to console Gidget. "Honey, I'm truly sorry. What an asshole. Are you gonna be all right?"

"I'll be fine, thanks. You were great, where'd you learn to fight like that?"

"Different places," Clay said. "It's a long story, I'll tell you about it sometime."

About that time, Susan walked in, chuckling to herself. "You two should have seen this guy in the parking lot. He looked like somebody had just hit him with a car. I asked if I could help him and he promptly told me to get lost."

Clay and Gidget rolled on the bed laughing. Susan looked at them as if they were crazy.

After spending time explaining everything to Susan, Clay said, "Girls, I think we should get the hell out of here. That idiot's liable to come back with a bunch of his buddies, and they're apt to be caring guns."

Susan said, "Grab your things, Gidget, let's go."

"I'm coming, I've got to get my hair dryer, it's in the bathroom."

The girls slept as Clay drove through most of the state of Arkansas. They were on their way to Oklahoma City, Oklahoma. It was a little after lunchtime when they decided to stop for a bite to eat. Gidget still looked a little rough around the edges; but give two women make-up and a little time, and its remarkable what they're able to accomplish.

Clay marveled at the difference in people. Susan was six feet tall and strong as an ox, but she ate very little. On the other hand, Gidget, hardly five feet and a little porcelain doll type, could eat her weight in cheeseburgers three or four times a day and never gain a pound.

After brunch, Clay and Gidget napped as Susan drove. When Clay woke up, it was getting dark. "How're we doing, Susan?"

"Great, we're only fifty miles from Oklahoma City. Clay, can we go to the Cowboy Hall of Fame tomorrow?"

"I don't know why not."

Gidget chimed in, "Hell, I don't care where we go; I just want to have some fun."

The girls had decided earlier that it was Clay's turn to get laid and they intended to make sure it happened. After checking into their motel, they talked about how they could look out for each other and still have a good time. Clay asked at the front desk for the name of a nice place, and was given a couple of options. When they got to the place they had chosen, they decided to go in separately. The girls would go in first and then Clay would come in a few minutes later and sit alone. The girls would find out the lay of the place by talking to the other ladies. When Clay finally entered the bar, Susan and Gidget were sitting at a table with three other girls. He watched them as he found a booth next to the door.

Clay knew they were talking about him and he knew what the plan was. He was trying very hard not to look their way. The waitress came to his table carrying a beer. She sat it in front of him.

"I didn't order that," he said, looking at the waitress.

"It's from the table by the window, the one with the five girls. They think you're cute."

"How nice. You go back and thank them for me. Give them each a drink and put it on my tab," he instructed.

The waitress did as he asked.

In a couple of minutes Susan came over to ask him to join them.

"Damn, Clay, it's working like a charm. When you join us, stick around for a few minutes and then excuse yourself and go to the bathroom. That'll give us time to find out if they like you or not. When you return from the bathroom ask Gidget to dance and she'll fill you in on everything, okay?"

"No problem," he replied, "I hope, I don't start laughing."

"You better not, or I'll kick your butt. Let's go."

By the time Clay had spent just a few minutes with the five ladies, he was enjoying the conversation, but he hadn't forgotten about the bathroom. He waited a few more minutes, and then, asked to be excused. When he returned to the table, just as planned, he asked Gidget to dance. While they were dancing, she told him what the girls had decided. The girl who had bought him the beer was supposed to get him for the night, if he guessed who she was. It wouldn't matter who he guessed, for they had all agreed that they would all swear that the one he guessed was the correct one. Clay laughed, for that was even a twist on their plan. This was working out great and the night was young. When they returned to the table and sat down, everyone was in a big hurry to find out whom he was going to pick.

"Let me buy us one more drink," he insisted. "I need more time."

It was time to order again, and the girls wouldn't wait any longer.

Clay said, "I'm going to ask one of you to dance. I hope she'll be the one."

He reached for Gail's hand and she blushed. He couldn't believe she really blushed. When they got to the dance floor, Gail was really nervous.

"How'd you know it was me?" she asked.

"You were the only one I wanted. I decided if you were not the one, I'd simply leave with regrets."

She smiled and snuggled closer to him as they danced. Clay told her the truth about himself, explaining, that he was traveling across country to see what he could see. He also told her that he'd be returning to school in the fall.

When they left the bar, he asked if she wanted to go to his place or her own. They went to the motel. Clay put the "Do Not Disturb" sign on the door knowing that would keep the girls away until they were finished. Gail was very pretty. She was a cheerleader at the University of Oklahoma, in Norman, and she certainly had the body for it. He pulled her close to him and they kissed.

He said, "You know, Gail, if a person doesn't kiss well, nothing else really matters, does it? It's a prelude to everything sexual, don't you think?"

"I never really thought about it, but you're absolutely right," she replied. "If a guy's a bad kisser, things aren't going any further."

Gail backed away and began to unbutton her blouse. Her bra seemed two sizes two small. Clay put that little girl through position after position and she kept on coming.

"Look, Gail, it's really late, and, I have to be out of here early in the morning.

She reluctantly began searching for her clothes. "I'll give you my number, call me sometime. Okay?"

"Sure, I'd give you mine, but I won't really have one until I start classes in the fall."

"I understand. I hope you'll remember me," she said. "I won't forget you."

Clay removed the sign from the door and took her home. When he returned, both Gidget and Susan were sound asleep. No questions.

The questions started first thing the next morning and he told them everything. Clay could tell that they were very proud of themselves for having concocted such a marvelous plan.

They played the same game on Gidget's behalf in Albuquerque, New Mexico and the following night it was Susan's turn. They were in Phoenix, Arizona. With Susan, it was a whole new ballgame. However, those two young ladies were masters at the craft.

It was a little past noon, two days later, when they arrived in Los Angeles. By the time they got checked into the motel and settled, it was almost dark. They decided to drive to the famous street corner of Hollywood and Vine to get a look at the freaks. Many people had told them it was a real sight to behold, and it was.

The next morning, it was off to Disneyland and Knott's Berry Farm. They took a whole day at Disneyland and decided Knott's Berry Farm would have to wait. The following day was Saturday and a good day to see a Dodgers game. Not one of the three of them had ever seen a major league baseball game, live. The Dodgers had just moved from Brooklyn, New York, to Los Angeles. They all had a wonderful time at the game; Susan even caught a fly ball. On Sunday morning they were back in the car. This time, they were on their way to San Francisco. That was Susan's ultimate destination.

San Francisco was a beautiful and a most interesting place, and according to Susan, they were going to spend at least a couple of weeks there. They checked into a motel close to the airport. Knowing they were going to be there for a while, they rented a suite with two bedrooms and a living room/kitchen combo. It didn't take them long to unpack. Both girls had to spend half an hour in the bathroom getting their face on. Finally, they were headed to dinner. On their way, the local police pulled them over.

"What did we do wrong?" Gidget asked, not really looking for an answer.

Clay said, "Damned if I know, I wasn't speeding."

"Maybe they don't like red cars," Susan chimed in.

The policeman asked for Clay's driver's license. He took the license back to his patrol car, got on the radio and talked to someone for a long time. Then, he came back to the car.

"Mr. Smith, will you follow me to the station please?"

"Are we under arrest?" Clay asked.

"No, of course not. If you will fall in behind me, I'll try not to lose you," the officer replied.

Clay began following the police car. In a minute or so, another police car fell in behind them. Clay was beginning to get nervous, and so were the girls.

When they arrived in front of the police station, they were directed to a parking spot and escorted inside. After about ten minutes of standing around feeling very foolish, they were taken into the office of a Captain Briggs. The captain asked the girls if they would mind waiting in the outer office. With that, the girls were ushered back into the hallway.

Clay said, "Look, Sir, I don't know what we're supposed to be guilty of but I think you have the wrong party."

"Have a seat Mr. Smith. Policemen from Virginia to California have been on the lookout for your vehicle." Captain Briggs got up from his chair and walked around the desk. "Mr. Smith. You do know a General Essex from Military Intelligence, don't you?"

"I know a Colonel Essex, but what does that have to do with anything?"

"Mr. Smith. The general has been trying to find you for days. I've been asked to put you on an airplane back to Washington D.C as soon as possible. The general himself told me that this is a matter of national security. I assume you're going to cooperate." The captain concluded.

"May I talk to my friends and see to their needs?" Clay asked.

"Certainly, Mr. Smith."

Clay tried to explain what little he knew to the girls. He told them to take the car back to the motel, and said he would call them as soon as he knew what was going to happen next. Susan and Gidget were certainly worried, but they agreed to do whatever he needed them to do. He hugged them both, and off he went to the airport with lights flashing and sirens blaring. The police treated him with the utmost respect; like someone really important.

This must be something truly big, Clay thought. There was even a military jet waiting for him. In less than fifteen minutes, they were on their way, headed to Andrews Air Force Base, just outside Washington D.C.

Chapter 10

Upon his arrival in D.C. there was a car waiting to take him to the general's office. Sergeant Hensley was the first to greet him, and then the general walked in. General Essex grabbed Clay and gave him a big hug. "It sure is good to see you, even under these circumstances."

"It's nice to see you too, Sir. Congratulations on making general, I'm not the least bit surprised."

"Clay, I'll get right to the point. Captain John Murphy has been taken hostage, and I need your help to get him back in one piece."

The general went on to explain that Johnny had been on a mission in the Bahamas when he was caught, quite literally, with his pants down. He was having a little fun with a dark haired beauty when four Latin speaking gents took him away. From what they had been able to find out, Johnny was being held on the Island of Bimini.

The Island of Bimini is very small. There were only a few buildings on the island: The Bimini Hotel, consisting of about twenty rooms, the Rod and Gun Club and the largest building on the island, that being the home of Mr. Adam Clayton Powell, a New York politician.

Clay had to go in at night. The island was closed to tourists at this time. Although he had been able to demonstrate many physical feats, swimming was a sport in which he did not excel. He had no problem jumping from the plane; but when he hit the water, his body became entangled in the lines, and he almost drowned.

When he finally got to shore, he buoyed all his escape gear just off the northeast corner of the island. Thank God for night vision equipment. There was no moon out, and it was so dark he could barely see the beach. Clay knew where he was headed. The entire island was only about five hundred yards across, and maybe half a mile from end to end.

Stripping to his bare essentials he went hunting for someone who could give him information. It was only a moment or two before he found such a friend. When he came up behind the man, Clay put his right arm around the man's neck. In the same motion, he jerked backwards and to his left. With great force, the man came down across Clay's right knee. The man's spine snapped, rendering him helpless. Clay began to question him. The man was alert, but unable to move. Unfortunately, he had no intention of telling Clay anything. Clay's Spanish was severely lacking, and the man pretended to understand very little English. Being severely pressed for time, Clay was in no mood to play games. He began to perform his own brand of surgery on the man by using his knife and removing the skin from the man's fingers, one finger at a time. It took only seconds for the man's English to improve. When he had the information he so badly needed, he afforded the man a quick and painless death. It was to Clay, the only humane thing to do.

Clay had just a little more than three hours to find Johnny and get off the island. Johnny was being held on the opposite side of the island about forty yards from the rear entrance to the Rod and Gun Club. Johnny was tethered between two trees and just hanging there like a sack of potatoes. There was an enormous bon fire and only two guards were present. Clay had to do this as quietly as possible. The guards had their backs to him. Johnny's head was hanging down and his body sagging as though he were unconscious. Clay circled around behind him to let him know help had arrived, but it was useless. Johnny didn't know the world he was in. Clay immediately turned his attention to the job at hand, disposing of the two guards. The first guard's neck broke easily. The second took a bit of doing.

Throwing Johnny across his shoulder he headed for the point where he had left his gear. Clay shook his head. *This had been way too easy.* In minutes, he had Johnny in the rubber raft and they were on their way out to sea. Clay turned on the homing signal and waited. Before long a navy helicopter was there to take them to safety. While waiting for the helicopter rescue team, he tried to bring Johnny around, but, no luck. He said, "Johnny, I don't know what they've got you pumped full of, but keep breathing, Partner, please. We'll have you some help real soon, I promise."

They were taken to Homestead Air Force Base, near Miami, Florida, where Johnny was placed in Intensive Care. The doctors informed Clay that it would be sometime before they would have a prognosis on Johnny's condition: however, they would let him know immediately when a change occurred.

After a huge meal, Clay was escorted to the BOQ where he was to sleep for as long as was needed. The sun was peeking over the horizon, and as soon as he was able to report everything to the general, he was in the shower and then to bed for some badly needed sleep.

It was two PM when he finally rolled over. *Holy shit, I need to call the girls*, he thought, in somewhat of a panic. He picked up the telephone. "Operator, I need to make a call to San Francisco, California."

"I'm sorry, Sir, but you can't make long distance calls from that phone."

Clay said, "Look, Operator, all you have to do is get the long distance operator to call you back with the time and charges when I'm finished. I'll come pay you immediately."

"I can't do that, Sir. You'll have to use another phone." At this point the operator was getting a little testy.

"What is your name, Young Lady?"

"Private Jaynes, Sir."

"Well, Private Jaynes, where is your switchboard?"

"I'm in the admin office, Sir."

"Thank you, Private."

When Clay got downstairs he could hardly wait to confront someone with brass on his collar. "Where's the Duty Officer?" he asked the young lady behind the front desk.

"That would be Major Mayfield, and he's in the back office. Could I help you, Sir?"

"No offense, Young Lady, but I don't think so. Now, if you will please get the major."

"Yes, Sir, right away, Sir."

"I'm Major Mayfield, and who might I be addressing," he said smugly.

"Major, my name is Clay Smith, and we have a problem."

All the color drained from the major's face. "I'm sorry, Mr. Smith. How can I be of service? General Essex called my office this morning and instructed me to give you anything you wanted. What seems to be the problem?"

"You have a telephone operator; a private Jaynes, I believe. I'm sure she was only following orders when she refused to allow me to make a long distance call. I told her that I would come down to pay for the call straight away, but that wasn't good enough. I don't think the general will be impressed, do you?"

"Yes, Sir, I mean, no Sir."

"Well, Major. What form of action do you think we should take?'

"Mr. Smith, if you will come to my office, you may use my direct line, and you may take all the time you wish."

"Thank you, Major. Lead the way."

They entered the major's office. "Have a seat, Mr. Smith. You will have to dial nine, wait for the dial tone and just dial the number you wish to reach. Will there be anything else, Sir?"

"Just a little privacy, Major."

"Certainly, Sir. Please, let me know when you're finished, and I'll be delighted to buy you a drink. Take all the time you need."

When Clay got off the telephone, the major informed him that the doctor from the hospital was trying to reach him.

"Major, will you please return his call, and tell the good doctor I'm on my way to the hospital. We'll have that drink some other time, Major. Thank you, for your assistance."

When he arrived at the hospital, the doctor was waiting for him. "Mr. Smith, your friend, Doctor Murphy is going to be fine in a few days. He would very much like to see you."

"Thank you very much, Doctor."

When Clay opened the door to Johnny's room, he was trying to sit up. He still looked like hell; but at least, this time, he knew where he was and to whom he was speaking. "Clay, you saved my ass. Thank you, Old Buddy."

"You'd do the same for me, wouldn't you?"

Johnny just nodded. He had tears in his eyes.

"You know, Clay, very few people would risk their own life for a friend. You're the only person that ever actually did anything for me."

"Forget about it," Clay replied, a little embarrassed.

"Clay, you're the one person for whom I'd risk my own life, and you know how selfish I am." Johnny tried to stick out his hand, but he was still shaking badly.

Clay grabbed him. "Friends forever; right, Kemo-saabe?"

The nurse brought in Johnny's dinner tray and Clay realized he was also rather hungry.

"Look, Johnny, eat your dinner. I'll come by in the morning, before heading back to San Francisco to be with the girls. I hope they haven't destroyed my car."

Johnny tried to laugh, "You must tell me about those gals sometime."

Clay smiled. "I'll be glad to, when I think your heart can take it."

When Clay returned to the BOQ, he was told that General Essex would be there within the hour. The general wished to have dinner with him. He felt sure the government owed him something and a free meal is better than nothing.

When the general arrived, Clay was waiting in the lobby. They went to the Officer's Club where they had a great meal. They also had quite a few drinks.

The general was his old self, once again. "Clay, I've been keeping track of you for some time, and, for some reason or another when you left Nashville, Tennessee, I lost you."

"Well, I'm sure glad you found me when you did. Johnny might not have lasted much longer."

"You're so right, My Boy. That was fortunate for everybody, but, most especially, Captain Murphy."

"You know, General, freeing Captain Murphy was too damn easy. I must have taken those guys by complete surprise."

General Essex put his hand on Clay's shoulder. "Son, when you are through running around, there's a job waiting for you."

"I know, Sir, but the University of Maryland is calling me," Clay said, with a big grin on his face. "However, I'll stop by to see you before classes begin, if that's okay?"

"I'll look forward to your visit," the general replied, looking at his watch.

"What time is it, General?"

"Its 0300 hours, and I have to be back at the Pentagon by 08:00." The general pushed back his chair. "Thank you, My Boy, for all you've done. Let's go, I'll drop you at the BOQ on my way to the airfield. Get some rest, and I'll have a plane waiting for you between two and four this afternoon to return you to your friends."

The general paid the check, put his arm on Clay's shoulder, and ushered him to the waiting vehicle.

Clay was given a free ride back to San Francisco. The girls were at the airport waiting for him. Susan and Gidget were so glad to see him they could barely contain themselves. Everybody tried talking at the same time. They wanted to tell him everything that had happened to them in his absence. They also asked lots of questions about what he had been doing. All he would say was that everything went fine. The girls had no idea what he had been doing and that's the way he wanted it. They picked up some fast food on the way back to the motel and settled in for the night.

Susan and Gidget had found some great places in which to hang out. They had told everyone about Clay, and they wanted to show him off to all their new friends. Clay was certainly ready to have some fun, and tomorrow night the fun would begin. It was nearly dawn when they turned out the lights and stopped talking and it was late in the afternoon when they finally began to stir. By the time everyone was showered and ready to go, it was dinnertime.

Their first stop was a place called the Satellite Club. The Spinners were there that night. Clay thought they were great. Clay had become a good dancer; at least he had rhythm and could dance to the music, and he could spin like a top. This wasn't one of those nights when they had to play their game. He had his choice of any woman in the place.

It was time for a huddle. The three of them had to decide who would go where. There were three couples, and they had only two bedrooms. They drew straws. Susan lost.

Susan and Gidget were ready to party again the next day. Clay, on the other hand, was tired of all the free love and all the other crap that went with it. He was thinking about Taylor and how much he missed her. Even after all this time, she was on his mind quite a lot.

Susan noticed him sitting quietly on the end of the bed. "Clay, is everything okay? You sure were deep in thought."

"Yeah, I'm fine, where's Gidget?"

"She went for a walk. She said she was gonna call home. I told her to use the telephone in the room, but she said she'd call from the front office."

About that time, Gidget opened the door and walked into the room. Both Clay and Susan could tell she'd been crying.

"What's wrong, Gidget?" Clay asked, as he and Susan went to her side.

"My mom is real sick. Dad says I need to come home. I told him I'd be there tomorrow. Clay, will you take me home?"

"Of course. We'll leave first thing in the morning," he replied, looking at Susan for her approval.

The three of them left for Sacramento the next morning. Saying good-bye to Gidget was damn near impossible. The three of them had become so close. They loved each other selflessly. They kissed, they hugged, they cried, they parted.

Next stop for Clay and Susan was Reno, Nevada. He and Susan had decided to take Interstate 70 back across the country. By taking the northern route eastward, they would be traveling through many beautiful places including Reno. While there, he and Susan tried their hand at gambling. Clay was good, especially at blackjack. He instinctively knew what was coming next; and his ability to count cards was a great help.

Susan lost the hundred dollars she had set aside for gambling and came to watch Clay. He had won about thirty-six hundred dollars and he kept on winning. When his winnings reached ten thousand, he decided to call it a night. He cashed in his chips and put the money in the hotel safe.

The two of them decided to take in one of the floor shows. It was more to their liking than was the Grand Ole Opry in Nashville. The headliner was a comedian named Don Rickles and he was funny, in a strange sort of way, insulting almost everyone in the audience, including Susan and Clay. Mr. Rickles was on stage when they came down the isle to their table. Their table was right up front so he saw the two of them together.

Mr. Rickles said, "Hey, young man, you must have something more than money in those pants if you can handle that big beautiful doll, or does she just sit on your face and see how long you can hold your breath?"

Everybody laughed. It was a little embarrassing. Then there were two girls walking back to their table. They had obviously been to the ladies room.

Mr. Rickles said, "Hey, Ladies, when you were in the bathroom, could you hear us from in there?"

"No," they answered.

Mr. Rickles promptly replied, "Well, we could sure hear you."

Again everybody laughed. The ladies were obviously embarrassed.

It was almost daylight when he and Susan finally got to their room. There were lots of advertisements in the room. One particular ad informed them that Elvis Pressley was playing at the Sands in Las Vegas. Since he had won so much money, they decided to hop a plane the next day and see the show. Elvis put on the greatest show so the money spent seemed well worth it. It was one of those "once in a lifetime" sort of things. Unfortunately, they were unable to get a flight back until the next morning so they decided to go bar hopping in downtown Las Vegas.

"Susan, drink all you want. I'll stay sober. I don't want to miss our flight." Clay was not a big drinker anyway. By four o'clock, Susan was pretty drunk.

Susan grabbed his arm and motioned toward a woman sitting some twenty feet away. "Look at her," she said. "Isn't she gorgeous?"

"Not bad, Babe. But she's nothing when compared to you, Susan."

"You're sweet." Susan pecked him on the cheek and walked a little unsteadily over to the woman's table. "I hope I'm not intruding," she said. "You've probably heard this before, but I wanted to tell you how stunning you look."

The woman smiled. "Why, thank you."

The woman's male companion glared at Susan. "You some kind of dyke or something? What the hell you trying to pull?"

Susan steadied herself against the table. "Nothing, I just —"

Clay was suddenly by her side. "I think you owe the young lady an apology, don't you?"

"Hell no, I don't owe some lesbian bitch any apology."

Clay moved closer, his face inches from the man's ear. The man's mouth fell open, but nothing came out. His face turned red, sweat beading on his forehead. "I'm sorry," he squeaked.

Clay's hand uncoiled from around the man's genitals. "That's a little more like it." He looked at Susan. "Come on, Honey. Time to leave these nice people alone."

When they were finally outside Susan grabbed his arm spinning him around.

"What on earth did you say to that man?"

"I told him if he said one more word I was going to let you kick his ass, right there in front of God, and his girlfriend."

Susan laughed so hard she damn near fell face down on the sidewalk.

Clay said, "C'mon, Susan. Let's have some breakfast, I'm starving."

She leaned against him. "You know something, Clay? You're really mad when you're cute. I mean, cute when you're ... "

"Steady, Girl, I know what you mean." Holding her arm he led her to a nearby table in a beautiful restaurant. They still had two hours to kill, so they ate and talked until it was time to go.

The flight was twenty minutes late getting into Reno. When they finally got back to the hotel, they were so tired they could barely get undressed without falling asleep. They slept straight through to the next morning.

The city of Reno, Nevada had shown them all they wanted to see. Clay was ready to head for Denver, Colorado. Soon, they were on the road and trying to figure out what there was to see.

They stopped for lunch in a small town called Steamboat Springs, Colorado. It was one of the prettiest places either one of them had ever seen. For a big tourist town, the people there were nice and overly friendly. They arrived in Denver a little before dark. They checked into one of the nicer hotels downtown, The Sheraton. Susan wanted to find a bar that catered to the alternate lifestyle and she wanted him to go with her. But when they arrived, Clay immediately felt uncomfortable.

"Susan, you didn't tell me there were going to be gay men here. I feel like a fish in a barrel."

"Sorry, Clay. We can go somewhere else."

"No, no, that's all right, but I'm not dancing with any of these guys, got that?"

"Yeah, I got it. Are you gonna be okay if I dance with someone?"

"Sure, I'll just order something to drink."

The waiter sat a drink in front of him. "From the man in the last booth," she said.

He threw five dollars on the waiter's tray. "I buy my own drinks."

"Yes, Sir."

"Clay, you shouldn't have done that. You insulted the guy."

"Sorry, Susan, but I really don't care. You go dance, and I'll be fine. If you run into any straight women on the dance floor, send them over."

A gorgeous young lady asked Susan to dance. Susan accepted and stood. "Clay, let me dance one dance and we'll leave."

Clay nodded.

Susan came off the dance floor, eyes glowing. "Clay, I'm going to a party with Vivian. Isn't she beautiful?"

"She sure is," he replied, shaking his head. "I'm going back to the hotel to get some sleep, don't wake me when you come in. Here's the room key, I'll get another one from the front desk. You have a good time."

As Susan bent down to kiss him on the cheek, she was shoved into the booth.

"What's with you two? You're too good to let me buy you a drink, and then you're making out with this cross/dresser."

"Cross dresser?" Susan began coming out of the seat, and Clay shoved her back. "Sir, and I use that term loosely, you have thirty seconds to apologize to this beautiful young lady."

The man came closer. "Who the hell do you think you are?"

The man's head hit the table with Clay's hand firmly attached to his throat. "I don't guess you'll be sucking on much tonight will you, Old Sport. Susan, it doesn't look like you're going to get that apology after all. The man seems to be all choked up."

Susan said, "Clay, I can handle this, let him go."

"Okay, Babe." he replied, releasing the man, and allowing him to slide down to the floor and just sit there. "Susan, take your friend and I'll see you outside. Go!"

Clay stood, bent over, and helped the man to his feet. Then he headed toward the door. Once outside, everything was fine.

"Clay, you all right? I could have taken care of that guy."

"I'm fine, Susan. You two go have some fun. I'll see you later."

"Mr. Clay, you are more than welcome to come along," Vivian said. "There will be straight people there as well."

Clay laughed. "I don't think so, but I appreciate the offer."

He drove back to the hotel, had a drink in the hotel lounge, and went upstairs. As he entered his hotel room, he noticed the message light blinking by the phone. Picking up the receiver, he dialed the operator for his message. The message told him to call a particular telephone number at six AM his time. It was an east coast number so that would be eight AM, wherever he was calling. He dialed the operator once again and asked her to wake him at five forty-five. That would allow him a few minutes to remove the cobwebs before making his call.

The phone woke him from a dead sleep. Clay realized quickly that Susan had not yet returned. He decided to make his call and worry about Susan later.

"Government operator, how may I direct your call?"

"My name is Clay Smith, and I have been instructed to call this number at exactly eight AM. It is now eight AM."

"What's the name of the party you wish to reach?"

"I don't know the name."

"Then, Sir, I'm afraid I can't help you."

"It was probably General Essex, or Sergeant Major Russ. Do you know either party?"

"Sir, I'm unable to find either party in my directory. Please call back when you have the correct name."

"Yes, Operator, I'll do that. Thanks a bunch, for all your help."

About that time a key went into the lock on the door. Susan walked in, looking a little tattered but happy.

"What are you doing up this early?" she asked. "I thought you would be sound asleep."

"I was trying to return a phone call."

"Who called?"

115

"That's the problem, they didn't leave a name."

"Well, maybe they'll call back," she said, trying to be helpful.

He got up walked across the room and kissed her on the cheek. "I'm going downstairs to get some breakfast and read the morning paper. You try to get some sleep. I'll put the "Do Not Disturb" sign on the door, that way you won't be bothered. I think we should stay here for at least one more day just in case whoever called tries to call again, okay?"

"Sure, Babe, I'll be fine," she answered, undressing all the while.

Clay returned to the hotel just before noon. He wasted no time getting to his room. When he opened the door, a telegram was lying on the floor, just inside the room. The note told him very little, but now, at least he knew who was trying to contact him.

Susan was really sleeping soundly. He could hear her breathing from across the room. Walking back to the elevator, he returned to the lobby, and headed straight to the bank of pay phones to dial the number printed on the telegram.

Johnny answered. "Clay, I received a call from General Essex, he'd like for you to be back in Washington on the eighteenth. There is some kind of huge conference at 0800 hrs that morning, and he wants you to attend."

"Why does he want me there?"

"Look, Old Buddy, the general has assured me personally that there'll be no more assassinations. Unfortunately, I owe him one. Please, just listen to what he has to say; I think you'll be glad you did.

He also told me that you'd still be able to attend the university if you took the job.

Clay agreed to be there and the conversation ended.

He went to the front desk and asked if he could have a late checkout. The desk clerk told him that if he could be out by two PM, there would be no extra charge. Clay went back to the room and woke Susan. He explained to her what was happening and that they had less than an hour to vacate the room.

"C'mon, Susan. You can sleep in the car. I'll drive. Move that pretty butt."

"Okay, I'm moving. Look, Clay, I may be talking, but I'm still asleep."

Chapter 11

It was just after two PM when they pulled out of the hotel parking garage and headed east on Interstate 70. Clay had five days before he had to be in D.C. His plan was to take Susan to Long Island, New York, to be with her family. Then he would proceed directly from there to Washington D.C., figuring, that with any luck, he would be there a day early.

Now there was no time for messing around. They would eat, sleep, and drive. By daybreak the next morning, they had driven through the entire state of Kansas.

It was early evening on Saturday when they reached New York. They arrived at Susan's home just as night was approaching. She had called her parents from Pittsburgh and told them they would be there sometime early evening.

There must have been fifty people in that little house, and there was enough food to feed an army. Susan's family was of German descent; therefore, there were items on the table that Clay didn't recognize. In an effort to be nice, he ate some of everything and for the most part, it was damn good. He was also quick to realize that

Susan's parents had no idea their daughter was gay. Everyone seemed to think he and Susan were going to be married. Clay just smiled a lot.

He asked Susan if he were going to be spending the night. If he was, he wanted to find a place to fall down. If he wasn't, he wanted to make his excuses and go to a motel and then fall down; although, it would be nice if he could fall down on a soft clean bed. She said he was indeed spending the night. Susan also agreed to help him say goodnight and then she would show him where he was to sleep.

She began announcing to the crowd that they were very tired, and as much as they wanted to spend the rest of the night talking to everyone, they had to get some sleep. Clay had to be back in Washington D.C. the very next day. Susan showed him to an upstairs bedroom and a place to shower. In less than ten minutes, he was in and out of the shower and in the bed. He had just gotten under the covers when Susan came back into the room.

"Clay, I need to take a quick shower. You go on to sleep, and I'll try to be quiet."

He was about half asleep when she came out of the shower and sat down in the chair beside the bed. He thought she must wish to talk to him so he sat up in the bed.

"Lay back down, Clay, and go to sleep."

"Hey, Girl, I thought you wanted to talk to me."

She looked bewildered, "Clay, I have to sleep in here tonight. That's what my parents expect."

He was amused, and knew this shouldn't be happening, but what the hell. Susan could deal with it later. He took a blanket and pillow, lay down on the floor with his pillow and blanket and motioned for her to take the bed. It was a very small bed.

Susan bent down and kissed him on the forehead. "Clay, you're one of a kind and I'm sure glad you're my friend. I'll wake you for breakfast around eleven. That'll give us a little time together before you have to leave."

He just grunted and rolled over.

At breakfast the next day, there were very few probing questions. Mr. Weidenberg just kept shaking his hand and Mrs. Weidenberg just kept hugging him around the middle. In contrast to Susan, Mrs. Weidenberg was a short, tiny woman.

After eating a hearty breakfast, He and Susan went onto the back porch to say their good-byes. They decided to call Gidget and chat for a few minutes. When they had her on the phone, they all cried. Even Clay shed a few tears. They expressed their love for each other and said their good-byes.

"Clay, I've never loved anyone as much as I love you," Susan said, her voice breaking. "I will forever be your friend. My time, and anything I own, will always be available to you. Please don't forget me."

"Susan, you know I feel the same, and if you ever need me, I'll always come to you, regardless of my circumstances." At that moment, he felt especially close to her. He wanted to express what he was feeling, but he simply couldn't find the proper words.

She put her arms around his neck, and for the first time, she kissed him right on the mouth. "Don't you go doing anything stupid, you hear me?"

"Yeah, I hear you, you big bully."

Susan held him close. "I will never forget the time we've spent together. I swear I wouldn't trade the last few months for anything."

"I know how you feel," he said. "When I close my eyes, I can still see you standing in the lobby of the hospital, with mud on your face, and the most beautiful, and the warmest smile ..." He couldn't go on; anyway, it was time to leave.

As she walked him to the car, He told her that he would be staying at the Guesthouse at Fort Belvoir, Virginia. That was as close to D.C. as he wanted to get. It would be inexpensive and clean. In addition, he promised to let her know if there were going to be any major changes to his current lifestyle.

Clay arrived at Fort Belvoir late that evening, and checked into the Guesthouse on the base, trying to think as little as possible about his meeting the next day. He picked up the telephone and called Leila, hoping to hear a pleasant voice. They talked for over an hour and decided to meet for dinner the next evening.

When the driver picked him up at the guesthouse, the limo he was driving was the longest car Clay had ever seen. The driver headed off base.

"Where're we going?" Clay asked.

"To the Pentagon," he replied.

Clay was already impressed and they hadn't even arrived at the Pentagon yet. They entered at the garage level entrance and were greeted by two more soldiers, a captain, and a lieutenant, who took him up the elevator to the general's office.

The captain said, "Mr. Smith, will you please wait here, someone will be with you shortly."

Before he could sit, a beautiful young girl headed his way. "Will you follow me please, Mr. Smith?"

She led him into General Essex's office. He was now thoroughly impressed. The office was the most beautiful one room he had ever seen. The walls were mostly cherry wood with crown molding that must have been 12" wide. Sections of the walls were covered in stain glass and ivory figurines. The carpeting was a deep burgundy, and so plush it felt like a firm mattress under his feet. He was sure that Ethan Allen himself must have designed each and every piece of the furnishings. The desk at which the General was sitting must have been at least five feet wide and maybe eight feet long. There were maybe ten telephones on his desk. There was even a *red* one.

This is no bullshit session, he thought. *Serious things, and decisions, must happen in an office this fantastic.*

General Essex watched the expression on Clay's face. "How do you like my new office, Clay?"

He replied instantly, "Who'd I have to kill to get an office like this?"

The general just smiled and waved it off; walking around the huge desk he extended his hand. "Clay, my boy, I never did thank you properly for the job you did in retrieving Captain Murphy from the islands down south. I want you to know that a lot of important people hold you in very high regard. We have a number of those people waiting for us in the briefing room. Come with me."

"Yes, Sir."

The general stopped abruptly. "Clay, you're about to meet some very important people, at least many of them think they're important. Look, Son, let's be serious. These people move the world in which we live. You just watch and listen and don't be intimidated by the surroundings or the conversation."

"I understand, Sir, and I'll try not to embarrass either one of us."

This time they both laughed.

When they entered the briefing room, there were nine people seated around a huge conference table, eight men and one woman. He and the general made eleven. The remaining seat at the head of the table was vacant. The general put his hand on Clay's shoulder and announced, "Lady and Gentlemen, this is the young man I've been telling you about." As the general made the introductions, Clay made mental notes concerning each individual with intent to put it on paper as soon as possible. There were two high-ranking military officers, two congressmen, four senators and a gentleman from the Justice Department.

The general began: "Clay, in the governmental structure, the left hand simply doesn't trust the right hand. The CIA has its own agenda and so does the FBI. G2, which, as you know, represents the military, is without the proper support to officially do much of anything. We need certain information, and we desperately need operatives that we can trust. Clay, you are just such a man, absolutely above reproach. A man who cannot be bought or swayed from the task at hand."

Clay flushed, "Thank you, Sir."

After a great deal of banter between all parties present, the general said, "Clay, if you will be so kind as to wait for me in my office, I'll be with you in a few minutes."

He returned to the general's office, and asked the pretty young receptionist for directions to the men's room. As he was washing his hands, one of the senators walked in. It was Senator Lazar from the State of Minnesota.

"Welcome aboard, Young Man. I know you idolize the general; however, if you ever find yourself in need of a friend, or just someone to talk to, please let me be that friend. My door will always be open."

"Thank you, Senator." he replied, "I'll remember that."

When he returned to the office, General Essex was waiting for him.

The general began to speak. "Clay, money and equipment are not a problem, but good people are hard to find. I would love to talk to you further, but I'm expected across the hall at a meeting of the Joint Chiefs. Follow me to Sergeant Hensley's office and he'll give you all the necessary details. Don't fret, my boy, there'll be no more assassinations."

"Thank you, Sir. I think I can live with that arrangement."

"Mr. Smith," Sergeant Hensley said, as Clay and the general walked into his office. "I sure was happy to hear you were going to be on the team."

"It's nice to see you too, Sergeant."

The general put his arm on Clay's shoulder. "Sergeant, you take good care of my boy. When you're finished with his briefing, show him to the quarters we've secured for him." The general turned and extended his hand. "It's a great day, My Boy. Get settled in and I'll talk to you again real soon."

"Thank you, General."

Sergeant Hensley began, "Mr. Smith —"

"Hold it, Sergeant. I think you should call me Clay, don't you. After all, you've seen me at my very worst."

"Okay, Clay. We've set up a number of situations in order to test your photographic abilities, and Sergeant Shackelford will, again, be brought in to work on your physical side."

Clay said, "That will be the hardest part, due to my injuries, but if anyone can get me into shape, Shack can. Also, I'll be enrolling at the University of Maryland in about two weeks, and I was told that that was no problem, right?"

"We will make every attempt to work around your schedule. I don't see any problem there."

Clay smiled broadly. "Terrific, that's terrific."

A handsome salary and great benefits were also part of the position. Clay's checks would come from a company called PR&M Inc. He would be listed as the Director of Operations for the company. He knew nothing about the company except that the president was a certain Dr. John W. Murphy.

"Clay, why don't I show you to your new home, we can finish talking on the way. Did you drive, or were you brought here?"

"Are you kidding? I rode in the longest limousine you ever saw. My car is at the guesthouse at Fort Belvoir."

"No sweat. Let me take you to your new place of residence, and then I'll take you to get your car. That way you'll know where you're going." Sergeant Hensley stood, picked up some paperwork from his desk, and they were on their way.

Clay's new address was 1111 Massachusetts Avenue in downtown Washington D. C. He even had a private parking space reserved just for his vehicle.

The apartment was nice, but unfortunately, it couldn't compare to the general's office. The apartment was fully furnished and whoever put it all together had very good taste. There was a huge living room/den combo with a fireplace. Fireplaces were one of Clay's favorite things. There was also a dining area that led to a large balcony with its own dining table and chairs. The kitchen was relatively small but well furnished, and the refrigerator was fully stocked. The bedroom was large with a spacious walk-in closet. The bathroom was almost as big as the bedroom. The towels were even his favorite two colors, burgundy and blue with just a hint of gray. The entire apartment was obviously decorated with a man in mind.

"What do you think, Clay?" Sergeant Hensley asked.

"Its fine, it will do nicely," Clay replied, trying not to sound like an overly impressed child.

"Well, c'mon, I'll take you to get your car, and you can get settled in," the sergeant said, handing him the key to his new home.

When Clay was finally unpacked, it was almost seven PM. Suddenly he remembered he was supposed to call Leila. He dialed the number and one of the children answered. They informed him that she was in the shower. He left his number and continued to inspect the apartment. There were lots of clothes in the closet. Most of the clothes still had the tags on them. He began trying things on and found that everything seemed to fit him perfectly. This he could not explain.

The telephone rang. It was Leila. She really was taking a shower. The two of them made plans to meet at the base housing area at eight-thirty. They would go from there in one car. Leila arrived about five minutes late, complaining about the traffic. When she got out of the car, she was smiling from ear to ear.

She was wearing a red dress with a single silver chain around her neck. She had on dark stockings and high heels that really complimented her legs. She didn't look a day older. If anything, she may have even looked better than he remembered. When she got into his car, the red dress looked great in contrast to the black leather seats.

"Where are we going?" she asked.

"I was gonna take you back to my new apartment; however, you look so fantastic, I'd like to go somewhere and have a drink first just so I can show you off. Do you mind?"

"Of course not. I know just the place."

127

They ended up at the lounge in the Shoreham Hotel. He was right. Not a man in the place could keep his eyes off her. Clay was over six feet tall with a beautiful tan and dressed to kill. The two of them were quite an item. The lounge was pretty crowded but they were able to find a table on the far wall looking out onto the street.

"Clay, you sure do make a woman proud. I like your new suit."

"How'd you know it was new?"

"Well, I should know. I picked it out. How do you think all those new clothes got in your closet?"

He reached over and gave her a little hug, "I thought it was magic."

She slid her left hand under the table, and between his legs. "Actually, I had a lot of help. The person who helped me probably knows more about you than anybody else alive, especially, when you consider she's never met you in person, until now. It just so happens she's standing right behind you. Let me be the first to introduce you."

As Clay stood and turned, Pamela, the young lady from the general's office, stood directly in front of him.

He said. "We've met. Today, at General Essex's office, but it's, indeed, a pleasure to see you again. Thanks for your assistance this afternoon."

Pamela seemed a little awe struck as he motioned for her to sit.

"Did things turn out well for you in the meeting?" She asked.

"I certainly hope so," he replied, rather matter of factly. "If not, I'm certainly wasting a lot of people's time and a lot of the government's money."

"Well, we wouldn't want to do that now would we?" Pamela replied, in the same tone of voice, mimicking him.

"So, Pamela," he continued. "Leila tells me that you know a great deal about me. Is that true?"

She blushed. "I guess it's true. You've led a very interesting life; unfortunately, your life has been filled with a great deal of sadness and tragedy."

Leila interrupted, "I certainly hope the last year or so wasn't so terrible. Was it Clay?"

"No, it most assuredly was not," he replied, as he took a long drink from his glass. "May I buy you a drink, Pamela?"

"No, thank you," she replied. "I'm here with a couple of my girlfriends. I think I'd better get back to them. It would be nice; however, if you'd walk over with me so that I could introduce you to them."

"Go ahead, Clay, Leila urged, do the polite thing. I'll wait for you, but, don't be gone too long, I might get lonely."

He took Pamela by the hand and escorted her across the room. When they reached the table where her friends were sitting, the introductions were made. He was about to excuse himself when Wanda, who looked to be the youngest of the group, spoke.

"Clay, you seem to be just as Pamela described. You're all that Pamela has talked about for the last two weeks and you're really pretty for a guy."

Everybody at the table blushed and that included Wanda. When she realized what she had said, she hid her face in her hands.

He walked back across the room, fully aware all six eyes were watching him. "Leila, I'm sorry it took so long."

Sitting down close to her, he could feel her strong, muscular leg against his own and they both knew it was time to leave. When the two of them were outside and walking toward the car, he continued. "Leila, I hope it wasn't a problem running into Pamela the way we did."

"No, not a problem," Leila replied, as she slide her arm around his waist. "Pamela knows we're good friends. That's why she asked me to help her get your apartment ready. Anything else she may think she knows doesn't really matter, does it?"

"I guess you're right, Love," he said, as he opened the car door for her.

On the ride from the hotel to his apartment very few words were spoken. They didn't even listen to the radio. Inside the apartment they sat on the floor in front of the fireplace. The fireplace was gas so there wasn't much heat to be concerned about. They didn't even turn on the lights. Holding each other they quickly demolished a good bottle of wine.

Leila finally broke the silence. "Clay, you'll always be very special to me. I feel like I was able to help you at a time when you really needed a woman's help. Tell me I'm not just imagining that."

"Leila, I'm truly grateful. Without a doubt, I would yet be floundering out there somewhere if you hadn't reached out to save me. You'll always be deep in my heart."

"Clay, my husband is coming home in a few days and I'd like for you to meet him." Leila almost cried as she spoke. "This will probably be our last night together. I must think of my husband and my children. Clay, tell me we'll always be friends, very special friends."

"Of course we will, and as I said before, your husband is a fortunate man. I'll always love you, Leila, in a most special way."

She kissed him. "Clay, do you want to make love to me?"

"Of course I do," he whispered as he returned her kiss.

The two of them enjoyed each other for what he thought would be the final time, and Leila was insatiable!

Afterwards, he drove her back to her car. "Leila, please call me when you get home. I want to know you're home safely."

"Sure, I'll call, but you worry too much," she replied.

Gosh, Clay thought. *In a little over twenty four hours my training will begin, maybe, I'll just sleep til then.* When he entered his apartment, the telephone was ringing.

"It's me, and I'm home safe and sound," Leila said, giggling. "Clay, you ought to ask Pamela to join you at the club dance a week from Friday. It'll be a lot easier to introduce you to my husband if you have a pretty girl on your arm."

"What makes you think she'd go with me?"

"You've got to be kidding," Leila replied. "Honestly, you men can be so slow sometimes. You ask her. She'll go. I'll guarantee it."

Clay laughed out loud. "Listen, Smarty Pants, I'll talk to you later."

Fatigue swept over him. He took a quick shower and went straight to bed. When he rolled over in the bed, he noticed a red light blinking by the telephone. *When did the phone ring?* He wondered. *I guess it rang while I was in the shower, and I just never noticed the light.* Having never had an answering machine before it took him awhile to figure out how it worked. When he finally pushed the right button, he heard Johnny's voice. He dialed the number Johnny had left for him.

Johnny answered immediately. "Hey, Boy, did things go well today? Are you on the team?"

"Yes, Johnny, things went well, and I think I'm on the team. It depends largely on my doctors and how well I perform on the tests they're about to administer."

"Piece of cake," Johnny replied. "You'll do great and you know it."

"I hope you're right my friend."

"Look, Clay, I'll call you later in the week to see how you're making out. In the meantime, if you need me for anything, give me a call."

"Thanks, Johnny, I appreciate your concern. But, tell me, how are you doing?"

"Hey, Man, I'm doing great."

"Well then, I guess I'll talk to you later in the week. You take care." Clay hung up, and in only minutes, he was sound asleep.

The telephone rang so loud Clay almost jumped out of his skin. This time it was Pamela, and it was almost noon. He knew she could tell he had been asleep, and she began to apologize.

"It's okay. I must tell you, however, I was dreaming about you. Now I'll never know whether or not I can catch you."

Pamela got so nervous she nearly forgot why she had called. "Oh yes, you are to report to a Doctor Delong in the morning. He's at the base hospital at Fort Belvoir, Virginia. Do you need directions?"

"That won't be necessary, I've been there before. I'll be there."

"Thank you very much," she replied, and promptly hung up the phone.

He tried to stop her but it was too late. Grabbing the general's card from his wallet he dialed the number.

"General Essex's office. May I help you?"

"Yes, you may. I'm new in town and very lonely. Would you go to the club dance with me a week from Friday? I'd be ever so grateful. You could even introduce me to some of your friends. I'm really not a bad guy and I'm cute as hell and a great dancer."

There was a long pause on the other end of the phone. "I'd be ever so happy to introduce you around. Maybe we can find someone right for you." There was a definite chuckle in her voice.

"I think maybe I already have; however, she has me at a disadvantage. She knows a great deal more about me than I know about her. Is there any chance we could correct that, maybe even before a week from next Friday?"

"Clay, I'm going to give you my home telephone number. If you live through tomorrow, I'll be home after six. Now, I've enjoyed our little chat; but if I don't get back to work, the general will have me shot. I will, hopefully, talk to you tomorrow night," and with that, she was gone again.

133

Chapter 12

Clay couldn't remember the last time he had eaten but he was sure it had been way too long. Shaving and showering went fast, and after brushing his teeth, out the door he went. His travels had taken him to hotels and motels for so long that he had forgotten he had food in his own refrigerator. When he remembered, he was already outside so he decided to walk around town until he found a place to eat. *That shouldn't take very long. Surely I can survive a few more minutes,* he thought to himself.

He found a place a block away called the Waffle House. It was certainly no five star restaurant, but the food was damn good. Bacon, eggs, and waffles were good any time of day as far as he was concerned.

By the time he returned to his apartment, it was getting dark. After eating, he was feeling much better about everything. The apartment was very quiet; so quiet in fact, it was beginning to get on his nerves. He tried watching television but that only confirmed his theory that people who watch a lot of television are mostly brain dead. Exercising came next and lasted for less than thirty minutes. The balcony looked promising, and the fresh air felt grand, and the view was really quite good. By the time he had calmed down, his telephone began to ring.

"Hello."

"Hi, Sweetheart, I could actually smell you this morning on my skin, it was great."

"Who is this?"

"I'll get you for that," she screeched.

"Leila, I'm so glad you called, I'd love to see you. Why don't you come over?"

"Sorry, Honey, but I have no babysitter. Why don't you come here?"

His response was immediate, "Okay, Love, but you'll have to give me directions."

The directions were easy to follow; however, he had to wait until the children went to bed, and he even had to park some distance away. Leila told him to enter off the back porch so he wouldn't be noticed. That was the first time he realized just how wrong this was. Unfortunately, it didn't stop him.

He went inside and locked the door behind him. Down the hall he could see a light from underneath Leila's bedroom door. It was a good thing that her bedroom was in another part of the house away from the children. When he entered the room, she was already under the covers with a book in her hand, motioning for him to come to her.

Moving to her side of the bed, he leaned down to kiss her on the forehead. She was already trying to undo his trousers. In a matter of seconds, she had him completely naked. She lay back with her head

135

on the pillow, and she pulled him down on the bed with her. For a long time they enjoyed the taste of each other until they were both full to overflowing.

He and Leila wore each other out. What little talking they did was in whispers.

"I just couldn't wait to see you one more time. I wanted to taste you, just as I smelled you this morning. I'm gonna miss you, Clay. My husband is a fine man, but you, My Love, are incredible."

"You're not so bad yourself," he said, pushing her hair from her face.

He left the way he had arrived, through the back door. Within twenty minutes, he was back in his own apartment.

When the alarm sounded, he thought he had only been asleep for a few minutes. He turned off the alarm and was suddenly excited about seeing Dr. Delong again, arriving at the hospital more than fifteen minutes early. The staff was already prepared for his arrival.

The first thing was a bunch of paperwork; then to the X-ray clinic for numerous pictures. The vampires came next. That's what he called the ladies who drew blood. He was then resigned to spending his time running on the treadmill, running, until he couldn't run anymore. Of course, there was also time for peeing in a cup.

Dr. Delong walked in while Clay was resting. "Boy, it's good to see you. I've often wondered how you were doing."

"You look good, Doc. The wife must be taking good care of you."

"Yes, I'm doing just fine. Karen is expecting our first child in about six months," Dr. Delong responded with a serious gleam in his eye.

Clay said, "Just a little proud, are we?"

Dr. Delong continued, "I think we best get serious about the state of your health. Have you had any particular problems other than the pain?"

"Look, Doc, as long as I continue to do my stretching exercises and don't try lifting any Volkswagens, I can handle it," he replied. "As a wise man once said, pain is only in the mind."

"Well, at least you haven't lost your sense of humor." Dr. Delong responded. "Clay, in my opinion, you can do anything as long as you remember your limitations, and that'll be in my report to the general." He patted him on the shoulder and smiled.

Clay smiled back. "Well, in that case, my next stop is mental hygiene, you know the headshrinkers. Look, Doc, you know how much I like you and how thankful I am for all the help you've given me. If you ever need me for anything, all you need to do is call, and I'll come running."

"Thanks, Clay. It was great seeing you again, and let's keep in touch."

Mental hygiene was a snap although it took the rest of the afternoon.

It was after six when he got back to his apartment. He was anxious to talk to Pamela. If for no other reason, he would find out what was in store for him the next day.

He dialed the number. "Gerard residence, this is Pamela."

"Well, I made it through the day. Would you like to meet somewhere for a couple of drinks?"

"I'd like that. How about the same hotel lounge?"

"I'll see you there at eight-thirty, if that's okay?"

"See you at eight-thirty," Pamela replied.

When Pamela arrived at the lounge, Clay was already sitting at the bar. He found them a booth next to the one he and Leila had sat in the previous evening. Pamela looked pleased. She was wearing a scotch plaid, pleated skirt and a white blouse with cuffs. With high top socks and penny loafers, she looked like a young schoolgirl. Her hair was almost in a ponytail or more of a French braid. Pamela was five feet four and probably weighed one hundred and ten pounds. She looked very athletic and yet a bit helpless and demure. She also had the biggest green eyes he had ever seen.

"Before looking at you makes me forget, what is my schedule tomorrow?" Clay asked.

"You are to report to room two-ten in the Pentagon at nine AM. They're going to do some psychological testing, or some such thing. Wear comfortable clothes." She reached into her purse, removed a piece of paper and handed it to him. It was his itinerary for the week, neatly typed on one sheet of paper.

He looked at it briefly, thanked her and put it in his pocket. He ordered drinks for the two of them and continued to enjoy the view from across the table. Just as she was about to ask another question, a big guy came strolling up to their table.

"Hey, you Prissy Little Bitch, you're coming with me." He grabbed Pamela by the arm and almost jerked her out of her seat.

Clay's reaction was instantaneous. "That's no way to treat a lady," he said as he brought the man to his knees. "You'll apologize now or you'll most certainly be sorry you ever opened your filthy mouth."

"Okay, okay, I'm sorry. I won't bother you anymore. Damn, Man, let go of my finger." The man pleaded, trying hard to get off his knees.

"Let him go, Clay, please," Pamela entreated.

"I think you were just about to leave, ain't that so, Fat Boy?" Clay scowled.

The man was still on his knees trying desperately to rise to his feet, rubbing one hand with the other. "Yes, I'm going."

"Then go," Clay said shoving him toward the door.

Pamela apologized at least a dozen times. There was no question about it she was pretty shaken. She went on to explain to him how she had met this guy at the lounge. When she allowed him to buy her a drink, he thought it gave him the right to paw her. She told him to stop and he got pissed.

"Hey, the world is full of assholes; you just have to know which ones to avoid,"

"I know, I should have never accepted a drink from him in the first place."

"Well, I imagine that's a mistake you won't make again. Ah, what the heck, let's have another drink. I'm buying, and I promise not to paw you at anytime during the evening. Okay?"

139

He finally saw a smile return to her face.

"I like that face much better," he said, raising his glass.

"Clay, when I was reading about you, I knew you were a really sweet person in spite of all you'd gone through, and I was fine until you walked into the office the other day." she paused. "You must promise not to take advantage of me. I'm a little out of my league, and you'll be sorry to know that I have absolutely no experience of any kind."

"I have no intentions of taking advantage of you," he replied. "I simply thought it would be nice to have a friend my own age to spend some time with. The fact that you're cute as hell is just a bonus, at least in my way of looking at it."

"Clay, I'm sorry. I didn't mean anything by that statement."

"Pamela, would you like to have dinner with me tomorrow night and Friday, Saturday, and maybe Sunday brunch? Or, maybe that's just too much food to think about all at once."

She smiled again. "I'll take all four, if you're serious."

"Of course, I'm serious. If you'll take all four, this night has been a big success as far as I'm concerned. Now, tell me about Pamela. Where do you live? Father, mother, sisters, brothers, and pets, I really want to know everything."

She began, "I live at home with my mom. My dad passed away two years ago from a heart attack. I have one older sister and no brothers. My older sister is married and lives in Chicago. I'll be attending American University on a part time basis in the fall. I have no steady boyfriend, and I love football and cooking."

"That's a pretty quick history lesson, Young Lady. Maybe you can cook me a meal sometime, if your mother wouldn't mind."

"How about Friday?" she replied. "What do you like to eat?"

"You promise not to laugh?"

"I won't promise but I'll try not to. Tell me."

"Meatloaf, I like meatloaf and mashed potatoes."

She looked relieved, "Let me draw you a map to my house."

When she was finished drawing the map, she informed him that she should be getting home. "It's a week night, and I have to work tomorrow. You may finish your drink; I'm not in that big a hurry." The waitress brought the check. Clay gave her the money and out the door they went.

Clay was just about to kiss her goodnight when he caught a glimpse of the big guy in the mirror coming from behind them. He shoved Pamela into the car, turned sideways and stuck his right leg straight out catching the man dead in the throat with his right foot. The big guy dropped like a stone. He then came across the right side of the man's face with his forearm and put him on his back.

Clay said, "Have you had enough, or shall I finish the job?"

The big lumbersome oaf crawled away. When he got to his feet, he took off running and never looked back.

"Pamela, are you alright?" Clay asked.

"My God, Clay Smith, you really are something else."

With that said she got back out of the car and put her arms around his neck. She gave him a goodnight kiss. The kiss was so sweet and innocent. Clay had a sudden rush of emotions stemming from more than two years back.

"I'll call you tomorrow night, after six. Dinner is on me tomorrow night," Clay reminded her.

When he returned to his apartment, he was sure glad he had made a new friend. It didn't hurt matters any that she was as cute as a button.

The telephone rang.

"I thought you might be worried, so I wanted to let you know that I'm home safe and sound. I'm even in my little pink jammies. My father would have greatly appreciated what you did for me this evening. Thank you again."

"Okay, Babe, but next time, it's your turn to rescue me."

"Don't hold your breath, Clay."

"Pamela, why don't you let me pick you up at your house tomorrow night? Then, on Friday, I'll know the way. I'll see you at seven-thirty, okay?"

"Seven-thirty will be fine. See ya."

"Wait a minute. I want to know more about those pink jammies."

"Goodnight, Clay, I'll see you tomorrow night."

The next morning, he was in room two-ten a little before eight. Being on time was very important to him. Someone he admired very much once told him that if you are late, you insult whoever you're going to meet.

That day, they tested him for hours. Not only did they find he had a photographic memory, but he was also a little psychic. At times he seemed precognitive. Only seconds earlier, but sufficient time to save his life, or the life of someone else. When he was finished, he was told that the doctors' reports would be sent to the committee.

He arrived almost twenty minutes early at Pamela's house, allowing himself extra time since he had never been there before.

She lived in a nice but very modest home. It was a two-story frame house painted white with dark red shutters and a black roof. Ms. Gerard, Pamela's mother was very pleasant. It was obvious she knew a little about Clay and his background. She asked him a lot of questions about what he thought his future would be like and what he was studying at the University. Before things got too deep, Pamela appeared, looking as cute as ever.

Ms. Gerard told them to have a nice evening, and of course, to be careful.

Clay opened the car door as Pam slide in on the passenger's side. Then he walked around the car and jumped into the driver's seat.

"Where do you want to go?" he asked.

She looked him over. "I hear you're a great dancer. Is that true?"

"Yes, as a matter of fact, I love to dance. So, Girl, lead me to the music."

"I know this place that has the best band around, but all they serve is mostly hamburgers and the like. Will that be okay?"

"Sure, it sounds great to me. Point me in the right direction."

She gave directions and he followed them to the letter. The place was called the Thunderbird Lounge, and she was right. The band was great. The two of them danced almost every dance. They did stop for a few minutes to eat a burger and drink a beer. The band played mostly reggae and soul type music. That was, of course, Clay's favorite.

He took her home about midnight and kissed her goodnight at her door.

"Am I still invited to dinner tomorrow evening or did I flunk the test?"

"Of course you are, and you best call me when you get to your apartment and let me know that you're home safe." she warned him.

He did as she asked. They talked for only a few minutes. She reminded him that tomorrow was his first day with Sergeant Shackelford and he better get some rest.

The next morning, Clay was in the gym bright and early and Shack was waiting for him.

Sergeant Shackelford began to speak, "Clay, according to the doctors report, I have been given the go ahead on everything except lifting weights. Although, you can bench press and do a little bicep curls."

"Okay, but try not to kill me on the first day of training," Clay said. "I have a big date tonight, and the young lady will be very upset if I can't walk."

When Shack had finished with him for the day, he told him to return first thing Monday morning. He suggested that Clay continue his stretching and get into the pool over the weekend. Clay tried to walk out with his dignity in tact; but in truth, his lower back was killing him. He tried every position he could think of to ease the pain.

The aching just wouldn't let up regardless of the position he took. Canceling his dinner date was out of the question, he was afraid of hurting Pam's feelings. Anyway even with the pain present, he still looked forward to seeing her again, and he was sure the pain would go away after a hot shower.

The warm, moist heat did help a little. He also took a couple of aspirin thinking that couldn't do any harm. Upon arriving at Pamela's, he was feeling reasonably well; but right away, she knew something was amiss. He told her that it had been a very rough day; however, he was certain a good meal would make him feel much better. With that, she smiled and offered him a drink.

"What do you have?" he asked, "And whatever it is make it a double."

"I have scotch and soda, and I know that's your drink of choice."

"That's great. Boy, I sure hope you're a good cook. I'm about to starve. By the way, it better be good or the wedding is off." he laughed and winked at her. Unfortunately, Ms. Gerard walked in at that very moment and what a look she gave the both of them.

"Is there something you two need to talk to me about?" Ms. Gerard asked.

"Mom, Clay was only kidding around. We've only known each other for a few days. I swear, he was just kidding."

"Well, your Father and I only knew each other for a week when he proposed." Ms. Gerard replied, "And we were married twenty-seven years."

"Mother, please!" Pamela flashed a look at her mom and then turned her attention to Clay. "Anyway, dinner is ready. Now, you can be the judge, Wise Guy."

Clay knew that he was in for a rough time, and he deserved it. He went to the table and held a chair for Ms. Gerard.

"Oh no, Young Man. I'll be eating in my room this evening," Ms. Gerard quipped. With that having been said, Ms. Gerard was gone.

Pamela was not only a great cook but also excellent company. She even knew a great deal about sports, not just football. The two of them ate and talked for more than two and a half hours. He had almost forgotten about his back until he started to get up. There it was again. The pain had eased considerably during dinner; however, when he tried to help with clearing the table, he was in real pain once again.

"Clay, why don't you go and lie down on the sofa in the den. I'll be there in a minute or two," she pleaded.

"Thanks, Love, I think I will."

When Pam came into the den, Clay was lying on the floor. She motioned for him to roll over, and she began to massage his lower back; already knowing where the trouble spots were. Pamela had read his medical history.

"Does that help at all?" she asked.

"Yes, you have strong hands, don't stop." He was almost pleading.

"I can do this as long as you need me to. Right now, I'm going to take you home and put you to bed. Just let me tell mom where I'll be, okay?"

She drove him back to his apartment in his car, with no concern for how she would get home later. When she got him into the apartment, she gave him a couple of his muscle relaxers and told him to take another hot shower. He did exactly as he was told. When he came out, he put on a pair of pajama bottoms that he had only worn once or twice. Pamela had him lay on the bed. She rubbed his back with baby oil that she had warmed. He was really starting to feel better, but before he could do anything about it, he went to sleep.

When he woke up, it was morning and he was alone, or at least he thought he was. Getting up slowly, he headed to the kitchen for a glass of juice. There was Pamela, lying on the sofa, sound asleep. He went back into the bedroom and brought out a blanket to cover her. She looked cold as hell, so covering her was the least he could do. He very quietly got himself a glass of juice and went back to the bedroom. It was almost seven. He would have been more than happy to have given her his bed but he didn't know how to accomplish that feat without waking her.

He was no longer sleepy, so he sneaked to the front door, opened it, reached down and picked up the morning newspaper. When he had successfully accomplished that little ditty, he started looking for his note pad. "Pamela, you really are special. I'm awake and in the bedroom reading the paper. Come and get me and I'll take you home. P.S. I feel much better thanks to you." He pinned it to the sofa where it couldn't be missed.

He had almost fallen off to sleep again when he heard the bedroom door being opened. She was being very quiet. When she saw he was awake, she asked him if he had an extra toothbrush.

"Yes, Love, there's one in the medicine cabinet, still in the wrapper"

"I'll be right back. Don't you go anywhere?"

When she returned, she snuggled right next to him on the bed. Then all of a sudden she sat straight up. "Can you walk without pain, do you really feel okay?"

"Walking is not a problem. The doctor tells me it's good for my back," he replied. "Why do you ask? And, before you answer, does your mother know you're all right? Is she okay with your being here?"

"Yes, and yes," she replied. "Would you like to go to the zoo? I haven't been in years but it has always been one of my favorite places."

"I'd like that very much, but could I just lay here and hold you for a few more minutes?"

"That's what I had in mind, Silly. The zoo doesn't even open until eleven. I would, however, like to go home, freshen up and change clothes if you don't mind. Oh, by the way, I really liked the note."

He kissed her so tenderly she swooned. The more they kissed, the more their bodies seemed to come together. He touched her breast ever so gently and she stiffened but she didn't move away.

"Clay, I feel your body getting aroused. I'm glad that I make you feel that way, but I've never been with a man before. Well, I had sex with this boy in my senior year of high school, but it only took about two minutes and it really wasn't very good, at least not for me."

"Don't you worry, Love. I won't force you to do anything, now, or at any other time. You have my word."

"I really do want you to touch me. She put his hand on her breast. Would you let me touch you?" she asked, sheepishly.

He took her hand and placed it between his legs and she began to stroke him.

"Oh my goodness, it is really getting huge."

He moved, "I think I need a cold shower."

"Just do one more thing for me," she entreated. "Take off my bra. I want to feel your hands on my bare skin, just for a minute."

He was very quick to oblige. Within moments, she couldn't seem to get her breath. Now, her hands were in his pants. He actually tried to stop her but she was losing it. Her entire body stiffened. Pamela screamed, "Oh, my God."

He kissed her and continued to hold her as she finally relaxed her body. She couldn't look at him.

He very calmly and very quietly explained everything to her. Finally, he instructed her to go into the bathroom and take a shower.

"Can I make you do that too?" she asked.

"Of course you can, and you almost did."

She said, nervously, "That was the greatest feeling I've ever experienced. The guy from high school never made me do that. I'm sure glad my first time was with you even if I am embarrassed. I may never be able to look you in the eye ever again. Are you angry with me?" She was so nervous she couldn't shut up.

"Pamela, it's alright. Go take a shower. We have a zoo to visit."

She looked at him with such admiration he almost blushed. He thought, *I'm not about to screw this up just for a roll in the hay.*

They were off to the zoo. First they had to swing by her place for a change of clothing but that was almost on the way. Next, it was time to find a place for lunch.

"Clay, let's eat at the zoo. They have a great restaurant. If we go now it shouldn't be very crowded, not this early in the day."

"We don't have to eat leaves, straw and the like, do we?" He teased.

"Don't be silly. Of course not."

They had a great day at the zoo. When they returned to Clay's apartment, it was almost dark.

"I have tickets to the Washington Redskins exhibition football game tomorrow. Would you like to go?" She asked.

"Sure." he said, "I've never been to a professional football game."

"Okay, you go take a hot shower. I'll warm some more oil to rub on your back. Go on, do what I say," she insisted. "In the meantime, I'll get you something to drink along with a couple of pills. You'll feel better in no time."

Again, he did exactly as he was told. It seemed like the right thing to do. Actually, he remembered her great hands on his back from the night before. He wasn't about to miss out on that. He shaved, showered and brushed his teeth. When he emerged from the bathroom, she was ready for him. She even had the covers turned down on his bed. Clay was only wearing a towel, so he fumbled in a drawer for some more pajama bottoms; upon finding them, he retreated into the bathroom to put them on.

"Love, I'm ready for you," he said with a smile as he re-emerged.

He walked over to the bed and reached for his drink. She handed him his pills. "Take these," she said, putting a pillow under his stomach and starting to rub his back.

He sighed. "I swear, you're worth your weight in gold. That feels good, and believe me, I know good when I feel it."

"I'll bet you tell that to all the girls just to get a back rub."

"Look, Love, I meant every word. To be honest with you, I could lay here forever."

"Clay, I feel the same way."

"All I know is that I have enjoyed the last couple of days more than any other in a long time. You make me feel like I used to before Taylor died. The two of you look nothing alike but you have the same caring personality. I could learn to love you. I need you in my life, Pam, and I don't want to lose another person I care for."

"I'm not going anywhere, I swear. Clay, I think I loved you even before I ever saw you. Now that I've seen you, and touched you, and felt your touch, I'll never leave you, unless you tell me to go," she was shaking like a leaf.

He kissed her and pulled her close to him.

"Clay, I can't breathe."

"I'm sorry, Love."

"Okay, enough of this nonsense. I need to make your back feel better and that is what I fully intend to do. Turn over and let me take care of you. Or would you rather seduce me?"

"Maybe, I'll seduce you later. My back really needs those magic hands."

The next few minutes were heavenly. With the pills, the drinks and the massage, Clay was beginning to feel damn good. He must've fallen asleep. When he opened his eyes, she was curled up right next to him sound asleep.

She was wearing the top to his pajamas and not much else. He got up very slowly and went to the bathroom. He brushed his teeth, then turned off the lights, and crawled back into the bed beside her. Moving next to her he placed his arm across her midsection. She murmured and backed up just as close to him as she could get.

She pulled his arm further across her body and kind of wrapped up in it.

He whispered in her ear. "Pamela Gerard, I think I love you."

"I love you too," she replied.

She raised his hand to her lips and kissed it.

Clay awoke early; it was really cold in the apartment. He made coffee, read the paper, and wondered if this was what it was like to be married.

When he heard the shower running, Clay looked at the clock, it was almost nine. In a few minutes, she came bounding out of the bedroom and jumped right in his lap.

"Sweetheart, I had the greatest dream last night. I dreamed you said you loved me," she said excitedly.

"I did say that and you said you loved me too."

"You know that's true, don't you, Clay?"

"Yes, I think I do. There is one thing I do know for sure. You look absolutely fantastic in my pajama top."

"Do you need to go home before we go to the ballgame?" Clay inquired.

"Nope, I have the tickets in my purse and a change of clothes in the bedroom. Want to come and help me change?"

"Why don't you fix us a little breakfast and have some of my wonderful coffee while I take a quick shower?"

He pulled her close and kissed her.

Clay jumped into the shower and started to sing. When he stepped out of the shower, Pamela was standing at the door.

"Don't be mad. I just wanted to see you. Clay, you are the most beautiful thing I've ever seen; more beautiful than in my wildest dreams."

He walked toward her and put his arms around her. Then he stepped back and opened his robe, the one that she was wearing. She had nothing on underneath. She was literally breathtaking.

"Where is my breakfast Woman?"

He picked up the robe and placed it around her shoulders once again. She headed for the kitchen as he patted her on the rump.

He got dressed and went into the kitchen. Pamela was cooking eggs and bacon and crying so hard she was shaking all over.

He walked over, turned off the stove, picked her up in his arms and carried her to the sofa.

"What's wrong, Doll Face, what'd I do?"

"You didn't do anything. That's the problem. You don't even want to make love to me. I'm just not good enough for you, am I?"

Clay brushed the tears from her eyes. "Don't be silly. I want you so bad my whole body went numb when I saw you standing in front of me. I said to myself that you were far more important to me than just another piece of ass. I thought you understood." Clay continued to explain. "Look, Pam, I think I'm falling in love with you. I just don't want to do anything to jeopardize this relationship. When we do make love, I want it to be because you want me, really want me. Not because you just want to please me. Can you follow that?"

"Look, I may not know all the right things to say or do, but understand this. I don't walk into a man's bathroom on purpose to get a look at his body and then allow him to disrobe me if I don't want him. Is that clear enough for you?"

Clay threw up his hands in surrender. "I'm sorry, Pam; will you ever be able to forgive me? Pamela, you are one of the two most beautiful women I have ever seen. The other one died two years ago. If you were really mine, I'd never even think about another woman. Please believe me," Clay urged. "Taylor told me once that a person can make love to another person without even liking them. But, if you like them first, and then fell in love with them before you made love to them, it should last forever."

"Wait just one darn minute. I'll bet you a hot dog at the ballpark, you can't say that again," she said, poking him in the ribs.

"Pamela, listen to me. I like you a lot and I've never, ever enjoyed being with anyone as much as I enjoy being with you. Tell me again you love me and I'll do anything you ask me to do. Pamela, please, I beg you. Don't let me screw this up. I care too much for you already."

"Clay, I do love you and I'm not ashamed of that. Nor am I afraid to say it again, and again. Do with me what you will, just don't throw me aside."

He said, "Remember, this is not a contest to see who can do the best job of satisfying the other. I'll learn to take care of your needs and you'll learn to take care of mine, okay?"

She nodded, "Look, I'm sorry. I'll be okay."

He stood up with her still in his arms and walked back to the kitchen. After sizing up the situation, he smiled. "Maybe we'll eat on the way to the game. What do you say to that?"

"Okay, but first I think I had better get dressed."

He carried her to the bedroom and dropped her on the bed. When he did, the robe she was wearing fell open. Clay jumped on the bed and started kissing her playfully from head to toe.

"You are so beautiful," he whispered. "I just can't believe you're here with me."

"Do you want me Clay?"

"You know I do."

"Well, it's too late. We'll miss the kick-off. Get off me, Boy." She gave him a playful shove and he fell off the bed onto the floor. She began to get dressed while he lay on the floor watching. He felt very fortunate to be loved, yet again, by a beautiful, sweet and caring person who he already adored.

He could not believe how quickly she was ready. It didn't take her more than fifteen minutes to get dressed, brush her hair and put on her make-up. She was such a natural beauty all she really wore was a little lipstick.

Clay put his arm around her as they walked from the car to the stadium. "You know, Pamela, having you walking beside me just feels right."

"I feel the same way," she said, sliding her arm around his waist. "Now, let's go yell for the Redskins."

Clay was amazed at the way some of the fans dressed for a football game. He leaned over so others couldn't hear. "Pamela, these people look pathetic. They look a little like an Easter Parade gone completely insane."

She laughed; she was a real football fan. She even knew all the players by name. *Beauty, brains, a true sports fan, and she loves me.* Clay thought, *it doesn't get any better than this.*

When the game was over, the Washington Redskins had won. They were both hungry for almost anything, except stadium food.

"Do you, by any chance, like Chinese food?" Clay asked.

"I sure do," she replied. "I know just the place."

He said, "I'm only the driver here. Give me a clue, which way."

Clay really liked the restaurant and the food was good too. The really great part was being with Pamela. She was not the least bit pretentious, and happy just being who she was. *That's a very hard combination to beat*, Clay thought.

"Pam, will you rub my back again this evening? I have a feeling tomorrow may be a really tough day and I'm afraid I'll need all the help I can get. I promise not to go to sleep this time."

"Of course I will, you Poor Baby."

When they were back at his apartment, Clay headed straight for the shower, hoping that when he came out, she would be there waiting for him. To his dismay, the bathroom was empty when he exited the shower. He wrapped a towel around him and went into the bedroom, no Pamela. When he walked into the den, she was standing on the balcony.

"Hey, Love, a penny for your thoughts."

He didn't want to go out there with just a towel on.

She came back into the den and went straight to the kitchen where she was warming the oil.

"Okay, Handsome, to the bedroom with you."

He lay down on the bed with the towel over his lower body. She began to massage his lower back. After a few minutes, he reached around, took her by the arm and pulled her down beside him.

"Pamela, what's wrong? Have I done something?"

"No, Clay, it's just me. These have been three of the happiest days I've ever spent and they are quickly coming to an end."

He could tell she was serious, and he wasn't about to make any of his usual dumb jokes. "Pamela, I'll see you tomorrow and everyday for the rest of our lives, if you'll allow me?"

Carl R. Smith

"Clay, I love you so much my entire body aches. I just want to stay here with you forever and I'm so afraid I'll screw it up just like you said you were."

He pulled her even closer and began to unbutton her blouse.

Pamela responded, "Clay, make me feel like a woman again."

For the first time they were both naked and on the bed together at the same time. When he rolled onto his back, she knew he wanted her. Of that, there was no doubt in her mind.

Neither he nor Pam wanted the night to end; however, tomorrow was going to be a very tough day, and there would be many pleasant days and nights to come. Clay took her home and was in bed by midnight.

Chapter 13

At five AM, the alarm clock was not a welcome sound; however, Clay was shaved and in the shower by quarter past. Sergeant Shackelford was ready and waiting for him when he arrived.

"Clay, how did your back respond to the workout on Friday?" Shack asked.

"If it weren't for the work of my own personal masseuse, I don't think I would have made it."

"Let's do without any weights at all today," Shack suggested. We'll see if that makes a difference. Anyway, you are plenty strong. We'll spend most of our time on conditioning and flexibility."

"You're the boss, Shack."

They spent most of the day running, jumping, climbing ropes and practicing defensive techniques. The last two hours, Shack must have attacked him fifty times with and without a weapon.

Tuesday morning it was very hard for Clay to get out of bed. Fortunately, it was mostly stiffness. He knew that he could survive and even overcome that, and he was able to keep up with Shack for the most part. By Thursday afternoon, his lower back was hurting him so badly he could hardly sit at all. Even the stretching exercises were becoming intolerable. If it had not been for Pamela's great hands, he would never have made it through the week.

Friday morning he was sent back to Doctor Delong. A group of doctors, including Dr. Delong, decided to do a caudal block. Dr. Delong explained the procedure. Needles would be inserted into the spinal area, injecting Novocain to kill the pain, and then injecting Cortisone directly into the inflamed area to aid the healing process.

Clay was a bit apprehensive. However, he was sure that Dr. Delong would not suggest anything he didn't personally feel comfortable doing. He signed the permission slip and within the hour the anesthesiologist who actually performs the procedure was doing his thing. The entire procedure took less than an hour. When they were through sticking him, he was miraculously without any pain at all. However, his butt and legs were so numb he couldn't stand up. They told him that was normal.

The nurses stayed with him for about two hours. When the feeling came back in his legs, they got him to his feet. He was able to walk just fine and the pain didn't return. They told him to take it easy for the next twenty-four hours and then he should be fine. He was also told that sometimes this procedure must be performed three times in order to completely relieve the pain. The procedures must be done a week apart for the best results. The doctors wouldn't know for three or four days whether or not this one would do the trick. Clay could only hope and maybe say a little prayer.

It was almost three when he was finally allowed to leave the hospital and return to his apartment. Dr. Delong decided to drive him home in Clay's car. The MP's would follow them to Clay's apartment, pick up the good doctor and return him to the hospital. He knew Dr. Delong wanted to talk to him, and he probably wanted this opportunity to be alone, just he and Clay. Even before the two of them got out of the parking lot, the questions began.

"Clay, I hope you don't think I'm sticking my nose where it doesn't belong; however, I'm not only concerned with your physical health, but your mental health as well."

"What is it, Doc? Say what's on your mind. We're friends, remember?"

"Okay. I don't trust that general, and I'm afraid for you. I just don't want you to be used and then discarded like and old pair of socks. Clay, can you tell me what's going on? Or, is this some top secret bullshit that you're unable to talk about?"

"Honestly, Doc, I don't know. All I do know is the general and a few choice and highly influential people think I'm the man for this job. I guess they'll tell me what the job is when the time comes."

"Look, Clay, I know this is none of my business, but I'm your friend. If you need someone to talk to, just give me a scream, okay, will you promise me you'll do that?"

"You got it, Doc."

Dr. Delong gave him a bottle of painkillers. "You take these, as it says on the bottle, for the next couple of days. While the Cortisone is clearing up the infection, you could experience some pain. However, if you still have pain on Monday, call me."

161

"Damn it, Doc, you're too good to me," Clay replied, sticking the pills in his pocket. "I'll take some just as soon as I get inside."

When Dr. Delong finally reached Clay's parking space at the apartment building, the pain wasn't bad; however, he was very uncomfortable. He struggled getting out of the car, before the doctor could get to him.

Dr. Delong grabbed his right arm to steady him. "Clay, are you okay? I can see that you're still a little woozy."

Clay straightened himself as best he could. "Look, Doc, you don't have to walk me to my door. I'm all right and I can put myself to bed. But, thank you very much for all the trouble you've gone to, I appreciate it."

"Clay, you're not in the military anymore. Why don't you call me Robert? Most of my friends do."

"Okay, Robert, the MP's are waiting for you. And, I promise, I'll call you if I have even the smallest problem."

"Clay, take those pills and go to bed: Doctors' orders."

"Okay, Bossy. I will, I will," he replied. "You're not gonna make me kiss you good-bye right here with the MP's looking on, are you?"

"I'd kick you in the ass, if I thought you could feel it," Doc replied. "Now, get your butt upstairs and get some rest. I'll call and check on you tomorrow."

"See ya, *Robert*."

When Clay entered his apartment, he decided to let Pamela know what was going on. *There would be no dance tonight.* He thought, *I sure hope Pamela's not too disappointed.* While he was dialing her number, it occurred to him that he had two really good male friends and they were both doctors. Not knowing whether or not that mattered; he still wondered about the significance.

Pamela assured him that the dance was of little importance weighed against his health. She promised to be there as soon as she could leave work. It was now almost four o'clock and he was beginning to need a pain pill. He decided to take two. They were small.

When Pamela arrived, he was almost out of it. She leaned down and kissed him on the forehead. "How you feeling, Clay?"

"Well, I'm not in any pain, but my stomach is really upset. I think I'm gonna throw up. I took two pain pills about forty five minutes ago."

"You shouldn't take medication on an empty stomach," she scolded, I'll bet you haven't eaten all day, have you?"

"They wouldn't let me eat before the procedure, but they did give me a coke afterwards."

She made him some soup, and kept bugging him until it was all gone. Then she took his dishes and started towards the kitchen. He was almost unconscious by now. "Pamela, have I told you lately how beautiful you are and how much I love you?" As she turned back to see him sleeping, one lone tear rolled down her cheek.

Clay didn't even know when Pamela left. When he woke up, it was almost midnight, and she was gone. He looked all around the apartment hoping to find a note or something, but no such luck. Picking up the telephone, he dialed her number, but all he got was a buzzing signal. This wasn't like a busy signal; it was more like listening to a hornet's nest. He decided to take a fast shower; and maybe by the time he was finished, the line would clear.

When he had finished his shower, the buzzing was still there. He was feeling pretty good so he decided to walk down the street and try another telephone, hoping the entire neighborhood wasn't on the fritz. In the hallway, he ran into one of his neighbors who was just coming in.

The man looked at him. "Hey, Neighbor, how you doing? I'm coming in, and you're going out. Life sure is crazy, ain't it?"

Clay tried to smile. "Yeah, my stupid phone's messed up. I was just going down the street to find another one. I hope the whole neighborhood's not out."

"Maybe it's just your phone. C'mon in, you can try mine."

"Thanks, Neighbor. I'll take you up on that. Maybe, I'll get lucky," Clay replied, following him into his apartment.

"The phone's on the table by the sofa. Help yourself."

Clay picked up the phone and dialed the number.

When Ms. Gerard answered, she informed him that Pamela wasn't at home.

"Clay, don't you worry about a thing," she said. "I'll leave Pam a note on her pillow. She'll call you as soon as she arrives."

He explained to Ms. Gerard about his telephone problems and that Pamela might not be able to get through. Finally the decision was made to leave her a note asking her to call the following morning. Ms. Gerard assured him that would be done.

Putting the receiver back in its cradle Clay tried to get to his feet, but he was still a little woozy. "Thanks, for the use of the phone."

"Are you all right?" His neighbor asked, offering him a hand.

Clay steadied himself. "It's these stupid pain pills I'm taking. I had a minor procedure performed on my back today, and I think I need to go back to bed."

"You wouldn't have any extra's, would you? My backs been hurting for weeks, and I haven't had a good night's sleep for over a month. If you could spare a couple, maybe I could get a little rest tonight."

"Sure," Clay replied. "You did me a favor, that's the least I can do. Follow me to my apartment and I'll give you a couple."

They walked some fifty feet to Clay's apartment. He found the bottle and handed the man two pills. "If I have any of these pills left, come Monday, I'll give them to you."

"Thanks, and by the way my name's Harry. Give me a scream sometime and we'll have a beer."

"You got it, Pal, and my name's Clay. Thanks once again for the use of the phone. I hope you get a good night's sleep, but don't take those things on an empty stomach, they'll make you sick."

"You got it, Clay. See you later."

When Clay checked his phone again, it was working just fine. However, the light on the telephone was blinking again. He pushed the button.

"Clay, this is John. When you get this message, give me a call."

He dialed Johnny's number.

"Hello."

"Hey, Johnny. I just got your message. What's up?"

"I just called to see how you're doing. I told you I'd call back later in the week, well, it's Friday, that's about as late in the week as one can get."

"I'm a little fuzzy right at the moment. They did a caudal block on me today, and I'm under the influence, but having no pain."

"Those procedures usually work," Johnny said, with authority. "Give it a couple a days, you should feel a lot better real soon."

"Hey, Johnny, do you know what I'm being hired to do. I still don't know. Dr. Delong asked me, and I couldn't tell him."

Johnny said, "I figured you'd tell me all about it."

"I sure as hell will, if I ever find out." Clay promised.

They finished their conversation, and if they had not talked for so long, he would've called Pamela again. But now it really was too late. He decided to take a couple more pills and hit the sack. *I'll call Pamela first thing in the morning, if she hasn't called me already.* The pain pills were starting to take effect. Lying back on the bed, he was out in no time.

Clay lay on the bed like a dead man, his mind almost alert, but he couldn't seem to open his eyes. Although he was damn near unconscious, he knew someone was in his apartment or at least he thought so; although, he couldn't be sure it wasn't a dream. Feeling the presence of some thing or somebody, he was almost certain someone had touched him. He felt the touch, but he couldn't physically respond. Then, his mind went numb as well.

166

Awakened by someone pounding on his door, he stumbled out of bed trying desperately to answer. Unfortunately, before he could get there, it burst open, and cops were everywhere.

"Henry Clay Smith, you're under arrest for the murder of Colonel John Nordstrum." He was handcuffed and taken to police headquarters.

The officers in charge of the case began their questioning immediately. It seems that at the Club dance on Friday evening, Colonel John Nordstrum went outside for a smoke. While the colonel was standing at the corner of the clubhouse smoking, he was allegedly having a heated conversation with a younger man. The young man pulled a gun and shot him three times, then disappeared into the parking lot. There were a number of witnesses to the shooting. Clay knew he was innocent, and he also knew that when the witnesses told the police that he wasn't the man they saw everything would be all right.

Colonel John Nordstrum just happened to be the husband of a certain Ms. Leila Nordstrum. Clay had, of course, never met the man but knew who he was.

He was pleased when they escorted him to the line up. Consequently, he was certain that when the line up was over, the apologies would be forthcoming and he could get on with his life. After standing for what seemed like an eternity, instead of being released, he was fingerprinted, photographed and booked. He didn't understand why this was happening, and no one would talk to him. *Surely they know by now that they have the wrong person,* Clay

167

thought. *Maybe it was just a formality.* Nobody would tell him what was going on. They finally took him to a room where they told him he could have a visitor. Sitting quietly, he waited to see what would happen next.

When General Essex walked into the room a moment later, Clay felt a whole lot better. *Now, things would get straightened out.*

The general looked agitated. "My Boy, what the hell made you do it?"

"General, I haven't done anything. I was home in bed all night."

"Son, they have four witnesses who positively identified you as the person who shot Colonel Nordstrum. The colonel had your watch clutched tightly in his hand when they got to him. Now, who're you trying to kid?"

"That's impossible. I'm telling you, Sir, I didn't kill him. Hell, I never even met the man."

"Clay, you were at the dance last night with Pamela Gerard. The colonel's wife, Leila introduced the two of you, didn't she?"

"General, I don't know what's going on but I swear to you, I was not there."

"Clay, I want to believe you, but why would all of those people lie?"

"General Essex, I don't know what's going on but I was home all evening. Hell, I took a couple of painkillers that Dr. Delong gave me. They completely knocked me out. I know better than to lie to you, Sir. General, you have to get me out of here. Please?"

"Son, that might not be very easy to do, but I'll get you an attorney. You just get some rest. We'll talk again real soon."

Next, he was taken to a cell where he spent Saturday night. He tried to sleep, but he felt like a man backed into a corner with nowhere to turn. Clay remembered a time when he was a junior in high school. One afternoon during shop class, a young boy whom he had protected from time to time was excused to go to the bathroom. While there, two bullies walked in and began to harass him. One of the bullies pulled a knife to frighten him even more. As the bully slashed back and forth with great, sweeping motions, his victim became so gripped with fear that he lost total control. Rage enveloped him, a rage that only fear can summons to the surface of the frail and weak. He reached for the knife, grabbed it by the blade and managed to take it away from his assailant in spite of severely cutting his hand. Now he became the attacker, stabbing and slashing violently until his victim was dead. By the time teachers responded to the horrible shrieks coming from the boys' bathroom, it was too late for both boys. Two lives had been taken that day. One-boy dead and the other one institutionalized, maybe forever. Clay silently cried himself to sleep, partly due to his own predicament, but also in remembrance of the two young boys whose lives were so foolishly wasted.

Sunday afternoon, he had a visit from a Mr. Jim Mann. He was a very young lawyer who'd probably just graduated from law school a week earlier. Mr. Mann was; however, very nice and seemed to know what he was doing.

He explained to Clay what he could expect to have happen in the upcoming days. Also, explaining what he would be doing in the meantime. Clay's bail would be set, hopefully, the next day at the arraignment. He asked Mr. Mann to please call Captain John Murphy and gave him the number in Atlanta.

"Tell him that I need him now." Clay pleaded.

The next day at the arraignment, his bail was set at five hundred thousand dollars. There was no way he could come up with that kind of money. Even if he used a bail bondsman, he would still need to come up with about fifty thousand dollars and that was impossible.

On Tuesday morning, Johnny showed up. "I never thought I'd see you in this place. Clay, they set your bond so high it'll take me a couple of days to come up with the money, but I'll get you out."

"John, I don't have anywhere else to turn. You know I'm good for it." Clay paused, "John, you haven't even asked me if I did it?"

"Hell, even if you did do it, I'd still get you out and you know it. You didn't do it, did you?"

"No, I didn't do it. I swear to you on our friendship. I didn't have anything to do with killing that man. I've never even met the man."

"I believe you," Johnny replied. "Look, Clay, you've been set up big time. We're going to find out why and who is responsible. Of that much, you can be certain, Old Buddy."

"John, I know that you're my friend. I have eight thousand dollars hidden away. You may use that to help raise my bail." Clay told him where to find the money. "Johnny, one more thing. I need you to contact Susan and Gidget. You'll have to call Susan and she'll get in touch with Gidget. They'll help us put this together."

Johnny gave him a big hug. "Give me two days, Old Buddy, and I'll have you out of here. Don't worry, My Friend. The doctor is in."

"Johnny, I don't think you should talk to the general, or for that matter, anybody. I don't know who started this, but at this point, you're the only person I trust."

"No sweat. That's using your head, but what about Dr. Delong?"

"Way to go, Johnny. If you need someone to help raise my bail, call him, I'm sure he'll help as much as he can. Speaking of doctors, Johnny, can you test my blood? Would there still be traces of the painkillers? You know the ones Dr. Delong gave me?"

"When did you take it last?" Johnny asked.

"What time was it when we got off the telephone Friday night?"

"It was probably around one in the morning, Saturday."

"Okay, the last time was about one AM Saturday morning."

"It would still show up. The lab in Atlanta could check it but I didn't bring anything to draw blood with."

"No problem, Johnny, give me your handkerchief."

Clay bit the cuticle on his index finger, and it began to bleed, letting it drip onto the handkerchief. "Is that enough?"

Johnny just sat there shaking his head. "That'll be plenty, you Idiot."

They said their good-byes and Clay was left to his many thoughts.

One of the toughest things for him was realizing that Leila and Pamela were a part of this monstrous lie. He felt sure that the two of them were just pawns in this game of chess, but he was determined to expose the key players.

He hadn't slept very much since he'd been incarcerated, and for the first time he realized that his back wasn't hurting anymore. This night, he slept about as well as one could be expected to sleep, knowing the predicament he was in. Once again, he had the strangest dreams; however, this time when he woke up, he couldn't remember much about them.

Wednesday went by so slowly he thought he was going to scream. He paced the floor most of the day, trying very hard, but without luck, to make some sense out of all the mess he was in. When Thursday came, things were really looking up. The jailer came to inform him that someone had paid his bail and that he'd be released in a few minutes.

He knew it had to be Johnny. Although he'd not heard from him since Tuesday, Clay knew, just the same. This would be Johnny's way of paying him back for saving his life. He was always one for paying his debts. Clay knew; however, that Johnny would have done it anyway, that's what *best friends* are for. Gathering his belongings, what few there were, he walked the floor until the guard came to release him.

Chapter 14

When he walked out of the jail, Johnny was waiting for him.

"God, it's good to be out." Clay shouted.

"Let's get the hell out of this place," Johnny encouraged. "I have the girls stashed at a motel just over the state line, and they're real anxious to see you. Clay, keep your eyes peeled, I think someone is following me."

"Johnny, turn right and let me out in the middle of the next block. I'm gonna start walking through the alley. You go around the block and pick me up at the other end. If the guy gets out of his car and follows me into the alley, once we get past the point of no return, I'll start running to meet you at the other end. Hell, by the time he's able to get back to his car again we'll be long gone. Do you understand?"

"Yes, I understand. Get moving."

"If you don't see me, go around the block one more time."

"Good luck, Old Buddy, I'll see you at the other end of the alley."

Sure enough, the guy who was following them took the bait. The man parked his car at the curb and followed him into the alley. When Clay reached the critical point, he began sprinting for the other end. He and Johnny got to the same place at the same time. Clay jumped

173

into the passenger seat and Johnny hit the accelerator. It was a thing of beauty.

"Okay, now we can go see the girls."

"You bet your ass," Johnny yelled.

"Johnny what about the blood test?"

"I'll know sometime today. I sent it overnight to a friend of mine in Atlanta."

"Johnny, there's something else. When they gave me back my valuables at the jail, my watch wasn't there. You know, the one Taylor gave me for Christmas. They said I wasn't wearing it when I came in."

"Were you?"

"In all the confusion, I can't be sure. But, I remember thinking that somebody was in my apartment, that Friday night, and that somebody touched me. They took my watch; that's how they found it in the colonel's hand, after he was shot. They really are trying to frame me, aren't they?"

Johnny replied. "It sure as hell looks that way."

When they got to the motel and Clay saw Susan and Gidget, it was like a homecoming.

Johnny said, "Boy, I sure do wish somebody loved me that much."

"I love you that much, you big dummy," Clay replied.

It didn't take very long to catch up on all the news. In less than five minutes, they got right down to the business at hand. Between him and Johnny, the girls were brought up to speed. They pretty much understood everything that had transpired between the people in question.

Clay said, "If I don't get some real food and real fast, I'm going to die from malnutrition."

Gidget and Johnny went for the food. Susan and Clay stayed out of sight.

When the food arrived, it was devoured in record time. Everyone was anxious to tackle the problem at hand.

Clay began, "I'll go back to my apartment and continue to work with the General's group in hopes that something will turn up. Johnny can stay with me. Hell, whoever's doing this already knows about him. If they didn't know before, they know now. For sure, they'll know who posted my bail."

Susan poked Johnny on the arm. "Clay's right. Johnny, you shouldn't have done that, now, you're in *big trouble.*"

Clay went on talking, choosing to ignore Susan's comment. "Gidget, you try to get close to Pamela. At the very least you can follow her. I want to know where she goes and who she sees. Do you think you can do that, without putting yourself in danger?"

"Sure, I can. Give me her address and telephone number and I'll get started first thing tomorrow morning."

It came down to Susan. Everyone agreed that she should apply for work at the hospital as a civilian. She was to befriend Leila Nordstrum as well as Dr. Delong. It was convenient that they had known each other before.

Susan had been dying to say something. "Clay, this may come as a huge shock to you, but everyone at the hospital knew Leila was bisexual, well, everyone except you. Leila Nordstrum, liked sex equally well from either side of the fence, and Colonel Nordstrum didn't have a clue concerning her alternate lifestyle."

Clay was amazed at his own naiveté, but they all kept reminding him that he was only twenty-one at the time he and Leila first met.

"Why do you think this is happening?" Gidget asked.

Johnny said, "We don't really know. I'm betting that through Clay's association with the general and his cohorts, he'll be the first to find out."

Susan chimed in, "I think they're all dirty, the whole lot of um."

Clay said, "Okay, but why do they want to get rid of me? What possible reason could they have?" He was really hoping to get some kind of an answer. It seemed no one was willing to tackle that one, at least not yet.

They all agreed that the way to communicate with each other without being detected was through food delivery. Every other day Gidget would deliver Chinese to Clay's apartment. On alternate days, Susan would deliver pizza. This way they could all be kept up to date. If there was something extremely urgent, one of the girls would dial Clay's phone number and hang up, then redial and hang up again. If this were to occur, they were all to meet at a bar on New York Avenue. The name of the bar was Cap-n-Guys and they were to be there within the hour. Cap-n-Guys was a gay bar about a block from the Greyhound Bus Station. Both locations were only a few blocks from Clay's apartment.

On the way to Clay's apartment, Johnny said, "Clay, the eight thousand dollars is still hidden. I thought we might have a need for it in the upcoming days."

When they entered the apartment, it was a mess. They both knew the apartment was bugged and they were determined to find the equipment

After being unable to find the bugs, they also agreed that; when they had something important to say to one another, they would go into the hallway; sit on the steps, and whisper. They also felt it might be a good idea to find a new hiding place for the money.

On Friday, Clay reported to General Essex'. When Pamela saw him walk into the office, she had to hold onto the desk to keep from falling over.

She walked unsteadily toward him. "Oh, Clay, I'm so glad your okay. I wanted to come to the jail to see you but mom had a fit."

He pushed her away. "You really are a cool one," he snapped. "To think, I put you in the same class with Taylor. I must be the biggest fool in town. Tell the general I'm here, and stay away from me."

She reached for him. "Please, Clay, give me a chance to explain."

"Damn you, Girl. Call him, or I'll just walk in unannounced."

She slumped into a chair by the desk, crying so hard she could barely speak. "He's … he's not here."

Clay screamed at her. "Do you have my new itinerary or did you think I'd just rot in jail? Don't even bother answering. Tell General

Essex I want to see him ASAP. He may call me at my apartment, and it had better be real soon. You got that, Honey?"

Clay spun around, and out the door he went.

"Please ..." was all he heard as he hurried to the elevator.

When he returned to his apartment, Johnny was taking a shower. He hollered through the door to let him know he was there, and then he went to the kitchen to make himself a drink, noticing that Johnny had been there already. Dropping in the chair by the couch, he was haunted with the picture of Pamela's face etched in his mind.

When Johnny finished his shower, the two of them went for a walk. He explained to Johnny what had taken place. Johnny was just as befuddled as he was. However, he thought they had better get back to the apartment to wait for the general's call.

Johnny said, "Let's find a telephone first I want to call my friend in Atlanta."

When he got off the telephone, he said the analysis was inconclusive; although, there were traces of Demral, Valium, and Thorazine.

"Clay, in court they'd probably conclude that it was a result of the caudal block and nothing more."

"You're absolutely right, Johnny. That little piece of information is not worth very much, is it?"

"No, Clay, it's not; however, we must explore all possibilities."

All of a sudden, out of the clear blue, Clay remembered his neighbor.

"Johnny, c'mon, I want you to meet my neighbor. He can tell you about what time I was with him Friday night and early Saturday morning, and he knows all about the painkillers. I even gave him a couple; it seems he was having a little back pain of his own."

"I can't wait to meet him," Johnny replied.

When they returned to the apartment building, the neighbor's apartment was empty. There was no name on the door or the mailbox. The apartment manager told them that he had moved on Monday and left no forwarding address. They did, however, find out his full name and where he worked.

Clay said, "This is getting to be a bit bizarre."

"You got that right," Johnny replied. "I think the general is the key to this whole mess. I think you've been set up and pretty soon we're gonna find out why. I also believe that one of the reasons they're after you is because you have no ties to anyone, at least not anyone that they know about. For that reason, there won't be any questions or inquiries if you disappear."

"But, Johnny, they know about you and now they know how close we really are. I mean with you putting up my bail and all."

"Look, Clay, the general already knows how close we are. Remember you were the one he called when I was in trouble."

Clay dropped his head. "Look, Johnny, I may have put you in real danger," he said regretfully. "I had no idea what was happening when I had the attorney call you."

Johnny got up from the step, and brushed off the seat of his trousers. "Clay, I'm here for you."

Clay looked up and the makings of a smile crossed his face. "I still think Pamela cares for me. She seemed to be genuinely upset. You know, Johnny, sometimes I'm so stupid that it's laughable."

"Well, I'm glad you still have a sense of humor," Johnny mocked. "Clay, I'm going to check out the place where your neighbor works. I sure would like to talk to the guy. You stay here and wait for the general to call. I'll see you in a couple of hours."

"Okay, John, but you watch out behind you. If anything happens to you, I guess I'll just have to shoot myself."

"I'll be cool, and you do the same, Old Buddy." With that he was down the stairs and on his way.

Clay was getting angrier by the minute. One of the first things he'd been taught was never to let anyone or anything get him angry or upset. *The guy who gets angry loses. When anger builds up, the mind doesn't think straight. Most every question has a simple answer, but logical thinking is the key.*

General Essex called late that afternoon. He seemed genuinely happy to know that Clay was out of jail and back at his apartment. "Clay, meet me at my office, Sunday afternoon, at 1400 hours."

"I'll be more than happy to meet you at anytime, Sir. Thank you for sending Mr. Mann to see me. He seems like a very competent young lawyer."

"You are certainly welcome, and never fear. We'll all get through this together," the general assured him.

Clay thought, *I sure am glad I don't have to see the general today. Maybe in a couple of days I'll have some more answers. I think I'll have a drink, and if Johnny doesn't get back soon, I'll have two or three. I feel too damned vulnerable when I'm alone.*

When Johnny came strolling through the door, it was almost five PM. He didn't look happy, and Clay knew that couldn't be good. He made Johnny a drink. Clay was now on his third. The two of them walked out into the hall and sat on the steps near the fire escape.

"Clay, this is just too big for a couple of country boys from Tennessee."

"What are you trying to tell me?"

"The personnel director where your neighbor worked was super nice." Johnny laid his hand on Clay's shoulder. "Yeah, that's right, Clay. I said worked, not works. He really didn't know why the guy just up and quit. He told me the guy looked really sick on Monday, and that's when he walked out. The guy had a doctor's appointment a couple of days earlier, and he thinks the doctor gave him some real bad news, like maybe he's dying or something. Here's the real crazy part. I told him that the guy had left a bunch of stuff in my apartment and I wanted to return it, but I didn't know where he'd gone. I also told him that the apartment manager had no forwarding address. I asked him if he would look in his personnel file and give me the guy's mother's address or a telephone number. He said he thought that would be okay as long as I didn't tell anybody where I got it. I promised, and he went to get the file."

Johnny took a deep breath and continued, "Clay, I thought we'd finally gotten a break. Unfortunately, when he returned, he said he couldn't find the man's personnel file anywhere. I asked him if that

181

kind of thing happened very often, and I think I made him mad. He told me that he'd been in charge of those files for over fifteen years and that he had never lost one."

"Johnny, what do you think it means?"

"Hell, Clay. I think someone involved in this freakin' mess took those files. That poor guy may be at the bottom of the Chesapeake Bay for all we know."

Clay stood up and leaned against the wall. "Holy shit, where's it all gonna end?"

Johnny shook his head, "I don't know, Pal. You can be sure there are a whole lot of high-ranking muckety-mucks involved in this one."

"I think I need another drink. How about you, John?"

"Make me a real strong one; this is like trying to work the, Times Crossword, with an ink pen."

Clay returned with two drinks, and handed one to Johnny.

"Do you remember which one of the girls is bringing dinner?" Johnny asked.

"I can't say for certain, but they should be here any minute. For some reason, I think its Susan."

At five minutes past six, Susan got off the elevator. Clay ran down the hall to catch her. He took the pizza into the apartment, sat it on the table, and walked back out to the steps to join Susan and Johnny.

After the pleasantries were out of the way between the three of them, Susan was the first to speak.

"I don't really know much yet, but there's a whole lot of scared people out there. Dr. Delong has gone on thirty days emergency leave. No one knows why, or exactly when, he left. What's been going on with you guys?"

Clay and Johnny spent the next few minutes bringing Susan up to date. They told her all they had encountered in the last few hours. Susan listened carefully.

"Susan, have you talked to Gidget? Did she find out anything?" Johnny asked.

"No, she wasn't back when I left."

Clay put his arm around Susan's waist, "I think we need to have another meeting. Johnny and I will be at the motel by ten."

Susan hugged him, and reached for Johnny. "Don't worry guys, we'll figure this out. Eat your Pizza, and I'll see you about ten o'clock."

As Susan walked away, Johnny followed Clay's expression. "Okay, Clay. What's on your mind?"

"Nothing in particular. I just think we all need to brainstorm a little before someone else ends up missing."

Johnny knew what he was thinking. "Clay, we're all in this together. I don't think Susan and Gidget are going to leave you in this mess."

"Look at it from my side, Johnny. You must know how I'm feeling right now."

"I think I do know how you feel. If the situation was reversed and one of us was in this mess, what would you do?"

"Hell, you know what I'd do. I'd be right here with you guys until hell froze over. You know I would, or you wouldn't be here now.

Let's go eat some pizza, and maybe you'll stop asking me so many questions. I can't even remember whether or not we've eaten today."

"Okay, Old Buddy. Lead the way, but you're not getting off that easy."

As the two of them started down the hallway, Clay thought he heard his phone ringing. When he unlocked the door and walked into the room, he could hear Pamela's voice on the recorder.

"Clay, I need to talk to you. Please call me back. By leaving you this message, I may have sealed my doom, but having you hating me or thinking that I betrayed you is, to me, a fate worse than death."

He and Johnny looked at each other, but not a word was spoken until they got to the stairs once again.

"What do you think, Johnny?"

"I don't know what to think. It may be another set up. How well do you really know this girl? She sounds pretty desperate."

Clay said, "Let's go meet with Susan and Gidget, and we'll talk it over. I'm not sure what to do. I sure would hate to leave her hanging out there in danger if she's telling the truth."

He and Johnny spent the next few minutes eating pizza and trying to figure out how to get away from their shadows. The guys in the big black car were following their every move. Johnny came up with a plan.

"Clay, you get the car and pull around front. Give me the rest of that pizza crust and one of those rubber gloves lying on the sink."

"What are you going to do with that?"

Johnny smiled mischievously, "I know what I'm doing. You just give me about five minutes and then pull the car around as though everything were normal. I'll meet you out front when I'm finished. Trust me, Clay, I've done this before."

Clay waited five minutes and then went to the parking lot to get the car. When he pulled to the front of the apartment building, Johnny was standing by the curb waiting for him. He got into the passenger's seat.

Johnny grinned. "Okay, Old Buddy, let's get this show on the road. The girls will be waiting and I don't wanna be late. They might start to worry."

"What did you do with the pizza?" Clay asked.

Johnny slapped his chest. "Hell, I stuck it up their tailpipe. They won't get two blocks."

Clay headed for the motel where the girls were waiting. Sure enough, he could see the car was no longer following them. He started laughing.

"What's so funny, Clay?"

"Sorry, Johnny. In my mind, I could see you on your hands and knees stuffing that pizza up their tailpipe, and you a practicing physician, no less. You're a genius, Partner, and you never cease to amaze me."

"Thanks, Clay ... I think."

Getting to the motel only took twenty minutes. They parked on the other side of the motel, away from the girls' room.

As they entered the room Clay fell across the bed closest to the door. "Okay, who called this meeting?"

"You did, Dummy," Johnny responded.

Clay rose to his elbows. "Do you girls have anything different to report?"

No one spoke.

He continued, "I think that when I meet with the general on Sunday, we'll have a much better clue about what's really going on."

Susan said, "Clay, this is obviously the weirdest thing I've ever been involved in, but I don't trust that general. Do you trust him?"

Before he could answer, Johnny chimed in, "Clay, you'd better listen to the lady. General Essex likes you, but he'd screw his own sister if there were a profit to be made. Clay, I worked for the man much longer than you did, and I know what I'm saying is correct. When I informed him that I was getting out of the service and going into private practice, he went nuts."

"You don't really think he had anything to do with this do you?" Clay asked.

Johnny paused, "I wouldn't put it past him. He is, without a doubt, the most ruthless man I've ever known. Believe me, that's saying one hell of a lot."

"Johnny, I never asked, but how did you get involved with the general?"

Johnny hung his head. "Clay, you know how poor my family has always been. I was barely surviving, while going to college on full scholarship. Medical School, even with all the grants, was difficult.

Then I met this young lady, one of my classmates. She became pregnant, by 'guess who'. One, backroom surgical procedure, and a few extra dollars in my pocket, and the general had me. I had to survive, and he made it easy for me, as long as I was doing his bidding. I hope you don't want to know any more than that, because, I'm not going into any of the gory details. I did what he asked me to do, for a long time."

"That's enough. I guess you know the general a great deal better than I do, and I thought I knew him pretty well." Clay, put his arm around Johnny's shoulder and gave him a nudge. "Let's go on to other things."

Clay told the girls about the call from Pamela. He asked them what they thought should be done. There was a long silence.

Gidget said, "You need to let me check it out. I found out where she went to high school, and I called her pretending to be from her graduating class. I'm going to meet her at the Shoreham Hotel Lounge tomorrow at one o'clock. If I think she's clean, I'll tell her that I'm a friend. I'll bet she'll tell me everything, if she's one of the good guys."

Johnny patted Gidget on the leg. "If she is a good guy, she may not live until tomorrow. After making that phone call, she may be dead already."

"Look, everybody," Clay said, excitedly. "I don't want anyone else to get hurt. I'm pretty sure these people would do damn near anything to get what they want."

Susan came out of the bathroom. "Just for your information, I'm having lunch with Ms. Leila Nordstrum tomorrow at the, 'Shoreham Hotel'. She seemed very anxious to get together."

Clay said, "You know, the Shoreham Hotel is one place both Leila and Pamela have in common. Maybe you two should spend some time asking around before they show up. I sure hope you guys don't run into each other."

Gidget said, "Me, too. I will check around, though."

Susan said, "That's a good idea. I'll get there a little early and I'll do some of my own checking."

Johnny jumped in, "Guys, I think we better find a way to get back together tomorrow evening if we can. We should have a lot more information to share. Don't you think?"

"I think you're right," Clay agreed.

It was obvious to both Clay and Susan that Johnny and Gidget would like to spend some time together, alone. They had been playing, patty finger, and swapping looks, for the last hour.

Clay said, "Susan and I are going out for a little while. We'll be gone for a couple of hours. Why don't you guys stay here and get better acquainted?"

"Be careful, you guys," was Johnny's only response as he waved them toward the door.

Gidget simply looked pleased.

Susan and Clay went to a bar down the street. The bar was not very crowded for a Saturday night.

"You know, Susan, we're all a little crazy. Maybe they'll bury us side by side."

"Well, let's not rush that along, if you don't mind. I finally met someone I believe I can spend the rest of my life with, and I think he really loves me."

"Does he know your sexual preference?"

"No, he does not. But you can bet I'll try to be good to him and, furthermore, I'd like to have a child. If you haven't noticed, that's very difficult for two ladies to pull off."

He said, "Maybe you should go home, and leave this to the rest of us."

"That really hurts, Clay. We are friends forever, no matter what. We swore that we'd always be there for each other."

"Hey, Sweetheart, I was only thinking of you. You should know that, you, Big Silly." Clay replied, poking her in the ribs.

He always loved hearing Susan laugh. When the third round of drinks came, they knew it was time to get back to the motel. If Johnny and Gidget were not better acquainted by now, it would just have to wait for another day. Susan looked at him and punched him on the arm. They were both having the same thoughts.

She said, "Let's go see how much fun those two are having without us. Maybe, when this is all over, you can teach me what it's like to be with a man. I've never had a man make love to me. Well, not all the way anyhow."

"Susan, this may sound a bit strange, but, if anyone could ever handle me, I'm betting it'd be you."

189

She laughed, "Yeah, I might very well be the only woman that can handle you, Big Guy. I'm an awful lot of woman."

He slid across the seat in the booth where they'd been sitting. "I think we'd better leave before I throw you across the table and have my way with you, Young Lady."

This time, Susan hit him much harder and they both laughed. Clay gave her a big hug, and kissed her on the cheek.

When they returned to the motel room, Johnny and Gidget were fully clothed and laughing about something. Susan and Clay could hear them even before they got to the room.

Clay said, "Look you guys, I can never repay you for what you're doing but you can be sure I'll never stop trying."

Johnny said, "Gidget and I were just saying that we believe this might be all Leila Nordstrum. This just might've been the quickest way for her to get rid of her husband."

Clay said, "I've thought the same thing. But why me, or maybe I was just convenient. You know, Guys, she told me to ask Pamela Gerard to that dance and, for some reason, she knew that Pamela would accept."

Gidget jumped in, "Maybe they've been planning this for a long time and you just happened to come along at the right time."

"Do you think they're lovers?" Johnny asked.

Susan said, "I'll bet I'll have a better handle on that little question by this time tomorrow night. Even if I have to sleep with, Leila Nordstrum."

Clay gave her a nasty look. "Okay, we'll all meet here at nine o'clock tomorrow night. Girls, if we're not here by ten o'clock, head to Cap N Guys and stay there until one of us gets there. Do you understand?"

"Yes, we understand," they both chimed in at the same time.

He and Johnny headed back to the apartment. Everything seemed to be just as they'd left it. This time, the car that was normally outside was nowhere in sight, and they didn't see any other suspicious vehicles. Clay could tell that Johnny was pleased.

They decided to sit on the stairs and talk for a while. Clay was the first to speak.

"Johnny, you know if you're correct and this was all Leila's plan, the general will get me out of this mess."

Johnny said, "There's just one thing that bothers me about that scenario. If she and Pamela are the only bad guys, then why the hell are we being followed? Why is the apartment bugged? They don't have the power to do that, do they?"

"Maybe it's the police or the bail bondsman. They'd sure be mad if I took it on the lam. They'd be stuck for four hundred and fifty thousand dollars; however, that doesn't make sense either. They couldn't have bugged my phone and the apartment in that short amount of time, could they?"

Johnny looked deep in thought. "No, I don't think they could. I'm sure it's not the police. So now we're right back to the general."

Clay said, "My head hurts from all this. Let's get some sleep."

"Clay, do you know anything more about your job?"

191

He began to explain as much as he could remember about the meeting and what he knew about the people present. He also told Johnny everything he could recall about the mental testing ordeal. By the time he'd finished with the update, Johnny was ready for a drink. Johnny went inside to make both of them something really strong.

"Here, maybe this'll help," Johnny, said, returning with a drink in each hand. If it doesn't, you probably won't care as much. At least, once we've had a few, we'll sleep well."

"Johnny, did all those people get murdered who were on the list we had in France?"

"I was there for the first seven. Well, eight counting the one we did together."

"Did you ever find out what they all had in common? Was there a link of any sort that you could put your finger on?"

"Not really. It was all random as far as I could tell."

Johnny explained as much as he could remember about his trip to Cuba and his being taken captive. He could recall very little about his captors, but he did remember that the head guy spoke perfect English and he was, without a doubt, Russian. Johnny didn't remember being taken to the island or whether he gave them any information that was useful to them. All he could recall for sure was that they kept referring to his superiors as the "Ten Little Indians."

"The Ten Little Indians. Who the hell are the Ten Little Indians?"

Johnny said, "I don't have any idea. They seemed to think I was working for them. They were pretty insistent about it."

Clay jumped to his feet. "Holy Mackerel, Johnny. There were eleven of us in that conference room. If you remove me from the picture, maybe we have the infamous Ten Little Indians."

"Damn it, Clay, you may be on to something. Do you remember who they all were?"

Clay looked at him incredulously. "Have you forgotten who the heck you're talking to? Remembering shit is my best thing. Of course I remember."

Johnny finished his drink in one gulp. "Well, I was never invited to any of those kinds of meetings."

"I'll tell you what, Johnny. Since you have no prior engagements for tomorrow, you could spend some time checking them out. I'll get you the list."

Clay walked up the steps and across the hall into the apartment as Johnny followed. He walked across the living room and picked up the throw rug that was lying on the carpet in front of the fireplace. He pulled back the carpeting underneath. There was the list. The list had the names of all the people in the conference room the day of the big meeting. There were even little bios written beside each person's name. He handed it to Johnny.

Johnny said, almost whispering, "Boy, you really are paranoid, aren't you?"

Clay motioned for Johnny to follow him back outside. He didn't respond until they were again safely out of earshot.

"You bet your ass I am. I have another copy wrapped in plastic and placed neatly under the battery in my car. I also have a letter addressed to the Washington Post."

"What kind of letter?"

"It simply tells them everything I know. Even a hell of a lot that I merely suspect. Don't worry, Partner. You're never mentioned. I must tell you, Johnny, that I'm a little worried about the meeting with the general. It could be good or it could be the worst meeting of my life."

"I'm sure it'll go well. You be cool, Old Buddy. With the girls on our team, we have a slight edge. I sure hope those two don't give anything away in their meetings tomorrow. They could get us all killed."

Clay held his glass in the air. "I promise you, those young ladies are real cool customers. They won't get trapped into saying the wrong thing very easily."

"I'm sure you're right. They must also be able to act pretty damn stupid. Do you follow my drift? In other words, they can't let on that they know the trouble you're in."

Clay said confidently, "I know they'll do the right thing. Even if I wasn't completely sure, you guys are all I have going for me."

Johnny rose from his seat on the step. "Let's go inside and try to get some sleep. Tomorrow is already here and my butt is dragging."

They took turns in the shower. They were in bed in no time looking for the sleep they hoped would come. Clay said a little prayer of protection for his comrades. He said a second one of thanks for their friendship.

As he tossed and turned, trying to rest his mind as much or more than his body, he again realized that his back had not been hurting him for some time now. For that he was truly thankful. The procedure performed at the hospital on that terrible Friday was very simple; however, it seemed to be the answer to relieving the pain in his back.

Chapter 15

Sunday morning was upon them very quickly. The sun was out, and Clay knew it was going to be a scorcher. The little bit of rain that hit the area over night was already evaporating quickly. You could almost see the steam rise from the streets at nine-thirty AM, as he took a morning walk. He decided to stop at the deli to get something for him and Johnny to eat.

Johnny was taking his morning shower when Clay returned. He could hear him singing and, for some unknown reason, it made him feel more at ease. Johnny loved to sing and he wasn't half bad. Johnny loved good soul music, and could listen to the Four Tops and the Temptations all day. That's one of the things that the two of them had in common. The only difference was that Johnny had no rhythm. *Imagine that, a black man with no rhythm.* He couldn't dance a lick, but he certainly thought he could.

When Johnny emerged from the shower, breakfast was on the table. They ate in silence for the better part of ten minutes without even looking at each other. Clay had picked up some bagels, lox, and a jar of peanut butter from the deli. Johnny loved peanut butter on his bagels. More than once, Clay had seen him eat it straight from the jar.

Johnny finally broke the silence, "I need to find out if the library is open today. If so, that'll be my first stop."

"Johnny, I'm really nervous about this meeting today."

"Look, Clay, just answer his questions truthfully. Let him do most of the talking if you can. He loves to hear himself talk."

"Johnny, do you think he's gonna try to get me out of this mess?"

"Of course he will. He has a lot of time and money invested in you. Believe me he doesn't like to waste either one."

"You're right, Partner. I guess I worry too much."

Johnny threw up his hands. "No!"

"Okay, Johnny, you made your point," Clay threw him the car keys.

Johnny threw them back. "I'll catch a cab, the driver will know how to get to the Library; anyway, you'll need the car. Listen, Clay, I'll be back at the apartment by dark. If anything comes up, leave me a note." Johnny motioned for Clay to follow him to the stairwell. "Leave the note under the carpet of the second step and I'll do the same if necessary."

Clay's face showed concern.

Johnny continued, "Look, Old Buddy, it's going to be all right. Susan and Gidget are doing their thing by now, and they're trusting us to do the same."

"Hell, I know that, and you can be sure I'll do my part."

"Clay, you most certainly have the toughest assignment. That's just the way it is. Frankly, I wish that I could be there with you."

Johnny went back into the apartment. He had to wash his hands and brush his teeth. Then they parted company. All of a sudden, Clay, was alone again. He still had well over an hour before his meeting, and so he did his own bit for oral hygiene and then decided to walk for a while, hoping to clear some of the cobwebs away. Clay was acutely aware that the next few hours might very well decide his entire future, or whether or not he had any future.

When he hit the outdoors, he knew instinctively that he was again being watched. Frankly, that didn't disturb him very much. He smiled, knowing, that if they were still with him, Johnny was most probably in the clear.

When he started walking down the street, the guy following him didn't know what to do. So, just for fun, Clay took off running. The guy jumped from his car and began to run after him. Clay ducked into the Milner Hotel and then out the side door, running around the block he ended up back at his own apartment building, and perched himself on the wall in front of the apartment building. In a few seconds, the guy came around the corner. When he saw Clay sitting a hundred yards away, he stopped and tried to act nonchalant. Clay gave him a little wave and went back into the apartment. He watched as the guy went back to retrieve his vehicle. When he was out of site, Clay went down the hall and out the side door to the parking lot. By the time the fellow got back in place to watch his apartment again, Clay was on his way to see the general. "*Someday I'm going to be able to tell my grandchildren about this, and we'll all get a big laugh,*" Clay thought to himself.

It was twenty minutes before two when he reached the general's parking area. As he got out of the car and started the long walk into the building, he was sure he was going to throw-up. He hoped the general would offer him something strong to drink, thinking he sure could use a belt. Every footstep echoed in his ears, as he walked up the marble steps leading to the main entrance of the building. Informing the security guard that the general was expecting him, the guard waved him past after calling the general's office to confirm his arrival. Clay made a mental note of the guard's name and badge number just in case he were to need it in the future.

The general himself was waiting for Clay at the door to his office.

"I can always count on you to be on time." General Essex said, as he extended his hand. "That's one of the many things I like about you, Son."

"Thank you, Sir," Clay replied.

The general looked pleased. "I'll bet you could use a drink about now. Have a seat, My Boy, and I'll get us both one. You still drinking scotch and soda?"

"Yes, Sir. That would be terrific."

After handing Clay a drink and lighting his customary cigar, the general began.

"I really don't believe you had anything to do with the death of that colonel. Even if you wanted him dead for some reason, you wouldn't have been so stupid. You wouldn't have killed him in front of that many witnesses. Clay, were you screwing that Leila woman?"

"I'd rather not answer that question at this time, if you don't mind, Sir."

"Well, be that as it may, someone is trying to get a pound of your flesh the hard way and we're not going to let that happen."

"Thank you, Sir."

The general continued, "I think she just wanted to get rid of her old man and you were the best opportunity to come along. She set you up to take the fall. She's really a cool customer. The way it stands now, you go to prison and she's single with a colonel's pension and she collects his life insurance. That's a pretty sweet deal. It's like having your cake and eating it too. How does that little Pamela girl play into this? Are you pumping her too?"

General Essex was on a roll and Clay wasn't about to stop him.

"Damn, Son, you need to get control of those hormones. Also, how the hell does the doctor fit into all this?"

"Look, Sir, I don't honestly know but you can be sure I'm gonna find out. None of this makes any sense at all to me. They must all be in this together somehow."

General Essex leaned back in his huge leather chair. "I have given permission for your attorney, Mr. Mann, to hire some investigators to check this out. He was told to spare no expense."

Clay said, "I really don't have much money; but I'll give you what little I have. I guess I could sell my car."

The general waved his cigar back and forth. "No need for that, My Boy."

"General, do I still have a job?"

"Clay, I have assured the members of our organization that you will be cleared on all counts. Hell, this is America where you're still innocent until proven guilty. We both know you're not guilty."

"That's very kind of you, Sir."

The general rocked forward. "Clay, you just lay low for a few more days. We don't want to be answering too many questions."

"I'll speak to no one." Clay replied.

The general came to his feet. "Henry Clay Smith is a valuable member of my staff. He is in no way responsible for this terrible act. That was my press release. It was in all the papers. You knew that, didn't you, Son?"

"No, Sir. I'm sorry I haven't even read the newspaper."

Clay was so relieved he almost dropped his drink. The general was saying all the right things. Clay felt pretty darn good about his possibilities for some kind of a future. The general seemed to really be his friend. Clay was actually feeling badly about some of the things he had been thinking.

"Sir, you just tell me what to do and I'm your man."

General Essex returned to his chair. He looked like he was deep in thought as he reached to open a drawer on the right side of his desk, taking out an envelope and handing it to Clay. The general, indeed, had the strangest look on his face. At that moment, Clay wished he were a mind reader.

"Take this money and give it to Captain Murphy. He had to hock his ass to make your bail. The extra money is for you to live on until we get this mess straightened out."

Clay was overwhelmed, "Thank you once more, General."

"Stay close to your apartment and, for God's sake, don't leave town. Also, don't come here unless I call you. Don't talk to anyone, not anyone. Do you fully understand me, son?"

"Yes, Sir, I most certainly understand. I'll wait for your call."

General Essex said, "For your information, I would've fired that bitch, Pamela, but I think I can learn more from her if she is close by. You see, I'm not as stupid as many seem to think."

Clay hoped his emotions weren't showing. "One last thing, Sir, do you have someone following me?"

"Not on your life. Are you absolutely sure someone is following you? Maybe with all that's going on its just paranoia."

"I'm absolutely sure, General. With your permission, I'll very quietly find out whom. I just assumed you were looking out for your investment."

"Please do, and let me know. There is a special number for you to use written down on a piece of paper in that envelope. Always be sure you use only that number when you need to contact me."

General Essex stood, and Clay knew that it was time to leave. He came to his feet and stuck out his hand. The general walked around the desk and put his arms around him just like everything was normal.

"Clay, I may have a little job for you to handle in a week or so. Can I count on your help if I need some assistance?"

"Damn right you can." Clay said, hugging him back.

As he walked down the hall away from the general's office, he knew someone was watching his every move. *But who*, he thought.

When he got back to his car, he tried looking around without being obvious, seeing nothing out of the ordinary. He realized that it was almost five PM, so he thought he might do a little shopping for food on his way back to the apartment.

He pulled into the Safeway parking lot, and parked his car before opening the envelope. When he did, he couldn't believe his eyes. The envelope had the general's note just as he said, and seventy-five thousand dollars. The fact that he had doubted the general was really beginning to bug him big time. *The man is obviously on my side. Damn, that feels good.* He could hardly wait to let everyone know, and he hoped everyone's day had gone as well, but he had his doubts.

After shopping, he returned to his apartment a little before six-thirty. As he started up the stairs, he looked under the carpet but there was no note. Putting the groceries on the counter he returned to the car for the remaining two bags. That's when he first realized the person who'd been tailing him was nowhere to be seen. They were either doing a much better job or they had finally given up. He hoped it was the latter.

Sure that Johnny would be home any minute, he decided to take a quick shower, shave and clean up a little. When he was finished, he went into the kitchen to make himself a drink and wait for John. It was now seven twenty. Clay thought, *I'm not going to worry. Things have gone too well today to let anything mess it up now.* About that time, he heard someone turn a key in the door and he knew it had to be Johnny.

Johnny looked at him. "Sorry, I'm a little late."

"No problem, Partner."

The two of them headed for the stairwell.

Johnny put both hands on Clay's shoulders and looked directly at him. "Boy, you look like the cat that swallowed the canary. You must've had a great meeting."

Clay playfully punched Johnny in the stomach. "Yes I did, but first tell me what you found out."

"To be honest with you, Clay, I didn't find out much of anything. The library was closed and my friend at the airbase wasn't able to do much on Sunday. He promised me that, by tomorrow night, he'd even know how many fillings they had in their teeth; and I trust him to do that. There is one thing; however, he was astonished to find Senator Lazar's name on the list. He told me that the senator from Minnesota was very well thought of and considered to be above reproach, at least that's the scuttlebutt."

Clay began, "It seems the general is on my side, and he assured me that he's going to do everything possible to get me out of this mess. He believes my story."

"Well, that's good news."

"He also gave me this." Clay handed the envelope to Johnny. "Fifty thousand dollars of that belongs to you. He thought you might like to have your bail money back. The other twenty-five is for me to live on until we straighten things out. Now, how do you feel about the general?"

"Whoa baby, I'm sure glad we have rich friends," Johnny exclaimed.

Clay laughed, "I have to believe the general is on our side, don't you?"

Johnny looked away, "I still don't trust the guy but I'll gladly take his money."

It was almost eight and they were supposed to meet the girls at nine PM. He told Johnny that they should get moving and Johnny concurred. When they left the apartment, Clay nudged him, "Hey, Partner, our shadow is back."

"I know, he was here when I came in."

"The general said he wasn't having me followed. I told him that if I saw someone following me again I'd find out who he was working for. Let's catch the bastard."

Johnny looked puzzled, "What do you have in mind?"

"Let's walk right up to the car and ask him. Unless you have a better idea."

"Not me. I'm with you, Old Buddy."

The two of them began walking down the sidewalk. When they reached a spot directly beside the car, Clay dropped his keys and when Johnny bent over to pick them up Clay stuck his Walther 9mm PPK right in the man's ear.

"Look, Fellow, this is getting a bit old. Who the hell are you working for?"

"I don't know what you mean," the man replied.

"Johnny, get the pliers from my toolbox. They're in the trunk of my car."

"You got it, Old Buddy." Johnny answered, heading for the parking lot where Clay's car was parked.

"What the hell are you going to do with a pair of pliers?" the man asked.

Clay's jaws tightened. "I'm going to ask you the same question one more time; but this time, I'm gonna give you a reason to tell me the truth."

"I'm telling you the truth," the man said, nervously.

"We'll see."

By this time, Johnny had returned with the pliers. He handed them to Clay.

"Johnny, take my gun. If he makes any move at all blow his head clean off. Can you do that?"

"Watch me," Johnny replied, taking the gun from Clay's hand.

Clay grabbed the bridge of the guy's nose with the pliers and began to squeeze just enough to get his attention.

"If you struggle, this is really gonna hurt. I really don't wish to do you any damage; so tell me, who hired you?"

The man started to respond negatively.

"Don't be stupid," Clay said, increasing the pressure.

"Okay, Okay, I was hired to follow you and report your every move," the man said, bleeding profusely now.

"The name, that's all I want to hear. No more bullshit,"

By this time the blood was all over the man's shirt and his trousers.

"If you make me ask you again it will take a dozen doctors to repair your face," Clay scowled.

"Senator Lazar's office. Let me go, please."

Clay released him immediately.

"Johnny, go pull the car around. I have a First Aid Kit; you probably saw it in the trunk. Put the pliers back and bring me the kit."

When Johnny returned, Clay asked him to attend to the man. Johnny packed the man's nose. "Do you think you can get to the emergency room, by yourself?" Johnny asked.

The man's eyes widened, looking at Clay and spitting blood on the sidewalk. "I'll make it. You're friends a crazy man, you know that?"

Clay said, "I'll not mention this to anyone. For your own sake, you shouldn't either. Get yourself to a hospital and be glad you told me the truth." Clay holstered his weapon, and when they were finally in the car and leaving the area, Johnny broke the silence.

"That man was absolutely correct; you really are a crazy man. He's just lucky he didn't push it any further."

"Ah, I didn't hurt him all that much."

"You know, the work you did on his nose just might improve his looks. Look what it did for you," Johnny said, laughing so hard he couldn't get his breath.

"Oh, that's real cute and you're supposed to be my best friend. I think I need a better class of friends."

Carl R. Smith

Johnny was still amused. "You know, with that twenty-five thousand, you might be able to get a better looking nose. Ah ... But then, what would you do for character?"

"Johnny, enough of the bullshit. What did you think about his answer?"

"I don't know. You met the senator; and after what my friend said today, I guess, in a strange sort of way, it makes sense."

They agreed, and they decided to give the girls a chance to form another opinion. It was almost nine fifteen when they arrived at the motel. The girls were starting to worry. They knew that Clay was seldom late, and they were acutely relieved when he knocked on the door.

"Okay, Ladies, who wants to go first?" Clay asked.

Gidget said, "I'll start. My lunch with Pamela was a little unusual. Clay, I think that young lady really loves you. The girl is scared to death, and she asked me if I'd get a message to you. She even gave me your address and telephone number. I was told not to talk to you on the phone because someone would probably be listening, and I should also be careful about talking inside your apartment. They bugged it the night you took the pills and passed out on the bed. She's the one who let them in."

"Who are *they*?" Clay asked.

"She told me she thought they worked for the general. But things have happened in the last few days and she's not so sure he's even aware of everything that's going on."

Johnny said. "He's aware. You can bet on that."

Gidget continued. "She was even afraid to talk to me in her own house. We went to her backyard and that's where she told me all this stuff. Then she said that she was sure someone was following her and I think she's right."

"That may all be true but why did she lie about Clay?" Johnny asked.

Gidget went on, "They told her that they only wanted him out of the way for a couple of days. Then this entire mess would be straightened out. She was supposed to say that she and Clay were together at the dance. Colonel Nordstrum being killed was a total shock to her."

Clay said, "Wait a minute. When she found out, why didn't she tell the truth?"

"Pamela wanted to tell the truth. They told her if she opened her mouth they'd wipe out her entire family. It seems she has a sister who lives in Chicago and her mother, whom she lives with here. She was also told Clay would die, along with herself. The girl doesn't know whether to 'shit or go blind.' If even part of this is true, I don't blame her."

"Then what's your take on all this?" Clay asked.

"The girl needs help, I'm convinced. I do believe she loves you, Clay. We've got to do something to help her."

"Do you think there's anything going on between her and Leila?" Johnny asked.

Gidget replied, "No, I don't. I spent more than an hour asking everyone at the Shoreham Hotel about her. No one ever saw the two of them together. I also talked to two guys who dated her a time or two and they all said she is sweet as apple pie."

Clay said, "Yeah, I thought so too."

Gidget wasn't finished. "One of the waitresses told me that Pamela was head over heels in love with this tall blond guy who looks a little like Troy Donahue. I think that would be you, Clay. Although, I don't see the resemblance."

Johnny interrupted, "I think he looks more like Trigger."

Clay shoved Johnny off the bed. "Go ahead, Gidget."

"I also asked the waitress if she thought Pamela went both ways and she laughed out loud. She thought I was kidding."

Clay said, "I must assume, from all that you've told us, you think she's just another one of the pawns in this chess game. Is that about right?"

"Absolutely. If we don't do something real quick, she's gonna end up dead just like the colonel. Clay, you don't want that to happen. Look guys, when we met at the hotel and had one drink, her hands were shaking so bad she could hardly hold the glass. Also, she drove me back to her house and she almost got us killed twice. This young lady is not that good an actress, I promise you."

Johnny said, "Okay, Gidget, I think we all get the message."

"Are you ready for me?" Susan asked.

Clay said, "Go ahead."

"Let me start by saying Leila Nordstrum is the coolest cucumber I've ever met. I don't think she really wants to hurt you Clay, but she's going to get what she wants, of that I'm certain. It sounds like she and the general would make a good team."

Johnny said, "Maybe they are a team."

"We talked a lot about the hospital. That's where I'm supposed to be looking for work, remember? She barely mentioned her dead husband. I had to bring up the subject. And, she couldn't understand why Clay would do such a thing; although, she knew he was infatuated with her."

"Bullshit, she's the one who seduced me." Clay said, angrily.

Susan continued, "I tried to act nonchalant but it sure was difficult. She kept asking me if I remembered you from the hospital."

"What'd you tell her?" Clay asked.

"I told her that I remembered you very well and you sure didn't seem like the type of person who'd kill someone."

"Thanks, Babe."

Susan went on, "She said she would put in a good word for me at the hospital and that the hospital was really understaffed. In my opinion, Leila did this to get rid of her husband. I don't think she has any immediate plans for the future. She didn't act like she did."

"How'd she act when my name came up?" Clay inquired.

"That's what I was trying to tell you. Big old tears rolled down her cheeks when your name came into the conversation. That's the only time she showed any kind of emotion."

Johnny said, "Gee, she's awfully sorry that Clay may spend the next fifty years in prison; however, she's not sorry enough to tell the truth, is she?"

"I didn't want to seem too inquisitive for fear of losing her confidence. She and I are having dinner at the infamous Shoreham Hotel on Tuesday evening. I think she really likes me."

Clay thanked the girls for all they'd done. He went on to explain everything that had happened in the past twenty-four hours. Also, he wanted to know if either of the women mentioned the senator or the general. Both girls responded in the negative except for what had already been said.

Clay began walking the floor. "Tomorrow, Johnny is going to find out everything possible about the ten people that were in the conference room with me."

Johnny interrupted, "It may be that the good senator is the key player after all. He certainly has the power to cause all these things to happen."

There was something else Clay needed to know. "Did anyone follow you back here, Gidget? That goes for you too, Susan?"

"I think maybe they tried. I changed cabs four times after I left Pamela."

Susan said, "No, I don't think so. I, too, was very careful."

"Johnny, let's you and me go for a little walk around the motel parking lot and check things out. You girls stay right here. We'll be back in a few minutes."

"Okay, Boss, anything you say." Both girls spoke, simultaneously.

He and Johnny spent about twenty minutes outside in the parking lot. Even in the area adjacent to the motel, they found nothing that concerned either one of them. When they returned to the room, they informed the girls that everything was okay.

"What do you think the general wants you to do for him, Clay?" Susan asked.

Johnny said, "He probably wants someone killed or at least seriously hurt. That seems to be his order of the day."

Clay said, "I don't know, Susan. He'll tell me when the time is right. I sure would like to have a little talk with the senator."

Clay handed each one of the girls a thousand dollars to help pay their expenses. Gidget grabbed him and kissed him right on the mouth.

Johnny said, "Do you two want to be alone?"

Gidget said, "Look, Fellows, all jokes aside, what are we going to do to help Pamela? Clay, if you care for that girl, you better do something."

Clay said, "Give me a little time to think."

"Oh damn, I almost forgot the most important thing." Gidget was suddenly so excited she slipped off the bed to the floor, landing with a thud on her behind. She went fishing for something, and pulled a crazy looking key from her purse and handed it to Clay.

"What am I supposed to do with this?" he asked.

"That key fits a locker at the Greyhound Bus Station, just a few blocks from your apartment. According to Pamela, the contents will clear you of killing the colonel; although, if you use it now, Pamela will surely be killed. But, if anything happens to her, you're to use it immediately. That's why she was trying to get you to talk to her, so

213

she could give you the key. I think she'd rather die than to have anything bad happen to you."

Clay responded, "We could get her and hide her out somewhere."

Susan said, "If we did, wouldn't that put her mother and sister in even more danger?"

Johnny said, "The four of us can surely figure out a way to protect this young lady. Think, you guys, there must be a way."

The girls were thinking already.

Johnny said, "Well, don't think that hard, Susan. You'll hurt something."

Now everybody laughed; all except Susan. She didn't seem to find it very amusing.

Johnny jumped on the bed and kissed her on the forehead. "You know, I love you, Babe. Almost as much as that little squirt, Gidget."

Susan shoved him backwards and he landed on the other bed.

Johnny jumped up. "I've got a great idea, Clay. Let's rent another room and stay the night. That'll give us a lot more time to think of a solution and it might even be fun."

Clay gave him a dirty look. "Always thinking with the wrong head, huh John?"

"I like that idea," Susan chimed in.

"What do you say, Little One?" Johnny asked excitedly.

"I love the idea, you Big Jerk."

Johnny said. "Then, it's settled. I'll go get us another room. Maybe I'll register under the name, Smith."

Clay said, "You do that. While you get the room, Susan and I'll get us all something to drink. Gidget might have a much better time if she's a little tipsy."

Gidget said, "Don't hurry, I'm gonna take a quick shower." She started to disrobe in front of everybody.

Johnny headed for the office. Clay and Susan took off towards the only place open that time of night. On a Sunday, beer was all they could get but everybody seemed to be all right with that. When they were all back together in one room, Johnny gave Clay the key to the room next door. It seems the motel wasn't very busy. They had their choice of almost any room in the place.

The four of them talked and drank beer until after midnight. Johnny and Gidget were ready to be in a room by themselves. Clay took Susan by the hand and escorted her to the room next door.

When Susan and Clay were alone in the room, he was the first to speak. "Susan, don't feel any pressure. I don't expect anything to happen. Even though we're both a little drunk, I'd never take advantage of you, you know that."

"Damn it, you know I've never gone all the way with a man before; but if you'll have me, tonight's the night."

She put her arms around his waist. They kissed passionately. Susan could feel his excitement begin to grow, and pressed the lower half of her body even harder against his.

"I know that I'm a big girl, but I've never had a man inside me. You're gonna have to take it slow the first time."

He whispered, "You are a magnificent specimen. When it comes to shear beauty, you outclass them all."

"Thanks, Clay, I really needed to hear something like that. It's no wonder Pamela loves you. You can be the gentlest man."

"If I hurt you, Susan, you stop me. Sometimes I get a little carried away. The truth is we don't have to be in a hurry."

She slid her hands down his back while pressing her body firmly against him. "I want you to make love to me."

He took her hips in both his hands and pulled her to him so hard she almost lost control. When Susan finally reached her peak, she damn near crushed him with her powerful legs.

"Hell, Babe, you're gonna kill me. Don't squeeze me any harder."

"I'm sorry, but I thought you were going to rip me apart. When you reached your peak, I just wanted to squeeze the life out of you."

"You damn near did," he said, breathing heavily.

He rolled to his back and took a deep breath.

"Was I okay?" She asked.

Clay touched her cheek. "I think if we did this a few more times, you might really kill me. I always wanted to die with a smile on my face."

"But, was I any good?" She asked for the second time.

"Oh yes, you were much more than okay. I think you broke it."

She moved toward him. "Here let me kiss and make it better."

Susan decided that it was time for another shower. They both felt a little silly. They'd been through a lot together and as great as it was, they were both a little embarrassed.

"Clay, I may not be able to walk but you were great."

"I tell you what, Susan, if we both reach forty and are not married, we'll just marry each other and grow old together. I think that'd be the right thing to do. I like you better than anybody else and I even love you like a sister. Whoa, I've never had sex with any of my sisters. I guess our being able to have great sex would be a bonus, what do you say?"

"I think that's a great idea, you got a deal. And, I love you, too."

Chapter 16

When morning came, he and Susan each felt as though they'd been in a tug of war. But, they were both brandishing great smiles.

"Susan, I'm gonna call Johnny and see if they're ready to have some breakfast. How much time do you need?"

"Give me ten minutes, is that okay?"

"Sure, Babe."

He picked up the phone. "Gidget, it's you. Susan and I are going for some food do you guys want to eat?"

"Yeah, but Johnny's in the shower and I'm next. How about we meet you there in twenty minutes. I'm really hungry, but then, I'm always hungry."

"Okay, we'll wait to order until you get there. See ya later."

They were on their third cup of coffee when Johnny and Gidget arrived. They both looked a little worse for wear.

Clay began, "I want to see Pamela. How do we make that happen?"

The others agreed they didn't have a clue.

He continued, "If they found out she was meeting with me, her life wouldn't be worth a plug nickel. So, how do we pull it off?"

Johnny said, "Give me some time, I'm working on it."

Clay said, "Gidget you go to her office today. Have her meet you in the ladies room. When you're alone with her, tell her we're going to work it out. Tell her to play it cool until she hears from us in a couple of days. Do you think you can accomplish that? I mean, without putting yourself in jeopardy? I don't want anything to happen to you."

"Sure I can. I'll let you know what she says tonight. It's my turn to deliver pizza, or is it Chinese? I can't remember. I'll let you know around six tonight. Will that be soon enough to make everything work?"

"Yes, that'll work."

"What about me?" Susan asked.

"And you, my Big Beautiful Wench, you go by the hospital and very carefully see if you can find out when Dr. Delong is scheduled to return."

"Okay, I'll get the information to Gidget and she can fill you in tonight."

"You know," Clay said, with a silly grin on his face. "I should've been an officer. I'm really great at giving orders, don't you think?"

Johnny looked up from his coffee. "Yeah, but let's not forget I am an officer, and I guess my marching orders come next."

"Okay, Captain Murphy, you get the lowdown on the 'Ten Little Indians'. I'm gonna try to get an appointment with the senator, if he'll talk to me."

"You got it, Old Buddy. I'll do my best."

219

Clay added, "Come on you guys, I have a key to a locker that should keep me out of jail. It's a beautiful day. What more could a man ask for? Also, you guys keep thinking about a way to get Pamela out of this predicament."

Johnny said, laughing the whole time, "You're too damned cheerful in the morning, Clay. It just pisses me off."

Gidget, on the other hand, laughed so hard she spit milk through her nose.

"Now, that's attractive," Susan said, trying to get out of the way.

Clay was looking for a chance to regroup and get everyone back on track. He was afraid that, with the good news, they might let up and it could cost someone dearly. Actually, at this point, he was even more confused as to who was responsible for all the trouble he was in. *I think it's time to take the offensive,* He thought. *For the last few days, we've been stabbing in the dark and I think we can do better.*

He said, "Look, you guys, I want to get a listening device inside the general's office. That's the only way we're ever going to know what's really going on."

Johnny said, "Maybe my friend at Andrews can help us but we're gonna be taking a big chance. If we get caught, we're done for."

"Johnny's right. You girls are out of this one."

"That's not fair." Gidget muttered, looking hurt and dismayed.

Clay said, "Susan, it really would be nice if I could talk to Doctor Delong. Surely he's not seriously involved in this mess. You do everything you can to find him. At least get a clue when he'll be back on duty. I'm sorry, that was already on your agenda, wasn't it?"

Susan replied, "Yes, Boss, it was. But, I'll leave no stone unturned."

He turned his attention to Gidget. "Gidget, you already know what you have to do. If things work out, maybe Pamela can help us bug the general's office. I sure hope she's all right,"

Johnny screamed, "By God, I got it. I knew there was something that didn't make any sense. I know what it is."

"Well, what is it?" Clay asked.

"If Pamela let the guys in your apartment, and, if she's afraid for her life as well as her sister's and mother's, then who told her to do it? Who threatened her and who is she afraid of?"

Clay said, "I don't follow you, Johnny."

Johnny continued, "She said she first thought it was the general. Now, she's not sure. Then who did she, in fact, talk to? Furthermore, did the threat come by letter, by telephone or did someone talk to her personally? Did she leave Clay alone in the apartment with whoever bugged the place? We know for sure that she went to the dance. Who did she go with and was that the person who killed the colonel? Do you guys understand any of what I'm saying?"

Clay's expression saddened, "Yeah, I think you're exactly correct. None of that makes any sense. Also Johnny, remember what the general told me? He said that he would've fired her on the spot but he was keeping her around to see if she knew anything. Anything that could help get me out of this mess. Gidget, are you pretty certain that what you told us is exactly the way in which she said it?"

"Absolutely."

Clay said, "Let me write this shit down. Then I'm gonna give you a few, well-written questions for Miss Pamela. When she answers them, you watch her every reaction. If she's lying, I believe you'll be able to tell. If she's been telling the truth, she won't get the least bit rattled. Can you handle that, Gidget?"

"Yes, Clay, I can handle that."

Susan added her two cents worth, "Damn it, every time I think things are looking up, this hole just keeps getting deeper and deeper."

Johnny interjected, "You're correct, my tall and beautiful friend. But we're the Four Mouseketeers and we're smarter than the average mouse."

"I think you mean the Four Musketeers," Clay corrected.

"Hell, Mouseketeers, Musketeers, who cares? We're still smarter than they think we are. By God, I'm gonna figure this out, even if it kills me. Oops, bad choice of words. Sorry, Girls?"

Clay said, "Screw pizza at six. Gidget, I think we better meet here again tonight. How about seven o'clock? We'll eat together, somewhere other than here."

Everyone agreed to reassemble at seven that evening.

Clay hung his head in his hands. "I'm so confused by now I'm getting another headache. Things seemed a lot clearer before Johnny's revelation. He was absolutely right, though, and you girls must know it too. One minute, I think Pamela loves me and is an unwilling participant, and then I think she's as evil as sin. I have seen some puzzles in my time, but this is truly impossible to get a hold on."

"Until I have irrefutable proof to the contrary, the general is my culprit. I've seen his work, up close and personal," Johnny said, with that all to knowing attitude, he sometimes displays.

Clay told the girls to be careful. He'd always been the "den mother" type and it often showed. To be truthful, he knew the others didn't mind at all, at least he believed that to be the case.

"Johnny, when we get back to the apartment, you can take the car. If I'm lucky enough to get a meeting with the senator, I'll catch a cab. You have a lot further to go than I do."

"Thanks, Old Buddy, that'll make my job easier."

Clay restated, "Whenever I think things are really starting to come together, they just get more confusing. But, if Pamela is one of the bad guys, how do we explain the key."

"I know exactly what you mean," Johnny said. "The senator may be the real bad guy. Although, I know how many lives the general has destroyed. I'll just bet he's never lost a minutes' sleep."

"When you get to your friend at Andrews Air Force Base, maybe we'll find some of the answers. If we don't, we'll just keep on looking."

"You're right, but I keep thinking," Johnny said, with a small amount of urgency in his voice. "We need to solve this mess before the general tells you about the favor. Whatever it is, you're gonna have to do it for him."

They arrived back at Clay's apartment a little before eleven. When they walked in the door, they couldn't believe their eyes. Someone had turned the place into a huge mess. It looked like someone had just thrown a pack of wildcats in the place and left them there for an hour or so.

"Well, Johnny, that little 'piece of ass' last night cost us a great deal more than the price of another motel room. If we'd been here, this never would've happened."

"Don't lay this on me, Old Buddy. If we'd been here, we might look like this apartment does."

"Hell, John. I'm not mad at you. I'm just mad."

"That makes two of us."

"Why?" Clay screamed.

"Your guess is as good as mine, Clay. The key. I'll bet they know about the key. You know they can't let us find whatever is in that lock box."

He knew Johnny was right, but what now? Something was tugging at the back of his brain. All of a sudden it hit him. Clay turned pale as a ghost.

Johnny grabbed him, "What's wrong?"

"Oh my God, Johnny, do you know where the general's office is in the Pentagon?

"Which floor Clay? I'll find it,"

"No, we don't have time. I'll go. Gidget may be running into real trouble. If they got Pamela and she tells them whom she gave the key to, Gidget won't live much longer. My God, what have I done?"

Clay was heading down the steps. "C'mon, Johnny, follow me."

They headed for the car.

"Johnny, go to the corner. Turn left. The bus station is only a couple of blocks. Secure that information from the lock box and put it elsewhere. They may already have it; moreover, they may be watching the place. What the hell, they may have overheard my big mouth upstairs in the apartment. Be careful, Partner. I'll see you back here real soon, I hope."

Clay circled the block and found Johnny hurriedly walking toward the bus station. Johnny saw him and ran to the passenger's side and hopped in.

"What now?"

"Find a telephone booth and call the motel. We might get lucky. If Susan is there alone, tell her to get the hell out of there right now. If they get Gidget, she may tell them who and where Susan is. Tell her to catch a cab from a few blocks away and to meet us at the bar. You know, Cap 'N Guy's. Tell her not to leave there. When you're through inside the bus station, you go there as well. Be sure you're not followed. I'll call you there as soon as possible."

Johnny jumped out of the car and was on his way again.

When Clay arrived at the general's parking area, he made a mad dash for the northwest entrance to the building. He barely got off the elevator when he saw Gidget going in the door of the general's office. There was no way to catch her or get her attention. Clay waited in the little alcove about fifteen feet from the door. In less than five minutes she came out and headed for the elevator. He grabbed her.

Gidget jumped back against the wall. "Damn it, Clay, you scared the hell out of me. What are you doing here?"

225

He grabbed her again. "C'mon."

"Clay —"

"C'mon, Gidget."

When they were in the stairwell, he began explaining to her what was going on. She hung on his every word until he was finished. She was in a hurry to tell him something important as well.

"Clay, Pamela didn't show up for work today. The lady in the office told me that she had called her house but no one answered. She said that she was probably on her way."

Clay turned. "Let's go check her parking space. Maybe she'll show up."

"God, I hope so."

"There's a pay telephone in the garage," he said. "We can call Johnny from there."

They went running down the steps.

"C'mon, Gidget."

"Would you quit saying, 'c'mon'." Gidget screeched. "I'm right behind you."

Pamela's parking space was empty. He felt it would be. They called Johnny and told him they were together, and safe, for the moment at least.

Johnny said, "I've talked to Susan, she's fine, and on her way to meet us. I've not noticed anyone following me, either they're real good or they're not there. You guys take care, and we'll see you soon."

Clay was very careful driving to the bar. Neither he nor Gidget saw anyone suspicious, and that made him worry even more. *You're always better off knowing where your enemies are,* Clay thought.

It took he and Gidget less than twenty minutes to reach the bar. Susan was already there. She and Johnny were having a drink at a back table. They all hugged and no one even noticed.

Clay and Gidget told the others about Pamela. They also told them that they were sure that they had not been followed.

Johnny had already told Susan about the apartment. Clay, in all the excitement, hadn't told Gidget, so he brought her up to date.

Clay couldn't be still. "I want to hear about the lock box. Did you have any problems?"

Johnny said, "Bad news, there was nothing in the locker, nothing at all."

"Had it been broken into?" Clay asked.

"No, it didn't look damaged at all. Believe me, I looked very closely."

Clay finally sat back against the booth wall. "Why is it we're no longer being followed? What do you think it means?"

"Hell if I know," Johnny replied, strumming his fingers on the table. "But you're right. It makes no sense and I don't like it."

"Johnny, take Gidget across the street to the bus station so she can call the general's office to see if Pamela ever arrived. If someone traced the call to the bar, they might put it under surveillance. That wouldn't be good."

"Okay, Gidget, you heard the master. Move that pretty little butt."

227

"Little, *little*, that's how you guys see me, ain't it? There's a lot more to me than just the fact that I'm shorter than most people."

With that they were gone. Clay and Susan just sat there with their mouths hanging open.

He looked at Susan, "Who put a bee in her bonnet?"

"Forget it, Clay, she's upset about Pamela. She thinks that if Pamela's dead it's all her fault, because, she was unable to convince you to do something a little quicker."

"Oh my God. What could we have done any quicker? But, you know she may be right. Instead of having sex last night, maybe we should have been trying to find Pamela." Clay hung his head.

Susan put her hand on his neck, and they were quiet for some time.

When Johnny and Gidget returned from making the telephone call, they didn't look very happy.

Clay said, "She wasn't there, was she?"

"No, she was not," Gidget, replied. "They'd not heard from her at all."

Johnny reached for Clay's hand, "Sorry, Clay, but I'll bet she's dead. I'll bet she gave up the lock box before they killed her."

Clay had tears in his eyes. He tried to speak but the words just wouldn't come out. Susan put her arms around him and tried to comfort him the best she could.

He regained his composure. "You know, if she's dead, she's an innocent party. That would mean she really did love me, and that makes me a two-time loser; first Taylor and now Pamela. I'm not gonna let anyone else die because of my bad life choices."

"Clay, you're not a loser, and this is not your fault," Johnny said, slamming his fist into the wall. "If I hadn't been so flippant last night we would've all tried harder, and maybe we could've saved her. I'm truly sorry, Clay."

"Johnny, I don't know when you have to be back in Atlanta but you're leaving today. With your money and my thanks. You girls are going home too."

Johnny started to speak but Clay cut him off.

"They want me for murder. Well, if they're gonna fry me; one or two more won't make much difference. Will it? I'm gonna kill me a general. Maybe I'll get me a senator, too. The other eight people who were in that conference room best find a good hiding place. This old boy's gonna massacre a few Indians. Then, I'm gonna leave the country."

Johnny said, "Come to your senses, Clay. I'm not going to let you do that and neither are these gals. Now, let's get down to business; but first, I need another drink. How about you guys? I'm buying. You might not get this chance again."

"I'll take one," Gidget replied, feeling her own sense of guilt.

Susan chimed in, "Me too."

Johnny turned to Gidget, "Gidget, did you tell Pamela where you were staying? Is there anyway she could've found out?"

"No, definitely not. We didn't even talk about me, at least not in that sense. I never called her from the motel either."

229

Johnny said, "Susan, get a cab and head for the hospital. We really need the information on Dr. Delong. The three of us will meet you back at the motel or at least Clay and Gidget will. I've got to get to Andrews Air Force Base and talk to my friend."

Susan downed her drink and kissed Clay on the cheek. Then she headed across the street to the nearest taxi stand.

Johnny said, "C'mon, Clay, get off your sorry ass and take Gidget back to the motel. I'll see you there as soon as I have the information we so desperately need."

Johnny looked right at him. "Don't make me kick your butt. At least not right here in front of the girls and everybody. It would be an ugly scene."

Clay looked right back at him. He stood up and headed for the door with Gidget at his heels. He didn't say one solitary word, but did as he was told. Neither he nor Gidget had very much to say on the way back to the motel but he could feel her watching his every expression.

She finally spoke, "Pamela may be all right, Clay. If you'll stop at that drugstore, I'll try to reach her one more time."

"Try her home as well," he said, reaching for his wallet.

"Okay, I will."

He tried to hand her some money but she just looked at him.

"I don't need your money, Mister. I have rich friends and I'm a kept woman."

That finally brought a little bit of a smile to Clay's otherwise somber face. He patted her on the forehead like a *little* child. She wrapped both arms around his neck and just hugged the stuffing out of him. That brought a tear to his eye for the second time in the last little while. He patted her on the ass as she got out of the car.

When she returned, the news was just the same. Nobody had heard from Pamela.

"Gidget, when you were at Pam's house, did you see her mother?"

"No, as a matter of fact I didn't."

"Well, I sure would like to know where she is. Wouldn't you?"

"Yes, I would. Do you know if she works somewhere?"

"I really don't remember but I don't think she does."

Gidget said, "Well, she should be home sometime today even if she does work."

They were both a little puzzled.

She continued, "I don't think anyone else was home yesterday. I do remember smelling cigarette smoke in the house. I thought it was funny because I never saw Pamela smoke. Did her mother smoke, or do you know?"

"I don't think so. At least I never saw her smoke."

He told Gidget he was going into the drugstore and call the Senate operator to try Senator Lazar. Maybe, just maybe they could get together.

He said, "I'll be right back."

"Okay, I'll wait in the car. Hey, get me some aspirin and something to drink."

When he returned, he told Gidget that the senator would see him at ten AM the next morning. The two of them headed for the motel.

231

He had bought Gidget a coke and some aspirin. She was in the process of taking a couple when a news story came over the radio about a woman found floating face down in the Potomac River. They didn't identify the woman.

"I'll bet that's Pamela," he said, his voice shaking.

"You don't know that," she replied.

"I feel it in my bones," he said, slamming his hand hard against the steering wheel. "I'll bet she was killed last night."

He parked the car on the other side of the motel. The two of them walked around the end of the building to the room. Everything looked just as it should have with nothing out of place.

Clay put his arms around her. "It looks like we've kept this place a secret. At least I hope we have. I have plans for the rest of my life."

When they were inside the room, she slid her arms around his middle. "What do you say, Big Boy, want to fool around?"

He gave her this incredulous look.

She withdrew her arms. "Okay, shoot me. I guess being scared makes me horny."

No response. He was thinking about Pamela, and he knew that Gidget was only trying to take his mind off things. Clay turned on the television in the hopes of hearing some additional news about the woman they'd found. If they knew anything, it would probably be on the Six O'clock News.

"How is your back doing?" Gidget inquired. "I haven't heard you complain about it at all since Susan and I got here?"

"Thanks for asking. It's much better. I haven't had any pain since they did that caudal block, the day all this started. It really did the trick. I guess that's the one thing I can be grateful for."

"Do you know what I'd be grateful for?"

Indeed, he knew. "Come over here, you little nymph. I'll give you one of my famous foot massages. That'll at least take my mind off all this garbage."

She kicked off her shoes and jumped on the bed where he was sitting. "I don't feel like I'm being very much help. There must surely be something else I can do."

"Being here for me and being my friend is much more than I deserve. You know, I'm not sure I could've survived to this point if it hadn't been for the three of you. By the way, how do you feel about Johnny? I think he's pretty fond of you."

She never answered. When he turned to see why, she was sound asleep. He folded the bedspread back in order to cover her. It was chilly in the room.

It was almost five o'clock, so he decided to go for a little walk before the Six O'clock News. He very quietly opened the door and went outside. The air outside had cooled considerably. It looked like it might rain before nightfall. Maybe he'd try calling Pam's house from the little store on the corner. If she answered, he would simply hang up; conversely, he wasn't sure what he'd do if her mother answered. He just wanted someone to answer the damn telephone. No one did.

When he returned to the room, Gidget was still asleep and it was almost six. He turned the television on without hardly any sound.

233

Then he just waited and hoped. The weatherman said it was going to rain and probably rain for the next couple of days. NASA announced that within eighteen months they would send a man to the moon. *Yeah right.* Clay thought, *that's a bunch of bullshit, it ain't ever gonna happen.*

The anchorman began talking about a young boy who saw someone floating in the Potomac. When the rescue team pulled the body out, it was a woman, and they figured she'd been dead for twelve to fifteen hours. The woman was in her late forties to early fifties; however, they did not have a positive I D as yet.

Clay got so excited when he heard the news, he screamed, *Fantastic.*

Gidget sat straight up. "What's wrong?"

"Nothing's wrong, the body was that of an older woman. I just heard it on the news."

"That's great, how long have I been asleep?"

"A little over an hour. I'm really sorry about waking you up so suddenly but I'm glad you're awake now. How do you feel?"

"I dreamed you were sucking my toes. Were you sucking my toes?"

"No silly. I went for a walk while you were sleeping. I just got back."

"I tried to get an answer at Pamela's from the telephone at the little store down the street but no such luck."

Gidget said, "I figure we can try again when we go to dinner."

"Yeah, that's a good idea." Clay suddenly realized it was getting late. "I wish Susan and Johnny would get here with some news. I thought they'd be back by now."

"Me too," Gidget said, adjusting her clothes.

There was a knock at the door. It had to be Johnny for Susan had a key.

Clay opened the door for him. "Well, don't keep us hanging. What'd you find out?"

"A lot, but Susan's cab just pulled up. Let's wait for her."

Susan came through the door as Johnny was talking.

Clay said, "What is it, Susan? You don't look so very happy."

"Did you guys here about the woman they pulled out of the Potomac?"

"Yes, we heard. At first we thought it might be Pamela but the woman was too old," Clay replied.

"Well, she wasn't too old to be Pam's mother. At the hospital, they said her last name was Gerard. Isn't that Pam's last name?"

Clay said, "Oh my God, yes it is. Are you sure it's her mother?"

"I'm pretty sure, but we'll know for sure by morning."

Johnny said, "Has anyone heard from Pamela? Did she ever show up anywhere?"

"We tried her at work twice," Gidget said. "And three times at home, no answer."

Johnny pulled Gidget off the bed. "Let's go get some dinner and I'll tell you what I discovered at the base."

Everyone had to take his or her turn in the bathroom. Then they were on their way to dinner and, with any luck, a lot of conversation to go with it.

While in the back seat of the car, Gidget and Susan were having their own conversation.

Susan said, "Clay was sucking your toes? When did all this happen?"

"No," Gidget replied. "I said, I dreamed that he was sucking my toes."

Johnny jumped right into the conversation. "Exactly whose toes got sucked?"

"Nobody's toes got sucked," Gidget said. "It was just a dream."

Johnny said, "I need a drink. I think we're all getting a little squirrelly."

Chapter 17

The restaurant was almost empty on a Monday evening. They had their choice of seats, and took a huge table in the back of the place where they could talk more freely.

Johnny began to explain what he'd discovered. His friend at Andrews had found mostly financial information on the people in question. It seems that each one of them had considerable wealth and a great deal of money in foreign banks. They also had some very strong ties to the second highest office in the land. The group in question was considered to be "Fringe Patriots," America first, but only if it meant money in their pockets and great power with which to bend others to their will. The cleanest one, and newest member, was the senator from Minnesota. No one seemed to understand his involvement. The senator was also the only one whose wealth came before his involvement with the group.

Clay said, "What do you make of all this, Johnny?"

"I personally think the senator is the odd man out. I don't really know whether that's good or bad." There was a great deal of uncertainty in Johnny's voice.

"What does that mean?" Susan asked.

Johnny continued, "Well, if we look at what we know for sure, you have to believe the general is the culprit. He's the one person who would, for sure, take the last dime from an old ladies purse and then have her killed if she complained about it."

Clay said, "Damn, Johnny, you really believe he's that bad?"

"Damn it, Clay, I was there when eight of them bought it. I couldn't tell you why any of them needed to be eliminated. Well, all except the one we did together, Clay. Let me tell you why they had you kill that poor man. They wanted to control his son, and they only needed him out of the way for a few hours. Kill the father, so the son will have to fly home to attend the funeral. Therefore, they would have ample time to manipulate his company for a few hours. That's the type of people we're dealing with. Now, do you understand?"

"Calm down, Johnny," Gidget pleaded.

"I'm sorry, Guys. I didn't mean to get carried away."

"Its okay, Johnny, go ahead," Clay encouraged.

Johnny started talking very calmly, "Clay, you really need to understand how far this man will go to accomplish his goals. He told me that you were his pride and joy, and that he had molded you into the perfect hit man. If you ever did fail, you'd just disappear and there wasn't anybody out there who'd even care. He also knew that you really idolized him and he was going to take advantage of that. Clay, he wants you to do his bidding. As long as you do, he'll take good care of you. When you stopped after the one mission, he was ready to have you buried in Vietnam; but you survived."

"Johnny, I've known you almost all my life. You're trying very hard not to say something and I want to know what it is."

All this time the girls were just sitting there completely mesmerized.

"Okay, Clay, you asked for it. I think the general had the colonel killed as a favor to Leila. He framed you in the process so he could save your ass and make you so beholding to him that you'd do anything he wanted you to do. God, I hope I'm wrong. I also believe he may have had something to do with the death of Taylor. He could have arranged that with little or no trouble at all. I thought that, when he found out that I had bailed you out of jail, he'd probably find a way to have me killed, too. Then you would only have him. Fortunately, he hasn't been able to find me alone long enough to get the job done. Now! Ask me if I love you more than a brother." Tears began to roll down his cheeks. He had said all he had to say.

Clay stood in disbelief. "My God, Johnny, I had no idea."

The waitress came to the table to get their order. "Is something wrong?"

"Oh no, it's just a family thing, a reunion of sorts. We're just so happy to be together again and we're acting a little silly." Clay sat back down, winking at the others.

Johnny said, "Bring us all another drink. We'll be ready to order by the time you get back."

"Yes, Sir," she said, and hurried off.

Susan said, "Well, we made quite an impression on her, don't you think?"

"Johnny, I have an appointment with the senator tomorrow. I almost forgot to mention it with everything else that's happened in the past few hours."

Susan said hurriedly, "Decide what you want to eat. Here comes the waitress with our drinks."

Clay jumped straight up out of his chair and ran to the bar.

"Turn that up," Clay said, pointing to the television.

Susan was right behind him and the others followed.

"What's going on?" Johnny asked.

"Shh, wait a minute," Clay said, pointing to the television.

When the newscast was over, they all slowly walked back to their table. The man on the television had said Leila Nordstrum, wife of the same Colonel Nordstrum who was killed at the Officer's Club just two weeks earlier, had taken her own life at her home in Alexandria, Virginia, outside Washington D.C. Ms. Nordstrum died at approximately six-thirty PM. There would be more details about the apparent suicide on the Eleven O'clock News.

Johnny said, "Son of a Bitch. They're dropping like flies."

Gidget stared at him. "This is too incredible to believe."

Johnny stared back. "Well, you better believe it and anyone of us could be next. My friend told me that, at last count, there was over a trillion dollars involved. A trillion dollars will buy a lot of coffins."

Clay looked up with a start. "Did you say a trillion dollars?"

"You bet your ass I did, one trillion dollars."

"Pamela must be dead." Clay was shaking all over. "They just haven't found the body yet."

240

"You're probably right," Johnny reluctantly agreed. "We've got to figure out who's doing this. I think we know why."

Gidget dropped her menu and pushed away from the table. "Shit, I've lost my appetite."

Susan looked at her, "Well, I know this is serious. Gidget has never before spoken those words in all the time I have known her. She can eat anything anytime."

"Let's all try to eat something," Clay said, even though the thought of food made him nauseous. "We're going to need all the strength we can muster to deal with the next few hours."

Gidget grabbed her menu. "Okay, let's eat."

Susan laughed, "Damn I feel better. You had me really worried, Young Lady."

The four of them ordered their food. They ate without saying much of anything. When someone did speak, it wasn't relevant to the situation at hand. They left the restaurant a little before ten o'clock and headed back to the motel. When they arrived, Clay and Johnny told the girls to lay low and stay out of sight until they were contacted the next day.

He and Johnny headed back to his apartment knowing it would take a little cleaning up before they'd get any sleep. When they arrived, they both realized that there was a new watchdog on the job.

They looked at each other. Each knew what the other was thinking. *We'll deal with this guy tomorrow.* It was raining hard, so they both ran from the parking garage to the apartment entrance. Inside the apartment, it was still the same mess they'd left earlier.

241

Clay went into his command mode. "Johnny, you take the kitchen and living room. I'll take the bedroom and bathroom."

"You got a deal," Johnny replied.

Johnny walked toward the kitchen. As he passed the sliding glass door that led to the balcony, something caught his eye.

"Hit the deck, Clay, there's someone on the balcony." Johnny was already on the floor.

Clay dove to his left behind the couch. They were now only five feet apart. This time, Johnny tried to whisper, "Something moved on the balcony."

"Get the light, Johnny, its right above your head."

When Johnny turned the light off, Clay could see that someone was indeed on his balcony. He quickly made his way to the door, realizing it was Pamela, and she was soaked to the bone.

He put his fingers to his lips, looking at Pamela and then at Johnny. "Johnny, you big dummy. It's only someone's cat. Now, you've scared it away."

Johnny and Pamela played the game. Pamela was absolutely freezing. Clay took her into the bathroom and told her to wait quietly. "Johnny, this bathroom is the pits; they even broke the lid to the tank behind the commode. Bring me a beer, will you?"

Clay gave Pamela the biggest hug he could muster. She collapsed in his arms, sobbing quietly. Johnny showed up with the beer and handed one to each of them.

"Damn, it's nice to meet you," Johnny whispered.

Clay had turned the water on to muffle the voices. He saw that in a movie. "How did you get out there on the balcony?"

"I climbed up from the patio below. It's not very hard. That was before daylight this morning. When I saw what a mess the apartment was in, I knew they'd already been here and would probably not return, at least not anytime soon. I think you guys were here around lunchtime; but when I saw the other guy with you," she gestured toward Johnny, "I was afraid to show myself. You guys left in a hurry. Tonight, I heard you call him Johnny and I knew it would be all right. Clay, do you have anything to eat around here? I'm starving."

Johnny went to get her something to eat. He returned with a bunch of cookies and some slices of cheese and the only two crackers he could find.

"Johnny you take care of the watchdog. Pamela and I will meet you out front in fifteen minutes. Is that enough time?"

"That'll be fine," Johnny answered, and he was gone.

Clay had given her some dry clothes to put on. He put her wet clothing in a bag to take with them.

"I love you, Clay. If I have to die to keep you safe, I will."

He felt himself melting under her gaze. "I love you too. I'm sorry I didn't give you a chance to explain. Let's get the hell out of here."

When he pulled the car around the front of the building, there was Johnny. He looked as cool as a cucumber standing in the middle of the street.

"Everything go all right?" Clay asked.

"He'll be out for quite some time. Let's get the heck out of here."

Clay drove as fast as he dared. He didn't want to be stopped by the police for speeding. They arrived at the motel without a hitch. It was almost midnight when they knocked on the girls' door.

"Who is it?" Susan asked.

"It's me and Johnny. Open the door please."

Both Gidget and Susan were pleased to find Pamela was alive and relatively safe and unharmed. The five of them talked almost all night. They mostly rehashed all the things they'd talked about prior to Pam's arrival. Pamela did have a few new wrinkles to add to all the other scenarios. She was now almost sure that the general was the one putting this together.

When they told Pamela about Leila, she wasn't surprised. She did think, however, that Leila was not the type of person who would take her own life under any circumstances.

"Have you heard anything about Dr. Delong?" Pamela asked.

Susan answered, "No, not really. I asked about him at the hospital but no one seemed to know when he was scheduled to return."

"I overheard the general and that guy from the Justice Department talking. They were talking about an accident. I heard them mention Doctor Delong," Pamela added.

Clay said, "Jesus, I hope he doesn't end up dying for this mess, too."

The one thing that they were all avoiding finally came up. Pamela mentioned that her mother was still not home when she left for Clay's place that morning. She said that she was really worried about her.

244

"Did your mother know about the package you left in the locker at the bus station?" Gidget asked.

"No. Anyway, I took the information out and put it in another locker in case you were one of the bad guys."

"Wait just a darn minute. Me, a bad guy? Don't you think I'm far too cute to be a bad guy?"

"I was afraid that, after we parted company, I might've made a mistake. I've been so paranoid. I thought maybe the general had sent you. It's the kind of thing he would do. I'm really sorry; and no, you don't look like a bad guy."

Pamela reached for her pile of wet clothes and fished out two more keys. She handed one to Clay.

"I was just trying to protect you, Clay. Will you guys help me find my mom?"

Johnny spoke up, "I think we all know where your mother is."

Pam's eyes lit up and a big smile crossed her face.

"Where?"

Clay answered her while holding her as tight as possible. "She's dead, Pam. They found her in the Potomac. We thought it was you at first, until they told on the news how old a person it was. They didn't identify the body on television. Susan was at the hospital. She heard them say it was a woman by the name of Gerard. I'm so sorry. Maybe it's someone else."

Pamela looked up at him and just went limp in his arms. It took them several minutes to bring her around. When they did, she couldn't stop crying.

Clay asked Johnny to please go to the front desk and get them another room. Johnny returned in a few minutes with a key. It was to a room on the floor above.

"Susan, will you please come upstairs and stay with us. I have to go meet with the senator in just about three hours. I don't want to leave her alone."

"Sure I will. First, I'm going down to the restaurant and get us each a ham & egg sandwich and some coffee and juice. You're going to need the coffee, Clay. Otherwise, you won't be very alert for the next couple of hours."

Gidget picked up Pamela's wet clothes. "I'm going to the laundry room. I think I'll try to dry Pamela clothes while you're getting our food."

"I'll go with you, Susan," Johnny offered. "You may need some help caring all that food."

"Thanks, Johnny, but you go with Gidget. That laundry room is spooky. Don't worry, I'll be okay?"

When he got Pamela upstairs in the new room, they just held each other for the longest time. Pamela felt so good in his arms. He just couldn't let go.

"It broke my heart." He said, stumbling over the words. "When I thought you lied and deceived me."

"I know. I'm sorry. I thought I was helping."

"I'm sorry about your mother. We'll check on your sister as soon as I return form my meeting with the senator."

Susan was at the door with breakfast. She handed the food to Clay. "I'll come back up in about forty-five minutes. That should give you plenty of time to make your meeting."

"Thanks, Susan."

The food was consumed in record time. Then he quickly shaved and showered. He hated to leave Pamela but he had to make this meeting. It could be the turning point in all this mess, and he was very much aware of that.

When he emerged from the bathroom, Susan was already there. She and Pamela were talking.

"I've got to be going. Susan, you take good care of my girl. I'll be back as soon as possible."

"Okay, Boss, you be careful."

Stopping by the room downstairs he told Johnny and Gidget to wait for his return before doing anything else.

Clay reached the Senate Office Building about twenty minutes early. He told the receptionist who he was. She announced him and told him to go right in. The senator was waiting for him. After a little small talk, Clay got straight to the point.

"Sir, I don't know what's been happening the last few days. But I didn't kill Colonel Nordstrum. I've had nothing to do with all the other deaths in the past twenty-four hours either, but I think I know some of the answers."

"I believe you, Son."

"You do? You believe me, Senator. Thank God."

"I have a very long story to tell you young man. You should pay very close attention. There's a lot going on right under the President's nose. I think the Vice-President's going to pay the price for this when it's all over. However, I see no way to prevent that from taking place. There's a secret group of people. They are known to some as the 'Ten Little Indians'. They've amassed an enormous amount of wealth using their power and influence. One of those men died. It's been about a year and a half. I was fortunate enough to take his place. The U. S. Justice Department's behind me all the way. Now, you're the only other person who knows. I tell you this because, with your help, we're going to stop them. We may not be able to save the Vice President's job but we'll save his life. His and a lot of others."

The senator paused to light a cigarette. "Are you with me so far, Mr. Smith?"

"Yes, Sir, I'm following you."

"If they are successful, within the next two years these people will control nearly one-third of the world's wealth. With the flip of a switch, they could easily destroy the American economy. They could seriously cripple the European economy as well. These people must be stopped."

"What in the world can I do?"

"A great deal, Mr. Smith."

"What makes you think that I can be trusted with this information?" Clay asked.

"Do you remember Sergeant Major Russ?"

"Yes, of course I do."

"Well, Mr. Smith, he was our man on the inside. When he was discovered, he died suddenly in a house fire with his entire family. Sound familiar? I believe you lost someone very important to you in the same manner. Isn't that correct?"

"Yes, Sir, you obviously know I did,"

"Sergeant Major Russ was a wonderful man. He told me that when, and if, you ever discovered the truth, heads would roll. Son, I'm offering you an opportunity to make a real difference for a lot of people. However, it must be handled very carefully. Are you with me on this?"

"Yes, Sir, tell me what you want me to do."

"I've been having you followed but you keep crippling my men. The guy you clobbered last night lost five teeth. He has a broken jaw and collarbone. I think we must first agree to trust each other. Do you think that's possible, Mr. Smith?"

"Certainly, Sir, and please call me Clay, if you wouldn't mind."

"Okay, Clay."

"Will you answer just one question for me, Sir?"

"I most certainly will, if I can."

"Did they have my fiancée killed?"

"I cannot be absolutely sure. However, I believe that was an act of God that simply worked in their favor."

"One more question, if I may?"

"Go ahead, ask?"

"What about Sergeant Shackelford? What part does he play in all this?"

"To the best of my knowledge, he is strictly independent. He told Sergeant Major Russ that you were the most natural fighter he ever trained. Also, he said that you have a high pain tolerance and that you demonstrated a total lack of fear. That is very uncommon to most people and that's why you're so damn good. Lastly, he said that you were innately gentle, loyal and extremely kind hearted. I was told personally that you were able to sense things before they happened. Are you really that good, young man?"

"The sergeant flatters me. I appreciate the kind words but no one's that good."

"Well, if you're even anything close to being that good, I'm pleased to have you on our side. Clay, will you do something for me?"

"Certainly, Sir, if I can."

There was a slide projector sitting on a table on the other side of the room. The senator walked across the room and turned it on.

"Can you clearly see all those sets of numbers?"

"Yes, Sir, I can see them just fine."

The senator turned the projector off again and walked back to his desk.

"Write them down, if you will, please?"

Clay looked very puzzled. "Say again, Senator. I don't fully understand."

He handed Clay paper and pencil. "The numbers on the screen, are you able to remember what you saw? Can you write them down from memory?"

"I'll try to, Sir, but I really wasn't trying to memorize them."

"Do the best you can."

There were twelve sets of numbers and seven numbers to a set. Clay closed his eyes and tried to picture the screen in his mind. He sat quietly for about thirty seconds. Then he began to write. In less than five minutes he handed the paper to the senator.

"I believe this is correct."

The senator took the paper and flipped on the screen once again.

The senator had a huge smile on his face. "That's amazing."

"Clay, let me give you a number where I can be reached day or night and you call me if you need to. I'll contact you as soon as I have all my ducks in a row. It shouldn't be more than three days, max."

The senator wrote the number down and handed it to him. "Sorry, Clay, I guess you really didn't need me to write my number down. Do you think you might remember it?"

"I'll remember it, Sir."

"That's very good. Use it if you feel the need."

"Thank you, Senator, for letting me serve my country in this way. I promise, you'll not be sorry."

"Do you need any money or anything to get you through the next few days?"

"No, Senator, I'm fine." Clay answered quickly. But just as quickly, he said, "Well, there is one thing."

"What is it?"

"Someone searched my apartment and really tore it up. Could you send someone over to help me put it back together?"

"I'll have it done today, you have my word."

"Thank you. You may also tell whom ever you send to remove the bugs. I think they belong to you, don't they?"

A big grin crossed the senator's face. "I'll do that, Clay, and thank you for being so understanding."

"No problem, Senator. Only too glad to be of service."

The senator took a drag from his cigarette. "I'll talk to you real soon, Clay. Please be careful."

As Clay was leaving, the senator walked around the desk and offered his hand. The handshake was firm and friendly, but Clay knew he meant business. The senator was one of those rare men, who, when shaking your hand, made you feel like the most important person in the room.

Clay wasn't sure what to think, but for some reason, he trusted the senator. It took him close to thirty minutes to return to the motel. He took a number of routes; trying to be sure he wasn't being followed. When he was certain the coast was clear, he headed straight for the motel; hoping everyone was awake and ready to hear all about the meeting.

Chapter 18

Pamela's room came first. Susan was with her and opened the door for him. She told him that Pamela had been asleep for over two hours.

"Clay, she was having some awful nightmares that woke her up with a start on two or three occasions, but I was able to calm her down, and she went right back to sleep."

"Susan, go downstairs and wait for us. We'll be down in a couple of minutes."

"Okay, I'll tell the others."

He went over to the bed where Pamela was sleeping, and lay down beside her, kissing her on the cheek. She began to come around: and when she realized it was him, she held on for dear life.

"Sweetheart, I need to go downstairs and bring the others up to date on my meeting with the senator. I don't want to leave you alone. Will you come downstairs with me?"

"Of course I will. Let me get some clothes on."

Gidget had taken Pamela's clothes to the laundry room and washed and dried them for her. She was dressed in a couple of minutes.

"I can't tell you how happy it makes me just to know we're together and you're no longer angry at me."

"Pamela, I can't wait till this is over so we can be together and act like real people once more."

She walked into his arms and laid her head on his chest. "Clay, please don't leave me alone anymore. I'll try very hard to do exactly what you tell me to do. I love you with all my heart, please believe me."

"I do believe you. Let's go."

"I'm ready."

The others were waiting anxiously to hear about the meeting. It took Clay close to half an hour just to explain. Everyone started asking lots of questions immediately after he began. He asked them to wait until he was finished, and then there'd be time for all their questions. Clay was very thorough and he tried to tell them everything. When he was through with his little dissertation, he made one more request.

"I want to hear each person's slant on what I've just told you. We'll start with the ladies. Oh, Johnny, I forgot something very important. The senator is going to have you reassigned to the Bethesda Naval Hospital. You're to report there on Thursday morning. He's doing so to enable you to stay in the area and help bring this thing to a close. I didn't know that you were supposed to be back in Atlanta next Monday. Also, he told me that you wouldn't be charged any leave time."

"I hope you gave him a big kiss for me. Damn, Clay, every time you go out you bring me money or good news. Thanks, Old Buddy."

Gidget was the first to offer an opinion. "I'm not sure my two cents is even worth that much; however, I wonder if the general is aware of what the senator is up to. He seems like a pretty smart fellow to me."

Clay turned to her. "I really can't answer that question; but for the senator's sake, I certainly hope not."

"I really don't know who to believe at this point," Susan added. "I just hope no one else gets hurt."

Pamela jumped in, "I can tell you this much, the general does not trust him. The only reason they brought him in was on the recommendation given by the Justice Department guy; and of course, the senator does have a lot of clout. He's also the head of a number of committees and they desperately needed the information he could supply. It has something to do with NASA and what it means for the next presidential election."

Clay gave her a blank stare. "How could it affect the presidential election?"

"I don't know," she said nervously. "But, I'll bet the senator does."

He turned. "Johnny, you've been awfully quiet. Say something."

"The most important thing to me is probably obvious. You've known me for a long time, Old Buddy. Don't you already know?"

Clay looked a little puzzled, not at all sure what Johnny was trying to say. He thought it must be something that only the two of them should understand.

Johnny was squirming in his seat. "Do we have to give the money back?"

Clay grabbed a pillow and threw it at him. "Hell no, we got it and we're keeping it. I don't think anybody even knows where it came from and I'm sure as heck not going to ask."

Johnny looked pensively at Pamela. "I'm sorry, but, when I'm nervous I became silly, it helps. Anyway, I believe that, from all we know presently, this makes more sense than anything else we've heard. You told me Clay that you thought the senator was the most decent one of the lot and that there was something very different about him when compared to all the others. Let me go back to my friend at Andrews one more time and see if he can solidify any of this for us. He told us the senator was the best of the lot."

Clay smiled, "Will you do that first thing tomorrow?"

"Damn right, first thing. I'll be sitting in his office at 0800 hours in the morning waiting for him."

Gidget gave Johnny a funny look. "I believe you are forgetting something, aren't you sweetie?"

It was almost like someone turned a light on in Johnny's mind. "You're absolutely correct. Clay, you and Pamela stay here with Susan. Gidget and I have a couple of quick errands to run. When we return, we'll all go out and celebrate. I could sure use a drink. I'll bet we all could. Can I use the car, Old Buddy?"

Clay threw him the keys. "Be careful, Johnny. You may be the only male friend I have left in this world."

"What about me?" Gidget interjected. "I'm your friend, too."

Everyone in the room looked at her. "C'mon, what? What did I say?"

Gidget kept staring at everyone, and then, like magic the light went on. She covered her face, fell back against the door and slid down to the floor.

Clay reached down and picked her up. "Gidget, my little brainiac, I do have other female friends." Then he kissed her on the forehead.

She grinned, grabbed Johnny's hand, and almost pulled him out the door.

Clay stacked up the pillows against the headboard on one of the two beds. He lay back against them with Pamela lying across the bed and her head in his lap. Within minutes, she was sound asleep. Susan took the blanket from the bed where she was sitting and covered her.

"She is really worn out," Susan commented. "And you look a little tired too, Clay."

He touched Susan's arm thankfully. "She's been through a lot and now she's lost her mother. It's not fair. She hasn't done anything to anybody."

Susan said, "Oh, by the way, we talked to her sister. Well, actually, Gidget and Johnny did. I stayed with Pamela. She's coming down here from Chicago to identify the body and make arrangements for the funeral. I'm not sure how we should handle it. Johnny told her that we'd pick her up at the airport tomorrow afternoon."

"Does Pamela know?"

"Yes, we told her but she doesn't know what to do. She said you'd know what to do when you got back. Do you?"

"No."

"Well, we better think of something and real soon."

Clay's mind was working on all cylinders. "You and Johnny meet her sister at the airport and take her directly to the police station. Once she identifies the body and leaves the station, they'll try to get to her, with hopes she can lead them to Pamela. The police need to put her sister in protective custody until this is all over."

Susan sat up, "I know, suppose we have Johnny put her in the hospital at Bethesda as a patient. They'd never look for her there, would they?"

"Actually, if you guys can get away from the police station and the coroner's office without being followed, that might work. They'll have to keep her mother's body on ice for a day or two. That should give us enough time before the funeral arrangements would have to be made."

Susan was bouncing up and down on the bed. "Johnny can check her in under another name and then nobody should know. That makes sense doesn't it, Clay?"

"It all depends on whether or not you and Johnny can get her there without being followed. That's the real key."

Susan looked directly at him. "We can do it."

Just then the door opened. Johnny and Gidget came in with bags under both arms.

Johnny said, "She's still asleep, huh?"

"She's been asleep almost since the minute you left," Clay replied.

Johnny said, quietly. "Give me the key to the room upstairs. We'll be back shortly."

Clay tossed him the key, and started to speak.

Gidget put her finger to her lips. "Hush, Clay, don't even ask."

After they left, he looked at Susan. "What the hell's going on? Do you know?"

"Don't ask me either," she said, smiling.

As Pamela began to wake up, she just crawled into Clay's arms. "How long have I been asleep?"

"A little over an hour," Susan answered.

Johnny came back into the room with a big silly grin on his face. "Okay, Clay, you and Pamela come with me."

Clay said, "Susan, will you explain everything to Johnny, you know, what we've decided to do about tomorrow?"

Clay and Pamela followed Johnny out the door and up the stairs. When they got to the room and opened the door, it was unreal. Johnny and Gidget had borrowed a table from the laundry room and a white tablecloth from somewhere. They had purchased mountains of food and there was champagne and candles everywhere. Somewhere, they'd even gotten silverware and china. The champagne was iced down in the trashcan. Gidget had even turned down the bed closest to the wall, and Johnny had placed a condom on each pillow.

"You, Guys, are truly the greatest." Clay said, smiling from ear to ear.

"I think you're great too," Pamela said, hugging Johnny's neck.

Johnny bowed from the waist. "Master, we are your servants."

Clay laughed. "Gidget, Johnny, you guys are too much."

"We will guard the room throughout the night to insure your privacy." Johnny assured them. With that, he and Gidget were out the door.

Pamela looked up at Clay with tears in her eyes. "You have great friends."

Clay encircled her with his strong arms, kissing her over and over. His hands were searching every part of her body, a body he had known once, but now, he wanted to be reacquainted with her strength and beauty. She was just muscular enough to make every part of her one hundred ten pound frame, tight, yet soft to the touch.

He held her face in his hands. "You're so very beautiful. You take my breath away."

Her hands were searching his body, deliberately, but gently.

Clay held her at arms length. "I think we'd better eat before all the food gets cold. We have all night to make love, and I believe we'll need all the strength we can get."

Although the food was very tasty, neither one of them ate very much. They did, however, drink two bottles of champagne and were just finishing their third when the telephone rang. Clay answered it before the second ring.

It was Johnny. He apologized, but he wanted to be sure that Clay knew he'd be taking the car the next morning. He wanted to be at the air base by 0800 hours.

"Don't forget, we have to pick up Pamela's sister sometime tomorrow afternoon at the airport," Clay reminded him.

"I'll be back by noon," Johnny promised.

The entire time Clay was talking on the telephone, Pamela was disrobing, a little bit at a time. It was driving him crazy. He was sitting on the bed closest to the window. Pamela was on the other bed, the one with the condoms on the pillows. When he hung up the telephone, she jumped from her bed to his, landing, squarely on top of him in less than a second.

"I want you, Clay, make love to me. I have to know that you still love me. Clay, touch me, please."

He obliged. Pamela was so excited she was shivering. She wanted him so much she didn't quite know how to express herself.

"Clay, I don't care about anything else. Please, make love to me now."

With his strong hands at her waist, he picked her up and laid her on her back. He did just as she asked. As he looked down at her, he couldn't believe how incredibly beautiful she truly was.

"I don't want to hurt you. That should tell you how much I care."

"I know, but when I look up at you and I feel you, and we become one, the pleasure is much greater than the pain, do you understand?"

"I think I do. Come here."

261

This time she actually tried to pull away. When it was over, she knew for certain that he was her man.

"I love you, Clay." She snuggled close to him and fell asleep.

"I love you, too," he whispered.

The sun was up early and so was Clay. It was almost six-thirty. He knew that Johnny would be ready for some coffee. Downstairs Johnny was almost ready to leave the room when Clay arrived.

"I'll be right out," he whispered.

Clay walked over and leaned against a bright red Cadillac. He thought it must belong to a pimp. It was a little gaudy for Clay's taste.

Johnny was out of the room in less than five minutes. They decided to walk to the coffee shop. It was only three hundred yards away.

"Everything go well last night?"

"It was wonderful. Thank you for all the trouble you guys went to. Do you agree with the way we plan to handle Pamela's sister?"

"Yes, but as you know, the tricky thing is getting to the hospital without being followed. If we can pull that off, we'll be okay."

"Will you have any problem stashing her at the hospital?"

"I don't think so. I know two other doctors there and I'm sure they'll help me. But the tricky part is still getting there."

"Is there something I can do to help?"

"Yes, there is something. Run interference for us and we'll be sure to get away."

"Okay, I'll be more than happy to. Why didn't I think of that? Let's get back. I don't want Pamela to wake up and find me gone."

Johnny threw a five on the table and headed for the door. Clay was right behind him. They reached the motel parking lot a little before seven-thirty. In just a few minutes, Johnny was on his way to the air base.

When Clay got back to the room, Pamela was still asleep. He could still smell the food and the champagne from the previous evening. Deciding to clean up he carried the trash out and then took the table back to the laundry room.

He had just finished and returned to the room when Pamela began to stir.

"Clay, is that you, Babe?"

"Yes, Doll, it's me. Go back to sleep. It's barely eight AM."

Clay walked to the front of the motel and purchased a newspaper, returning to the stairwell next to his room he sat there reading his paper. He chuckled to himself thinking about how much time he'd been spending on stairwells lately. A door opened, he jumped up and looked around the corner. Susan was coming down the sidewalk.

"Hey, Clay, I thought you might be awake."

She sat down beside him.

"Pam okay?"

"She's fine."

He reached over and gave Susan a huge hug and then told her about the new plan. She didn't like it at all.

"Suppose you get picked up? That would be much worse."

"If they wanted me, they would've tried something before now. Anyway, you know that I'm like the Roadrunner. I'm uncatchable, beep beep."

"Look, if anything happens to you, I know a couple of people I'm gonna kill." There was no hint of teasing in her voice.

"I love you too, you big bully. I wouldn't want you after my skinny little ass."

He leaned over and kissed her on the cheek. "Do you think it'll be all right to leave Pamela and Gidget alone all afternoon?"

"They'll be fine. Gidget's smart, and a hell of a lot tougher than she appears. Pamela must be pretty tough too, she got this far, didn't she?"

"Yeah, you're right as usual. Is Gidget up?"

"She was awake when I left the room. She may be in the shower."

"Go check. I'll go check on Pamela. Call me from your room,"

"Okay, I'll talk to you in a minute."

As he walked into the room, Pamela sat up in the bed.

"You cleaned the room. You'll make someone a great wife someday," She was actually laughing and it sounded great.

"You sure do wake up in a good mood and damn, if you aren't still beautiful, even in the morning."

He asked if she'd mind staying with Gidget that afternoon. Then he explained the plan they had devised to protect her sister. She didn't like him taking chances but she was very grateful.

"I'll be all right with Gidget. I liked her even before I knew she was your friend."

The telephone rang. It was Susan. She said to give them about fifteen minutes and then to come on down.

"We got fifteen minutes. Hit the shower, beautiful. I think I'll finish my paper, if you don't mind?"

"I'll be ready in ten and you go right ahead and read your little paper. I don't mind at all. I like a well read man."

He and Pamela were downstairs in just under fifteen minutes. All three ladies said that they were hungry and they said it almost simultaneously, as though it was planned.

"Wow, how many guys can have breakfast with three beautiful women at the same time? Everyone will think I'm a pimp. That must be my big red Cadillac parked outside."

The girls looked at each other with a blank expression. Not a one of them understood the part about the Cadillac. Clay realized what they were thinking. He just chuckled to himself.

Breakfast went without a hitch, except for the fact that Gidget ate almost everything in sight and was still hungry. Clay and Susan had seen her do this before, but Pamela was amazed.

When the four of them returned to the motel, it was past eleven. Clay figured Johnny would be back any minute. He took Susan by the arm as the others entered the room. "We'll be in shortly. I have to explain something to Susan."

"What is it, Clay?"

"I'm going to steal some old car. When they start tailing you and Johnny, I'll ram them and then take off and catch a cab back to my apartment. When you guys are sure that Pamela's sister is safe, you two return to the motel. I'll find a way back here before dark."

Susan looked concerned, "Okay, but if anything happens to you, I'll be really disappointed and so will a lot of other people, people who love you a lot."

"I'm afraid to catch a cab back to the motel. They might be able to trace me." he stated. "That'd put everyone in danger. Do you understand?"

"Yes, I understand. Just be careful," she replied.

Before anything else could be said, Johnny came around the corner of the building. He was sporting a huge smile.

Clay greeted him, "Things go well with your friend at the base?"

"I think so. Everything he could tell me about the senator was good. His contacts in Maryland are certain he's clean."

Clay sat back down on the steps. "Do they still think the second in command is going to have a hard time getting out of the mess he's in?"

"I was told that, if the truth ever surfaced, he'd have to resign; but we both know the whole truth will never be known."

Clay laughed, "The President will protect him as long as it's in his best interest."

"I don't understand how any of this could be in the President's best interest." Susan said. "I'm sure he's a good man, at least, I think he is."

Clay continued, "The Republican Party and the American people will take the biggest hit. Those other guys will walk away laughing

266

with their pockets full. Then they'll retire and live a life of leisure. And it'll all be at the expense of so very many innocent people."

Johnny leaned against the wall. "I suppose you're right, Clay, but we've got to stop them if we can."

He looked first at Johnny and then at Susan. "I sure hope we don't die trying."

Susan said, "Me too. I'm just learning to live. I'm sure you feel the same way, right Doc? Say something."

"You know the way it is. The rich and powerful get more wealth and more power and the middle class Americans get screwed as usual."

Clay got up. "We just may be able to stop at least one group before they fleece all of America. It just makes me feel sad and angry to know that the American people put these guys in office."

"Think about this." Johnny stammered, "If the senator is honest, that's worth something."

Susan looked at Clay. "Do you think the President's involved?"

"I certainly hope not."

He patted Susan on the head and turned his attention to Johnny. "Look, I've explained everything to Susan. I'll meet you guys back here before dark, God willing."

Johnny nodded, "We should be at the morgue by three PM with Pamela's sister. Hopefully, the entire process won't take very long. Clay, you should probably be there by three-thirty at the latest."

"Don't worry. I'll be there."

"I never had any doubt, Old Buddy."

Clay reached to offer Susan an assist. "You guys had better come and say good-bye to Gidget and Pamela. I want them to worry as little as possible."

"Let's do it." Johnny said, as he took Susan's other hand.

When all the good-bye's had been said, Johnny and Susan were on their way. Clay stayed with the girls at the motel until he felt they understood and were fine with the plan. He was on his way before two. He wanted to be sure he had plenty of time.

Johnny and Susan were to meet Pamela's sister at two-twenty. If the plane was on time, they should be at the police station no later than three. The only problem with Clay's plan was the fact that he'd never before stolen a vehicle. He was just a bit angst-ridden, but what did it matter. If he was being charged with murder, what's a little Grand Theft Auto?

The cabbie dropped him off less than a block from the police station. It was almost three. As he began to look for the proper vehicle, Johnny and the ladies passed right by him. They'd made very good time. Now the dye was cast. He spotted the vehicle he intended to use. It was situated so he could see the others when they came out of the police station. Clay knew how to do this for he'd practiced it many times when he was in training. It was just one of the many ways they practiced getting away from the scene of a hit. Now, it should come in handy.

Clay was ready to make his move but he didn't see anyone suspicious hanging around. Although he was absolutely sure they'd have followed Johnny from the airport. Maybe the opposition wasn't yet aware of what was taking place but he doubted that. His mind was going a thousand miles a minute. As he began questioning his total thought process, there they were. This time, there were two of them in the car. They looked like a new group altogether.

Clay had found an old truck. This was to be his vehicle.

It was three-forty and he had to make his move. He opened the door of the truck and jerked the wiring from under the dashboard, preparing to start the engine. Johnny and the ladies were coming down the front steps of the police station. Clay started the truck and backed up as far as he could in order to gain as much advantage as possible.

He decided to change the plan just a smidge. Clay knew from the way in which the men were parked, if he could get beside them with the truck, they would be completely blocked in. As Johnny and the ladies were getting into the car and making their exit from the parking space, he simply pulled the truck along side the car with the two men, pulling so close they were unable to exit the car from the driver's side. Now, they were completely blocked in, with a car in front of them and one behind. Parallel parked against the curb. In the confusion, Clay jumped out of the truck and took off running across the street before the guys even realized what was happening. He was now inside the office building on the other side of the street and able to see Johnny and the girls make a clean getaway. *Hell, why wreck another man's truck when it's unnecessary,* he thought; standing at the window and laughing at the guys in the car. They were having a hissy fit.

Clay waited for sometime before exiting through the back of the office building. He realized after doing so that he was only five or six blocks from his apartment, and he began walking in that direction, going in one store after another just to be sure he wasn't being followed. He didn't consider himself paranoid, just careful.

When he arrived at his apartment, it was as neat as a pin. He'd almost forgotten the senator's promise. At least the senator was a man of his word. Out of the corner of his eye he noticed the light was blinking on his answering machine. The general had called and Clay was to meet with him the next morning at 0500 hours, at the general's office. He called the number he'd been given and left a message, telling the general to expect him.

So he decided to check his mail and his apartment thoroughly. Everything seemed to be in order. Now he had to find a way to return to the motel without being followed. Leaving his apartment he walked to the Greyhound Bus Station and hopped on the next bus going south, asking the driver to let him off on Highway 1, just south of Alexandria, Virginia; knowing he could walk to the motel from there. Surely they wouldn't follow the bus. He bought a ticket to Richmond, Virginia, just in case someone checked to see where he was going; although, no one seemed to be watching.

There was that feeling again of being all-alone and he didn't like it much. Clay had always been a loner but it sure was nice to have friends.

He bought a copy of the Washington Post, noticing the lead story had to do with certain contractors bribing government officials. The paper said there was an ongoing investigation. Clay thought it might not be a bad idea to have a newspaperman on his side just in case everything went to "Hell in a hand basket."

He exited the bus about half a mile from the motel, and he took every precaution in finding his way there. Gidget and Pamela were glad to see him safe and sound. It seems the others hadn't been heard from. It was only five-fifty and they had a little time before dark.

"Have you girls eaten anything lately?"

"We had a hamburger and some french fries at a little past one," they replied.

"Let's wait on the others to get here. Then we'll eat. Is that okay with you two?"

"Sure, I can last another hour. How about you Pamela?"

Pamela looked worried and he wanted to make her feel better. He told them the story about the truck and also about the general's message.

She said, "Clay, I worry about you going to the general's office at that time of the morning. Nobody will be around except for the guard at the door."

"I'll be fine," he assured her.

"I know."

"Pamela, what's your sister's name?" Gidget asked. "I hate to keep referring to her as your sister. She does have a name, doesn't she?"

"Janice, her name is Janice."

"She's older than you, isn't she?"

271

"Yes, three years. Why?"

"No reason, I was just curious."

Pamela caught on. "I'm okay, you Guys, but thanks for trying to help. I love you for it."

"Yeah, well, we love you too." Gidget replied a little embarrassed.

Johnny and Susan arrived just in the nick of time. They were running out of small talk. Pamela, even though she was trying to be strong, was getting even more nervous.

"Hey, Old Buddy, was that you in the truck?" Johnny asked.

"Yep, and I didn't even have to wreck it. Pretty cool, huh?"

Susan patted him on the back. "I'll bet the guy who owns that truck is still trying to figure out how it got there."

Clay said, "Well, how did it go? Is everything okay? Is Janice safely at the hospital, Johnny?"

"Pamela, your sister is in room three-twelve. I have her registered as a patient, and I have her listed under the name of Roberta Long."

Gidget started laughing. "I thought her name was Janice?"

Pillows were flying at her from everywhere.

Susan gave her a "how stupid can you be" look. "Anybody hungry? Johnny and I have hardly eaten anything all day, and I'm starving."

"Thanks, everybody. I'll never forget all that you've done." Pamela didn't think the words were adequate to express how she felt but those were the only words that would come.

"You're welcome," they all replied in unison.

"Let's eat," came from the *little* human garbage disposal.

"Pamela, after dinner we'll take you to see Janice. You can spend the night with her if you like. Since Clay has to be in the general's office at 0500 hours, it might be better for him to get some sleep tonight. Don't you think so, Girls?" Pamela squeezed Johnny's arm. "I think maybe I should, if it's okay with you, Clay?"

"Sure, Love, that'll be okay."

He pulled her close to him and gave her a kiss on the cheek.

Johnny said, "Would you guys hold that mushy stuff until I have some food in my stomach?"

They all started to laugh, even Pamela.

"Listen to us; we sure do sound happy tonight. The human spirit is a marvelous thing." Clay suddenly realized how that statement must have sounded. "Now, I sound like a philosopher."

Johnny said, "Why not, we just whooped those suckers again, didn't we? I'm buying drinks for everybody. Wait a minute! I'm becoming a real big spender. I better slow down. Well, I'll buy the first round. I don't want to set any precedents."

Everyone was in a pretty good mood, all things considered.

"Clay, with your permission, I'd like to ask Pamela a couple of questions," Johnny said. "That is, if she feels up to it."

"Do you, Pamela?" Clay asked.

"Sure, Doctor. If there's anything I can do to help, please ask."

"Okay! How did you get involved in all this mess? Gidget told us that someone threatened you and your family. How did that happen?"

"Well, Clay called me at work to let me know he was all right but that he'd be unable to attend the dance. I told him it didn't matter and

273

that I'd be over to check on him as soon as I could leave work. When I got to his apartment, he was sick from taking pain pills on an empty stomach. I made him some soup and crackers. He ate the soup and then fell asleep. I was cleaning up the mess I had made in the kitchen when someone knocked on the door. When I opened the door, these two men forced their way into the apartment. They told me they were with the CIA; and that if I didn't do exactly as they asked, I'd not live to regret it. I was to attend the dance with the tall, thin guy and introduce him to everyone as Clay. The other man was going to be with Clay and someone else was going to be outside my mother's house. If this tall, thin guy didn't bring me home between twelve-thirty and one o'clock, my mother would be killed. Leila must have been in on it because, when we got to the dance, she talked to me and introduced the guy to her husband as Clay, and she just winked at me. She acted like it was some kind of a game. When the guy took me home, I was told to speak to no one or they'd also kill Clay. It wasn't until the next morning when I tried to contact Clay that I found out he was being held for the colonel's murder. I wanted to go see him at the jail, but my mother had a fit. I didn't know what to do."

Johnny said, "Had you ever seen any of those men before?"

"No, never."

"That's enough, Johnny," Clay said. "Pamela, I'm really sorry. When I think of the way I treated you …"

"Clay, I don't blame you. We were both caught in the middle, but I do wish you had trusted me a little more."

"I know, Pamela. Please forgive me," he pleaded.

Johnny said, "Look, Pamela, I'm sorry, too."

"It's all right, you guys," Pamela said, trying to summon a smile. "Let's eat."

They talked and ate for two hours. Then Johnny decided they'd better get Pamela to the hospital before lights out at 2200 hours.

In a military hospital, everything was shut down at 2200 hours. Johnny didn't think it would be a good idea for them to be making much of a fuss after hours. He thought it might draw too much attention and that wouldn't be very wise.

Clay agreed, and everyone else went along with the program.

They headed back to the motel to drop off Susan and Gidget. Then the three of them were on their way to Beththesda Naval Hospital. When they arrived, it was almost 2200 hours. They wasted very little time getting Pamela to the room. She enjoyed introducing Clay to her sister.

"It's really nice to meet you, Clay. Pamela called me a week ago and told me she had had the most wonderful weekend of her life, with the most glorious man on the face of the earth. You, also seem to have marvelous friends."

Johnny said, "Look, you two, be very quiet and don't draw any attention to yourselves. Clay and I need to get going before anyone starts asking me any questions."

The girls nodded their understanding.

Pamela had moved real close to Clay, and was almost whispering, "Clay, I love you more than anything. No matter what happens in the future, don't you forget? It's very important to me. Now that both of my parents are gone, I need you to be by my side. I know you're the greatest, but please don't get killed. I'm not sure I could handle that one."

He pulled her close. "I don't want to lose you either. I've only loved two women in my life. If I were to lose you, it might just be the end of me too. You have a wonderful night with your sister. I'll be with you again real soon."

Johnny motioned for Clay to hurry.

"Hold me, one more time," she pleaded.

He hugged her and gave her a peck on the lips.

Chapter 19

They were back in the car and headed toward the apartment. Johnny laid his head back and quickly fell asleep. Clay stayed quiet. Most of his thoughts were centered around his meeting with the general in less than six hours.

Johnny woke as they were pulling into the parking garage. "I hope you don't mind if we wait until tomorrow to clean the apartment. I'm just too tired to do it tonight."

"No problem, my friend, it's already clean."

"Boy, you've had a busy day too."

"Actually, the senator sent someone over to straighten things. He also promised to remove the bugs."

When they entered the apartment it looked great.

"The senator has a great cleaning lady." Johnny said, turning his attention from the apartment, he continued. "Clay, something has been bothering me for a long time, and I want to get your thoughts."

"What is it?"

Johnny motioned for Clay to follow him outside.

"You've talked to the general and you've also talked to the senator. Do you think they know that you've been listening to both sides?"

"I've been having the same thoughts and I can only partly answer your question. The senator knows that I've been talking to the general but I hope the general doesn't know that I've been talking to the senator. Did you follow that?"

"Yeah, I understand. I think you're better off if the general thinks you're playing ball only with him. He needs to think you're only on his team."

Clay had this worried look on his face. "I guess I'll find out in the morning. I'm afraid he'll call in the favor I owe him."

"I think you're correct." Johnny said, "I can't imagine what it could be. I think I'll wait here for you, unless you feel you need me to be a little closer?"

"No, you stay here and I'll return as soon as the meeting is over."

"Clay, do you still have that little tape recorder? The one I gave you when we were in France?"

"Yes, it's in the drawer beside my bed. Do you think I should take it with me?"

"Perhaps, but if you get caught, the general will have your balls cut off. But, it would sure be nice to have everything on tape."

Clay headed for the kitchen. "I need a real stiff drink or I'll never get any sleep."

"Make me one too, if you don't mind?"

Clay brought the drinks and motioned for Johnny to follow him. They were once again back on the stairs.

"Johnny, Gidget and I put all the money in a safe deposit box at the bank next to the drugstore, the one right down the street from the motel. Here's your key."

"Do you have a key, too?"

"Yes, and by the way, there is a card for you to sign. It's in the glove compartment of the car. I'm gonna get it right now before I forget. Walk with me."

Clay headed down the steps. They walked out to the parking garage and retrieved the card.

"Johnny, we need to drop this thing off at the bank as soon as we can just in case something was to happen to me."

"I think you're safe as long as the general doesn't know that you may be working with the senator. As long as he thinks you'll do his bidding, he'll take good care of you. Clay, do you think Leila killed herself?"

"Why would she? She had everything to live for with the colonel out of her way. No, I don't believe it for a minute."

"Then what do you think happened?"

Clay said, "I think she might've had second thoughts about framing me and they killed her to shut her up. Tomorrow we'll go to the Greyhound Bus Station and gather all the evidence from the locker. I want to put it in the safe deposit box at the bank."

"There's one more thing that I don't understand. If they have four witnesses who will swear that they saw you kill the colonel, why do they care about Pamela or Leila?"

"I would suggest that the both of them knew way too much and the general was simply unwilling to take any chances," Clay responded.

As they walked toward the apartment, the paperboy ran up the stairs ahead of them. He dropped a paper in front of Clay's door and Johnny picked it up. He grabbed Clay by the arm and hustled him back to the stairway.

"What's wrong, Johnny?"

"Clay, look at the headlines."

"What does it say?"

Johnny handed the paper to him and pointed to the front page.

"WOMAN JUMPS TO HER DEATH"

"A woman jumped to her death from the Fourteenth Street Bridge. No apparent motive has been found." The article went on to say whom she was and that her daughter with whom she lived was also missing. The article stated that it may have been a double suicide and the second body has yet to be found.

"Boy, I know what they intend to do with Pamela if they find her."

Clay said, "Yeah, it's already set up. Johnny lets walk over to the Waffle House and get some breakfast. I can't sleep I'm too wired and anyway look at the time."

"Sure, Old Buddy. By the time we eat and you get back and shower, it'll be time to meet with the general. Hell, I probably couldn't sleep either."

Johnny punched Clay on the arm. "The only problem is, when we start eating, I'll start thinking about Gidget. I really like her a lot; do you think she likes me?"

"What's not to like? You're tall, handsome, and a doctor, and you have great taste in friends. Sure, she likes you, and I think maybe a whole bunch."

"I sure hope you're right, Old Buddy. But, you know, I'm not going to marry her."

Clay tried to ignore his last remark. "Speaking of doctors. I sure hope that Doctor Delong is all right. He's really been a friend to me, and I'd hate to think that I may have inadvertently caused his death."

Johnny said, "I can't believe there's been no announcement. You know the people at the hospital would be talking about it, if they knew anything."

The waitress came to take their order and brought them some coffee.

Clay looked at the waitress. "Keep the coffee coming, Sweetheart." His attention returned to Johnny. "Hey, Partner, I wonder what would happen if I fell asleep on the general."

"Even you're not that cool." Johnny replied. "You'll be sweating bullets and you know it."

"Yeah, I guess you're right."

"You know I'm right."

281

"Boy, I wish we could straighten out this mess. School starts in less than a week."

"I think you can forget this semester, Old Buddy."

When the waitress came back to the table, Clay ordered a cup of coffee and a Danish to go. Johnny was just finishing his last bite when the order was set on the table.

"What's the coffee and Danish for?"

"I thought our watchdog might need a little refreshment. He's been setting outside for over an hour waiting for us to make our next move."

Johnny bowed from the waist. "You know, for a killer, you're a real sweet guy."

"I guess we're just two of a kind."

As they exited the restaurant, Johnny stopped. "I have a better idea." He took the bag out of Clay's hand, and walked back into the restaurant handing the bag to the waitress. Then he handed her some money. She followed him outside and walked right past Clay to the car. Johnny waved at the man in the car. He then grabbed Clay, and they both took off running toward the apartment.

"That was real cute, Partner."

Johnny was out of breath. "I thought you'd like that."

"Johnny, I never asked and you never told me, but where did your family move to when they left Knoxville, Tennessee?"

"Ashland, Kentucky. It's about two hundred miles away. My mom still lives there. It's just south of Cincinnati, Ohio."

Looking out the window, Clay said, "I see the watchdog is back, in his normal place. I guess he'll follow me to the general's office but it really doesn't matter. With any luck, Johnny, you'll be fast asleep."

"Hell, I drank enough coffee to keep me up until noon at least."

Johnny headed for the liquor cabinet and Clay headed for the shower. When he finished his shower and got dressed, he was handed a freshly made scotch and soda.

"Here, Old Buddy, you might need this. I sure wish there was some way for me to go with you. I guess I could go and just sit in the car; however, I think I'd rather be lying on that sofa."

Clay turned quickly, "Oh shit, Johnny, did you report in while you were at the hospital? Do you have to be back there this morning?"

"Relax, Clay, everything's fine. I'll check in around lunchtime; and yes, I did report in. Otherwise, how would I have gotten a room for Janice?"

Johnny jumped straight up slapping his hand over his mouth.

Clay caught on, "Right," he said, waving his arms, and giving Johnny the high sign. "Hell, sometimes I think maybe I'm losing my mind." He paused, looking at Johnny. "Janice, is that the nurse from the third floor? Damn, Johnny. You've been there only a few days and you're already screwing one of the nurses."

Johnny nodded his head in agreement, and breathed a sigh of relief. "Well, I guess it's my boyish charm." He winked at Clay, and mouthed a, 'thank you'.

"I got to go. You take care of things, Partner." Clay turned and started toward the door.

"I'll just be sitting here getting drunk waiting on you to return."

"Thanks for being here, Johnny. I couldn't have gotten this far without you. See ya."

He exited the building and headed for the parking garage noticing the watchdog had started his engine. When Clay passed the car heading south, the guy fell right in behind him about a half a block later. Clay was in no hurry and he took his time getting to the Pentagon.

The parking area was almost empty. He wondered if he'd gotten there before the general. It was four-fifty AM and just beginning to sprinkle rain. Clay headed for the entrance and the guard who was on duty at that ungodly hour. The guard checked his credentials and told him the general was in his office waiting for him.

General Essex seemed genuinely happy to see him and that relieved some of the jitters.

The general turned and walked to the beautiful bar area to Clay's right on the far wall. "Would you like some coffee?" he asked.

"That would be great, Sir."

"It may not be very good. I made it myself. It never seems to turn out just right: but what the hell, it's better than none at all."

The general actually got Clay some coffee and then handed him a bottle of Irish whiskey. "If you put enough of this in it, you can even enjoy my coffee."

"Thank you, Sir."

"Clay, I'm gonna get right to the point. I'm sure you heard the news about Ms. Nordstrum. What a shame. I guess she just couldn't handle the colonel's death. I really don't understand any of that mess but never fear. I have your best interest at heart."

"Thank you again, General."

"When you were here a couple of days ago, I told you that I might need a favor. Well, I hoped I could find another way, but we have a traitor in the midst and I now have sure knowledge of that fact."

Clay sipped his coffee calmly. "A traitor, Sir?"

"Yes, My Boy, and I wasn't absolutely sure until yesterday. I now have irrefutable proof and it pains me to have to tell you."

"Who, in God's name, could it be, you must know?"

The general lit his customary cigar. "Yes, I know, and it makes my blood boil."

From Clay's observation the cigar could easily have been lit with the fire coming from the general's eyes.

"I want him dead," the general screamed. Then, calmly he continued. "And, it must happen within the next five days. Clay, you do this for your country and me, and you'll never hear another word concerning those ridiculous murder charges against you. You have my word and my undying gratitude as well."

"Why me, Sir? There are probably hundreds of people who'd do it for the right price."

The general looked somewhat irritated. "Damn, Clay, he's too well guarded. It would take anyone else too much time to get near enough to do the job properly. It must look as though he took his own life. That's imperative. Do you understand?"

Clay regrouped his thoughts. "Yes, I think so, Sir."

"If you need Captain Murphy to help, it's okay. He understands these things; and although we may not always see eye to eye, he's a real American and he knows his duty."

"Who is this person and how am I supposed to get to him?"

The general poured more coffee for the both of them, put whiskey in his, and handed the bottle to Clay. "Do you remember the senator from Minnesota?"

Clay's heart almost stopped! He hoped the general didn't pick up on it. He tried to act as though he had choked on his drink hoping to cover his expression.

"A senator, oh my Lord," Clay replied. "I do remember him. Yes, Sir."

The general proceeded. "Clay, our group is only six months to a year away from reaching our goals. This man could ruin over three years of dedication to the cause. You'll be paid a cool quarter of a million dollars and have your record cleared."

"Holy cow!"

The general's eyes sparkled. "That's a lot of money, ain't it, My Boy?"

Reaching behind himself on the desk, he retrieved a large manila envelope, and handed it to Clay. "There's a hundred thousand in that envelope. You may count it later, if you wish. The final one hundred and fifty thousand you'll receive when the job is finished. You may share it with Captain Murphy if you like."

Clay remained calm, as the general continued. "Clay, I have never asked you to do me a personal favor before, but this is a matter of national security. Will you help me?"

"Yes, Sir, I'll do as you ask, but you'll have to let me do it my way."

"No problem, but it must look like a suicide."

Clay put the envelope in his hip pocket. "Oh, by the way, Sir, it was the senator who hired someone to follow me. I convinced one of the gentlemen to spill the beans, so to speak. You told me to find out, if I could. As you can see, I always do as you ask, Sir."

"I'm glad to know that. That should make you understand all the more why this is necessary. Clay, if you'll work with me, I'll make you a rich man. I like you, Son, I always have."

"I appreciate that, Sir."

The general pushed another envelope across the desk. "Here is all the pertinent information on the senator and it's pretty damned accurate."

Clay took the envelope in hand. "General, if I were to need to find Sergeant Shackelford, could you help me?"

"I wouldn't wish you to take him into your confidence or anyone else outside of John Murphy. Is that clear?"

"Of course, Sir; however, he has in his possession some rigging equipment I may need."

The general began going through one of his desk drawers until he found the sergeant's file. He opened the file and copied his address and telephone number on a piece of paper and handed it to Clay.

Sergeant Shackelford was stationed at the Quantico Marine Base about thirty minutes south in Virginia.

"Thank you very much, Sir. I'll get to work on this right away."

"Oh, by the way, have you heard from Pamela Gerard? I heard on the news that they found her mother floating in the Potomac and that she too was missing. You didn't have anything to do with that did you Clay? I know that when you left here the last time, you were really angry with her."

"Absolutely not. I thought maybe you'd done me a favor, Sir."

Clay was looking very intently for any reaction from the general.

"I wish I had, but no, she simply didn't show up for work a few days ago. The police seem to think they'll find her body in the river also. The report I heard was a double suicide or some such thing as that. I'm glad you were not responsible."

"I appreciate that, Sir."

The general continued, smiling, and puffing on his cigar. "There must be an epidemic of some sort. With Ms. Nordstrum dead and I suppose the Gerard girl dead too, I guess the case against you will fall apart. How convenient that would be, My Boy."

Clay said, "I had nothing to do with that one either; however, I can see where you might think it possible or even logical."

"I know you're clean," the general said. "I just wanted to hear you say so. I'd think that the last victim of this epidemic should be the senator himself."

Clay grimaced, "Does seem only fair, doesn't it, Sir?"

"It's not only fair, but it's appropriate, don't you think?"

"Sir, do you think the senator played any part in all this?"

"Damn right, he's responsible for all those people dying. He'll get you too, if you don't get him first. You can count on that, My Boy."

Clay paused for a long while, "I'll have it done before next Monday. I do think it might look better if I could arrange for it to happen on Sunday evening. Then the other members of the team would think he was in over his head and couldn't face them at the meeting on Monday."

The general smiled, "That's good thinking. I can make that work. I'll spend the rest of the week laying the groundwork for just such an event. Brilliant, My Boy, and I'm counting on you to make it happen just that way."

Clay came to his feet. "I'll make it work, you can count on me, Sir."

The general extended his hand. "Great, now get going before the whole staff shows up for work. I don't think it'd be wise for us to be seen together just now."

He and the general shook hands, as Clay backed away. "Yes, Sir, I'm on my way."

When he finally got to his car, it was almost seven-thirty. He just sat there for the longest time trying to convince himself that this was really happening. Finally, starting the car he headed toward the apartment. Traffic was really a mess that time of the morning. It took him almost thirty minutes to go two miles.

When he walked into the apartment, Johnny was sound asleep on the sofa. He headed for the bathroom to get rid of some of the coffee he'd been drinking for the past three hours. Upon returning to the living room he noticed Johnny was trying to awaken.

Eyes half shut, he began to speak.

"How did it go, are you okay?"

"I'm fine, but you're not going to believe all I've got to tell you."

Johnny rubbed the sleep from his eyes. "I'd believe anything at this point."

"Come with me, I need to show you something."

Once they were outside on the stairs Clay began to explain. "He wants me to kill the senator and it must be done before next Monday morning's meeting of the group. Also, it must look like a suicide and he'd prefer I do it on Sunday evening. That would best fit his schedule."

Johnny just stood there for a moment. "Geez, you've got to be kidding. Tell me this is some kind of sick joke."

"It's the truth, every word. I guess we should've seen it coming. Think about it, Johnny. It all makes sense, don't you think?"

"Well, yeah, but I suppose it just seems too outrageous, even for the general."

Clay spent the next hour relating to Johnny every part of their conversation. Then he showed him the money. He had never seen Johnny at a loss for words until now. Clay had repeated the conversation almost verbatim in order for Johnny to get the full effect and have the proper appreciation for what had taken place at the meeting.

"Johnny, you take a shower. I'm going to put this money in the bank. I noticed a branch of that same bank about six blocks from here. I'll take them the card you signed and make another donation to our safe deposit box. On second thought, you come with me. When we're finished, we'll stop and get a quick bite to eat on the way back to the apartment."

"Let's go," Johnny said, "I'll take a shower later."

They were at the bank and back at the Waffle House having breakfast before ten AM. The waitress was different; but the food was still good and, for some reason, the coffee tasted great.

"Johnny, you take a shower and head to the hospital. After you've checked in, get Pamela and Janice and head for the motel. Hell, they'll be safe there; if anybody knew about the motel they'd have taken out Susan and Gidget by now. Try to get there by six PM. I'll get a few hours sleep and meet you guys there. Does that suit you okay?"

"Sounds like a good plan to me."

They paid the check and headed for the apartment. Something seemed just the least bit out of kilter, but Clay couldn't put his finger on what it was. All of a sudden, it hit him.

"Where's the watchdog? He doesn't seem to be around this morning."

"Right you are, Clay. I knew something was different."

Clay laughed. "Don't you take any chances, Johnny? They may still be there and we just don't see them."

"No problem. I'll be extra careful. I don't want to die now, I'm too wealthy and so are you, Old Buddy."

Clay looked at him, his eyes drooping. "Here's where we part company. I'm gonna walk down to the bus station and call the senator. I need to see him as soon as possible. They may still have a tap on my phone."

"That's a good idea he needs to help coordinate our next move."

"I want you at our next meeting, Johnny. That is, if you don't mind."

"Fine with me, if the senator doesn't mind."

Clay shook his head. "Johnny, if I don't make it to the motel by dark send out the Mounties."

Johnny became rather serious. "Clay, you be careful. As soon as I take a quick shower I'll be on my way to the hospital. Get some rest, you look really beat."

The senator answered on the second ring. "Sir, it's Clay. I met with the general this morning, and we need to talk, soon."

"Meet me in the parking lot of the Senate Office Building and we'll take the back entrance to my office. How about nine PM this evening? Can you wait that long?"

"Yes, Sir, and may I ask a favor? I'd like to bring Captain John Murphy along if you don't mind."

"If you feel it's appropriate, he's welcome to join us."

"Thank you, Sir. I'll see you at nine PM sharp."

Clay left the Greyhound Bus Station and headed toward his apartment for some much needed sleep. He knew he was being watched but it felt different somehow. Trying hard to notice everything around him, Clay saw nothing out of the ordinary. That really bothered him. So, he ducked into the Waffle House and purchased a couple of donuts and then took off out the back door with the manager's permission. He was back at his apartment in a flash; however, something still didn't feel right.

Deciding he needed sleep more than worry, he checked the apartment, set his alarm for four PM and fell across the bed.

When the alarm sounded, he sat straight up. Turning the alarm off, he was half undressed before he entered the bathroom. The shower felt especially invigorating, the hard spray felt especially good to his neck and back. He had forgotten to shave but, hell, it just made him look sexier.

It was now four-thirty PM and he had to find a way to get to the motel without being followed. He decided to try the bus again but this time he wasn't so lucky. The next bus didn't leave for hours. Catching a cab, he had the driver drop him off at the Military Police Station on the base at Fort Belvoir, knowing that if he were being followed, they would have to stop at the front gate, everybody did. Any vehicle not displaying a base sticker would be checked. That would give him the edge he needed. At the MP station, he told them he was to meet with General Essex and asked for a ride to the Base Exchange. They were only too happy to oblige. From the Base Exchange he took another cab and instructed the driver to exit through the back gate onto Highway 1, "Richmond Highway." He was now only a couple of miles from the motel so he made it their well before six PM.

The girls were fine, and he promised to bring them up to date as soon as Johnny arrived with Pamela and her sister. Gidget handed him a beer and Johnny pulled into the parking lot before Clay could take his first sip.

Everybody was there and everything seemed okay. Clay asked if everyone was ready to have some dinner, and Gidget, as usual, was the first to say yes. Johnny went to the front desk and rented another room for Pamela and Janice. When he was finished and had the key in hand, they all piled into Clay's car.

"Where shall we dine, Ladies?" Clay asked.

They chose a place with a bar. It seems everyone was more interested in drinking than eating. When they got settled in and placed their drink order, it was time for some serious conversation.

Pamela sat next to Clay and held his hand under the table.

Clay began. "The general called in his marker. Hold on to your seats ladies. He wants me to kill the senator, and I'm supposed to make it look like he committed suicide. It was decided that Sunday night would be the perfect time. That way, the general can make the announcement at the big meeting on Monday morning. He's going to tell the other members that I killed the senator, because, he was about to betray their cause. The General thinks that will keep everyone else in line."

When Clay was finally through, they were on their third round of drinks and they were ready to order their meal. The waitress was very patient and even made a few suggestions. When everyone had given his or her order to the waitress, the roundtable discussion began.

Janice spoke bluntly. "I realize that you guys have been living this hell for days, but this is the most unreal thing that's ever happened to me. I just hope we all come out of this alive and well."

"You are absolutely correct," Clay responded. "And I'm extremely sorry that things are as they are. The people we're dealing with would gladly kill each and every one of us if they could find us all together."

"What are you going to do about the general and the senator?" Pamela asked.

"It'll depend largely on what happens at my meeting this evening with the senator."

"What do you think would've happened if you'd said no to the general?" Susan asked.

"I don't honestly know. I believe he'd have tried to force me, using the murder charge as his weapon. Right, Johnny?"

Johnny shook his head. "I'll guarantee you one thing, if he could get his hands on you girls, he would then force Clay to do whatever he wanted him to do."

"You're right, Johnny. That's why we must keep you ladies safe at all cost. Janice, I know that it's very hard on you and Pamela, with your mother's death and the fact that you're unable to plan her funeral. But she would want the two of you safe."

"I've partially taken care of that. Mother's sister and two brothers are handling the funeral arrangements and we'll attend if possible. It's a hell of a mess."

"That was very smart, Janice. It must run in the family," Susan replied.

Clay said, "You, Gals, stay here at the motel. If anyone has to go out, let it be Susan or Gidget. I don't think anyone knows what they look like. It might even be a couple of days before Johnny and I can get back here; however, that might make it even safer for the four of you."

Pamela looked at Clay as though she was going to cry. "Clay —"

"It'll be okay, Pamela. I want to know you're safe and then I can concentrate on the task at hand."

She laid her head on his shoulder. "I understand. I won't be any trouble. I just hope this is over soon."

Clay reached in his wallet and pulled out a piece of folded paper. "All four of you commit this to memory. If you suspect someone has found your hiding place, call Sydney at this number."

He handed Susan the piece of paper with Sydney's number on it.

"Who is Sydney?" Janice asked.

"He would've been my brother-in-law if his sister had survived the house fire. Anyway, he'll hide you, and I'll know where to look if you're not here. He lives in Richmond, about two hours away. All of you memorize the number; and when you have done so, burn the piece of paper. I don't wish to put him in any kind of needless danger. Susan, I want you to rent a car and keep it close by. I've given you plenty of money and having a car available will help you make a quick getaway."

Susan patted his hand. "I'll do that first thing in the morning and we'll keep most of our stuff in the trunk, just in case."

Clay continued. "Good girl. Gidget, you stay with Pamela and Janice can stay with Susan. That way, if they were to get one room, they still wouldn't have both sisters. You should also make up some kind of signal from one room to the other."

Johnny interrupted, "Look, Girls, we're not trying to frighten you. Clay's just covering all the bases."

They had all pretty much finished their meal. It was almost time for Clay and Johnny to take off. There was just time for one more drink. The waitress brought the last round of drinks and Clay paid the check. Just to be safe, he handed Susan a handful of hundred dollar bills.

The six of them went back to the motel. Clay asked to be alone with Pamela for a few minutes.

"Pamela, I've thought about you all day. I don't want anything to happen to any of you. I love you, kiddo. You guys sleep in shifts and take care of each other."

"I love you, too." She smiled. "Please don't get killed."

"I'm glad to see that you can still make jokes. I'm a very lucky man. Now, stay out of sight."

"Kiss me and get going. By the way," she blushed. "My sister thinks you're cute."

They walked back into the room where everyone else was waiting. He and Johnny departed without much fanfare.

Chapter 20

The drive to the Senate Building took less than twenty minutes. Neither he nor Johnny had very much to say. The Senator was waiting for them in the far northeast corner of the parking lot, almost hidden from view. He motioned for them to follow and he led them to the north side of the building where they could enter without being detected. It took only minutes before they were safely in the senator's outer office.

"We'll talk here," he said. "If they were going to bug anything, it would probably be my office."

"Good idea, Sir," Clay replied. "This is Captain Murphy, or should I have said, Doctor Murphy?"

Johnny stepped forward, hand extended. "Just call me Johnny if you will, Senator."

The senator began, "I believe you called this meeting, Mr. Smith. What's on your mind?"

"I'm not sure how to say, what needs to be said. Can I have something to drink, Senator?"

"Will you do the honors, Johnny?" the senator asked. "Right thru that door behind you and to your right. Make mine scotch, straight up,

298

if you will please." The senator sat back in his chair and lit a cigarette. "Look, Clay, whatever you say here, will remain in confidence. You have my word."

Johnny returned with drinks for everyone. "Here you go, Gentlemen, bottoms up."

"Thank you, Captain Murphy." The senator dispensed with his drink in one swallow. "Clay, I believe you met with the general recently?"

"Yes, Sir, I was coming to that part. I met with him at five AM this morning and he called in his marker. Well, at least he told me what he wanted me to do for him in repayment for his getting me out of this mess."

The senator grew a bit impatient. "Well, what is it, Son? I don't think anything would shock me at this point. I told you the general would do anything to further his cause, or should I say increase his bank account?"

"There's some big meeting next Monday. Maybe I should say a meeting of the 'Ten Little Indians.' Is that correct, Sir?"

"Yes, that is correct. If you're interested, the name was taken from an Agatha Christie novel and the general's favorite movie. He thought it was fitting."

Johnny started laughing out loud.

"What's so funny, Captain?"

Johnny shuffled his feet, uncomfortably. "I think it's time for the first Little Indian to die."

The senator looked astonished. "The general wants you to eliminate one of the Ten? Just one of them?"

Clay finished his drink. "Yes, Sir, that's the assignment I've been given, and it must take place by Sunday evening."

Now, the senator looked very concerned and he almost dropped his cigarette. "We must move even faster than I'd planned."

"Did he admit having anything to do with the Colonel Nordstrum's death or Doctor Delong or Leila Nordstrum? How about that young lady, Pamela, and her Mother?"

"Not at all, Sir," Clay replied.

"Damn, who does he want killed this time?" The senator asked, point blank.

Clay stumbled with the words. "You, Senator, and I'm supposed to make it look like a suicide."

The senator came straight out of his chair. "I need another drink." He walked into the other room. "That, son of a bitch. He thinks he can kill a United States Senator and get away with it? Will you testify to that in court, Young Man?" The senator was almost screaming.

"Yes, Sir, but I'm already wanted for murder. Will my testimony be worth anything in court?" Clay asked. "The young lady, Pamela, has left material in a lock box that she says will clear me. Maybe that'll do the trick."

"That's great." The senator downed his drink, again, in one swallow. "She must have truly cared for you."

"Cares for me, Sir," Clay said proudly. "She is very much alive."

The senator swung around. "Give me your glasses, Gentlemen, I'll make us another, this is getting better all the time. Do you think she'll testify? If so, we must get her into protective custody, as soon as possible, don't you think?"

Clay handed the senator his glass. "I'll ask her, Sir."

Johnny chimed in, "What about her sister? She is also in danger."

"Certainly," the senator replied. "And, what about the two of you?"

Johnny took two glasses from the senator and handed one to Clay. "First things first, Senator. How do we handle this?"

"You have the ladies and the information in my office at six AM tomorrow morning. We'll let the FBI take it from there."

"Will they arrest the general?" Johnny asked.

"The information will go to the District Attorney and if he finds the evidence to be strong enough, he'll do exactly that."

Clay said, "And if he doesn't, then what happens?"

"I don't think that's even a possibility. Hell, we have entirely too much testimony and a lot of dead bodies. I think we have him." The senator continued, "I believe if the two of you are willing to testify along with the young lady, it's a done deal."

Clay said, "I sure hope you're correct, Senator."

Johnny was pacing the floor. "I don't like the idea of losing control of the situation, and furthermore, if the general finds out about our plan prematurely, we'll all be kicking up daises."

"Senator, if you're being watched, the general will know something's up," Clay said nervously.

The senator ran his hand through his hair. "Then what do you suggest?"

"Stay by your private telephone," Clay advised. "We'll call you before midnight with the right plan."

The senator took a drag on his cigarette. "You guys have been right so far. We'll do it your way. I'm sure glad you two are on my side."

Johnny said, "You should be glad, Senator. Otherwise, you wouldn't have very long to live."

Clay spun around and gave Johnny the most incredible look. "I'm sorry, Senator. Johnny didn't mean that the way it sounded."

The senator stood. "That's alright; a little levity never hurt anyone. And, I have no doubt he is correct."

A light just went on in Clay's head. "Senator, can we back up for a minute?"

"Sure, Clay, what is it?"

"When you were talking about people who have died, you mentioned Dr. Delong. Is he dead too?"

"Yes, he and his wife were killed in a small plane crash. Somehow, I thought you knew. Although, I don't think they've released the information to the press."

Clay almost fell into one of the chairs by the wall. "Oh my Lord. I have brought death to so many people." Clay was really struggling to gain control of his emotions. "I loved that guy, and his wife was pregnant with their first child. Jesus, we've got to nail this guy, before we're all dead."

The senator looked anguished. "I'm sorry, Son. I should have handled that more delicately. But, Clay, none of this is your fault. General Essex is the most ruthless man I've ever come across. Now, he wants me dead, and Fellows, I'm depending on the two of you to keep that from happening." The senator walked over to where Clay was sitting and put both hands on Clay's shoulders. "I promise you, with your help, we will get this bastard and the sooner the better. Think straight, Clay, the general's rein is about to come to a screeching halt."

"Thank you, Sir," Clay said, "Shall we leave as we came in?"

"Yes, and I'll wait for your call. Good luck, Men."

The senator extended his hand, first to Clay, and then to Johnny. "Please think carefully, Clay, and you too, Captain Murphy. This is huge. We're talking about bringing down two generals, an admiral, two congressmen, three senators and a highly thought of member of the Justice Department. Who knows what'll happen to the Vice President."

Clay and Johnny hustled out of the building. They didn't say anything until they were safely in the car.

"Clay, let's go by the Greyhound Bus Station and retrieve the information from the lock box before going to the motel."

"My thoughts exactly," Clay replied.

When they had retrieved the two envelopes from the locker at the station, they headed toward the motel.

"Look around, Johnny, we must be sure we're not being followed. This is not the time to do something really careless."

"I've been paying attention. Let's drive through the military base just in case."

"Good thinking, Partner. I did it to them once and we can do it to them again."

They went through the front gate and out the back gate on to Richmond Highway. They were at the motel before eleven PM. The ladies had been waiting anxiously for their return.

He and Johnny spent more than twenty minutes explaining the plan to the ladies and then asked for suggestions on how to pull it off.

Pamela looked at Clay, her eyes pleading. "I'd feel safer staying with you, Clay."

He held her close. "I know, but they'll protect both you and your sister. Let's face it; they do this for a living. I'll miss you but this should be over real soon."

Susan made a suggestion. "Why don't you take Pamela and Janice to the office of the FBI and have the senator meet you there, fifteen minutes later. That way, if he's being followed you guys will already be inside and they won't see you together."

"That's really good thinking." Johnny said, "It must be hard to be both beautiful and intelligent. I can hardly stand it. C'mon, Clay, lets go down the street and make the call." Johnny continued, "Clay, whatever else happens, we want a copy of the information in those envelopes before we leave them with anyone. Don't you agree?"

"Absolutely, Partner."

When Clay got the senator on the telephone, he told him that they would be at the office of the FBI by twelve-thirty AM, and that he should arrive no earlier than twelve forty-five AM.

The senator agreed. "I'll call from my private line and let them know you're coming. They'll be there waiting for you."

Clay and Johnny went straight back to pick up the girls.

"Everything is set and we need to go right away," Clay urged. "We have to be there by twelve-thirty and that doesn't give us much time."

The four of them arrived at the office of the Federal Bureau with more than ten minutes to spare and they were indeed expected. They were escorted to a room at the end of a long hallway and served coffee and doughnuts. The senator arrived right on time. He laid everything out for the agent in charge.

After receiving copies of everything they wanted, Clay and Johnny headed back to the apartment for some well-deserved rest. They were to meet again with the senator at eight PM that evening. They wanted to go over the details. This could be a very tricky operation. Also, they wanted to give the FBI a chance to look over the material from the envelopes; wanting to be absolutely certain that coupled with their testimonies the information was more than adequate to clear Clay and put the guilty parties "Out of Business."

When they got back to the apartment, everything was quiet and there were no watchdogs. But, just to be safe they sat on the steps.

"You know, Johnny, I feel like I might stay out of jail after all."

"I never had a doubt." Johnny replied, slapping Clay on the back. "Staying alive, now, that's a whole new subject."

"Yeah, if the general finds out what's going on too soon, he'll make every effort to shut us up. We could put him away for a very long time. With what we know about the people who were summarily executed, he could get the gas chamber. During the period when you were involved, did you make any notes, or keep any records, Johnny?"

"I do have a little green book with times and dates. I also have a lot of my own thoughts on everything that was going on at the time."

"Damn, Johnny, that's great. I always knew you were smart."

"Right, but what do you think that would do for my reputation. I don't exactly look like a saint in all this mess you know?"

"You're right, Partner, that wouldn't be good for either of us. We can't let that happen. I really don't think we'll need anything like that anyway. Let's hope we aren't forced to bare our souls to the entire world."

"Trust me, Clay. This shit is never going to be made public. It makes everybody look bad and politicians don't like to look bad."

Clay stood, "Let's go inside and try to get some sleep."

When they entered the apartment, the message light was on by the telephone. The message was from James Mann, Clay's attorney. He asked him to call the following day between nine AM and five PM, and he left the telephone number where he could be reached.

"What do you think that's all about?" Clay asked, not really looking for an answer.

"He probably just wants to touch base. You guys have only talked a time or two and he has to try to earn his money."

Clay was well aware of the way Johnny felt about lawyers. He'd say they were like Vampires. They only survived on other people's blood, draining their clients, a pint at a time.

Clay decided to fix a drink for the two of them. When he was finished, he once again motioned for Johnny to follow him to the stairs.

"What now?"

"Look, Johnny, this attorney is probably on the general's payroll. That makes me a little nervous. I'm gonna have to play it pretty dumb."

Johnny started laughing, "I think you can handle that, Old Buddy."

"Thanks, Partner, with friends like you a man doesn't need to worry about his enemies."

"Hell, let's get some sleep. Clay, you worry too much; however, as long as you worry, I guess I don't have too, now do I, Old Buddy?"

He pushed Johnny up the stairs. "I guess you're right, Doctor."

One more drink and they were tucked in for the night. It was almost three AM and they knew in a few hours all hell could break loose. The apartment was especially cold and Clay found himself shivering as he crawled between the sheets. He jumped out of bed and went to the closet to retrieve another blanket, taking it to Johnny who was already asleep on the sofa. He covered him with the blanket.

"Thanks, Mom." Johnny muttered, just loud enough for him to hear.

Clay made no comment, and he was back in bed in no time.

The telephone rang and Clay's heart skipped a beat.

"Hello!"

"Mr. Smith, this is James Mann, I hope you got my message yesterday?"

"Yes, I was gonna call you. What time is it?"

"Almost nine-thirty. Can you come by my office today? I think I may have some very good news for you."

"Sure, what time?"

"How about noon? Maybe we could have some lunch."

"That would be okay. Tell me how to find your office."

Mr. Mann gave him the directions and bid him a good morning.

Clay decided to take his shower and shave before waking Johnny and he almost made it. Just as he exited the shower, Johnny opened the door.

"Who the heck was on the phone?"

"It was that attorney. I'm meeting him for lunch at noon. Do you want to go with me?"

"Damn right. I could eat the north end of a south bound mule."

Clay wrapped a towel around his waist. "That's cute, Johnny. Your southern roots are sometimes a little too exposed. You're supposed to be the intellectual one, aren't you, Doctor Murphy?"

Johnny smiled, "Well, I am quite hungry, don't you know?"

Clay walked past him into the bedroom. "Take your shower and I'll make us some coffee."

Johnny jerked Clay's towel off as he went past. "Already done, help yourself, and I'll be out in a minute."

The coffee smelled good. It made him think about how great it was to be alive. He thought it really strange how little things sometimes seem to bring about a whole new way of thinking. Clay remembered how truly great it felt the day he walked out of that jail and could feel the sun on his face.

He and Johnny enjoyed the coffee and were looking forward to the day and what they hoped it would bring. They left the apartment and headed for the parking garage. There was no watchdog in sight. It was a beautiful day, not a cloud in the sky.

"Johnny, you just follow my lead and maybe we'll get through this lunch okay. We need to mostly listen."

"I'll only speak when spoken to. Anyway, I'm just going along for the food."

Mr. Mann's office was no big deal. It was apparent that he'd just begun his practice. According to his credentials, he graduated suma cum laude.

The excitement over Clay's arrival was quite evident on Mr. Mann's face, and he was almost giddy over the news he was about to pass on.

"They dropped the charges against you, Mr. Smith. It seems they have some new evidence and they are now quite sure you weren't even involved."

"Wow, that's incredible."

Johnny said, "Do you know what the new evidence is and how they obtained it?"

"Not really, but I'm sure they'll make public their next move very shortly. I'm very happy for you, Mr. Smith. I must say that I did believe what you told me about that night. I've been trying to get a lead on Ms. Pamela Gerard but I've had no luck. Did you know that that colonel's wife killed herself?"

"Yes, I know, but I'm not so sure about the suicide." Clay caught himself. He was saying entirely too much already. "What do I owe you, Mr. Mann?"

"Nothing, it's all taken care of and I hope if you ever need my services again, you won't hesitate to call."

Clay was enjoying this. "They can't change their minds and come after me again, can they?"

"I don't think you have anything to worry about, Mr. Smith, and the bail collateral should be released by tomorrow."

Johnny was smiling from ear to ear. He could hardly contain himself. Clay tried to remain subdued but it was difficult. They left Mr. Mann's office and hugged each other right there on the sidewalk. It felt incredible and they wanted to celebrate.

"Let's go tell Susan and Gidget." Johnny said, "They're going to freak out, and what happened to our lunch?"

Clay said, "We'll eat when we see the girls, okay, John? Let's go."

When they reached the motel, the girls were nowhere to be found.

"Where the hell can they be?" Clay screamed.

"I don't know, Clay. Let's check out the restaurant down the street."

They drove the short way to the restaurant with every horrible thought in the world going through their minds. As they pulled into the parking lot, Susan and Gidget came strolling out of the place as though they hadn't a care in the world. When they saw the guys, they came running toward the car.

"Hey, Fellows, everything okay?" Susan asked.

Gidget threw her arms around Johnny's neck. "Damn it, Doc, you're shaking. What's wrong?"

"Nothings wrong now, Little Bit. But you two scared the hell out of us. We thought something had happened to the two of you."

"You, big bear, you really do care." Gidget said, smiling at him.

Clay and Susan were also busy hugging each other. They started laughing that kind of nervous laugh.

"What's happened?" Susan asked, excitedly.

Clay couldn't stand still. "The police dropped the charges against me. My lawyer just told us the good news."

"When we get through with our meeting tonight with the senator, we're going to party big time and that's a promise," Johnny said enthusiastically.

"Oh shit," Gidget said. "I guess you won't need us any longer. I mean, I'm glad it's okay but I'm gonna miss you guys."

"There's still plenty of work to be done." Johnny said, "If the general finds out prematurely what is going on, all hell's gonna break loose."

Clay and Johnny got a sandwich from the restaurant, and the four of them headed toward the motel to wait. They parked the car and playfully headed for the girls' room. As they rounded the corner of the building, Clay grabbed Gidget by the arm and jerked her backwards.

Johnny grabbed Susan. "Oh my God, look at that door."

Clay shoved both girls down the sidewalk away from the room. "Jesus, they've found us," he said. "Girls, head for the laundry room and hide."

"No, follow me," Johnny said. "Go, Clay, I'll take care of the girls."

Johnny and the girls ended up behind the storage building adjacent to the motel. There they waited for Clay. In a couple of minutes, he came darting around the edge of the building.

"I'm sure glad you girls got hungry. Those assholes broke your door down thinking you two were in the room. When they realized their mistake they must've taken off. I don't really know what's happening. I assume the general wants the two of you. That way he can force me to do whatever he wishes. He no longer has the murder charge to hold over my head and therefore he wants some leverage, I think." Clay continued, "Johnny, go get the car and pick us up by the mailboxes. I think they're gone for now but they may be watching the front."

"Sure, Old Buddy, give me three minutes and then come running."

Johnny headed for the car and he was as good as his word. In less than five minutes the four of them were safely away from there. Clay and Johnny just looked at each other. Again, each knew what the other was thinking. *Both Susan and Gidget could've been hostages or even dead by now.* It made a cold chill run straight down Clay's back.

"Johnny, let's head south on Highway 1. We'll be in Fredericksburg, Virginia in about thirty minutes, and from there the girls can catch a bus to Richmond. When we get to Fredericksburg, I'll call Sydney and he'll pick them up. They'll be safe at his place. No one knows him, and they wouldn't expect the girls to leave town."

Johnny tried to smile. "That's what I love about you, Old Buddy, you always have a plan."

The girls had been uncharacteristically quiet and that bothered Clay, but he knew better than to talk about it right then. After ten minutes or so, he decided it was time to break the ice. "You girls were very brave back there. I couldn't be more proud of you."

Gidget punched him in the back of the head. "Stuff it, Clay. I was scared shitless and I don't mind admitting it either."

Susan said, "Me too. I almost wet my pants."

"I know, but we're all safe now. Johnny and I will see that you're in good hands."

Susan said, "I'm not worried about Gidget and me. It's you two that I'm concerned about. I know that you're going back and I don't want you to."

"We'll be fine Susan, you have my word, and Johnny's too. Right, Johnny?"

"Absolutely, I'm much too young and cute to die."

They arrived in Fredericksburg around six-fifteen PM and Clay placed his call. When he returned to the car, he was smiling and that made everyone feel better. The bus for Richmond was to leave in less than an hour. Clay hated to leave the girls, but he had just over an hour to get to the senator's office for their meeting.

Johnny had already purchased the tickets and was waiting for Clay to say the word.

"Johnny, we need to talk."

Clay walked away from the girls with Johnny right behind him. "Johnny, if you think it would be best, you can stay with the girls and meet me tomorrow at my place."

"No way, Old Buddy, the girls are okay and they'll be fine. I'm in this for the long haul. I think, however, we need to get moving."

"You're right again. Let's say good-bye to the girls."

Everyone knew what had to be done. Clay promised to call after the meeting. He told them to buy whatever they needed; knowing they only had the clothes on their backs.

He said, "Sydney will take you to get whatever you need. I'm sorry Susan, Gidget. Have a nice time with Sydney."

He and Johnny were back on the road by seven-ten PM. Clay knew they had adequate time. "Do you think the general knows about everything?"

"He must, it's the only explanation for what's taken place," Johnny answered. "Look, Clay, the general has a God-complex. He loves to show his power and he's not used to being backed into a corner. He would've killed them if it served his purpose. Then he'd have gotten a good night's sleep. Clay, you just don't understand how ruthless he really is, but I do."

"Damn it, Johnny, I just can't imagine anyone being that evil and I don't want to either. Can you understand that?"

"Yes, I understand, but the general's mind doesn't work the same way. He has no regard for anyone's life other than his own, and that is that."

"You know if he hurt those girls, I'd kill him without remorse. Does that make us the same?"

"Clay, you told me once that you would never again let anyone hurt you. Do you remember that?"

"I remember. We were just kids."

"The difference is very simple. You only fight back, usually in someone else's defense. The general needs no reason to kill. But you, my friend, must have a damn good reason. You are basically just a pussycat."

"Thanks, John, I needed to hear that."

"No problem, Old Buddy."

They pulled the car into the parking space and looked for the senator.

Clay said, "Should we try the back entrance?"

"I guess so. I thought the man would be here to lead us inside. Damn it, Clay, I hope something bad hasn't happened. This shit is driving me crazy."

They tried to enter but the door was locked.

Clay turned to Johnny. "Let's go around to the front and see what happens. They're not going to shoot us. We do have an appointment you know?"

As they turned the corner back into the parking lot, the senator's car pulled into the space next to them.

"Sorry I'm late, Gentlemen, but I couldn't get off the damn telephone."

Clay held the senator's door. "It's okay, Sir, we were just worried about you."

"Let's get inside before someone spots us. It's been a real crazy day, and I'm not talking about my senatorial duties."

Johnny said, "The day we had, I may never forget. No matter how hard I try."

In moments, they were in the senator's outer office and ready to share the day's experiences. The senator offered them a drink and they were quick to accept.

"How are Pamela and Janice?" Clay asked.

"They have them stashed somewhere in Chevy Chase, Maryland. I talked to the Bureau Chief this noon and he assured me everything was going along smoothly."

Clay said, "May I start?"

The senator handed out drinks. "Certainly, Clay."

"My attorney called this morning and we met with him at noon. The charges against me have been dropped but I guess you know that. How did that happen so fast?"

"The FBI told me this morning that a copy of what they received from you last night had already been sent to the local District Attorney's Office. They received it by special messenger yesterday morning. When they read the girl's, I mean, Ms. Gerard's statement, it was clear. Then they played the telephone tapes. They were convinced that you were in no way involved. They would be obliged to inform your lawyer."

"Pamela must have sent them a copy. She was probably afraid she'd be killed before she could get me the key to the second locker. She never mentioned it to us, or to me." Clay said, pacing the floor. "The general must have found out soon thereafter. That's why he tried to kidnap the girls."

The senator jumped. "He what? How'd he find them?"

"Not those girls," Clay cautioned.

Clay and Johnny spent the next few minutes explaining. They told the senator all about Susan and Gidget and the part they had been playing. Well, maybe not everything.

Clay took another sip of his drink. "The general must think by now that I'm not going to carry out his orders."

The senator interrupted, "I'm sure that he thinks he knows. But, we need to convince him otherwise. According to the FBI, we don't have enough to make an arrest. We need him to become reckless and the only way to do that is to challenge his ego. They wanted you to meet with him and get everything on tape but I convinced them that he wasn't that stupid. I also told them you weren't that stupid either."

"Thanks again, Sir. Would you please explain to me how this all works? Why have they taken so many lives and why in all parts of the world? I simply don't understand. I do know that a small part of it has to do with contractors who deal mainly with the military."

The senator began, "I'll try to make it clear. It began for me when I finally came to realize that a great many people were making more money outside the political arena than inside."

"What does that mean?" Johnny asked.

"Well, to be precise, the amount of bribe money to people in decision making positions is incredible. I thought the group we know as the "Ten Little Indians" was mainly responsible, but that was only the tip of the iceberg. The salaries these people receive are just like receiving a tip at the end of the month. They make their real money elsewhere."

"How much money?" Johnny questioned.

"Millions of dollars. When the group found out that through the deaths of a few people at a given time, they could control the currency in a particular area, or the stock of a particular company, they jumped at the chance. By doing so, for only a day and sometimes, even minutes, they were able to turn millions into billions. That much money can even affect the Stock Exchange for a period of time. Think what that would accomplish. If left unchecked for another year or so, they'd be the most powerful people in the world. Money is power, make no mistake about it."

Johnny's glass was empty. "May I fix us another drink, Senator?"

"Sure, Captain, but you were about to say something, weren't you?"

Johnny nodded, "I was told that those who had to be eliminated were a threat to American security."

"That was my understanding as well," Clay added.

The senator fumbled in his pocket to retrieve his cigarette lighter. "I must admit, at one time they had me convinced and I was ready to be a part of the program, as a patriot. At least that's what I thought. You can blame all, or at least a great part of it, on the new computer age. In the fifties, this would never have been possible; but now, in the late sixties, it is becoming easier by the day. There are very few safeguards. That will probably change in the next few years."

Clay said, "We must stop them now, right, Senator?"

The senator took a long drag on his cigarette. "If we can indict the general, they'll fall like a house of cards, but we must get him. He is the catalyst and he supplies the muscle, as you well know. If we can get that Ms. Gerard before the Grand Jury and document her testimony, we have a chance. Without her, you both must testify and the general will try to destroy your life and any hope of a future you may think you have. We may have to let him think you have killed me. I know how that must sound, but it may be the only way to flush him out into the open. If we can do that, then everyone will see him for what he really is." The senator paused for quite sometime. "Clay, you call the general, and thank him for getting you out of the mess

319

you were in. He'll not know how to react. That'll give us a little more time."

"I'll call him first thing in the morning," Clay replied.

"Tell him that you've met with me and you're trying to gain my trust. Then, ask him for a big paycheck. He identifies with greed; so hit him with something he can believe. Tell him you want a million dollars. For that much money, you'll make it happen. The FBI is not releasing anything about you, or why they dropped the charges against you. The general should go along with the program. You need to be convincing, and show no fear."

Johnny interjected, "He can do that, the man doesn't even sweat, that's why he's so good. Clay can be the proverbial rock. That always gives him the upper hand."

"Cut it out, John, nobody's that good." Clay insisted.

The senator raised his glass. "I hope Captain Murphy is correct. You're going to have to be one hell of an actor, Young Man."

Clay squirmed in his seat. "I'll do my best, and I'll call you tomorrow, Senator, just as soon as I've met with the general."

"One last thing, Fellows," the senator said grimly. "If the general thinks you're about to betray him, he'll probably try to eliminate the both of you, and soon."

Clay said, "We'll be okay, won't we Johnny?"

"Of course, I told you that I'm too young and pretty to die."

"I have made arrangements for the two of you to stay at the Air Base. Here's a key to room twenty-one. You'll have to share for a couple of days, but you'll be safe. If you don't show up there tonight,

I'll personally have your butts kicked. Do we understand each other?" The senator was smiling. "In your quarters, you'll find the keys to another car, use it. That car of yours is very pretty, Clay, but it stands out like a sore thumb."

"Thank you again, Sir." Clay said, "You seem to have thought of everything."

The senator shrugged, "I sure do hope so, My Boy. I guess that's why they voted for me back home in Minnesota."

Clay and Johnny got to their feet. Clay said, almost as an afterthought. "We'll talk to you sometime tomorrow, Sir."

The senator shook hands with the both of them and he patted Clay on the shoulder. "You can exit through the back like you did the last time. Be very careful, gentlemen. The general is probably having you followed. Be sure you give his men the same treatment you gave mine... I'm just kidding, Fellows. His men might be instructed to kill you, mine weren't."

"Sir, before I go, could you get a message to Pamela for me? Please tell her 'Ditto.' She'll understand."

"I'll see to it personally, Clay."

As they exited the building, Clay inquired, "Johnny, do you have to be at the hospital tomorrow?"

"No, not until Friday. Are you trying to get rid of me, Old Buddy?"

"Of course not."

Chapter 21

When they got to the car, Clay looked at, Johnny. "Would you mind driving, Johnny? You know the way to the Air Force Base better than I do."

"Okay, but can we stop for food on the way? I could die from malnutrition at almost any moment. Do you remember when we last ate?"

"We had a sandwich about five hours ago. I think I could eat something too." Clay continued talking, "Before we eat, let's call Susan and Gidget. They'll be worried about us, and we promised we'd call as soon as our meeting was over."

They found what looked like a nice restaurant. The hostess led them to a table and they ordered drinks. The server brought the drinks just as the waiter was taking their order.

Clay touched the waiter's arm. "Do you have a pay phone?"

"Yes, Sir, it's next to the restrooms, in the front of the building."

"We'll be right back. Don't let anyone steal our table."

He and Johnny found the telephone booth and placed the call to Sydney's. Everything was fine. Susan told them that Sydney had the most beautiful house she had ever seen and he really was taken with

Gidget. Clay laughed, but he thought it best not to pass along that little piece of information to John. *Hell*, Clay thought, *everybody is taken with Gidget.*

They returned to their table to find the salads they had ordered with their meal had already arrived. The waiter asked them if they wanted another drink and of course the answer was yes. They began to eat in silence. The restaurant was a place called the Jolly Ox, and it was very nice. The décor was old English with maybe a little touch of Germany thrown in just for good measure. They had both ordered prime rib. When the waiter sat the entrée in front of them, they just looked at each other.

"That's the biggest piece of meat I've ever seen," Johnny said. "If I eat all of that, it may kill me, but I'm gonna try."

The meat was so tender it could literally be cut with a fork, and the baked potato was the size of a football with at least a half-pound of butter and sour cream on top. The two of them ate for nearly an hour, but neither one could finish everything on his plate. When the waiter asked them if they wanted dessert, they were too full to answer.

"May I suggest an after dinner drink. We have a drink that'll make you feel as though you could eat once again."

"I'll take one of those," Johnny said.

"Me too."

"I hope its Alka Seltser, that might just work," Johnny mused.

When the waiter returned to the table, he sat two small glasses in front of them. The drink was actually blue.

"What is this stuff?" Johnny asked.

"It's minty, and you must drink it in one gulp. It'll burn a little but it'll do you very much good."

"Hell, I'm game. C'mon, Clay, let's do it together."

One, two, three, and down went the drinks.

"Damn, that takes your breath away," Clay said, almost whispering because he couldn't seem to breathe.

Johnny looked at him. "I feel great. That's some great stuff, and, it did me very much good."

Clay laughed. "I don't think our waiter's from around here. But, I've got to get me some of that blue stuff."

"Well, get enough for me too. That's the wildest thing I've ever experienced."

"Well, I don't know if I can agree with that statement," Clay said, laughing.

Johnny looked at him, "Yeah, I get your point."

They left the restaurant and made their way to the Air Force Base. The room was quite small but it did have two beds, a bureau and one nightstand between the beds, with a lamp and a clock.

Johnny said, "I need to take a shower, badly, but I sure do hate to put dirty underwear back on."

"Wash your underwear while you're in the shower, and it'll be dry by morning."

"Good idea," Johnny replied, slapping Clay on the back.

The two of them showered and washed their shorts. They took the cord from the lamp and strung it between the beds for a clothesline. Unfortunately, they now only had the overhead light in service.

Clay jumped in bed. "I beat you; you have to turn out the light."

"Thanks, a bunch."

Johnny turned out the light and scurried across the room. As luck would have it, he hit his big toe on the bedpost. Clay almost fell out of bed laughing. Johnny was dancing around the room and screaming bloody murder.

"Oh you, big baby, it couldn't hurt that bad," Clay snickered.

Johnny screamed a few more obscenities, at Clay this time, and then climbed into the other bed.

"I'm sorry, Partner, but if it were me, you'd have laughed just as loud, and you know it."

"Yeah, yeah, get some sleep," Johnny grumbled. "I know, what you're thinking, Clay, it'll feel better when it quits hurting. Ha ha!"

Clay spoke, ignoring Johnny's statement. "You know, facing the general tomorrow will be no small task."

"I know, but you can handle it."

"How am I going to convince him that I'm on his team?"

"Let me sleep on it, and I'll tell you in the morning. Goodnight, Clay."

"Goodnight, Johnny."

Clay was up before seven. He went down to the lobby to read the newspaper. He didn't want to disturb Johnny. In less than thirty minutes, Johnny was looking for him.

"Let's go get a bite of breakfast," Johnny suggested. "Believe it or not, I'm hungry."

Clay said, "I tried to find the car the senator left for us, but I couldn't. According to the little tag on the keys, it should be a brown Chevy."

Johnny said, "C'mon, after we have breakfast, we'll find it. No problem."

"I want to call the general before nine. The best time to catch him is when he first comes in and he usually gets in before then."

"Sure, Clay, we'll call him before we look for the car."

He and Johnny went to the Officer's Club to have their breakfast. Clay could make his call from the bank of pay phones in the lobby of the club. When they'd finished eating, he rang the general's number.

"General Essex's office, may I help you please?"

"Yes, Ma'am, this is Clay Smith, I need to speak to the general."

"I'm sorry, Mr. Smith, but the general is on another line. Would you like to hold?"

"Yes, Ma'am, I'll hold."

"Essex's here, how may I help you?"

"Sir, its Clay. I didn't know anyone else answered your private line."

"Only during business hours. What can I do for you?"

"Thank you, General, for getting me out of this incredible mess. I don't know how you did it so fast, but thank you very much. And, Sir, I need to talk to you in private. I think my plan is in place, and I hope you'll be pleased."

"Sure, I'll see you at 1800 hours this evening?"

"That'll be fine, Sir. Are we to meet at the same place?"

"Yes, I'll see you then. Be careful, Clay, there's a lot of nuts out there."

"Yes, Sir, Thank you, Sir, I'll see you at 1800 hours."

Johnny said, "You handled that very well. How'd he seem?"

"He seemed a little taken back at first, but when he got the idea that I was still on the job, he seemed to mellow out and was even friendly. We need to find that car and I need to find a toothbrush."

"Me too." Johnny said, "And maybe a little deodorant."

They headed back to the BOQ and began to scour the parking lot. No luck, there was no brown Chevy anywhere to be found. Just as they were about to leave in Clay's vehicle, a young shavetail, (second lieutenant) pulled in driving a light brown Chevy and parked right by the front door. When the lieutenant got out of the car, another car pulled in and picked him up.

Clay said, "I think that must be the right car."

"Let's try it. You have the key, don't you?"

The key fit and they were off to find a drugstore. It was another beautiful morning and they were both hoping it would be a good day. The car was big and bulky, but it was free and full of gas. Clay didn't like the idea of leaving his own car parked at the BOQ, but he assumed it would be safe.

"Hey, John, we have well over a hundred and fifty thousand in the bank and the senator thinks I should ask the general for a million. We'll be rich. Do you think I should ask for that much?"

"I don't really know, but the senator seemed to think it'd be a piece of cake."

"I'm gonna tell him that the senator means nothing to me and why shouldn't I look out for myself. I'm also going to tell him that I hope Pamela is dead, for she betrayed me. Maybe that'll get him off her back."

"That might just work. Maybe you should tell him that I convinced you to ask for the money and that we're going to share it."

"You think he'd believe that?"

"He just might."

"Damn, Johnny, I should have asked if I could bring you to the meeting."

"I think you should drive your car to the meeting place. He'll know something is up if he sees you driving this."

"You're correct again, my friend. And it would only take him a few minutes to find out where it came from."

"I also think you need to mention what happened at the motel."

"Are you crazy, Johnny?"

Johnny turned sideways in the seat. "No, hear me out. The general may think you know, and he probably thinks you suspect him; however, if you come right out and tell him that you think the senator tried to kidnap our girlfriends, he'll think you suspect the senator and that'll calm his fears."

"That's pretty good, John."

"You have to admit, Clay, it does make sense."

"Absolutely, it makes perfect sense. When I get through this evening, we're going to Richmond and spend the night with the girls. What do you think about that, Partner?"

"I think we'd better call the senator before you go, but I can think of nothing I'd rather do then spend a little more time with Gidget."

"Johnny, how about introducing me to your friend at the base?"

"That's a good idea, just as soon as I buy a toothbrush."

"You know, Johnny, my back hasn't bothered me for over a week. That caudal block really worked." Clay slammed his fist against the dashboard. "When I think of all the people that have died ..."

They found a drugstore, and Johnny spent the next twenty minutes trying to find the right toothbrush. Clay bought one for himself, but it took him only a minute. Then they had to buy a razor and some shaving cream, and of course Johnny had to have deodorant. Then they went to J. C. Penney's and bought some more underwear.

"Boy, are we going to be spiffy when we see the girls," Johnny said, jokingly.

Johnny drove them back to the base. He knew how to get to his friend's office and Clay didn't have a clue. Clay was thinking that he'd heard so much about Johnny's friend at the air base that he could almost picture him, even though he'd never met the guy. He was shocked. The guy was about five feet tall and weighed close to nothing, and he could easily have been the poster boy for nerds. Without a doubt, he was one of the very first computer geniuses. The man talked about three feet over both their heads and that made Clay feel a bit stupid. They decided to have lunch with the guy, and when lunch was over, they headed back to the BOQ.

"Johnny, what do you wanna do this afternoon? We've still got five hours to kill. Sorry, Johnny, another bad choice of words."

"Let's go watch the Senators. The Oriole's are in town, and I think Palmer is pitching."

Clay knew he was talking about the Washington Senators baseball team. The Senators had a player by the name of Frank Howard who was the biggest man Clay had ever seen in a baseball uniform. He could hit the ball a mile; however, the Baltimore Orioles were by far the better team. They had people like Brooks Robinson, Frank Robinson and Jim Palmer, and they were incredible. The ballgame was the activity for the afternoon, and it was a well-needed break and Big Frank Howard hit a monstrous homerun. It was almost five PM when they left the ballpark, but they still had plenty of time to make the meeting. They'd almost forgotten that they needed to return to the base to change vehicles.

"What's your plan for taking out the senator?" Johnny asked.

Clay put his hand to his head. "I've been working on that in my head all day."

"Well are you finished working on it, Clay? What's the plan?"

"Don't rush me, Johnny. Do you have any ideas?"

"Not really."

"I think I'll just wing it. I'm sure something will come to me when the time is right. If it doesn't, I'll tell the general that I'm still working on it."

"Oh, that's really great, Clay. I'm just brimming with confidence now."

"Don't worry, Johnny, sometimes being a little vague makes you look smarter than you really are. I don't wish to sound lame in front of the general."

"Okay, Old Buddy," Johnny, said calmly. "I know you'll come up with something before he has us dumped in the Potomac."

"Well, I guess it's only fair. You practice medicine, and I'm practicing to be a hit man, or spy, or something of the sort. They do call it, 'practicing medicine', don't they? That always makes me a little nervous. You'd think doctors would know what they're doing by now," Clay started laughing out loud when he saw the look on Johnny's face.

"Okay, Smart Ass, I get it. I hope I get to 'practice' on you sometime."

"Don't wish that too hard, my friend. I don't think either one of us would enjoy that, at least I know I wouldn't."

"Right, I guess we ought to be careful what we wish for, huh?"

They pulled into the parking lot with more than ten minutes to spare. It was almost dark, but that was probably because it had gotten rather cloudy and it looked like it might rain at almost any moment.

"C'mon, Johnny. I think we should go in together. If the general doesn't like it you can return to the car and wait. Hell, what's he gonna do, shoot us?"

They entered at the front of the building and signed in. The guard announced their presence on the phone to the general's office. Clay

331

heard the guard mumbling something over the telephone but he couldn't understand what he was saying.

The guard said, "The general asked me to have you wait. He said it would be only a few minutes and he'd come out to get you."

Clay and Johnny walked across the huge foray to the sitting area. Clay hated marble. It was so very cold and this place had marble everything. There were marble steps, marble floors and even marble wainscoting around the walls. The entire structure appeared to be marble, stone, glass or wrought iron. Nothing could be much colder than that.

It was nearly twenty minutes before the general came from his office to invite them in.

"It's very nice to see you Captain Murphy, how have you been?"

"Fine, General, and you?"

"I'm doing just great. Keeping the world safe from those commies but that's why I get the big bucks."

"Yes, Sir. I reckon that's true."

"How's the medical field? Cure any major diseases, lately, Doctor?"

"Not lately, Sir."

Clay was really getting sick of all this bullshit. Johnny and the general didn't like each other very much, but they were determined to be polite, regardless.

When they were inside the general's office, things changed.

"Doc, you're good with your hands. How about fixing everyone something to drink?"

"Do you still drink Bourbon with a splash of water, General?"

"That'll do nicely, Captain."

The general reached for a cigar, smelled it, licked it, and snipped the end off.

"Would either of you like a smoke?"

"Yes, I believe I would," Johnny replied.

Clay knew Johnny liked a good cigar and he'd even smoke a cigarette sometimes, when he was drinking.

Clay began, "I want to thank you once again, General, for pulling whatever strings you had to pull to get me out of the mess I was in."

"No problem, Clay, that was, as I understood it, a vital part of our agreement."

"Did the police or your attorney tell you how I pulled it off?"

"I never talked to the police. Mr. Mann, the lawyer you hired for me, just told me that I was free, and that you'd taken care of everything."

"That's nice." The general said, with a half-hearted smile. "Look, Clay, I know that you've met with the senator more than once. Do you think he suspects anything?"

"Oh my Lord, no. He doesn't have the foggiest idea, but he continues to dig for information like a mole in a hole."

The general frowned. "Yeah, I know he keeps digging. That's precisely why we're going to dig his grave."

"Johnny and I have a couple of friends. Girls, you know? Today the good senator tried to kidnap them. I don't know why, but the man has a few screws loose. We sent them back home. It scared the hell out of um."

"I'll bet it did," the general said, looking uneasy for the first time Clay could ever remember. "Did they ever find the body of that little bitch, Pamela Gerard? I know they found her mother."

When he heard the general use the words, bitch, and Pamela in the same sentence; it was all he could do to control himself, but somehow he managed.

He said, "Not to the best of my knowledge. Who do you think had them killed? It must have been the senator, but I don't understand why, do you, Sir?"

The general seemed a little lost. "I don't know, Clay. I suppose it must've been the senator, or at least someone in his association."

Johnny said, "Did that Pamela lady have any information that could hurt us in any way, General?"

"It's possible, I can't be sure." The general replied, puffing hard on his cigar. "Actually, I thought she'd probably try to contact you, Clay. Maybe the police have her. She needs to be eliminated that's for certain."

Clay said, "If she contacts me, I'll do the job myself. I owe her big time."

The general eased back in his chair. "I understand you have a plan in place to take care of the senator."

"Yes, Sir, I do. I promise you he'll be in the headlines come Monday morning. It will look like a suicide and only the three of us will ever know the difference. There is one thing, however. Johnny and I feel like we should be paid a little better."

Johnny interrupted, "I have a slew of medical bills, and you know that I'm going into private practice real soon. I don't wanna have to work for the next ten years to get out of debt. Anyway, Sir, I know you have more money than God."

The general was obviously irritated. "How much more do you want?"

"We want one hundred and fifty thousand more now and seven hundred and fifty thousand more on Sunday night, when it's finished. Sir, with that much money, we can pay off Johnny's medical bills and pay for my return to the University to finish my education. C'mon, Sir, you'll make that back in a day."

"I'll check with the committee and let you know tomorrow," the general responded.

"C'mon, Sir, you make all the decisions, and we both know it." Johnny was pretty emphatic, "I've always done exactly as you've instructed and you know that you can trust me. It's just pocket change to you, General."

The general got up from behind his huge desk. "Wait here, I'll be back in a couple a minutes."

He left the room. When he returned, he was carrying a small satchel. He handed it to Clay. "Don't let me down. This money won't be worth much to you in the grave."

Johnny said, "Never fear, you've made a very wise decision, General. Clay and I will do a perfect job, and we'll all be happy."

"I'll meet you here at midnight on Sunday with the rest of your money." The general said, looking a little agitated.

Clay said, "You know, General, killing a United States Senator is a lot more complicated than killing a little nobody school teacher in France."

The general said, "You be here Sunday evening. I'm not unhappy with our deal, just do it."

"Yes, Sir," they both answered.

He and Johnny exited the general's office and headed for the car. The parking lot was nearly empty. Only a handful of cars were present.

Clay was almost giddy. "My God, Johnny, we are rich and I do mean rich!"

"You were great in there, Old Buddy. My God, when the general called Pamela a bitch, I was afraid you'd jump across that desk and rip his tongue out. But, you were cool as a cucumber."

"Thanks, John. I want to call the senator and then go to Richmond. We're gonna have a party."

"I'm with you, Clay. Do you realize we already have more than three hundred thousand dollars?"

"Yeah, I got it, Partner. I'm shaking on the inside. You just can't tell it."

They found a telephone and placed a call to the senator. He set up a meeting for the following evening at nine. It was now Wednesday, and Sunday night was drawing closer. Clay knew that whatever move they were going to make would have to be made very soon.

"Should we take my car, Johnny, or do you want to go back to the base and get the government car?"

"We still have our toothbrushes," Johnny quipped. "Why don't we just go? We can be there in a couple of hours, and anyway, I'm more comfortable in your car."

They stopped to place a call to the girls. After filling the tank and buying nearly twenty dollars worth of junk food, it was time to settle in for the trip. It was late and there wasn't much traffic.

"Damn it, Johnny, I think we have a tail."

"You've got to be kidding."

"I don't know who or why, but they're back there," Clay said, shaking his head in disbelief.

"Can you lose them?"

"I'm sure as hell gonna try, Johnny, otherwise we're not going to endanger the girls by going to Richmond."

Clay was a superb driver. He'd been trained by the best and now he was going to find out how well he was trained. Hitting the accelerator he passed a few slower vehicles but the other car was still there. Now, he was certain they were being followed.

"Any ideas, Doc? I don't seem to be losing um."

"Let them catch us, Clay."

"Okay, but your plan better be a good one," Clay said, a little uncertain.

Clay decided to pull off at a truck stop, just outside of Fredericksburg. When he stopped, the tailing car pulled into the parking lot and stopped about two hundred yards away.

"Okay, Johnny, they caught us. What's your plan?"

"Sorry, Clay, but I don't really have a plan. Then again, we couldn't let them follow us to Richmond."

"C'mon, Johnny, let's go inside and see if they follow us?"

Clay started toward the entrance and he stopped in his tracks. The car began to head right for them. He and Johnny stood their ground and the car stopped right next to where Johnny was standing. Two men exited the vehicle and walked toward them.

"Are you Clay Smith and John Murphy?"

"You know who we are," Clay replied. "Why are you following us?"

"We need to talk to the both of you. We were afraid to try and stop you for fear you might panic and someone would get hurt."

Johnny said, "Okay, talk. We're listening."

The taller of the two men reached for something in his pocket but before anyone could blink an eye, Clay's gun was pointed at the man's head.

"I'm just reaching for my identification. Don't do anything stupid."

Clay said, "Go ahead pull it out."

The man handed him his ID.

"As you can see, we're agents for the Federal Bureau of Investigation."

Clay said, "Okay, we know who you are and you know who we are. Now, what do you want to talk about?"

The agent said, "Would you mind if we went inside and maybe had some coffee?"

Clay moved toward the door. "That's fine, c'mon."

The four of them went inside the truck stop and found a booth where they could sit down. After ordering coffee for everyone, the older and shorter of the two agents began to speak.

"We've been guarding two young ladies that were delivered to us by the two of you. About three hours ago, they were killed along with two of our best agents. The Bureau Chief asked us to find you and make you aware of the situation. I'm truly sorry. The chief said you two would probably be next and that you needed to be apprized of the situation ASAP."

Johnny said, "Oh my God, are they both dead?"

"I'm afraid so," the agent replied.

"Was anyone left alive?" Johnny asked.

"No, they were all found shot, execution style, by the two agents who went to relieve them. They had only been dead a short while."

Johnny said, "I suppose you have no clue as to who did this, do you?"

"No, Sir, not at this moment."

Johnny started to stand. "Thank you, gentlemen, for letting us know. I'm sorry about the two agents."

"Sir, you don't seem to understand. We have been ordered to take the two of you into protective custody. You need to come with us."

Johnny threw up his hands. "Not a chance."

Clay looked up from his coffee. He was trying to compose himself. "The last two people you had in protective custody are dead. Now you want the two of us to believe you can protect us?"

Johnny threw ten dollars on the table. "Tell your chief that we simply refused to join you. We can take care of ourselves and we will."

"Okay, Guys, but you're making a big mistake."

Johnny said angrily, "Maybe so, but it's our choice and this way no more of your agents will get killed. That's a plus, isn't it, Fellows?"

"I guess so, but the chief isn't going to be happy about it."

Clay's chair went backwards, and coffee went everywhere. "I'm gonna kill that son of a bitch." Clay burst out the door and into the parking lot with Johnny and the two agents on his heels.

"Clay, stop." Johnny screamed. "I'm not gonna let you do this."

Johnny grabbed him just as he reached the car. Clay whirled around. "Damnit, Johnny, don't make me hurt you. That bastard deserves to die, and you, above all people, know it."

He grabbed the keys from Clay's hand and threw them to one of the agents. The look of hate, anger and frustration on Clay's face was easy for them to see.

"Mr. Smith," the taller agent said, "please come back inside and let us handle this. I promise you, we'll get the people responsible for this terrible act."

"Look, Agent," Johnny said, "I know you mean well, but Pamela, the younger of the two girls that was killed, risked her life twice to save my friend. They loved each other and now, she's paid the supreme sacrifice, she's given her life. How the hell do you expect him to feel?"

"You're right, Mr. Murphy. I'd feel pretty bad. I told you my supervisor is going to be real angry if we come back alone."

"You're breaking my heart," Clay shouted. "Now, leave. Give Johnny my keys, and go away, and don't follow us anymore."

The agents walked around the car and extended their hands. "We're really sorry about the young ladies."

Within minutes, Johnny and Clay were in the car and on there way again. Johnny took the wheel.

CHAPTER 22

Clay felt like he was going to explode. "I'm gonna kill that son of a bitch, and I'm gonna enjoy it."

"I'm really sorry, Old Buddy. I'd kill him for you but I know you need to see his face."

"You're so right," Clay said, squeezing the door handle so hard you could hear it. "I want to look him right in the eye and tell him what a bastard I think he is. I want to watch his soul descend into hell."

"I know how you must feel," Johnny said, as he slammed his fist into the seat.

"God, why?" Clay yelled. "He didn't need to do that. He has killed her whole family, just like he did Sergeant Russ."

"What'd you say?" Johnny said, with a look of terror on his face.

"I said he killed her whole family."

"No, you said something about Sergeant Russ."

"I said he killed her whole family like he did Sergeant Russ, and his whole family."

Johnny pulled to the side of the highway, banging his head against the wheel. "You mean the house fire wasn't an accident?"

Clay reached to touch him. "According to the senator, it was set to shut him up. Sergeant Russ, was the inside man for the Justice Department."

"Holy Cow! Why didn't you tell me, Clay?" Now, you could see the anger on Johnny's face.

"I would have Johnny, but I didn't even realize you knew the man that well."

"Are you kidding? He helped me many times, and he loved you."

Clay gave him an apologetic look. "Well, I'm sorry, Partner. I really didn't know."

"The general needs to die. I told you he was black hearted, Clay. I hope you don't mind if I give his soul a little push toward hell."

Clay looked at him with understanding, his face marked with the same seething hatred. "We'll both watch him die, and then set fire to his grave. Maybe we'll even toast marshmallows?"

Johnny said, "You got the right idea. You toast the marshmallows, and when were through, I'll piss on the grave."

They were just outside Richmond, Virginia, and headed west of town, to Sydney's. Clay had never been to Sydney's new house, so he was giving Johnny the directions he had been given, and trying not to make a mistake. When they pulled up to the front of Sydney's house, they were really impressed. It was a very dark night but the lighting around his home was exquisite. From the road there was a half circle driveway that led to the right where the four-car garage was located. As they pulled into the driveway, they were looking straight at the front of the house. It was three stories tall with a doublewide staircase spiraling upward to a landing and then on upward to the huge double door entrance. They were huge doors with sidelights, making it look like there were four doors. The stairway was brick with oak railings and the doors were solid oak. From a distance, they looked like they had been hand rubbed, and the sidelights were stained glass and leaded with his initials.

One of the garage doors opened just as they pulled in. Johnny drove the car into the garage. Before they could even exit the car, Susan and Gidget were down the inside stairs leading from the living area.

"Damn, it's good to see you guys," Gidget yelled as she jumped around Johnny's neck.

"Damn, it's great to see you too," Johnny, replied.

Clay and Susan hugged each other as they ascended the stairs. When they entered the living area at the top of the stairs, it was even more beautiful. The entire back of the house was all glass with doors leading to a huge patio and deck. There were stairs going both left and right leading down to the pool and spa. This area was connected to the pool in such a manner that the overflow would spill into the pool like a huge waterfall. The entire pool and deck area was granite and stone. It was similar to the ones seen in the old biblical movies in the Egyptian Pharaoh's palace. It was not unlike the area where the wives and concubines went to bathe. The house had five bedrooms with a balcony off each one. They each had their own bathroom. Some of the bathrooms were enormous, having their own separate shower and tub area.

Johnny's eyes were big as saucers. "Boy, Sydney must be loaded."

"Where is Sydney?" Clay asked.

"He's gone to the State of Washington on business. He'll be back on Friday. He called about an hour ago and we told him you were coming down," Gidget replied.

Susan said, "He said he hoped to see you real soon and to make yourself at home. Boy is he a nice guy. You have great friends, Clay."

"Yes, I do. I am very blessed."

"Are you guys hungry? We have a little of everything." Susan said.

Clay replied, "Actually, we bought a bunch of junk food when we stopped for gas but we haven't touched any of it. Something took away our appetite,"

Gidget said, "What happened?"

"Johnny, you tell them. I need to go to the little boy's room."

Clay went into the bathroom and threw some cold water on his face. He felt like he was going to be ill. As he sat on the side of the tub he could hear Johnny explaining everything to the girls. His body slid into the floor and the tears began to flow, silently at first; and then he could no longer control himself. He was crying so hard his entire body began to shake. Susan came in and held him for a long time. She sat in the floor beside him with his head in her lap. The crying continued, as she smoothed his hair with her hands and let him cry, never saying a word.

He didn't know how long they'd been in the bathroom but it seemed like hours. When they finally returned to the living area, Gidget came over and sat in Clay's lap and put her arms around his neck.

"We love you, Clay."

And with that, tears flowed again.

"I love you too, *little* one."

Johnny said, "I'm fixing drinks for everyone, if Gidget'll show me to the bar. With a house like this, the man must have a bar."

The others knew Johnny was trying to break the mood. All four of them were good at knowing when and what to say. That's why they sometimes said nothing.

He put his arms around Gidget and hugged her tightly. "I'd really like something to drink. Gidget, show him the bar."

"You got it, Boss. Come with me, Doctor."

She showed Johnny to a huge armoire. It was loaded. There were bottles of damn near anything. The booze flowed freely for the next little while.

"Why did he have to kill her? Somebody answer me that?" The strong drink had begun to numb Clay enough to enable him to talk.

Johnny spoke up. "He was afraid of what she'd tell the courts; and he wasn't going to take a chance, so he eliminated them both."

Clay gritted his teeth. "I'm gonna enjoy taking him down. I hope it takes him a month to die."

Johnny continued, "Clay, I hope you know that when you're of no further use to him, he'll have you killed too. He's also going to kill me, just for giggles."

Clay put his arms around Susan from the back. "Yeah, I'd already thought of that, when we show up Sunday night, we're as good as dead."

Susan whirled around, her face only inches from Clay's. "Show up where, Sunday night?"

Clay said. "We're supposed to meet at General Essex's office for our final payoff. Johnny and I are supposed to assist the senator with his suicide. Then the general is supposed to pay us the last of the money he owes us. If we show up, he's gonna try and eliminate us as well. I'm sure that's his plan."

Gidget chimed in, "I think this whole thing stinks."

Clay said, "Me too, but we have to play the final hand."

Susan looked emotionally drained. "Okay, then lets figure out a way to protect your ass as much as we can."

"I've got an idea!" Gidget said, "Suppose we put everything in writing. Then we'll tell the general that when the last payment is paid and we're safe in another country, we'll send the envelope to him. We'll tell him that we don't want to be in the country any more until this all blows over."

"That's not altogether bad, Gidget. At least the idea is sound. What do you think, Johnny?"

"I think something like that might actually work. Of course, if the general's arrested for attempting to have the senator killed, that'd work even better."

Clay was beginning to realize how little he'd eaten. "If I don't get something other than booze in my stomach real soon. I'm gonna puke, and that won't be a pretty sight."

Susan moved closer to him. "You love breakfast food. How about I fix you guys some pancakes and sausage?"

"Can you do that?" Johnny asked. "Clay didn't tell me you knew how to cook."

Clay sighed, "She loves to try, and she's pretty good at it."

Gidget said, excitedly, "I can set the table."

Johnny grabbed Clay by the hand. "C'mon, Clay, let's go check out the spa. It must be warm. I can see the steam coming off the water. The girls' don't need our help."

"I didn't bring any trunks."

"Hell neither did I. Do you think the neighbors will mind, Girls?"

Susan said, "There aren't any neighbors, at least not for a mile or two."

"Okay, Johnny, let's do it." Clay was still a wee bit modest.

Johnny was half way down the steps, and disrobing as he went. Clay took off right behind him, and in a minute or so, they were in the water.

"Boy, this feels great." Clay said, resting against the side of the spa, eyes closed.

"This is just what the doctor ordered," Johnny replied.

"Anything else you wish to prescribe, Doc?"

"I would say a good meal and about three good hours in the sack with that long legged blond would make me feel like a new man."

"Johnny, that's all you ever think about. Give it a rest."

"Ah, c'mon, Old Buddy, do you think she might give me a chance? I'll bet she's great in the sack. What do you say?"

"Go ahead and ask her. She won't hurt you, at least not for asking."

"Do you think Gidget would get angry?"

"I don't think so, but you might want to ask Susan privately first."

"You get Gidget away for a minute and I will. Will you do that for me?"

"Sure, Johnny, as soon as we're through eating."

The girls called down from the deck that the food was almost ready and that they should come to the table. Gidget threw them a couple of towels and told them to hurry. When they got out of the water, they almost froze. It was about forty-five degrees, but it felt like zero.

They ate in silence.

Clay said, "Kudos to the chef. The food is really good."

Johnny took the opportunity to offer his compliments as well. "Susan, you are beautiful and brainy, and you can cook. You really are something else. What more could a man; oops, or a woman ask for?"

"Well, I'll be damned," Clay said, sheepishly. "I don't think I've ever seen Susan blush before. Have you Gidget?"

349

"I don't think so."

"Hey, Gidget. Come help me get all the junk out of my car, would you?"

"Sure, Clay, but shouldn't I help with the dishes?"

"Let Johnny help, he ain't done a darn thing all day."

"Okay, I'm coming."

He and Gidget went down to the garage to empty the car of all the things he and Johnny had bought earlier.

Gidget said, "Johnny wants to put a move on Susan, doesn't he?"

Clay nodded. "That would mean you and me, Babe. I hope that doesn't upset you. Nothing has to happen you know?"

"Clay, you asshole, I have wanted you forever. Something better happen."

He smiled. "Do you think Susan will play along?"

"Yes, she likes Johnny. She might be afraid of hurting your feelings though."

"You tell her I know she loves me and that's okay, but do it carefully,"

"I can handle it, don't you worry," she assured him.

"Shut that door and let's go back upstairs," Clay said, sounding a bit agitated. "They've had enough time, don't you think?"

Gidget grabbed him around the waist and gave him a big hug. "Don't fret, I'll be gentle, Darling."

"Get moving, you little twerp." Clay replied, chasing her up the stairs.

"Clay, stop. I don't like being chased."

When they got back upstairs, Clay said, "I need a drink, Johnny, do you think Sydney has any of that blue stuff?"

"I doubt it, but I'll look in the liquor cabinet," he replied.

Gidget said, "There is some kind of blue peppermint drink in there."

Johnny pulled out the bottle, and low and behold, the man had everything.

"I didn't see you eat that much, Clay. But, Ladies, this is some great stuff." Johnny went on to tell the girls the story about the night at the restaurant.

Susan said, "Give me some, I'm about to burst."

Johnny handed her a little shot glass. "You have to drink it all at once at least that's what the guy told us."

She turned it up to her lips and drank. "Whoa, that is some powerful stuff."

Johnny said, "Yeah, it will curl the little hairs on the top of your feet."

"I love those stories," Gidget replied. "When I was in school, I read the entire trilogy."

Susan glared at her. "What in the hell are you talking about?"

"You know, J. R. R. Tolkien, the writer. The *Hobbit*. You know, the little guys, with curly hairs growing out of the tops of their feet."

Johnny said, "Gidget, you amaze me. I'm sorry, but until now, I never thought of you as an intellectual. I'm impressed."

"Thanks, Doc. I told you I was more than just another pretty face. What do you say; let's all go for a swim before turning in? C'mon, Guys, you didn't eat that much."

They all headed for the pool. When they started outside, Susan pulled Clay aside and asked him if it would be okay for her and Johnny to spend the night together.

"Susan, you know I love you more than damn near anything. I won't love you one ounce less either way. I just hope Gidget doesn't kill me."

"I'm more worried about you killing her. She's so tiny."

"I love you Susan. It'll be all right, don't you kill the doc."

They had a wonderful time playing in the pool. Gidget was just like a little water bug. It seemed, she could stay underwater forever.

She swam over to Clay. "Let's go to the bedroom," she whispered.

"Okay, make me another drink and I'll be right behind you."

She jumped out of the water and headed up the stairs to make his drink.

"Gidget and I are turning in for the evening. Don't you two do anything we wouldn't do?"

Gidget handed him a fresh drink and motioned for him to follow her. She took him up the stairs to a bedroom in the southeast end of the house.

"I need to take a quick shower, but I have to shave first."

"Go ahead," she said. "I'll take my shower while you shave. Is that okay?"

He began to lather his face when he noticed she was watching him.

"What! Did I do something wrong?"

"I've never been able to tell you how strong and beautiful you are."

Clay corrected her. "Men are not beautiful, they're handsome,"

"You're beautiful to me."

"Well, you're a handsome little filly and you have a great butt. Now, we're even."

"I'm not really that *little*, am I, Clay?"

"No, you only seem little when you are standing next to Susan."

"Well, I'm five feet one and I weigh one hundred and five pounds. Look at these boobs; they aren't small, are they?"

"No, as a matter of fact, they are quite beautiful, and the rest ain't bad either."

Clay was through shaving when she came out of the shower. He began to brush his teeth when she walked up behind him, reached around and grabbed him with both hands.

"Let me take my shower, and then you can do that all you want, okay?"

"Go!"

When he came out of the shower, she was already in the bed. He pulled the covers back and lay down beside her.

She began to massage him. Clay's body knew what to do but his heart just wasn't in it. He kept thinking about Pamela. Tears began to roll down his cheeks before Gidget realized what was happening.

"I'm sorry, Clay. You're thinking about her, aren't you?"

"I can't help it."

"I know," she whispered. "It's all right."

"She wanted to stay with me but I thought she'd be safer with the Feds."

"Clay, how did they find her? Do you know?"

"I have no idea."

"Susan and I talked about how much she cared for you. She must have loved you very much."

"Loving me can be hazardous to your health. It seems like every woman who ever loved me has ended up dead."

"Well, I love you, and Susan loves you and we're not dead."

"Gidget, I'm gonna kill that son of a bitch. You can count on it."

She said, "Wouldn't it be better to have him spend the rest of his life in prison? That general wouldn't last five years in prison, and they'd be horrible years."

"You're probably right. My mind is just going a million miles an hour and I can't seem to slow it down."

She said, "Roll over, let me massage your neck and back. Try to go to sleep we can have sex some other time."

He rolled over and she began to massage his neck. Before he could get things straight in his mind, he was out like a light. When he awoke, he was alone in the bed. But, he could hear talking coming from downstairs. On the way to the bathroom he acrobatically put on his trousers, washed his face and hands and brushed his teeth. As he started down the stairs he could hear Johnny saying something to Gidget.

"How are you, little one?"

"I'm okay, but Clay had a very rough night."

"Pamela, huh?"

"Yeah, and he's just sure that something bad is going to happen to Susan and me. He says that everybody who ever loved him has ended up dead."

"I'm still alive, and I've known him for over twenty years, but I understand what he means. His problem's the fact that he made her go with the feds, when she wanted to stay with him. Now, she's dead, and he thinks it's his fault. You know, if she had not left, you guys would've probably been in your room when those thugs came by to pay you a visit and you'd all be dead, or worse. If there is a worse?"

"You may be right. I wish I had thought to tell him that."

About that time Susan came in. "What are you guys talking about?"

Johnny said, "Clay had a really rough night."

"I was afraid that might happen. He blames himself, doesn't he?"

"Yes, I'm afraid he does," Gidget replied.

Susan said, "We should let him sleep as long as he can. Than we'll try to talk some sense into him."

Johnny said, "I agree, how about some breakfast? You worked me awfully hard, Susan, and those pancakes are long gone."

"I can do cereal," Gidget said, with a giggle.

"Cereal will be just fine. How about you, Susan?"

355

"Cereal's okay with me."

Gidget proceeded to set the table. "Who cleaned the kitchen?"

"I did," Johnny said, "and don't start with me."

"You did a mighty fine job, Doctor."

Susan got up from the table. "I'm going upstairs to check on Clay. I'll be back in a minute."

"Okay, but don't wake him," Gidget ordered.

Susan looked at her. "I'll be very quiet."

Clay got up from the steps where he was listening and hurried back to the bedroom. He threw off his trousers and jumped under the covers.

When Susan entered the room, he acted as though he was just waking up.

"Good morning, Susan. I hope you had a good night."

"Clay, you big boob, are you all right?"

Susan lay down beside him and put her head on his chest.

"Clay, I wish I'd been with you last night. I don't want to be with any other '*man*'."

"I love you too, Susan."

"Johnny is a nice guy, but if I'm gonna be with a man, it has to be you. Otherwise, look out ladies, here I come."

He started to laugh. "You always make me feel better and nothing happened between Gidget and me. I swear."

"Well, Johnny had a great time, but it meant nothing to me."

"I hope he doesn't know that?"

"Clay, I really wanted to be with you. Will you make love to me again sometime?"

"Are you kidding? It would be my pleasure. I wish we had time right now."

Susan reached over and touched him. He was hard as a rock. It wasn't that he didn't love Gidget, but somehow, with Susan it seemed to mean something more.

"You really do want me, don't you, Clay?"

"Yes, I believe I do. I promise you, I'll return tonight after my meeting with the senator, if you want me to."

She kissed him for a very long time. "Does that answer your question?"

"Thanks, Susan. I'll be here tonight. Johnny won't be able to come. He has to be on duty at the hospital Friday morning. I'll be alone, and it'll be very late. My meeting with the senator is not until nine PM and it could last an hour or better. It may be after midnight."

"I'll wait up for you."

"I'll be here, don't you worry about a thing."

She said, "The others are downstairs having cereal. You ready to join them?"

"As soon as I use the bathroom, I'll be right down. Are you all right?"

"I'm just wonderful now," she said, hugging him gently.

He kissed her on the forehead.

"I want you now," she said.

"Me too, but we can make it. Eat lots of breakfast that might help."

Susan punched him hard in the stomach. "I'll see you downstairs."

"I'll be there in a few minutes, if I can catch my breath."

When he came downstairs, only Susan was sitting at the table.

"Where is everybody?"

"They're downstairs playing pool. I guess they got tired of waiting."

"Well, that's just fine." He said, as he reached over and patted her on the hand.

"Hey, Susan, will you fix me a piece of toast?"

"Sure, Clay, coming right up."

"This will all be over soon; and when it is, I'm gonna take you on a vacation, just the two of us. Could you handle that?"

"Can we go on a cruise?" Susan's eyes started dancing. "I've always wanted to go on a cruise."

"Why not? I hear the food's great."

Johnny and Gidget came up from downstairs.

"Hey, Clay, how did you sleep?" Johnny said in a way that seemed to be almost too sincere.

"Not bad."

"I made breakfast, how was your cereal?" Gidget asked.

"Best cereal I ever ate. Johnny, we need to get back before the bank closes. I want to get this money in the bank. We also need to go by my apartment and get a change of clothes."

"That's a good idea. I could use some fresh clothes myself."

Clay looked at Susan, "You, Ladies, don't have any transportation, do you?"

"Sure we do," Susan replied. "Sydney left us the keys to his new Jaguar. It's in the first garage. Wanna see it?"

"Is it an XKE?" Johnny asked.

Susan looked questioningly, "Damned if I know, let's go look."

It was indeed a brand spanking new Jaguar XKE, and one of the most beautiful cars Clay had ever seen. It was silver with black interior, and it had all the bells and whistles.

Clay said, "I sure am glad you girls have something to drive. It bothered me to think of you two way out here on the west end with no way to get around."

When they went back upstairs, Clay dug into his stash. He pulled out a wad of bills and handed the girls another thousand dollars. "You girls can spend this anyway you want, just try to play it cool. We don't want to draw any attention to ourselves."

Gidget said, "You guys are very generous and I, for one, appreciate it. I know Susan does too. I guess it'd be nice if we were to restock Sydney's liquor cabinet."

"Give them some more money Clay."

"Okay, but what for?"

"You, Gals, buy something really nice for Sydney." Johnny insisted, "Maybe something for his house, and tell him it's from all of us."

"Thanks, Johnny, that's a great idea. Johnny, we best get going, I'll bet the bank closes at five."

In a few minutes they were on their way back to Washington D. C.

"Clay, I've been thinking about a way in which we can protect ourselves against the general. I think we should leave a letter with my friend at the Air Base. We'll instruct him to take it to the newspaper and the District Attorney if he doesn't see us in person at noon on Monday. We'll tell him to leave town until then, and to let nobody, including us, know where he is. That way, they couldn't force us at gunpoint to call him in order for them to get their hands on it. We'll give him a couple hundred dollars and he'll be a happy camper. What do you think?"

"I think that'll work. We need to let the general know this before we go to meet him on Sunday. We'd certainly hate to get blown away, before the fact."

"Right you are, Partner."

They went straight to the bank, and it's a good thing they did. They arrived there at four twenty-five and the bank was supposed to close in five minutes. Clay felt sure that everyone deserves to get lucky at least once a day. After putting the additional money into their safe deposit box, they went straight to Clay's apartment. It looked just like it did when they left it two days ago.

"I don't think anyone has messed with anything, do you, Johnny?"

"It doesn't look like it, but let's be careful anyway," he whispered.

"I gotcha, Partner."

He motioned for Johnny to follow him outside to the old reliable stairwell. "I'm going back to Sydney's after we're through with the senator this evening. You can use the BOQ quarters and you might as well use the car too."

"Okay, but is everything all right?" Johnny asked, looking a wee bit uneasy.

"Nothing's wrong. I promised Susan that I'd come back tonight, but I realize that you have to be at the hospital in Bethesda, Maryland tomorrow morning. It's a good thing the senator gave us another car, isn't it?"

"Are you going to be all right by yourself, Clay?"

"Yes, Daddy, I'll be just fine. How about you, Son? We'll meet back here at the apartment by six PM tomorrow night."

Johnny grinned, "I should be able to be back from the hospital by then."

Clay winked, "If you're delayed, I'll wait for you."

"What do you want to do until our meeting?" Johnny asked.

"I think this is as good a time as any to get our message to the general. What do you think?"

"Why not." Johnny replied. "What's the old saying; there's no time like the present."

"I guess we can call from the apartment. We'll tell the senator our plan, so if someone is listening, it really won't matter."

Clay placed the call. "This is General Essex, how may I help you?"

"It's Clay, Sir. Everything is all in place. The job will be done as planned. Dr. Murphy and I have placed an envelope with a third party, instructing him to leave town until noon on Monday, letting no one know where he is, including us. If for any reason he does not see us at that time, he is to turn the envelope over to the Washington Post, and certain other people."

The general growled, "I don't like this, Clay."

"I'm really sorry you feel that way, Sir. I told Dr. Murphy that I trusted you with my life. But, then I thought you probably wouldn't even care. You've always taken care of me, Sir, and I won't let you down, General. I'll personally deliver the envelope to you on Monday."

"I should have known this was Captain Murphy's doing. Well, don't you fret, My Boy, I'm not angry with you."

"Thank you, Sir. I'll see that everything works out for you, General. Please, you know I wouldn't let you down. I owe you everything."

"Clay, don't you tell the captain that I was the least bit concerned. Do you follow my drift? America and I are depending on you, Son."

"Don't give it another thought, Sir. I'll see you Sunday at midnight, and you'll be proud of me, General."

"I'm always proud of you, My Boy. I'll see you Sunday."

Johnny had been pacing the floor during the complete conversation. He grabbed Clay by the arm, put his hand over Clay's mouth and almost drug him out to the stairwell. "That was an Academy Award performance. I never thought I'd see the day, but you played him like a violin. He bought every word, didn't he?"

"I think so. I think he now believes I'm really on his side, and that's exactly the way it should be, right?"

Johnny couldn't stop grinning. He grabbed Clay and gave him a massive hug. "Fantastic, absolutely fantastic."

Clay backed up stuck out both hands, palms out, as though he were stopping a school bus. "Johnny, I want to go to the police station and find out what's happened to Pamela and Janice's body. I don't want them to be buried in a pauper's grave. That's what the city will do without a next of kin around."

Johnny thought for a minute. "I don't think that's a very good idea. Wait until we meet with the senator tonight and let's see what he can do to help us. If the general found out you were arranging Pamela's funeral, he'd know something was wrong. Clay, do you understand what I'm saying?"

"I understand, Johnny. Why don't we go over to the Shoreham Hotel and have a drink or two at the bar. I promise not to make a scene."

"Sure, Clay, I'm all for that."

It was nearly dark when they got to the bar, and boy, was it crowded. They finally found a seat about halfway back. The waitress remembered Clay from before; but thank God, she couldn't remember who he was with.

"Boy, Johnny, I'm glad she didn't ask any more questions."

"I thought she was going to say something about Pamela but you guys were only here a couple of times, right?"

"I was in here twice with Pamela, and once with Leila."

"Maybe this wasn't such a good idea, Clay."

"Johnny, look who's sitting at the end of the bar."

"That's, Sergeant Shackelford, isn't it.?"

"It sure as hell is."

About that time the sergeant saw them and started toward their table. He looked good, but Clay thought he seemed a little worn out.

"Clay, it's great to see you, and you to, Captain Murphy, isn't it?"

"Yes, that's correct. How are you, Sergeant?"

"I'm okay, but with all these people dying around me it's starting to give me the willies."

Clay said, "Yeah, I know what you mean."

"I don't mean to be rude, but could I talk to you in private, Clay? It will only take a minute. I hope you don't mind, Captain?"

Clay stood, and he and Shack walked outside into the hotel lobby. The sergeant sat down on a sofa and motioned for Clay to sit beside him. "Clay, I know you didn't kill that colonel. I tried to tell the general that, but he didn't want to listen."

"Thank you, Shack, but they already dropped the charges against me."

"That's great news, but what the hell are you still doing in this damn town. Clay, you get the hell out of this town, and as far away from General Essex as you possibly can."

"Look, Shack, can we go back inside and talk? Captain Murphy has been my friend since I was a little boy and he knows absolutely everything. Please?"

"Okay, if you think it's all right."

The two of them walked back inside to the table where Johnny was sitting.

"What's the deal?" Johnny asked.

Clay motioned for Shack to have a seat. "Shack was unaware that we've been working on this together. He didn't want to say the wrong thing in front of the wrong person."

"That's okay." Johnny said. "I understand completely."

"Shack, are you still doing work for the general?" Clay asked.

"He has tried to recruit me on several occasions but I wasn't interested. I haven't done anything for him since Dr. Delong died, and that was no accident. Even the Department of the Army, hasn't issued the news to anyone. I don't think anybody at the hospital even knows yet. The doctor and his wife were both killed in a small plane crash. The FAA has not given out the names yet. I heard the general telling that guy from the Department of Justice all about it."

Clay dropped his head. "Well, I knew he wasn't one of the bad guys. Damn, I liked that man."

Johnny turned his attention to the sergeant. "Do you think the general had them killed?"

"I sure do." Shack replied.

Clay finished his drink. "Shack, do you know any of the other members of the general's group?"

"I'm not sure what group you mean. Do you mean his staff?"

Clay shook his head. "No, I'm talking about the group called the Ten Little Indians."

"I never heard of that bunch." Shack replied. "Who are they?"

Clay shrugged, "Oh, it's not important. You're probably better off not knowing."

Shack's eyes brightened, "How is your back doing?"

"Thanks for asking, Shack. I'm doing really well ever since they gave me that caudal block."

The waitress came, "Can I get you guys another drink?"

"Yes, bring us two more and whatever the sergeant wants." Clay gestured toward Shack.

"I'll take another beer, Ma'am."

Clay looked straight at the sergeant. "Actually, Shack, I thought you might be the one the general would call when he was ready to get rid of me; and that concerned me a great deal."

"The general knows how much I like you, Clay. He wouldn't come to me. There is a group of guys he has used in the past, but they're just thugs. They are the ones who killed all those ladies."

Clay and Johnny sat straight up. "Do you know where to find those guys?" Clay asked.

Shack looked at Clay and then at Johnny. "Not really, but I'll check around if you want me too."

Clay reached across the table and placed his hand on Shack's arm. "Please do, and if you find out anything at all, please give me a ring. It would really mean a lot to me."

"I sure will, Clay. Do you think the general is after you?"

"He could be I'm not really sure."

"Well, if he hires those guys, you're in luck. There are three of them and they'll try to take you head on. They think they're bad, but they ain't bad enough to take you. And, if the doctor's as good as I've heard, you've got them out numbered."

"I hope you're right, Shack," Johnny replied.

It was as though the sergeant came alive. "Look, Clay, I'd be glad to help you take those assholes down. Let me work with you guys?"

"Shack, give me a number where you can be reached on Sunday. I just might give you a call, if you really want to help." Shack wrote his number down and handed it to him. Johnny punched Clay, and pointed to his watch.

"Shack, we have to meet someone in just a few minutes. I'll call you Sunday morning. I don't think you should mention this conservation to anyone, just to be on the safe side."

"Okay, Clay, not a soul. It was real nice talking to the both of you. I really hope you'll call me. I owe that bastard." Shack looked rather serious.

"It was really nice talking to you too, my friend." Clay gave him a big hug right there in front of everybody.

Shack stood proudly, "You take good care of yourself, Clay. I'm glad to know we're friends."

They shook hands, and Clay and Johnny headed for their car.

"Clay, when you called him friend, it really meant something to him. You really have a way of making people feel good and you make them feel important. People like that, Old Buddy."

"Well, I meant what I said."

Johnny stopped in his tracks. "That's why it works. They know you mean it."

Chapter 23

It was almost eight-thirty PM when they reached the car. They drove to the senator's office in less than fifteen minutes. The parking lot was almost empty but the senator's car was already there, at least it looked like his car. In a moment they saw a light come on in the car. The senator stepped out and motioned to them.

Clay thought, *another one of those important meetings. Will this one be the most important, or will there yet be another?* When they were inside and settled with drink in hand, Clay could barely keep a handle on his emotions.

"What the hell happened?" Clay said, heatedly. "I thought the ladies would be safe with your people. Hell, Pamela wanted to stay with me but I thought she'd be better off with your guys. What … happened?"

The senator hung his head. "I'm truly sorry, Clay. I don't know what to say. I don't know how they found them, but they did."

"Do you know those two FBI agents tried to take Johnny and me into protective custody? They said it was for our own protection. What a laugh. I told them to go to hell and to quit following us."

The senator said, "There's a leak somewhere. We just need to plug it."

Johnny was pacing, "Pardon me, Sir, but isn't that a little like closing the barn door after the horses have already gotten loose?"

The senator stammered, "I guess you're right, Captain, but we still need to know who gave them up."

Clay interrupted, "We met with a man this evening who knows the guilty party. As soon as he can find them, he's gonna give me a call."

The senator perked up. "Clay, the minute he calls, you let me know and we'll have them picked up."

"Not a chance, Senator. I'm not gonna let those bastards get away. I'll take care of them personally."

"Clay," The senator pleaded. "Let the law take care of them. They can probably give us all kinds of information. Information we can use against the general, and maybe the entire group."

"No offense, Senator, but if I turn them over to the police, they'll offer them a deal. If those guys testify against the group, they'll go free and you know it's true. Well, not in my lifetime, Sir."

"Clay, sometimes you must let the little fish go in order to catch the bigger ones."

"Bullshit, it just makes it easier for the police and the D.A. What the hell, they didn't kill anybody they knew. Well, I knew all six people they killed, and they are gonna pay. Everybody will just have to bust their butts a little bit harder to catch the rest of those sons-a-bitches." Clay was so angry he was damned near frothing at the mouth.

The senator said, apologetically, "I'm not saying its right, but sometimes you simply have to play the game. That's the way the world works."

Clay threw both hands in the air. "Maybe that's why the world's such a mess."

Johnny stopped pacing and stood between them, looking back and forth. "I don't want to become a referee here. Let's stop arguing and try to get our plan together. How about it guys?"

The senator sat back in his chair. "You're right, Captain Murphy, but I really am sorry. If I hadn't talked you guys into letting the FBI take over, those girls would probably still be alive. Their blood is on my hands."

"Senator, I know you didn't mean for it to happen. Clay is hurting right now and so am I, but we still want the same things." Johnny's voice was, purposely, as calm as a summer breeze.

"You're right, once again, Captain. As a United States Senator, I try very hard to do the right thing and my hearts usually in the right place, but I don't have all the answers. I'll get those bastards if it kills me, and it may very well do just that."

Clay began his own form of pacing. "I know you're trying to do the right thing, Senator, and I truly believe you mean well. We're both feeling guilty and I didn't mean to take it out on you. It's just that I want to hit something or someone really hard. I want them to feel the pain that I'm feeling."

The senator put out his hand, to Clay. "We'll get them, Son, I promise."

Clay shook his hand and the senator reached for Johnny's hand as well. "Clay, I know this won't help very much, but I have something for you." The senator got up, walked across the room, and removed his jacket from the hanger where he had placed it. He slid his right hand into the appropriate pocket, retrieving a small envelope. "Here, Clay, I believe this belongs to you."

Clay took the envelope, his lips beginning to quiver. "Oh my God, I don't believe it." He threw both arms around the senator's neck. "Taylor gave me this watch for Christmas before she died. How did you get it, Senator?"

"I called the police and requested they return it to you," the senator replied. "One of my men went down to the police station this afternoon to pick it up. It was the very least I could do. I hope it helps a little."

"I really appreciate your having done this, Senator." Clay turned bright red. "My Lord, Johnny, I just hugged a United States Senator."

Clay looked at Johnny and he was smiling as though he had just been given a great gift of his own.

Johnny reached for the senator's hand. "Senator, Clay was certain he'd never see that watch again. My thanks also, Sir, that was a very nice and personal thing to do."

The room was filled with emotion; even the senator couldn't hide the effect. "You're both more than welcome. It doesn't make up for all that has happened, but I knew it would mean something." The senator paused, "Let's get down to business. Clay, you and Captain Murphy show up at my home about nine PM Sunday evening and I'll blow my brains out. My wife will hear the shot, and after investigation, she'll call the police."

"Does your family know what's going on?" Johnny asked.

The senator nodded. "My wife does, and the children will be away for a few days. We have to make this seem as real as possible or it won't work."

Clay raised his hand like a schoolboy asking permission to speak. "What are the police going to do when they get there and there's no dead body?"

The senator lit a cigarette before continuing. "The FBI will arrive at nine-thirty PM, and they'll take over jurisdiction. I'll have a body from the morgue. The head and face will be so badly destroyed from the shotgun blast that immediate identification will be impossible. I'll leave a note. Clay, you can tell the general that you forced me to write it. Tell him that you threatened to kill my entire family if I didn't cooperate. Also, tell him that I begged you not to kill me, and that I told you he was the bad guy. He'll buy that, I know him."

Their conversation was suddenly interrupted by a knock on the door. Clay had gun in hand and jumped in front of the senator. Johnny was headed toward the door. The senator quickly explained, "Its okay, Clay. I invited a friend of mine to join us for a few minutes. Open the door, Captain, let him in."

Johnny opened the door very cautiously. It was a little, short, frumpy guy in a dingy, wrinkled overcoat. His frock of matted hair and unusual spectacles hid a child-like face. He was, in fact, Tim Siler, a reporter for the Washington Post. The senator had explained the scenario to him and he was going to see that the newspaper carried the story on the front page Monday morning. The general's meeting with the group was scheduled for eight AM; and with any luck, there would be a retraction by the newspaper before noon. After a quick round of introductions, Johnny was the first to speak.

"I'll bet a lot of people are going to be shocked when they hear of your death, Senator. I hope most of your friends and colleagues don't read the early edition."

The senator smiled, "That makes two of us."

Clay jumped right in. "Let me get this straight. If the general calls the police, say after eleven PM, Sunday evening, they will verify that you took your own life. Is that correct, Senator?"

"That is the idea, My Boy. On Monday morning, the FBI will walk into the general's meeting. They'll arrest him for conspiracy to commit murder. They'll have all the evidence and sworn statements from the both of you, statements, saying that the general hired you to commit this horrible crime. The meeting room will be bugged. We hope the general will brag about his feat to the rest of the group. It's an ego thing with him, plus he'll use it to put the fear of God into everybody else in attendance. Do you get the idea? If he'll admit it on tape, you two won't even have to testify."

Clay clapped, "That's a damn good plan, Senator."

The senator looked pleased with himself. "I think it'll work, don't you?"

Johnny looked uncertain. "I certainly hope so."

Mr. Siler finally entered the conversation. "Do you have doubts, Captain?"

"Not exactly. I'm just the incurable pessimist."

Mr. Siler turned his attention to, Clay. "How about you, Clay?"

"I think I can improve on it some if the senator will permit me?"

"Please do." The senator replied.

Clay began. "Suppose I suggest to the general that I attend the Monday meeting. I'll explain to the group how the general and I disposed of the senator. We'll also tell them it was to protect the entire group and to preserve the cause, whatever the hell that's supposed to be. The general will go along with that in a heartbeat. Then, we'll have him on tape admitting everything. What more could the D. A. possibly want? We'll have tied the entire case up in a ribbon, and handed it to him. Surely they can't screw that up, can they?"

Everyone was silent. Then, Mr. Siler smiled. "Gentlemen, that is magnificent. With the ego General Essex has, he couldn't shy away from that. He'll also think that, if Mr. Smith is willing to admit his guilt in front of the whole group, he's got him forever. That'll make him want to do it all the more."

The senator stood; all smiles. "It's agreed then. Clay, you'll talk to the general before Sunday and that's the way we'll play it."

Clay stood also. "Okay, Sir, after talking to General Essex, I'll call you on your private line just to let you know it's a go."

The senator lit yet another cigarette. "That'll work, Clay. Now, is everyone in agreement?" Everyone either nodded or said yes. "Clay, I'll wait for your call, and I'll see you and Captain Murphy at my house on Sunday evening at nine."

This time Johnny waved his hand. "Senator, may we use the car you loaned us for a few more days? I need to be at work in Bethesda tomorrow and Clay needs his car. We'd certainly appreciate it."

"Of course, Captain, no problem at all."

Clay wasn't quite finished. "Senator, there is one other thing. I want to assign someone to stay with you and your family until Monday morning. With this man, you'll be as safe as in your mother's womb."

The senator tried to take a sip from his empty glass. "I already have people watching over me, but I am grateful."

Clay looked determined. "Look, Senator, the general may have some sort of backup plan, and I don't think we should take any unnecessary chances. He won't get in your way, and you'll like him a lot. Humor me, Sir. Please!"

"Okay, Clay, who is this man?"

"Sergeant Shackelford, he really wants to help."

Johnny chimed in. "Senator, he really wants to be of service, and I agree with Clay. You could be making a big mistake if you don't accept his help."

Mr. Siler added. "Senator, I think you should listen. Better, safe than sorry."

The senator reached for a tissue. "Okay, Fellows, if it would make you feel more comfortable."

Clay sighed and shook Mr. Siler's hand. "May I use your phone, Senator?"

The senator sat back down in the chair, from which he had just risen. "Go ahead."

Clay proceeded to the desk and dialed the sergeant's number. Clay told him to bring his toothbrush and to meet them at the senator's office as soon as possible.

Clay turned. "Senator, he's on his way. May I have another drink, Sir?"

"Certainly, and I'll take another. Clay, you best fix one for Johnny and Tim."

Clay, tended bar for the next few minutes. When everyone had a fresh drink in hand, Clay continued. "Senator, do you know what has taken place concerning Pamela's funeral? I want to see that she and her sister have a proper burial. That's the least I can do."

Before the senator could respond properly, Mr. Siler jumped right in. This was right up his alley. "I think it might be easier if I took care of those details. I'll write the obituary and plan the funeral for Tuesday. Don't worry Clay I'll do the job as if it were my own family."

Just then, the telephone rang.

"Hello, what is it, Harry? The senator looked puzzled. "Oh yes, I know who he is, send him to my office. That's okay; I'll have someone meet him in the hallway. You did fine, Harry. Thank you.

Yes, Harry, we'll be leaving real soon. I'm just lucky you were on duty."

Clay said, "Is something wrong, Senator?"

"No, not at all. Harry has been one of our security guards for over twenty years. However, sometimes he gets carried away, but he means well. Captain Murphy, will you step into the hall and wave down the sergeant?"

"Certainly, Senator."

Sergeant Shackelford walked in beaming. "I hurried as fast as I could, but that guard's a little strange, or maybe I just look like a bad guy?"

The senator extended his hand. "I'm Senator Lazar, and I don't think you've met Mr. Siler, he's with the Post."

"Nice to actually meet you, Senator. And, you too, Mr. Siler."

"It's nice to meet you too, Sergeant, and you can call me Tim."

Sergeant Shackleford turned to Clay. "Clay, what's this all about? How can I help?"

Clay put his arm around the sergeant's shoulder. "I want you to guard the senator for the next few days. I told him, that with you on the job, he would be as safe as it's possible to be. Will you do that for me, Shack?"

Sergeant Shackelford was standing tall, smiling like a kid who had just got his first base hit in Little League. "You know I will, Clay. Senator, it will be a great privilege, and I'll try very hard to stay out of your way."

The senator smiled at him. "Thank you, Sergeant." Clay directed his attention toward Mr. Siler. "Tim, I'll be more than happy to pay for the cost of the funerals, and you may include the mother if it hasn't already been taken care of. I'm confident, you'll do something real nice, and I thank you."

The senator interrupted, "Clay, the government will pay for the funerals, whatever the cost. This should be their expense considering all that has taken place."

"That's very kind of you, Senator," Clay replied.

The five of them started to go their separate ways when Clay grabbed Shack by the arm. "Shack," he whispered. "Have you found out anything about those thugs yet?"

"No, Clay, but I should know something by the day after tomorrow."

Clay patted him on the back. "Okay, but, you find me the minute you know anything, you hear?"

"Absolutely, I promise."

Johnny was eavesdropping. "If you can't find Clay, you call me at the hospital."

"Okay, Doc, will do."

Clay sat his empty glass on the sidebar. "Senator, I'll talk to you soon, and I'll see you Sunday evening, if not sooner."

The senator was holding the door for everyone. "Okay, My Boy. I'll have everything in place."

Clay and Johnny headed for the car. "Johnny, I really want those bastards."

"I know."

"Johnny, you drive. Are you going to stay at the air base tonight, or are you going to check in at the BOQ in Bethesda?"

"I think I'll stay at the air base." Johnny paused for a moment. "Clay, you know you're my only real friend, please be careful."

"Hell, Johnny, it's you I'm worried about. Those bastards won't know where I am, but they'll know where to find you. If anything happened to you, it would be my fault. I don't think I could live with that. I have entirely too much blood on my hands already."

"Damn it, Clay, this is not your fault."

"Yeah, but if I had never fallen for Pamela, she'd still be alive."

"It's the general's fault, that's all there is to it. He's the bad guy in all this and you've gotta remember that, Old Buddy."

"I know, but I really feel like shit."

"You'll feel a lot better when we send those sons-a-bitches to hell."

"Damn right I will."

Johnny dimmed his lights, and the guard at the gate waved him through. It was almost eleven-thirty PM when they finally got to the BOQ. Clay took the flashlight out of the glove compartment and he and Johnny inspected the government car thoroughly. They determined it had not been bothered. They figured that, to date, no one knew where they were. He followed Johnny inside to retrieve his personal items. It was obvious that the housekeeper had been in to straighten up, but everything seemed okay.

Clay grabbed Johnny's hand, and then pulled him close. "You get a good night's sleep, Johnny. I'll meet you at my apartment on Sunday at six PM. If you hear from Shack, call me at Sydney's. Don't give anyone else his number, not even the senator."

"Clay, do you really think telling me that was necessary?"

"Of course not, Johnny. I'm just all strung out. All this shit has me doing and saying a lot of things that don't make much sense. Sorry, Partner."

"Clay, you call me tomorrow morning at exactly eight-thirty, at the hospital. Ask for Doctor John Wayne Murphy. You can hang up once you've asked for me. I just want to know that you and the girls are okay. If you screw around and wait for me to answer, they could be monitoring my calls."

"I'll do that, but how will I know you're okay?"

"When I get the message, I'll call you back from another phone. Don't worry if it takes me awhile. I might be involved with a patient. However, if it's more than a couple of hours, send in the Mounties."

Clay grabbed him again; this time he kissed him on one cheek and then on the other. "You're a dear friend, Johnny."

Johnny backed up. "Cut that out. Clay, I saw a great definition for a friend on the back of a matchbook. It said that a friend is that person who walks in when everybody else walks out. How do you like that?"

Clay was still laughing. "I think that's beautiful and, in your case, absolutely correct. I will repay you someday."

"Who saved whose life in Bimini? I'm just trying to get even, Old Buddy."

Clay stepped forward. "Don't make me kiss you again." This time, Clay was really cracking up. "Okay, John, I'm outta here. See ya Sunday."

Clay headed for the car. He kept thinking about the matchbook definition of a friend. It was simple, yet perfectly correct. It was almost midnight when he hit the highway; he was constantly looking to see if he was being followed. When he pulled into the driveway at Sydney's house, as before, the same garage door opened.

The girls came running down the steps. "Is Johnny all right?" Gidget asked.

"He's just fine, and he sends his love to the both of you."

Susan said, "Are you hungry, Clay?"

Clay headed for the steps, allowing the ladies to go first. "I'm starving as usual. Can either one of you make me a grilled cheese sandwich?"

"Sure I can," Susan replied.

Gidget turned, almost tripping. "How about a beer, Big Boy?"

Clay reached to steady her. "I'll take one now, and one more with the sandwich."

"Coming right up."

When they got upstairs, Gidget brought him a beer and Susan commenced preparing his sandwich. He sat in the big overstuffed chair next to the fireplace and Gidget sat down in the floor, at his feet.

"How did the meeting go with the senator?" she asked.

Clay explained everything, right down to the very last detail. The girls were really interested; and when he was finished, Susan brought him his sandwich. She had put lots of butter on each side, and cooked it slowly in a skillet until each side was a golden brown.

Clay smiled up at her. "Thanks, Beautiful. Is there any milk in the fridge?"

"Yes, why?"

"This would taste much better with a cold glass of milk. I'll drink the other beer later."

Susan put the beer back in the refrigerator and poured him a big glass of milk. It was relatively quiet for the next few minutes, while he ate his sandwich and drank his milk.

Susan couldn't wait any longer. "Clay, are you really going to kill those guys if you find them?"

"You mean when I find them; and the answer is, yes, I'm gonna kill 'em. Do you think I'm wrong?"

Susan was becoming emotional. "It's not that I think you're wrong, but I don't want you to kill anybody. I know they deserve to die, but I don't like to think of you killing someone."

He pulled her down beside him. "I'm sorry, Susan, let's talk about something else."

"I think you should kill them," Gidget said. "But that's just my opinion and it ain't worth much. If they hurt either one of you guys, I'd want to kill 'em."

Susan just sat there shaking her head.

"What are we gonna do this week-end?" Clay asked, trying to be perky. "I want to do something really fun."

Susan said, "I'd like to go to Williamsburg. I'd like to ride the horse-drawn carriages and see the sites. I've heard that it's gloriously beautiful. Can we do that, or would that be too boring for you?"

He laughed, "Sounds good to me, and boring might be fun, for a change."

The three of them sat, drank a little, and talked until almost dawn.

Clay noticed Gidget was falling asleep on the sofa. "I think it's about time to call it a night; however, we probably should set the alarm. I need to call Johnny at the hospital at exactly eight-thirty AM, and I really don't want to miss that."

Gidget stirred, "I just need a blanket, and I'll sleep right here on the couch."

Susan tossed her a blanket from the downstairs closet and motioned for Clay to follow her upstairs.

He put his arms around her waist and almost pushed her into the bedroom. "If I shave and shower quickly, will you give me a massage?"

"Only if you let me shower too." She replied.

"That might be fun, but you have to let me shave first."

They both fell across the bed. Susan said, "No one's holding your butt on this bed, Clay Smith, get moving."

He said, "Oh, that's real cute. I'm going already. It won't take me long."

"You go ahead and shave. I'm going downstairs to be sure everything is locked up tight. I think I should take Gidget a pillow."

Clay undressed in the bedroom, down to his shorts, before heading to the bathroom. He was almost finished shaving when Susan came in.

She stood at the door, posing. "You're mighty pretty. If you had big boobs, and a little pug nose, you'd make a pretty woman."

Clay acted hurt. "Boy, that sure makes a guy feel good, especially the remark about the nose."

"You know I love your crooked nose. It gives you character."

He turned and threw water at her. "O boy, like, I've never heard that before, at least not more than a thousand times."

Suddenly, Clay felt an incredible chill, like a cold wind. He couldn't explain it, but he knew instinctively something wasn't right.

"What's wrong, Clay?"

"I don't know, but something is amiss, and I don't know what."

He ran from the bedroom toward the stairs with nothing on except his shorts. Susan was right behind him. He reached Gidget in a matter of seconds. She was sound asleep on the couch.

He covered her mouth. "Gidget, don't ask questions, just get upstairs with Susan, now."

Susan said, "I'm right behind you, Clay."

"Then, both of you get upstairs in the bedroom and lock the door. Susan, Sydney keeps a gun in his bedside table. Don't be afraid to use it."

The two girls went flying up the stairs as fast as they could run. Clay needed his gun but it was in his car. *Good move, dummy,* he thought. He grabbed the poker from the fireplace and sat in the shadows waiting. Five minutes or so passed, and nothing. Then ten minutes passed and still nothing. He looked at the clock across the room. It was after six. It would be daylight soon. Clay decided he could wait. Something moved in the shadows by the door leading from the kitchen to the patio. He didn't move, not wanting to give his position away. Surely he could get one or two of them, and maybe with any luck, Susan would shoot the other one, figuring it was the three thugs he was looking for.

It was now almost seven o'clock and nothing. *Damn it, make your move.* He heard someone messing with the back door. It was starting to get light outside. Clay heard the noise again at the door. Meow, and then again, meow. Heading for the stairs; in only seconds, he was by the bedroom door.

"Susan, it's me. Open the door."

The door opened slowly. Susan grabbed him. "Clay, are you all right?"

"I'm fine. Does Sydney have a cat?"

"Yes. His name is Ike, like the President."

Clay fell into the wall, slid down to the floor, and just sat there. "Well, I think it just stole ten years of my life. God, I hate cats."

Gidget said, "Ike is real sweet, but he doesn't come around very often."

He rose to his knees. "Well, I think he is trying to get in."

Susan snickered, "He usually scratches on the door and meows."

Clay purposely ignored her. "Susan, did you find Sydney's gun?"

"No, Clay, this is not his bedroom, and I was afraid to go after it."

Swearing loudly, he said, "You two wait here. Where is his bedroom?"

"It's downstairs, the big bedroom off the living room. You know, the one with the enormous bathroom and hot tub," Susan answered.

He headed down the stairs. It was daylight. When he found the bedroom he realized he was right next to it the whole time. The gun was in the bedside table. Clay searched the house and the grounds, and all he found was a cat named Ike.

When he came back upstairs, Susan and Gidget were sitting on the bed. Susan declared, "Clay, I've never seen you this jumpy before."

He collapsed on the bed beside them. "I know, but I thought I might've brought them here. If anything ever happened to the two of you, I'd shoot my own self."

The three of them headed back to the kitchen. Susan filled the cat's bowl and placed it on the patio.

Gidget looked at Clay. "Well, he won't be back around for a few days. You can relax now."

He slid the gun across the table. "Here, just shoot me."

Susan intervened, "Would anybody like anything to eat or drink? Clay, you have to call Johnny in less than an hour. No sense going to bed now."

Clay said, "I'll take some coffee, if it's not too much trouble."

Gidget got up and kissed him on the head. "I'll do it, Susan. I make the best coffee anyway."

"Look, Girls, I'm really sorry for scaring the hell out of you. What time is Sydney supposed to be getting home?"

Susan sat down in the floor and laid her head on Clay's knee. "He said it would be between eight and nine this evening."

"I'll sure be glad to see him. I haven't seen him since before Taylor died."

They talked for a while longer, and then, Clay made his call. Now, all he could do was wait.

Gidget was lying on the couch again, trying to sleep.

She said, "You guys go on to bed. There's a telephone in the bedroom. When he calls, it'll wake you; and anyway, I need some sleep too." She rolled over and covered her head.

"That sounds like a good idea. C'mon Susan, lets go to bed."

"I'm with you. I can hardly keep my eyes open."

When they got upstairs to the bedroom, Clay headed for the shower. Susan was right behind him.

Just then the phone rang. Clay stopped, "I'll get it."

"Everything okay down your way, Old Buddy?"

"Just great, Johnny. You make it to work okay?"

"Yeah, I was here early."

"Have you heard anything yet?"

"Nothing, Clay, but I'll let you know the minute I hear something."

"I know you will, Partner. You take care, I'll see you Sunday."

"Okay, you have a good time with the girls."

Just as they hung up, Susan came out of the bathroom. Clay walked over to her and they kissed. She reached out and pulled him close.

Clay said, "Please, Babe, let me take a quick shower."

"Okay, but don't keep me waiting long."

He was in and out of the shower in less than five minutes. Susan was patiently waiting.

When he came out, the telephone rang again. Susan threw a pillow at the phone.

Clay grabbed the receiver.

"Clay, I just heard from Sergeant Shackelford. He gave me the location of the three men. They are staying at the Milner Hotel, a few blocks from your apartment. What do you want me to do?"

"What time will you be finished at the hospital?"

"I should be through by five-thirty or so."

"Meet me at my apartment at six-thirty. We'll have some dinner and work out the details. Is that okay with you?"

"Sure, I'll see you there. Be careful, Old Buddy."

"Okay, Partner, I'll see you then. Thanks, Johnny."

"I know, they found the bastards, didn't they?"

"Yes, Babe, they sure did, and I couldn't be happier. Just hold me, and let me get a few hours sleep. You're not angry with me, are you Susan?"

"If you mean the sex, it's all right. I'm concerned about you getting hurt. You're the best friend I have in the world and I don't want anything bad to happen to you. It is okay if I worry just a little, isn't it?"

He kissed her tenderly. "I guess, as long as it's just a little."

She shoved him onto his stomach. "Let me massage your back."

"Thanks, Susan, you're the best."

"Yes, Clay. Shut up and get some sleep, but you owe me one."

"Sure, Babe," Clay mumbled …

Nightmares galore! It was almost two PM when Clay awoke to find himself, once again, alone in the bed. He jumped up, put on some clothes and hurried downstairs. Susan and Gidget were eating a late lunch.

"Good afternoon, Clay." Both girls spoke in unison.

Susan said, "Do you want something to eat?"

"Yeah, I think I'll have something. What are you guys eating?"

Gidget said proudly, "Tuna salad sandwiches and I made them. I also made the tuna salad. Are you brave enough to try it?"

"Sure, why not?" He replied. "I guess you already know, Gidget. They found the guys who killed Pamela and her sister. They're probably the ones who killed a bunch of others too."

"Yes, I know, and I'm just as nervous about it as Susan."

"Would you two stop? I'm gonna be fine; and God willing, I'll be back soon."

Susan handed him some milk. "Clay, I don't think you should mention God. I'm sure, he wants nothing to do with what's about to happen."

"You're right, Susan. I didn't mean any disrespect."

Gidget placed a sandwich in front of him. "Okay, but if you get killed, I want your car." She wasn't laughing.

He looked at her and then at Susan. "Oh, that's precious. Well, if I do, I'm coming back to haunt the both of you, so there."

Clay was aware that the three of them had been through a lot together and they were all too nervous to be anything but silly.

He kissed both girls. It was time: he had to go.

Chapter 24

Clay arrived at his apartment just after six PM and everything seemed to be in order. He knew Johnny would be there at any moment, and he could think only of getting his hands on those three men and very little else.

Johnny arrived at twenty past the hour, and he seemed a little fidgety. Clay thought that he'd been through enough of this, and that it wouldn't bother him at all.

"Are you all right, Johnny?"

"Clay, I need to tell you something. All those other people that were killed, well, I just assisted with the details. I never really killed anyone personally."

"This is one hell of a time to tell me, don't you think?"

Johnny looked ill. "I guess so, but I'll do my part. You just tell me what you need for me to do."

Clay said, "What about the guy who was following us? You sure took care of him in short order."

"I just hit him twice with a brick that I found laying beside the steps."

"Johnny, you help me plan it, and I'll do the dirty work. I know you're good at that part. Can you handle your gun if it becomes necessary?"

"Yes, I'm a damn good shot; and believe me I will shoot those bastards without blinking an eye."

"Before we kill the last one, I want to know who hired him."

"But, Clay, you already know the answer to that."

"I want to be absolutely sure." Clay said. "Do you have a silencer for that weapon?"

"As a matter of fact, I do."

"Then I suggest you use it. We don't want to make too much noise. At least, not until I find out what I want to know."

Johnny tried to smile. "You got it, Old Buddy."

He and Johnny made their plan. It didn't amount to very much. Just find out if they're in the room, then go in and kill them. Pretty darn simple. They headed for the Milner Hotel and this time Johnny was as nervous as a "Cat on a Hot Tin Roof."

"Johnny, there's probably a detective somewhere in the hotel. If we run into him, we'll ask him where we can find some girls. When it's over, we'll walk out separately. Johnny, you go out the side entrance and I'll go out the front. We'll meet at the car."

It was a Friday night and the hotel was really jumping. That made it much easier to get lost in the crowd. Clay had parked about a block away. "Johnny, when we're finished, you exit through the side entrance and start walking toward my apartment. I'll get the car and pick you up."

They headed for the hotel lounge.

"Johnny, go in the bar and order a drink. I'm gonna call their room to see if they're there."

"What are you going to say if they answer?"

"I'm going to ask them to please check their bathroom. I'll tell them that the guest below them has complained about a leak and we need to know if it's coming from their room."

Johnny smiled, "That's pretty good. I guess that's how we're going to get into their room later, right?"

"Very good, Johnny, you catch on fast."

Johnny went to the bar. Clay went to find the house phone. When he returned to the bar Johnny was having a drink.

He sat down and motioned for the waitress. "We hit the Jackpot. At least two of them are in the room, and maybe all three. I asked them if it would be all right if someone from maintenance came up with a stethoscope to listen to the pipes in the bathroom. I assured them that it would only take a minute. Also, I told them it might be a few minutes before I could send someone."

The waitress came. Clay ordered a drink and another for Johnny.

Johnny finished his first drink and pushed the glass to the center of the table. "Clay, that ought to work. It's a good plan. You didn't even need me."

"Well, I'm still glad you're here."

He and Johnny had a small toolbox with them. Johnny had taken the stuff from his medical bag and put most of it in the toolbox. He had also procured some drugs from the hospital that he thought might come in handy. At least, it might make the three of them talk a little more freely, and it reportedly worked very fast.

Just as they started out of the bar, someone grabbed Clay's arm. "Shack, why aren't you with the senator?"

"That is well taken care of and I knew damn well you guys would show up here tonight. I thought you might want a little help. Those are some real bad dudes."

Clay and Johnny brought him up to date on the plan and he was anxious to participate. Shack had a gun but no silencer. They decided that Clay and Shack would act as the maintenance men. When they walked into the room, they would leave the door ajar. Johnny was to count to five, which would give Clay and Shack time to get to the bathroom. This way they'd have the three men in a cross fire. Just to make sure they didn't shoot each other, and since the door to the rooms opened in and left, Johnny was to take anybody out to his right and Clay would take anybody out to his right. That would cover the entire room.

Clay said, "If we kill them all quickly, it's okay, but I hope at least one of them last long enough for me to question him."

"If I'm close enough to get my hands on one of them, I'll take him down by hand and we can question him all we want," Shack commented.

Clay looked at him. "Okay, Shack, but don't take any unnecessary risk."

"Don't worry, Clay. I'll be sure before I make my move."

"That's good enough for me. You ready, John?"

Johnny said, "I'm having an adrenalin rush! Let's do it! But let me go on record and say that I'm sure glad you showed up, Sergeant."

"Thanks, Doc."

Shack stopped. "Clay, aren't you afraid these guys will recognize you two?"

"I don't think that's a problem," he replied. "The people tailing us were hired by the Senator, and just to be safe, I'm wearing glasses and a cap, and they won't see Johnny until he's shooting at them. Do they know what you look like, Shack?"

"No, there's no way they'd know me from Adam," Shack answered. "I guess it's that time. What room are they in?"

Clay said, "They're in room four-fifteen. I'll take the stairs. You two take the elevator. I'll meet you in the hallway."

"Okay, Clay." Johnny said. "We'll be there."

They met in the fourth floor hallway. Johnny passed out the surgical gloves. "We don't want to leave anything for the police to find. Remember that, and don't leave anything behind."

Johnny stood to the right of the door with his back against the wall. Clay knocked on the door, "Maintenance, we're here to check your bathroom."

From the room, "Keep your shirt on, I'm coming."

The door opened.

Clay viewed the room. "We'll only be a minute."

With toolbox in hand, he and Shack crossed the room and went into the bathroom, counting to five under their breath. One of the men followed them into the bathroom. Clay was praying that Shack would know instinctively that this was his man.

Clay reached five just as he sat the toolbox down and flipped it open. He had maneuvered himself to one knee beside the sink with the man to his back. When he heard Johnny say, "Five" he already had his weapon in his hand and knew where his target was. He took his man down with one shot and so did Johnny. Shack had his man semi-conscious and lying on the bathroom floor. Johnny shut the door as he entered the room. Clay walked over to each of the two men and put a bullet in their heads. Shack and Johnny had dragged the last man out of the bathroom and placed him in the only straight back chair in the room. They taped his feet and hands together and gagged him. Johnny took some smelling salts from the toolbox and brought him around.

Clay began, "I want to know who hired you to kill those two women and the FBI agents the other night; if you tell me this'll be easy. If you don't, you're gonna suffer something awful."

Clay removed the gag,

The man said, "Go to hell."

Shack shoved the gag back in his mouth. Johnny took out a syringe with needle and proceeded to stick it in the man's arm.

"In about thirty seconds, he'll tell you everything you want to know."

Clay said, "I'm tired of messing with you, scumbag, who hired you?"

Shack removed the gag.

"I'm not telling you any …"

Clay said, "I'm losing my patience."

The man's eyes rolled back in their sockets. "Okay, okay. It was a bunch of Indians. General Essex is the big chief."

Clay shoved the gag back in his mouth. "Now, that wasn't so hard, was it?"

"I think we need to be going." Johnny whispered nervously.

Clay said, "Untie him and put him on the bed. Stick the tape in your pockets. We don't want anyone to know we've been questioning him."

Johnny and Shack did as they were told and placed the third man on the bed. Clay removed the gag once more, stuck his weapon in the man's mouth and blew his brains out the back of his head. They checked the room and exited quickly. Shack went down the stairs at one end of the hallway while Clay went down the stairs at the other end. Johnny took the elevator. Clay walked to the newspaper stand and bought some gum. He then walked casually out the front door. Walking to his car he met Shack on the way.

"Shack, get to your car and meet us at my apartment in ten minutes."

"I'll be there."

Clay got to his car and picked up Johnny three quarters of the way around the block. They drove directly to Clay's apartment without saying anything. When they parked the car and began walking toward the entrance, Johnny inquired. "Did you see the sergeant?"

"Yes, he should be here any minute. I thought the least we could do is give him a drink. He earned it, don't you think?"

"Absolutely."

"By the way, Johnny, you were quite the professional back there. I'm proud of you."

"Thanks, Clay. But, for your information I almost threw up on the sidewalk outside the hotel."

"Thanks, Johnny, for telling me that. I appreciate it."

Shack showed up just as they reached the top of the stairs. He was coming in the front entrance.

"Johnny, go on in and fix you and me a drink. I'll wait for Shack and find out what he wants. We'll be there in a minute."

Shack took the stairs two at a time. He was in great shape for a man pushing forty.

"What would you like to drink, Shack?"

"Beer, if you have it. I don't drink much of the hard stuff."

When they walked into the apartment, Johnny handed Shack a beer and Clay a scotch and soda.

Johnny said, "I heard him say he wanted a beer. I'm not psychic."

Clay motioned for the guys to follow him. When they were outside the apartment, he hugged them both. "Guys, I can't begin to tell you how much your friendship means to me. I do thank you from the bottom of my heart; and I'll be there for you, anytime and anyplace. You can take that to the bank."

Shack said, "Clay, you are the coolest customer I've ever known. You weren't the least bit nervous tonight and I was sweating bullets."

"Me too." Johnny said

"Come Monday, when all of this is over and I have my life back, I'll personally speak to Santa. You two can be sure that there'll be something very special in your Christmas stocking this year, and I'm not talking fruitcake." Clay said, with a smile that would light up the room.

Johnny said, "Shack, you get back to the senator and don't let anything happen to him. We'll see you Sunday evening. Thank you again. I'm not sure we could've pulled this off without you on our team."

Clay said, "He's right, Shack. I love you, my friend."

Shack excused himself and headed back to Chevy Chase, Maryland, and the senator.

Johnny said, nervously. "Shack's one hell of a guy, isn't he?"

"Damn right he is. He's as loyal as a good dog, just like you Johnny. By the way, do you have to work Saturday?"

"No, I don't. I'm not even on call this weekend. You wanna go see the girls?"

"Yeah, I thought we might. I think I need to call them right now and let them know that we're all right. Let's go down the street to the bus station and use the pay phone. Then we can stop by the Waffle House."

"I'm with you, Old Buddy."

When Susan answered, Clay could tell by the sound of her voice that she had been sitting by the phone, waiting for the news, good or bad. "Susan, its all right, everything went just as planned. I know you've been concerned."

Susan said, "Clay, Sydney missed his flight, and he can't get another one until tomorrow."

"That's a shame I think I can finally talk to him now, about Taylor. I would really like to ask him some questions."

"I think he feels the same way," Susan said. "I know he was very disappointed. I think he's looking forward to spending some time with you."

Clay and Johnny loaded the car with what provisions they needed and they were again on their way. He told Johnny the story about the cat. Johnny couldn't stop laughing. "I always knew in my heart that you were afraid of a little strange pussy."

"Oh shut up, Johnny. You've waited your whole lifetime to pull that one; although, I gotta hand it to you, that was quick. Only a warped brain could work that quickly."

"Well, if you say so, Old Buddy."

It was late, when they arrived. The girls were still faithful. As soon as they pulled into the driveway, the garage door opened.

He and Johnny spent the next hour telling the girls; only generally, what had taken place and about Sergeant Shackelford's willingness to help.

Susan said, "We're just glad you're both okay. Gidget and I have been worried sick."

Clay said, "I'm sorry for what I've put you girls through the past few weeks. I guess I'm really not the friend I ought to be; however, you must admit, it hasn't been the least bit boring."

"Bullshit, Clay, except for being scared out of my wits a time or two, I've had the time of my life," Gidget said. "I'll probably tell my grandchildren about this someday. Of course, I'll play a much bigger part when I retell the story."

Susan laughed, "Me too."

Johnny said, "Damn, Susan, I'd have never dreamed you ever thought about having grandchildren. That's a kick: no offense."

Gidget's eyes were dancing with excitement. "Did you guys use that Sodium Pentagon stuff to make those guys tell you what you wanted to know?"

Johnny shook his head. "Not sodium pentagon, its sodium pentothal, and yes, that's what we used,"

Gidget stuck out her lower lip as though she was pouting. "I had the right thing, didn't I?"

"Yes, you did," Johnny said. "I'm very proud of you."

Clay said, "Johnny where did you put those gloves?"

"They're under the front seat of the car in a plastic bag. I'll go get them. The syringe and tape are in the same bag."

Clay nodded, "Susan, doesn't Sydney have a leaf furnace in his backyard?"

"Yeah, it's right next to the pool house."

"Good. That's where we'll destroy the evidence. Susan, while John and I go down and get rid of this crap, will you please make me another one of those great toasted cheese sandwiches?"

"I sure will. Do you want milk to drink?"

"That would be great."

Johnny walked in with the stuff. "Can I have one too?"

Susan said, "I guess so, but I must tell you, they're addicting."

"That's okay, I'll chance it."

He and Johnny found the back yard furnace. They placed the gloves and tape in the kiln and ignited the gas. Within minutes, the remaining evidence was completely destroyed. They returned to the living area.

Clay said, "I sure would like to see a copy of the Washington Post. I wanna see how they report the death of those guys."

Susan said, "You can get a copy at the drugstore. It's on Midlothian Turnpike, about two miles back towards town."

Johnny said, "I doubt that they've even found the bodies. It'll probably be in tomorrow's paper or maybe not until Monday."

"How do you think the general will take the news, Johnny? Do you think he'll suspect us?"

"Yeah, I think he'll not only suspect us but he'll feel pretty certain. I'm concerned that he'll no longer trust the two of us, but I'm not sure he trusted us to begin with. He thought you hated Pamela for lying to the police and getting you in this mess."

"That's true."

"Then, don't you think he'll wonder why, we'd want to kill those guys."

"I see what you mean," Clay said. "I was so mad, I didn't think properly. Why didn't you stop me? I wish you'd said something earlier."

"I didn't actually think it through at the time; however, even if I had, I couldn't have stopped you and you know it. I think we need to call that reporter, the one we met in the senator's office, and maybe he can get them to hold off printing the story until Monday."

"Do you think he can do that?"

"I don't know, but it's worth a try. If we explain our reasoning he'll probably try to help. It would be in the best interest of the senator. He should accept that," Johnny said, with a measure of insistence in his voice.

"How are we gonna explain knowing about it without accepting the responsibility for killing them?"

"Look, Clay. He's like a lawyer, he can't tell anybody. Okay, he can, but he won't."

"Let's find a pay phone and I'll give him a call," Clay said nervously. "I'm not gonna make the call from here."

"I'm with you, Old Buddy, let's go."

Clay paused, "I think we might want to wait til morning, or at least until daylight."

Johnny stood reaching for his wallet. "I think his home telephone number is on the back of his card. I think we should call him now and give him as much time as possible to stop the story. He won't mind. If we wait and someone leaks out any part of the story, we're in trouble."

"You're right again, Johnny, let's do it. Susan, are there any grocery stores open this time of night? It might be nice to replenish Sydney's refrigerator, and you girls would probably like to get out of here for a while."

"Sydney told me the Safeway is open twenty-four hours a day, and its right next to the drugstore."

"Okay then, finish your sandwich, Johnny, and we'll get the hell out of here for a little while."

"I'm almost finished, Clay. It'd probably be wise if someone made a grocery list. How about it, Girls?"

Gidget jumped up. "I'll do it."

"I'll help you," Susan replied.

Clay stood and adjusted his clothes. "Well, I'm going to the bathroom and brush my teeth, among other things."

When he returned, everyone was ready to go. They piled into Clay's car and headed for the Safeway with everyone, except Clay, talking at the same time.

"What is it, Old Buddy? Something's eating you and you need to share it with the rest of us."

"It's nothing."

Susan said, "I know he's thinking about Pamela, aren't you Clay?"

"Well, actually, I was thinking about Taylor and Pamela. I can't seem to win. Every time I fall for someone, they die. It's not even safe being around me, as you know."

Susan touched his hand. "It'll be all right, Clay. God has someone out there and you'll find each other. Some day, you'll be able to forget, or at least the pain will go away."

"Thanks, Susan, you're really sweet."

They reached the Safeway and the girls went grocery shopping while he and Johnny used the pay phone. Clay explained the entire situation to the reporter and Mr. Siler assured him it would be handled.

"Thank you for calling so quickly, Clay. If you had waited much later we'd have been in big trouble; however, I think you've given me enough time to take care of everything. Clay, when this is over I want an exclusive. Do we have a deal?"

"Deal, and thanks a bunch, My Friend. I'll talk to you real soon."

Clay patted Johnny on the back. "You were right, I'm glad you encouraged me to call now. Mr. Siler is going to take care of everything."

"Damn, Clay, we make a good team, let's go find the girls."

The girls' had two buggies full of groceries. When they returned to the house, it took the better part of an hour to unload and put everything in its proper place. Clay and Susan did most of the putting away, it seems Johnny and Gidget had other things on their mind.

When they were finished with the groceries, the two of them sat on the sofa in front of the fireplace, not saying a word. Clay gave

Susan a kiss on the cheek and laid his head in her lap. Susan began to stroke his hair.

"Clay, I promise you, everything will work out for the best. I have a lot of faith in God and he always knows exactly what he's doing."

"I wish I could believe that."

"I assure you, if you'll only look, you'll find him."

He was asleep in minutes. When he awoke, it was light outside. Taking the blanket that Susan had evidently covered him with, he went upstairs, and found her sound asleep. Lying down beside her, he put his arm around her, kissed her on the shoulder and went back to sleep.

When he woke the second time, Susan was gone. It was cold in the bedroom. He wrapped himself in the blanket and went downstairs. Susan was making coffee.

"Susan, are you okay? What time is it?"

"It's almost noon and I'm feeling good, how about you?"

"I feel much better, thanks to you. May I have some coffee?"

"Sure, just a little sugar, right?"

"Yes, Ma'am."

"You call me ma'am again and I'll spit in your coffee."

"Sorry, Kiddo, I lost my head. I guess Johnny and Gidget were awake for a while. They may sleep til suppertime."

"They were still awake when I went to bed and that was nearly dawn."

"Gosh, Susan. You must have sat with me a long time. I looked at the clock and it wasn't quite four o'clock when I fell asleep."

"Yeah, I sat with you for awhile. Do you want something to eat, or do you want to wait on the others to come down?"

He got up from his chair, walked across the room, and put his arms around Susan's waist from behind. He kissed her on the back of the neck. "I'll wait, if you will?"

"That's fine with me. I'm not very hungry." She turned to walk away but Clay wouldn't let her go. "What's your problem, Clay?"

"Just be still for a minute. I want to tell you how wonderful you are, and if I could put it into words, I'd tell you how much I care for you. Susan, you are at this very moment the most important person in my life. I'm really sorry if I've hurt you. I know I've taken you for granted, and I'll try never to make that same mistake again. It's never funny when you hurt someone you love. Forgive me?"

"Look, Clay, I know it'll sound stupid, but I really wanted you, and more than that, I wanted you to want me." Susan took his hand and walked to the table. "Drink your coffee. I'm acting plum silly."

He held her chair, and when she sat down he plopped down right in her lap and kissed her as only he could. "Susan, would you be my girl?"

"Yes. I think I'd like to try real hard, maybe it'll work."

Clay got up to get the two of them some more coffee. He brought the pot to the table and set it on a towel.

Susan noticed, "That was very thoughtful. I told you that you'd make some one a great little wife someday."

"Yeah, you did tell me that didn't you?"

He began to laugh and it must have been infectious, Susan began to laugh as well, wiping a single tear from her eye.

"What's so funny? I need a good laugh," Johnny said, entering the room.

The four of them had a great time just being together. On Sunday, when it was time to leave, there was a great deal of mixed emotions. Clay gave them all the details about what was going to take place and told them to tell Sydney that they'd return on Monday or Tuesday.

Clay said, "You two keep your noses clean and give Sydney a big hug for me. Susan, keep praying it's almost over."

"I'll pray too," Gidget said. "You two be real careful."

Clay pulled Susan to the side. "Guys, I need to talk to Susan for a minute, wait here and we'll be back shortly." He took Susan by the hand and walked her back up the steps to the living area. "Susan, when this is all over, would you go on a cruise with just me?"

"Of course I will, don't be silly."

"Could you stand to be alone with me, for a week, or maybe two? I'm talking, same cabin, same bath, and same bed."

Susan put her arms around his waist and moved as close as possible. "You bet your sweet ass I can. Do you promise, Clay?"

"You bet your sweet ass I do. Now, take care, Cutie, and I'll see you in a day or so. Pray for me, Babe." He hugged and kissed her good-bye, and down the steps he went.

CHAPTER 25

It was early afternoon when he and Johnny headed once more towards Washington D. C. They were a little apprehensive about what was supposed to take place in the next few hours. Once again, they each knew what the other was thinking. They did that quite often, it was almost uncanny.

"Clay, tonight will be the ending of a tumultuous time in both our lives. I'll go back to doing what I've been trained to do, and you'll begin a collegiate journey. Take your time and do it right. Don't be in a hurry to get on with your life. Enjoy the moment."

"Thanks, Johnny, for the advice. I'll try to make you proud."

"Clay, you're gonna be years ahead of the other students when it comes to experience so don't judge them too hastily. Let your experience make you a better student and, even more so, a better person. Don't waste this time. You've worked very hard to get to this point in your life."

"I'll try to take it slow and live in the present, not in the past. I hope never to have to hurt anyone else for as long as I live. I promise to walk away if there's any possibility of doing so, no matter how it makes me look to others."

409

"Clay, I've never known you to harm anyone that didn't deserve it. I've also seen you walk away without recourse, unless someone else was in peril. I wish your brother and sisters could see you as I do. I know you'll always be there for them. Maybe some day they'll reach out to you without wanting something in return."

"I wish they could know the truth about what's been going on in my life. They think I was AWOL, and they'll never know the real truth. I could've used a little understanding from them when Taylor died. They'll never even know she lived."

"I know. I've wanted to talk to them myself, many times. I'm sure they love you Clay, and maybe someday they'll want to know the real you."

"I appreciate the thought, Johnny. They have their own lives, and I do love them. My brother-in-law, Robert, wanted to fight me one day, and I walked away from that. I must say, however, that my sister, Lucy, tried to prevent it from happening. The rest of them just egged it on. Robert was right, and I was wrong. Maybe everyone would have felt better if I had let him belt me once. If I had, we'd have both been sorry. It worked out for the best."

"Clay, remember what you said Susan told you, there's someone out there for you. In God's own time, you'll come together and produce the most glorious children. One of them may find the cure for cancer. Maybe one of them will bring peace to the world. I wish I could tell you when it will happen, but I can't. Don't give up. There is method to this madness. Keep the faith, Old Buddy."

"What about you? Gidget told me that you've met someone. I'm told that she's from Ontario, Canada and you think you might marry her. Is that true?"

"Yes, it's true. If I had told you about her you would've given me a hard time where Gidget is concerned."

"I only hope she's enough woman for you. Don't marry her, John, if you can't be true to her. Your appetite for women is the strongest I've ever seen. If you're gonna marry her, be sure you can be faithful. If you continue to want every woman you see, it'll drive a wall between the two of you. Don't do that to yourself, or to her."

"I don't want every woman I see."

"Yes, you do, Johnny."

"Look, Clay, I can be a one woman man if that's called for."

"I think it's supposed to be that way when you get married."

"Women are attracted to me. Can I help that?"

"No, Johnny, I guess not. All I'm saying is that you should sow your wild oats while you're single. When you decide on one woman, be sure you can be true to her. That's all I'm saying."

"Okay, okay. Let's change the subject."

Clay tried not to laugh. "Johnny, are you the least bit worried about what we're about to do?"

"As a matter of fact, I'm scared to death, aren't you?"

"Hell yes, I just hope everyone does their part correctly. If there's one mistake, we could blow the whole deal."

Johnny turned in his seat. "With you and the senator running the show, everything will go smoothly. Clay, you should be an actor. You can play any role. I'm more worried about the reporter. He had better be as good as the senator thinks he is. You know he holds the keys to most of what is about to happen?"

Clay shook his head. "Yeah, but I think he'll be very professional. He seems to know exactly what he's doing, and the senator will be watching his every move. If he screws this up, he'll have to move to another country. His professional life will be virtually over."

"You're right, Clay. Now I'm worrying enough for the both of us. Boy, that's a switch."

He and Johnny arrived at the apartment just as the sun was going down. They had not said another word to each other for the better part of half an hour. It was pretty chilly and it looked like it might rain again. When they entered the apartment, Clay was the first to speak.

"I've made a decision. I'm going to give my portion of the money to the kids at the orphanage. I'll keep enough to pay my tuition and to live on for a while. I know I could be set for life but I just don't want any reminder. I don't need anymore pain in my life."

"What about all the good times? There have been times we will never forget."

"I'll remember you and the girls, the wonderful friendship we've shared and I'll know in my heart that I couldn't have made it without the lot of you. Johnny, you'll always be my best friend."

"Clay, let's go to the Waffle House and get something to eat I'm starving."

When they exited the apartment building, it had started to rain. It was only a short distance so they ran for it. There was not another soul in the place. All the help, the cook and two waitresses were sitting at a booth drinking coffee. The younger of the two waitresses got up and walked across the floor to take their order as the cook walked behind the counter. After taking their order, she turned and hollered their wishes to the cook. He thanked her and turned toward the grill. She brought the coffee and then whispered something to the cook that made him laugh. The other waitress continued to sip her coffee and smoke her cigarette while still sitting at the same booth. It was so quiet it was almost spooky.

Clay said, "I've never seen this place so quiet. Its suppertime, but I guess this is more of a morning place."

The waitress brought the food and went back for Clay's milk. As the cook walked back to the booth where the other waitress was sitting he lit his own cigarette, and the three of them freshened their coffee and began talking amongst themselves.

"Johnny, do you feel something?"

"What do you mean?"

"I don't know. I've got that weird feeling again. Damn, I hate that feeling."

"You're just worried about the next few hours."

"I don't think that's it. Have you noticed we no longer have a tail?"

Johnny looked bewildered. "If it was the senator having us tailed, then it makes perfect sense. Why on earth would he be having us followed now?"

Carl R. Smith

Clay said, "That's it. Casually look across the street. Those two men have been sitting in that car since we came in here. If they're tailing us, then something is really screwy."

"Don't let your imagination get the best of you. They're probably waiting for someone. What do you say, let's find out for certain. Are you with me?"

"Sure, Johnny, I'm through eating. What'd you have in mind?"

"Let's pay the check and head back to your place. If they're following us, they'll have to move and then we'll know."

Clay paid the check and Johnny left the tip. When the waitress took their money, she touched Clay's arm. "I need to talk to you, act like you're going to the bathroom and I'll meet you in the back hallway."

"Do what?"

"Tell your friend to wait, and go to the bathroom. I'll meet you in the hallway in just a minute. There's something you need to know."

"Johnny, wait for me. I need to go to the bathroom."

"No problem, I'll wait right here. Take your time."

When Clay got to the hallway just outside the bathroom, the waitress came through the swinging door.

"Look, Fellow, it's none of my business, but I think someone is following you guys. When you two came running in here, that car outside rolled up across the street with its lights off and it's been sitting there all this time. I've seen you in here before and I just thought you'd like to know. Is there anything I can do to help?"

"My partner and I were just having the same thoughts. I live in the apartments on Massachusetts and, if you're right, I may call on you later. Would that be okay?"

"I get off at eleven. Do you need my home number?"

Clay kissed her on the cheek and put ten dollars in her hand.

"I'll let you know before you get off. If you don't see me, everything is okay, and I'll talk to you later, okay?"

"That's fine. My name is Hannah."

"Thanks again, Hannah. I'll see you later."

When Clay came out of the hallway, Johnny was waiting by the door. He didn't want to say anything to Johnny until they got outside.

"What's going on, Old Buddy?"

"I'll tell you later."

When they exited the building and headed toward Clay's apartment, the car didn't move. Clay thought they looked like they were simply having a conversation.

"The waitress said that car rolled up with its lights off just as we came running in. She thought we ought to know, and she even offered to help. I told her I'd call on her later, if there was anything she could do."

"Hell, Clay, she was hitting on you, but she's probably right about the guys in the car."

When they got into the apartment, everything looked the same as before.

Johnny said, "Turn the light on in here and I'll go to the bedroom and see if the car has been moved. I think I can see them from the bedroom window."

"You took the words right out of my mouth. Go ahead I'll make us a drink."

When Johnny returned from the bedroom, Clay handed him a drink. The car had indeed been moved and it was now across from the apartment. The two men were still inside the car. It was very puzzling.

Clay said, "It must be General Essex' idea. He wants to be sure we're going to the senator's. Maybe we should let them follow us."

"Maybe, but I need to think about this for a minute. What are the pros and cons?"

"I'm going to shave and shower, Johnny. That'll give you time to think."

Johnny waved his arm. "I'll make us another drink. Shall I bring it to you in the bathroom?"

"Yeah, that'd be great."

It was only a couple of hours until they had to be at the senator's residence. Clay was ready to get it over with. He felt like his stomach had been churning long enough. Johnny had not said very much but Clay was pretty sure he felt the same way.

Johnny came in and handed him a drink.

"Thanks, Partner."

"Clay, are you as nervous as I am?"

"I think so. I'm taking it real slow; otherwise I'm probably going to cut my own throat. I can usually shave in a couple of minutes, and I've been at this for more than five."

Clay finished his drink in two gulps and was ready for another. Johnny took his glass and headed toward the kitchen. He knew what to do and, anyway, he was ready for another drink as well. Johnny brought Clay his third drink just as he was getting into the shower.

"I'll set it here on the sink, Old Buddy."

"Okay, John. I'll be out in a minute."

Johnny walked back into the bedroom. Clay could hear him mumbling to himself, even with the water running. He took a quick shower, and when he came out Johnny had a lot to tell him.

Johnny pulled him back into the bathroom and turned on the water. "Clay, there are now two cars, and four men. I saw them talking to each other while you were in the shower. I'll bet these guys are going to hit us when this is over tonight."

"What about the letter?"

"Clay, I think the general is about to call our bluff."

"But why would he think we were bluffing?"

"He has probably figured out a way to explain everything to the press. With us dead, they'll believe anything he tells them, especially if the senator has just been murdered."

"Murdered?"

"Think about it, Clay. He could just as easily say we assassinated the senator, and that we tried to blackmail him and his associates.

Don't you see he could make it work? He'd end up being the damned hero."

Clay became red-faced. "Neither me nor God will ever let that happen. They'll have to kill me first."

"Of course they will, Old Buddy. That's the idea."

"Right." Clay said, pacing back and forth. "Do you think they'll try to take us when we leave the senator's house or will they wait until we're away from there?"

"I don't know. I think they may try to take us as we leave the house, but that might draw too much attention. If the general were still going to claim the senator committed suicide, killing us at the senator's home wouldn't make any sense. How would he explain our being there?"

"You're right, Johnny. If he kills us somewhere else, he can spin it anyway he wants. He could even blame us for all the other deaths. It won't do any good to lose those guys. They'll just head for the senator's house anyway. I do think it might be wise to narrow the odds a little. I'd rather take them two at a time than face all four of them at once."

"That makes good sense," Johnny agreed. "Let's take two of them here. I don't think the others will come to their aid. If they do, it'll screw up their entire plan. They need for us to take care of the senator; otherwise the whole thing falls apart."

Clay said, "I'm tired of playing the invincible hero. Let's call the FBI and tell them we have spotted two of the guys that killed their two agents including Pamela and her sister. They'll take them into custody for at least twenty-four hours."

"Hell, if you're gonna do that, let them get the whole bunch and we'll be in the clear. By this time tomorrow, it should be over."

Clay said, "Maybe we'd better call from the Waffle House. If they're listening in on my phone, it won't work. They'll be long gone before anyone gets here. You stay here, Johnny. I'll go make the call and have them meet me at the restaurant. Where's the second car and what does it look like?"

Johnny gave him all the information he'd need, and Clay took off for the restaurant. He knew Johnny was watching, and if anything weird took place, Johnny would find a way to let him know.

When Clay entered the restaurant, Hannah, smiled from ear to ear. "Do you need my help?"

"Not yet. Where's the pay phone?"

"It's in the hallway next to the bathrooms."

"Thanks."

When he got the FBI on the line he explained who he was and what he wanted. They told him someone would be there very soon. He told them he'd wait inside the Waffle House in order to draw less attention.

Clay sat on a stool at the counter. "Hannah, give me a cup of coffee." Before he could finish his coffee, he saw a car pull up out front. He got off the stool and headed for the bathroom. "Hannah, you see those two guys headed this way? They're with the FBI, send one of them back to the hallway, but tell the other to wait here. Don't point, I think someone is watching."

"No problem, I can handle it. I won't give anything away."

In the hallway, Clay explained to the agent where the cars were parked.

"Look, you need to let me get back to the apartment before you leave here," Clay said. "If they suspect something's wrong they may take off."

"Go ahead, Mr. Smith, I'll use the bathroom, and me and Jimmy will drink a cup of coffee before doing anything. We'll handle it from here. They won't get away."

Clay exited the restaurant and headed toward his apartment. When he got inside, Johnny was full of questions.

"I don't know exactly what they're going to do, but the agent promised me they wouldn't get away." Clay was whispering, just in case. "Johnny, turn off the lights, I want to see what happens."

In a few minutes there were cops everywhere and they had both cars blocked in and surrounded. Clay and Johnny saw the FBI and the local police load the four men into police vehicles and pull away.

Johnny said, "That was easy. I guess knowing a senator really pays off. I can take my shower now. I do think one more drink is in order. You want one?"

"I sure do. Go take your shower and I'll make the drinks."

Johnny was almost undressed before Clay finished speaking. He knew how much better he felt and Johnny was surely feeling it too.

Clay was tired of having to hurt people. When Johnny emerged from the bathroom his drink was waiting for him.

"How much time do we have, Clay?"

"We need to leave here in about thirty minutes."

"Clay, I think we're going to pull this off. By this time tomorrow, we should both be able to relax for the first time in weeks."

"Yeah, I can't wait for you to meet Sydney."

"That's great, but I can't wait to get back to my hospital duties. Saving lives is much more calming. I just want to be bored for a while."

"I think I'll go back to Tennessee for a short time. Maybe I'll find a way to communicate with my sisters and my brother. I'm older. Maybe things will be different." Clay paused for a long time. "You know, Johnny, sometimes, I'm not very realistic."

"Ah, c'mon, Clay, give it a try. You have absolutely nothing to lose."

Clay turned off the water in the bathroom where they had been talking. "I think we'd better be moving." he said, grabbing his gun and sticking it in his back pocket. "I'll go bring the car around. Meet me out front."

"Clay, should I take my gun?"

"Of course, Johnny. We're not completely out of the woods yet."

"Okay, get the car and I'll be down in a minute."

As Clay left the apartment building, he noticed someone was towing one of the two cars vacated by the four men the FBI had taken into custody. Clay checked his own car thoroughly before getting

421

inside. It had become a habit with him. When he drove to the front of the apartment building, Johnny was waiting patiently.

"Let's do this, Partner?"

"Yes, Old Buddy," Johnny, replied. "It's almost over."

"I can hardly wait until tomorrow morning. I'll be watching the general's face when the Justice Department, the FBI, and the senator walk into that conference room. That should be priceless. Revenge is certainly sweet."

"I wish I could be there."

"Ask the senator. He probably won't mind letting you tag along."

"I think I will. The worst he could do is say no."

They drove the rest of the way to the senator's house, with Johnny navigating. He was in charge of the directions. They arrived almost fifteen minutes early and they parked across and down the street from the senator's residence. When they rang the doorbell, a very beautiful woman, who looked to be in her early thirties, invited them inside. She introduced herself as the Senator's wife, and led them to the study. The senator got up from his desk to welcome them. He looked very calm for a man who was about to commit suicide.

"Did you have any trouble finding the place?"

"No, Sir," Clay replied.

The senator began, "The body's in the other room. It'll only take a few minutes and this part will be over. You two bring the body in here and set him in my desk chair."

Clay and Johnny did as they were told. When the body was sitting upright in the chair, the Senator went to the gun cabinet and produced a double-barreled shotgun. He took two shells from one of the drawers and loaded it. "I can't pull the trigger. One of you guys will have to do it."

Clay said, "Have you written the note, Sir?"

"Yes, I have." The senator handed him an envelope.

"This is perfect, Senator. I believe the general will buy it. Johnny and I will deliver it to him by midnight. He should be very pleased."

Johnny said, "Give me the gun, Senator, and step back out of the way."

"When my wife hears the shot, she'll wait one minute and then telephone the authorities. She knows what number to dial. You fellows will have to get the heck out of here. This place will be crawling with agents from the bureau."

Clay said, "Sir, forgive me but could we go over this just one more time. I don't want any mistakes. I'm sure you feel the same."

"Okay, let's rehash."

Johnny said, "Allow me. When Clay and I leave here, we'll go directly to Clay's apartment and then, at the proper time, we'll head to the general's office. We'll hand him the note and collect our blood money. Tomorrow morning, at exactly 0800 hours, the general will break the news to the committee, with Clay at his side. The general will inform them that he and Clay are the responsible parties, although the public will view this as a suicide. At 0830 hours sharp, you Senator, along with the Justice Department and the FBI will walk into the committee meeting and proceed to make the arrest. At that time you'll applaud Mr. Smith for his help and his loyalty to his government and the American people. Then, I'm personally going to sleep for a week. Does that explain everything fully or did I miss something?"

The senator looked at the dead body. "That was perfect, Captain. Any questions?"

Johnny reached into his pocket and pulled out a pair of surgical gloves. He put them on and took the shotgun from the senator. "You know this is going to make an awful mess. Do you have some plastic around here somewhere?"

Clay said, "What about the container the body came in from the Morgue?"

"That'll help," Johnny replied.

The senator waved his arms. "Wait a minute. I have some old drop cloths in the garage. They are pretty thick. They were used while the house was being painted. There are more than a dozen of them."

Clay said, "I'll get them, Senator. You shouldn't go outside. Someone may still be watching the house. Tell me exactly where to find them."

The senator gave him detailed directions. Clay went through the inner hallway and made his exit through the kitchen. When he returned from the garage, the senator's wife was sitting at the kitchen table. She was as white as a sheet.

"Are you all right, Ma'am?"

"I'm just a little scared. What if something goes wrong?"

"Everything is gonna be fine. I got this stuff from the garage so we wouldn't make such a mess. Don't you worry about a thing," Clay assured her, as he reached out to touch her cheek.

She grabbed him, with hands as cold as ice and she clung to him with all her strength. He patted her hand. "It'll be over real soon, I promise."

"Thank you, Young Man. My husband told me that you were very nice. Please don't let anything happen to him."

"Don't you fret, he'll be just fine. You're gonna hear a shot in the next few minutes. Can you do your part? Do you need any help?"

"I'll be okay. You go on and do what you have to do. I'll make the call."

He gave her a little hug and headed back to the study. When he entered the room, the senator and Johnny were talking to Sergeant Shackelford.

"Where have you been, Shack?"

"I've been walking the grounds for the last hour or so."

Clay said, "Well, is everything quiet out there?"

"I haven't seen a soul. Actually, I did see you guys pull in, but I was too far away to get your attention."

Clay said, "Good job. Has the senator been good to you?"

Shack seemed a little embarrassed by the question. "He has been very nice to me. I've tried real hard to stay in the background. Are you two doing okay?"

"Yes, we're doing just great," Clay replied.

425

This was the first time since their arrival that Clay had given any thought to the men in the cars. He thought he should share the information with the senator, and he spent the next several minutes explaining what had taken place.

The senator actually applauded. "You handled the situation correctly. Before the general knows what has happened to those guys, he may be in the same cell. I wish you had done the same with my men instead of beating them up so badly."

Johnny flushed, "Sorry, Senator, but the situations were somewhat different. The guy with the broken jaw was my fault."

"Its okay, Captain. You did what you thought best at the time. I don't want to make you guys angry with me. If I do, you'll let me know, won't you?" The senator gave Johnny a big smile.

Clay said, "Has Shack been brought up to speed? If so, let's get this over with. It gives me the shakes."

"I didn't think anything would do that to you, Mr. Smith," the senator responded.

Clay ignored his comment and went straight to the heart of the matter.

"Senator, you go to your hiding place and please stay out of sight. We'll make as little of a mess as possible. Shack will stay here and see that your wife is all right. Good luck, Sir. I'll see you in the morning at 0830 hours sharp."

"I'll look forward to it. By the way, I have given Captain Murphy permission to enter the committee room with us tomorrow. Good luck to you, Gentlemen."

Clay and Shack hung the plastic over the curtain rod hoping it would catch most of the mess. Johnny backed the chair up within about three feet of the hanging plastic. He got down on his knees in front of the chair and tried to stick the barrel of the shotgun in the mouth of the corpse, it wouldn't work.

Shack said, "Rigormortis has set in. You'll have to break his jaw, Doctor. When you break his jaw, his mouth will fall open. I heard breaking jaws is what you do best."

Clay and Shack began to laugh.

"Thank you, Sergeant. I know how it works. I am a doctor, you know."

Johnny put the end of the barrel under the man's nose and pulled the trigger. Flesh and bone went everywhere but there was very little blood.

"Well, I guess his jaw is broken now, ain't it?" Johnny quipped.

Clay moved away from the desk. "Shack, you go assist the senator's wife. Johnny and me, we're outta here."

Johnny threw the shotgun to the floor, and he and Clay headed for the car. They walked rather fast, but they didn't run. Clay drove very carefully, and they were half way to his apartment before anyone spoke.

Clay said, "Let's stop somewhere for a drink or two. I need to calm down and I'll bet you do, too. Let's go to the Shoreham, what do you think?"

"I think that's the perfect place. How ironic, don't you think? Isn't that where a lot of this crap got started? Oh, sorry, Clay, I didn't realize what I was saying. You sure you want to go there?"

"Yeah, I really do."

Johnny said, "We only have time for one drink before we have to go see the general. It's almost ten-thirty."

"You're right, Johnny. We'll stop by the apartment for a quick drink. When we are through with the general, we'll have time to go and have another drink."

Clay circled the block twice before finally pulling into the parking garage. He wanted to be sure they weren't being watched anymore. Neither he nor Johnny saw anything suspicious. They were very cautious going from the garage to the apartment. They were even more careful opening the apartment door.

"Johnny, will you fix us a drink? I have to go to the bathroom. I'll be right out."

"Sure, Old Buddy." Johnny said, heading toward the kitchen.

When Clay entered the bedroom, he noticed the light was blinking on his telephone. He continued to the bathroom. Coming out of the bathroom, he walked across the room to get his message.

"Hey, John, come in here."

Johnny walked into the bedroom and handed him a beer.

"Sorry, Clay, we're out of scotch. What do you need?"

"I don't know who'd be calling me here, but, as you can see, I have a message. I thought it best if we heard it together. I checked the wiring and the receiver. Everything looks the way it's supposed to."

"Then let's hear the message."

The message was from James Mann, the attorney. He said that he had a package to deliver to Clay Smith and Doctor John Murphy before midnight. The package was from General Essex. Mr. Mann said if they got this message before eleven-thirty PM they were to call him at his office immediately. It was now ten fifty-five PM.

"What do you make of that Johnny?"

"I don't know, Clay. Dial his number."

Mr. Mann answered on the very first ring.

"Is that you, Mr. Smith?"

"Yes, it's me; I just got your message."

"The general is very sorry that he couldn't meet with you personally but he has been detained. Can you and Captain Murphy meet me at my office?"

Clay said, "I'll meet you at the Shoreham Hotel lounge in forty-five minutes. Does that meet with your approval?"

"That'll be just fine, Mr. Smith. I'll be there at eleven forty-five. I trust, you'll bring Doctor Murphy with you?"

"He'll be with me."

"Then I'll look forward to meeting with the both of you. See you there."

Clay hung the receiver in its cradle. "Johnny, we need to meet Mr. Mann at the Shoreham Hotel by eleven forty-five. Let's get going."

"Wait a minute, Clay. We can be there in ten minutes. How are we gonna do this? I'm very happy not to have to meet with the general: however, this makes me a little nervous. I know you want to

429

get there quickly so you can scout the place out. I do think we'd be wiser if we had a plan. We always have a plan, and that's the way I like it."

"Okay, Johnny, but let's do it on the way."

They were out the door and in the garage area very quickly. They took the time to check the car. They were never in that much of a hurry. They got to the hotel at eleven-twenty PM. Clay was going to check the restaurant and the lobby while Johnny checked the outside entrances as well as the lounge. They were to meet in the front of the lobby in fifteen minutes. It didn't even take that long and neither he nor Johnny found anything the least bit out of order. Hell, the restaurant had closed at ten PM and the lounge was only open due to some private club to-do.

Clay and Johnny were headed for the lounge when Mr. Mann come down the hallway from the side entrance and waved to them. They stopped and waited for him to catch up. He had his usual smile and he was carrying a rather large briefcase.

"It's really nice to see you again, Mr. Smith, and you too, Doctor. Shall we go inside and have a drink?"

Clay said, "I'm sorry, Mr. Mann, but the lounge is closed to the public. There's some private party going on. Is General Essex alright?"

"He's fine he had some kind of airplane trouble. He'll be back in a couple of hours. I'm supposed to tell you that I've brought you all the available cash. The rest will be waiting for you in the morning. You are to meet General Essex in his office at seven forty-five tomorrow morning." Mr. Mann handed the briefcase to Clay. "I had a hard time getting this much together on such short notice. The general didn't call me until four hours ago. I hope everything is still okay. I did the very best I possibly could."

Clay moved in order to place Mr. Mann between he and Johnny. "You seem a little nervous. Are you okay, Mr. Mann?"

"I need to be going. I have to meet the general's plane in just over an hour."

They shook hands. Mr. Mann was very fidgety; however, it was all very friendly. As Mr. Mann walked away, Clay and Johnny just looked at each other.

Johnny said, "Let's get out of here. I want to open that briefcase and see just how short they are. Does it feel heavy?"

"It's pretty heavy." Clay paused. "You don't think this thing is booby trapped, do you?"

"I don't know. Maybe that's why Mr. Mann was in such a hurry to get the hell out of here. We should have opened it while he was still sitting here."

"You're right, Johnny. What do we do now?"

"If it's not ticking, we're gonna take it to the hospital and X-ray it."

"That's a great idea."

When they got to the car, Johnny got his stethoscope from his bag and listened to the briefcase as best he could. When he was fairly certain it was safe, they were on their way to Bethesda Naval

Hospital. Clay laughed as Johnny X-rayed the briefcase from every angle.

"I'm sure it's all right. Open it, Clay."

Clay flipped the latch and it fell open. He dumped the money all over the floor.

"Damn, Johnny. There's a lot of money here."

When they finished counting, they were one hundred and twenty thousand short.

"Holy cow! Six hundred and thirty thousand dollars." Johnny began jumping and hugging Clay's neck. Clay just grinned at Johnny and hugged him back. They quickly placed the money back in the case and were on there way again.

Clay said, "I ain't never gonna be able to sleep tonight. Let's go to the Waffle House and get some food. I've suddenly developed a mighty appetite. How about you?"

"I could eat a horse," Johnny replied.

"We'll call Susan and Gidget from the pay phone and let them know how we're doing. They're probably still awake."

"Clay, where are we gonna stash this money till the bank opens?"

"We'll stick it in a locker at the Greyhound Bus Station. It should be safe there until tomorrow."

"Good idea, Clay. We can call the girls from the telephones there. They have booths where we can have a little privacy."

Chapter 26

As they drove back to D. C., they were still looking over their shoulder, but no one seemed to be following them. In fact there was hardly anyone else on the road. It was going on two AM. They reached the bus station without incident. They had enough change for the locker but they had to make the call collect. Hell, it was two AM on Monday morning, and Sydney was probably sound asleep. They called anyway.

Susan answered on the first ring. The operator had to go through her little spiel and Susan said she would be more than happy to accept the charges.

"Clay, are you okay?" Susan said, getting her breath.

"I'm just great. I hope we didn't wake Sydney. Is everyone okay on your end? Johnny says hello and wants you girls to know we are rich men. More importantly, we are still alive and kicking."

"Sydney has been in bed for hours. He was dead on his feet when he finally got home. He has to leave again tomorrow afternoon."

"Damn. When's he coming back this time?"

"He'll be back sometime Thursday. Clay, Gidget's driving me crazy, she wants to say hello."

433

"Put her on, Susan, but don't go too far away."

He could hear Gidget giggling in the background. "Gosh, it's good to hear your voice. Is Johnny all right?"

"Here he is. Ask him yourself."

"Hi, Little One, this is your rich doctor friend. Things went even better than we could've imagined. I'm gonna buy you something really expensive. See you guys in a day or so. Think about what you'd like to have."

"Johnny, I like expensive presents." Gidget said, emphatically. "You be really careful. Don't let anything happen to you before I get my present."

"I'll be careful, and, if you're lucky, I'll see you tomorrow, Tuesday at the latest."

"Yeah, I know if I'm lucky. Do take good care of yourself and, if you're lucky, I'll be waiting. I seem to do that well."

"Okay, Gidget. I'm putting Clay back on."

"Clay, you know I miss you most of all. I really do wish you were here, with or without the, big lug. Susan wants to talk to you again. Here she is. Bye, Clay."

"Good-bye, Sweetie."

"Clay, are you there?"

"I'm here Susan. Are you crying?"

"Yeah, just a little. I'm so happy to hear your voice. I wish you were here. I know it may sound silly but I'd just love to talk to you all night."

"I'll be there soon. We're still going on that cruise, right?"

"You bet your sweet ass we are."

"You, Girls, get some sleep. Johnny and I will talk to you sometime tomorrow. You have my word, okay, Babe? Don't cry anymore."

"Whatever you say, Clay. I'll talk to you sometime later today, right?"

"That's right, Susan, this afternoon. Good-bye, Babe."

Clay looked at the clock on the wall. They'd been on the telephone for nearly thirty minutes. Johnny was leaning against the wall smoking a huge cigar. He had bought a five pack. Clay lit up, and the two of them stood there laughing at each other.

Clay poked him, "We better get out'a here before these people think we've lost our minds and call the police. Waffle House, here we come."

Johnny was looking a bit green around the edges. "Let's go. I need something in my stomach. This cheap cigar is making me sick, and I hate to throw up with my stomach empty."

"It is a pretty lousy cigar. You'd think we could afford better. I'm a very rich man, you know?"

"So am I," Johnny replied.

They headed for the car, like a couple of giddy school kids. Clay didn't even care who noticed. Actually, the place was just about deserted. There was a poor old beggar sitting on the curb. Johnny walked over and handed him a twenty-dollar bill. He then took one more puff off his cigar and handed it to the guy.

Clay had this real throaty laugh. "Johnny, you sure are a generous sort. You're not one of those philanthropists, are you?"

Johnny stepped back, "Wow, I'm impressed. That's a pretty big word. To be honest, I think I'm more of the philanderer."

Clay stuck out his hand. "Way to go, Partner. That is the absolute, unvarnished truth."

They were finally at the restaurant. By this time, they were both pretty hungry. Again, the place had very few customers. They found a booth and ordered some coffee. When the waitress returned with the coffee, they were ready to order their food. They ate and talked for two hours.

"I guess we'd better go home and get ready for the big finale," Clay said, looking at his beautiful watch.

Johnny had this astonished look on his face, "Clay, did you hear what you just said? That's the first time you've ever mentioned this place as being your home. Do you think that was a Freudian slip?"

Clay eyes widened, "I don't know. I guess it's possible. Do you think I really feel that way down deep inside? That's a little scary."

Johnny took another sip of his coffee. "Don't analyze it to death, Clay. It probably doesn't mean a thing. It's quite possible that you're just as crazy as the rest of us."

"With all that's happened in the last few weeks, who wouldn't be crazy?"

Johnny raised his coffee cup, "I think I need one more cup of coffee. We have to stay awake for at least the next four or five hours.

Hell, I'm supposed to be at the hospital at 0800 hours. I guess I best call and let them know I'll not be in until Tuesday."

Clay looked at him, "Can you call them this time of the morning?"

"Yeah, sure, someone will relay the message to the right party. I'll go use the phone. Order me another cup of coffee. No cream this time."

Clay motioned for the waitress and ordered two more cups of coffee. It kept bothering him that the general was out of town. Whatever he was doing must have been pretty damned important. Clay thought, *If I live through tomorrow, I might very well live forever.* That could very easily be a curse. Clay was a young man and, already, he was sick and tired of all the lies, deception, and bullshit. Dying may simply supply the only rest for the weary. *Wow*! Clay thought. *I'm even becoming profound.*

Johnny returned from making his call looking a might grim.

"Is everything all right, Johnny?"

"Yeah, I just had a hard time getting to someone who was willing to help me. I sure hope the right person gets the message."

"Hell, it's the Navy. I don't think they'll fire you."

Johnny reached for his wallet, "Let's go get ready for the hell to come. In a very short time from now, we'll either be relieved, dead, or in so much trouble it won't even matter."

Clay stood, "You got that right. Let's go."

They got into the car and drove the block or so to the parking garage. It was almost daylight on a Monday morning and a great many people were just getting their day started. There were a number of cars already on the streets. Clay wondered who they were and where they might be going to begin their day's work. Were they happy, were they sad, or were they just going through the motions, and did anyone really give a damn?

Someone was parked in Clay's parking space, so he decided to park on the street in front of the apartment building. This time of day, that was not a problem. When they got inside the apartment, Johnny went straight to the kitchen to make some more coffee. Clay ran to the bathroom.

When he returned, to the kitchen, Johnny handed him a fresh cup of coffee.

Clay said, "You don't happen to have anymore of those lousy cigars, do you?"

"Sure, there were five in the package." Johnny went fumbling through his pockets. "You're not gonna smoke one of those awful things in here, are you?"

"As a matter of fact, I'm going out on the balcony. Do you want to come?"

Johnny handed him the cigars. "Sure, let me get a refill on my coffee."

Clay took the package of cigars from Johnny and unwrapped one as he slide the patio door open; walking outside he lit up. It didn't taste so bad this time. He took a couple of long drags and Johnny decided to join him. It was going to be a beautiful morning. The sun was coming up and there were just enough clouds in the sky to make the scene even more glorious. Johnny lit his cigar and was taking a sip of his coffee when the balcony shook. There was a sound like the falling of a brick wall on concrete.

Johnny said, "What the hell was that?"

Clay put his hand over his heart. "It sounded like a major wreck. Let's go out front. Maybe we can see what happened."

They headed through the apartment and out the front door. They looked both left and right. Everything seemed to be okay. About that time, there was a flash of light to their right.

"Clay, call the fire department. I think one of the apartments is on fire."

He ran for the telephone and Johnny ran toward the blaze. After making the call, Clay ran back outside. Johnny came around the corner of the building and ran toward him.

"What happened?" Clay shouted.

"The car in your parking space was just blown to hell and back. Let's get back to the apartment. There's nothing we can do for the person in the car."

"Clay, did you give them your name?"

"Who?" Clay asked.

"The fire department."

"I said there was a fire at the apartment building located at 1111 Massachusetts Avenue and that they'd better hurry. Then I hung up and ran after you."

"That's good," Johnny said, expressing a sigh of relief. "Maybe we won't have to answer a bunch of questions. That bomb was meant for us, you know?"

"I figured that much."

The two of them stood in Clay's living room puffing away on their cigars.

"Johnny, do we have anything to drink in this place, other than beer?"

"There's plenty of bourbon. Clay, you know these cigars are going to make this place stink for a week."

"Yeah, I know. Let's have some bourbon, my nerves are really shot."

Johnny made the drinks and motioned for Clay to follow him to the balcony. When they were once again standing outside the apartment, Johnny spoke.

"The general is going to be very surprised to see us this morning. That, son of a bitch! Maybe when he sees us, he'll drop dead with a heart attack. That would save everybody a lot of trouble."

"You know, Johnny, it could have very easily been us in that car. Somebody up there likes us. That's the first time anyone has ever parked in my space. Give me your glass, Johnny. I'll get us one more drink. It's almost time to get this over with."

Johnny handed him his glass and took another drag from his cigar. Clay returned with the drinks and handed one to Johnny.

Clay puffed on the cheap cigar. "I wonder why the fire department is not evacuating the building."

"The fire wouldn't have spread. It's all concrete. It doesn't present any danger to the tenants. They probably put it out in five minutes," Johnny replied.

Clay looked thoughtfully at Johnny. "Doesn't it matter to General Essex that we might have had all that money in the car with us? I guess he figures it's gone either way."

"Remember, Clay, the senator told us that one million dollars was only pocket change to the general. He must have been speaking the truth. Let me go freshen up. I'm gonna meet the senator about the same time you're going to the general's office. Clay, do you have the suicide note on you. I'd give him that letter, first thing."

"Yeah, I have it in my vest pocket, and I have every intention of giving it to him the minute I walk into the office."

Johnny went to the bathroom. He was only gone a few minutes. Clay had almost finished his cigar, and he desperately needed to brush his teeth again.

"Johnny, let me go to the bathroom, and then we're out of here."

He was back in a flash. "Let's go, Johnny."

"I'm ready. You know, whoever planted that bomb has never seen your car before. They must have told him to look for your parking space because that car didn't look anything like yours."

"Is there a point to this, Johnny, or are you just rattling?"

"No point. I was just thinking out loud. Clay, drop me off at the Senate Office Building. I'll see you at about eight-thirty, God willing and the creeks don't rise." Johnny smiled, "Don't you just love my southern charm?"

"Keep it up, Johnny. I need something to relax me, no matter how inane. I really do need you to keep talking. Sing me a song. You love to sing, and you're not all that bad."

441

"Thanks, Old Buddy. Now you tell me what a beautiful singing voice I have, just as I'm about to die. Some friend you are."

"Wait a minute. I didn't say you had a beautiful voice. I said you weren't bad. There's a major difference."

Johnny punched him on the arm. "Clay, I know you really love my singing."

They were approaching the Senate Office Building. Johnny stuck out his hand. "Be cool, Old Buddy. I'll see you in about an hour."

"Thanks, Partner. I hope I'm still alive and breathing."

Johnny exited the car and walked away. Clay was having a little difficulty keeping his focus. He swung around the corner and in no time he was pulling into the visitor's parking area, not wanting to park in the restricted lot. If he parked there, they would have to telephone the general for approval and he wanted his arrival to be as much of a surprise as possible. It was seven-thirty-five AM. With barely ten minutes to compose himself he began thinking about how much he hated what the general had done. He thought about Pamela and her family, Sergeant Russ and his family; all the while, getting angrier and angrier, that was not normally a good thing. In this case, however, it made his knees stop shaking, and now he was ready to face whatever was about to happen.

Clay opened the door to the general's office. The new receptionist looked up from her desk. "May I help you, Sir?"

"My name is Clay Smith. The general is expecting me."

"Just one moment, Sir. I'll tell him you're here. Could I get you some coffee?"

Clay smiled at her. "No, thank you."

When the woman returned, she had a strange look on her face. "Sir, the general will be right out."

The door behind Clay opened. It was Sergeant Shackelford.

"Hi, Maggie. Can I have a cup of coffee?"

"Sure, Sergeant. Help yourself."

The sergeant winked. "Hello, Clay. It's really nice to see you."

Clay walked across the room and stuck out his hand. Shack grabbed it and smiled.

"I didn't think you'd mind if I dropped by for a few minutes," Shack whispered.

Now, Clay was whispering, "Is everything all right with the senator?"

"Everything is great, couldn't be better. You keep your cool, Clay."

At that very moment, the general walked through the other door.

"Well, Clay, on time as always," the general said, forcing a smile. "What are you doing here, Sergeant?"

The sergeant came to attention. "Just getting a cup of coffee, Sir."

"Well, I see you have it. Shouldn't you be getting back to work?"

"Yes, Sir. Thank you, Sir. Nice seeing you again, Clay. Take care of yourself."

The general said, "I'm so glad you made it, Clay. Follow me. The committee will be meeting any minute."

Clay followed him into his office. General Essex turned and handed him an envelope. "I think this is what you're looking for, My Boy."

Clay, in turn, handed him the letter from the senator. "I know this is what you're looking for, General."

The general opened the letter and read it very carefully. "This is absolutely perfect. He must have believed every word you said."

"I assure you he did, General. It was much easier than I thought it would be."

The general said, "I think it's time to face the committee. Are you up to it or should I go in alone?"

"I'm ready, Sir. They need to be told what they can expect if they become traitors. They'll think you're God. Isn't that the way it should be, Sir?"

"You're right, My Boy. Come with me and let's put the fear of 'God' into everyone present."

"I'm right with you, General."

He followed the general into the conference room. Everyone was present. The general walked over to the chair where the senator usually sat and leaned it against the table. Almost everyone in the room had this puzzled look on their face.

The general began, "Gentlemen, and Lady, the senator will not be joining us this morning."

He continued by reading the suicide note. Clay was watching the faces of the other members of the committee. They went from puzzled to pale and then to "Oh my God." Some even had a look of relief, and many didn't seem to care at all.

General Essex went on to explain to them what actually happened. That seemed to get their attention. He told them that treason or traitorous acts would not be tolerated. Clay could tell, everyone in the room got the message. Lastly, the general told them that they owed Clay Smith a debt of gratitude.

It was 0835 hours. *Where was the senator?* Clay thought. About that time, all three doors to the conference room burst opened. Everyone just stared in disbelief as the senator walked into the room with FBI agents, Military Policemen, and a number of men from the Justice Department. Clay could even see Johnny and Shack standing just inside the double doors.

Senator Lazar pointed directly at General Essex, "General, you're under arrest."

The general never moved, and everyone else was too shocked to move. Two of the FBI agents walked around each end of the conference table and took the general into custody.

The older of the two agents said, "I think you need to come with us, General. Everyone else keep your seat. You're all going to be here for quite some time."

Senator Lazar walked over to Clay and extended his hand.

"Thank you, Young Man. This would never have been possible without your help. The entire country owes you a great deal, and I owe you, my life. God bless you, Clay."

As the agents were escorting General Essex out of the conference room he suddenly turned to face Clay, with fire in his eyes. The silence was deafening, as the general screamed. "You bastard, I thought you were a loyal American. You're a traitor and a Judas. Do you even know what a Judas is?"

Clay walked toward him, with Senator Lazar desperately pulling at his arm. "I most certainly do, General. In this case, it's a man I worked for, respected, and would have died for ... a man, I loved like a father ... a man, who betrayed his country and disgraced the uniform he wears. Yes, General, I damn well know what a Judas is."

THE END

EPILOG

Three months had passed and Clay was enrolled at the University of Maryland. It was a Saturday and it was just beginning to snow. While standing on the balcony, thoughts of Leila walked through his mind. The snow reminded him. A tear rolled down his cheek as he again recalled the last day with his friends. It was at the funeral for Pamela and her sister.

Johnny was now a civilian doctor and practicing medicine at a hospital in Redding, California. He was a very promising anesthesiologist. Susan was working as a physical therapist at a hospital in New England. Gidget, with the help of the good doctor, was beginning a career in pharmaceutical sales. She had moved to Chicago. The four of them talked almost weekly.

Many of the past events were wafting their way through the recesses of his mind. He remembered the good times as well as the scary times. Now he was alone, and the loneliness was pulling at his very existence.

Clay had spent the last three months of the year in Knoxville, Tennessee. He had returned to his childhood homeland in an effort to reconcile with his sisters and his brother. Things didn't work out as he had hoped, but they were at least talking to each other. His thoughts were cut short by the ringing of his telephone. Clay had to shove a chair out of the doorway in order to reach the phone. It was a certain Senator Lazar.

"Mr. Smith, it's so nice talking to you again. I'm glad I caught you at home on this cold and snowy morning. My wife and I would like to invite you to dinner this evening at seven."

"Thank you for the invitation, Sir, but …"

"Clay, this is very important. I have a major situation here and I need your assistance. Please don't turn me down. You're my only hope, and the food will be excellent. At least come for dinner, and hear what I have to say."

"Okay, Sir. I'll see you at seven."

The story continues!

About the Author

Mr. Smith is an army veteran. He served during the Berlin Wall Crisis, the Cuban Missile Crisis, and the Vietnam War. The decade of the sixties was spent in government service, not a good time for that sort of thing. After putting that life behind him he has been a very successful hotelier, president of two corporations, CEO and founder of another. Alex Haley, the author of "Roots" encouraged the writing of this work more than ten years ago.

Printed in the United States
1366800002B/34-1008